T0283266

KALYNA
THE
CUTTHROAT

BY ELIJAH KINCH SPECTOR

Failures of Four Kingdoms
Kalyna the Soothsayer
Kalyna the Cutthroat

FAILURES OF FOUR KINGDOMS

KALYNA
THE
CUTTHROAT

ELIJAH KINCH SPECTOR

EREWHON

an imprint of Kensington Publishing Corp.
erewhonbooks.com

EREWHON BOOKS are published by:

Kensington Publishing Corp.
900 Third Avenue
New York, NY 10022
erewhonbooks.com

All Kensington titles, imprints, and distributed lines are available at special quantity discounts for bulk purchases for sales promotions, premiums, fundraising, educational, or institutional use.

Special book excerpts or customized printings can also be created to fit specific needs. For details, write or phone the office of the Kensington sales manager: Kensington Publishing Corp., 900 Third Avenue, New York, NY 10022, attn: Sales Department; phone 1-800-221-2647.

Erewhon and the Erewhon logo Reg. US Pat. & TM Off.

ISBN 978-1-64566-090-3 (hardcover)

First Erewhon hardcover printing: December 2024

10 9 8 7 6 5 4 3 2 1

Printed in the United States of America

Library of Congress Control Number: 2023944514

Electronic edition: ISBN 978-1-64566-091-0 (ebook)

Edited by Sarah T. Guan
Interior design by Cassandra Farrin and Leah Marsh
Map by Virginia Allyn

For Grandpa Everett, who would have been confused by the fantasy and disgusted by the violence, but I hope would have recognized the politics.

"It is not love to my neighbour—whom I often do not know at all—which induces me to seize a pail of water and to rush towards his house when I see it on fire."
    —Peter Kropotkin, *Mutual Aid*

"It was my destiny to see the disjointing of a world."
    —Younghill Kang, *East Goes West*

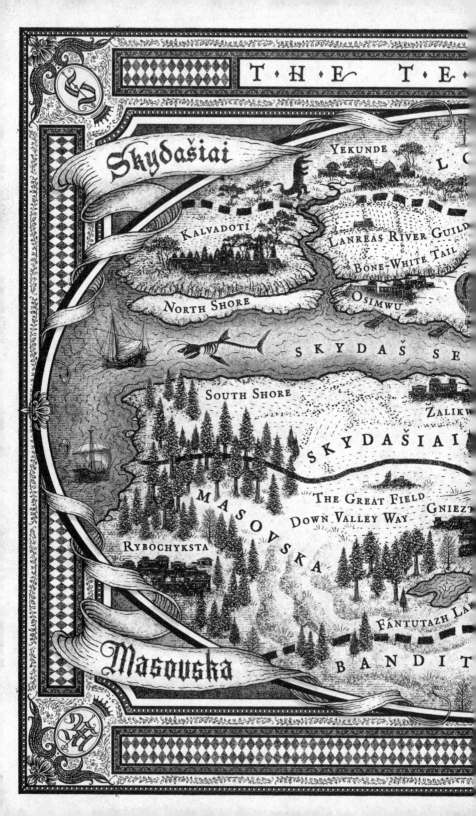

ARCHIA

QURUSCAN

HT

GALIAG

KEÇEPEL

QOYUL

ABATHÇODU

SEBEK

QURUSCAN

DESGOL

SUNSET PALACE

TURMENBACH

GLAIZATZ LAKE

ROTFELSEN

STATES

Rotfelsen

Figures of Note,
for Your Reference

Those from the Tetrarchia

KALYNA ALJOSANOVNA: The Tetrarchic schemer at the center of my story.

ALJOSA VÜSALAVICH: Her father.

DAGMAR SORGA: A mercenary from Rotfelsen.

ŽYDRŪNAS: A mercenary from Skydašiai, and friend to Dagmar Sorga.

MANTI DUMPLING AKRAM: My first friend in Quruscan.

VIDMANTAS: A stylish Skydašian thinker.

IFEANYAS: A quiet Skydašian thinker.

ADOMAS: Founder of the Lanreas River Guild.

ŽYDRĖ: An early member of the Lanreas River Guild.

YALWAS: An early member of the Lanreas River Guild who tends to disagree with Žydrė.

Those from Loasht,
with Names Translated into Skydašiavos

SILVER PETALS ALIGHT ON SAND: My spouse. Of the Zobiski people.

CASABA MELON WATER SOOTHES AT NOONTIME: My good friend from the Academy. Central Loashti, but a mix.

ALOE PRICKS A MARE UPON THE MOUNTAIN BLUFF: An acquaintance from the Academy who went on to bigger things. Central Loashti.

THE SIMURGH RULES AIR, WIND, AND SEA: A crackpot inventor. Central Loashti.

THE BINTURONG WILL EAT ALL THINGS, SO WHY THEN SHOULDN'T WE?: A Zobiski from further north than me.

ECHOES IN THE GINGKO-WREATHED VALLEY SOUND LIKE GRANDFATHER'S VOICE: A Kubatri in face-paint with an odd vocation.

KALYNA
THE
CUTTHROAT

Chapter One

Just Before Everything
Went Wrong in Abathçodu

The first thing anyone from Quruscan said to me that wasn't blandly polite was: "How are you still alive?" This was so puzzling that it made me doubt my understanding of their language.

By this time, I had spent a month and three days traveling through that windy and mountainous kingdom to the south, guided first by a fellow Loashti, and then by a somewhat out-of-place Rotfelsenisch sellsword. Truth be told, I preferred the sellsword to my countryman. The Loashti guide worked very hard at assuring me that he considered my people to be just as Loashti as his. The darkly blonde sellsword made it very clear that she hardly cared for me one way or another, and I found this refreshing—but we'll come back to her soon enough.

In my travels over Quruscan's dry and dusty mountain roads, I found its people to be unfailingly polite: sometimes friendly, sometimes suspicious, but never saying anything that could lead to an uncomfortable conversation or potential embarrassment. Throughout the Greater Eastern Tetrarchia—that cobbled-together country of which Quruscan was one-fourth—my native Loasht had always been seen as a threatening, monstrous thing; yet the only questions posed to me about my homeland were over its weather or its food.

"Beautiful day! Do you have days like this in Loasht?"

"Yes, but it depends on the region."

Or:

"You *do* have lamb's meat and lychee drinks up there, I hope."

"Certainly! Although we import the lychee from you."

And so forth. My answers would often be followed by a subtle look that suggested relief—as though the Quru were pleased to know Loasht was civilized enough for clear skies and lamb's meat. Loashti civilization is, of course, far beyond ancient when compared to that of any in the Tetrarchia.

The famed Quru disdain for nosiness was one of the chief reasons I had chosen to study there, rather than in any of the other three Tetrarchic kingdoms. Another reason was, of course, the famed Library of Abathçodu, with all of its crinkled old volumes on rituals from throughout the known world: blessings, thanksgivings, rites of passage, and, of course, curses. My specialty.

On that trip, I saw a number of wonderful sights (some of which I jotted down in my Commonplace Book and may reproduce in another volume someday), but I was most enchanted by the zip lines. Many of Quruscan's mountains were bound up in great cords—as though they needed to be held to the ground, lest they fly off into the sky—which sometimes supported whole cities on nets and platforms, hanging precariously in the air. The zip lines also served as conveyances from upper to lower cliffs: the Quru would sit in small metal carriages that sped downward at, I fancy, the fastest speeds that were not fatal. I was both disappointed and relieved to learn that my trip would not require their use.

Upon reaching the city of Abathçodu, I said goodbye to the blonde mercenary and spent a few days getting to know my new, if temporary, home. A mishmash of wooden buildings and yurts, Abathçodu, with its mostly homogenous population of middling size, would have been a notably minor city in Loasht, but its cultural life was wonderfully rich. During my first week there, I came to feel great confidence in my mastery of Cöllüknit, the Quru language: I enjoyed a number of poetry readings, performances, and unveilings of flimsy, purposefully impermanent statues. Did I catch every meaning in these pieces? Of course not, but I felt I fit in quite well. I had learned the language by way of many books and the tutelage of a long-retired dragoman—that is, a traveling interpreter—who liked to hang about the halls of my branch of the Loashti Academy, auditing classes for fun.

But it was on my sixth day in Abathçodu, after the locals had begun to realize I was in no hurry to leave, that I was asked the question that made me doubt my mastery of the language. After carefully retranslating in my head and getting nowhere, I winced and managed to cough out, "Excuse me?"

"I asked," the broad Quru man began, slower this time, "how you are still alive."

I must have stared.

"How," he tried again, "did your head become so broken? And how have you survived it?"

I stared a bit more. Hearing the words again brought no more *sense* to the conversation. Certainly, I was not as beautiful as I had once been, but I had no great scars, nor was I extraordinarily wrinkled for a person north of forty.

The possibility dawned on me that this was a preamble to the man breaking my head. After all, only months earlier had the Tetrarchia stopped seeing Loasht as, officially, a perpetual threat.

He sighed, frustrated with my lack of understanding, batting dust off his burgundy robe as though it would clear his mind. It seemed we were frustrated by the same thing but could find no common ground.

I began to chide myself for the great arrogance with which I had traipsed across our newly open border. I'd simply shown my papers to a tired Quru official, who comprehended none of what their words or their pink coloring said about my provenance beyond: "BORN IN LOASHT." After that, I'd worried about hatred, yes, and brigands, and falling to my death, but I'd been *confident* I could at least speak to these people in their language.

In Abathçodu, on that sixth day, I felt myself begin to sweat profusely even though the mountain air was too cold for me all year round.

"How . . . how is it broken?" I gulped out, expecting him to crack my skull in answer.

Instead, he replied, "That is just what I am asking!" He then forced a laugh that I think was meant to be friendly, screwed his mouth to one side, and tried to explain himself.

"This," he said, waving a large, callused hand over my face, "is not the way a skull breaks, you know?" He pushed back his little blue skull-cap, and lifted the straight, dark hair that covered half his forehead. I saw there a tattoo, shaped like a small explosion. "*This* is. From when I fell as a child."

"And the ink . . . ?"

"Marks where my skull was broken, and how. What else?"

"I see." I began to understand our impasse. "A record for your doctors, yes?"

"Of course!" He clapped his hands happily. "But to have your face and neck covered so, you must have endured *terrible* calamities. And your doctors must speak an odd language of brokenness."

"Ah!" I cried. "Now, you see, I am from Loasht—"

"Yes, I'm aware. It's a popular subject."

"Well, in Loasht—or at least in Yekunde, the city I'm from—we do not use tattoos to mark old injuries."

He blinked. "What in the world do you use them for?"

"For . . . fun? You should see my arms." I almost offered to show him the rest of my body, but that was the flirt in me, which I did not expect to be welcome in the Tetrarchia.

He looked puzzled for a moment, and then he laughed. I also laughed, and then we got drunk. He showed me the sorts of places where the Quru actually loosened their tongues and gossiped, even yelled a bit—where they "shared their mysteries," meaning any personal or impolite subject.

He told me his name was Akram, and that people in Abathçodu called him Manti Dumpling Akram, in order to distinguish him from anyone else with his given name. Quru family names were kept secret from all but one's closest friends (another "mystery"), a fact I had already learned in preparation for my journey.

"Named for my favorite food when I was a child," said Manti Dumpling Akram. "But I can't stand them anymore."

Later that night, Manti Dumpling Akram and his friends came up with the idea of asking a local doctor to attempt to read my "nonsense" tattoos. I agreed, because it sounded fun.

"But quickly," slurred Akram, "before the whole town learns your secret!"

I was quite tickled at the thought of my extremely visible facial tattoos being a secret.

The next morning, we were all quite hungover when I was introduced to a woman called Doctor Eldor. In Quruscan, I learned, the profession of "doctor" had followed so closely on the heels of older "healer" traditions—without those previous traditions being condemned as "witchcraft" or something similar—that nearly all their doctors were women.

Doctor Eldor took one look at the swaying lines crisscrossing my cheeks and laughed us out of her office. She did not even get to the upright crocodiles and marula trees on my arms, nor the stylized map of ancient, pre-Loashti Yekunde on my back.

From then on, Manti Dumpling Akram and I were great friends. Until, of course, he turned on me.

But before it all went wrong, I spent three seasons in Abathçodu, studying in its sprawling library, seeing the students and locals every day, asking after their families in the subtle and circumspect way of Quruscan. I felt as though I was liked, or at least tolerated. I had traveled there in the early summer, and stayed in that city through its dry warmth, the unending rains of autumn, and the freezing avalanches of winter. (In Yekunde, where I'm from, we hardly had a winter at all.) When their beautiful, if still quite wet and chilly, spring started, I truly felt comfortable in Abathçodu.

My name is Radiant Basket of Rainbow Shells. Which, in the manner of Loashti names, is fully translated, as a phrase, into every language in which it is said. In Loashti Bureaucratic (and also in the Skydašiavos in which I'm writing this), it sounds just fine, but in my native Zobiski, it is beautifully alliterative. You will just have to trust me on that, as I worry the Zobiski language is disappearing from the world.

This is my record of the time I spent with Kalyna Aljosanovna. I only knew that odd child of the Tetrarchia for a short time, but in those months, she changed the course of history on both sides of our border. I am both excited and scared to see what else will come of her work.

But before we meet Kalyna herself, we must understand the precarious days in Quruscan that ultimately led me to her. So, Abathçodu.

Abathçodu really was a wonderful city. I say this even now, despite the harrowing way in which I left it. Though the city was almost entirely Quru, with hardly any dwellers from the other Tetrarchic kingdoms (Masovska, Rotfelsen, and Skydašiai, respectively), it gathered together inhabitants from throughout Quruscan's mountains and steppes. This was thanks to its wonderful library, the school that sprang up around that library, and the artistic works that bloomed from said school.

The art was the biggest surprise to me. Not the plays and dances and poetry readings—I had expected those—but the statues. A friend of Akram's was a distinguished professor called Crybaby Vüqar, and he told me that the Quru people on the steppes loved statues. They, apparently, had statues everywhere: of generals on horseback, of unnamable gods dispensing laws, of famous ghost hunters and mystics, of anyone they could immortalize in stone or metal. But up in mountainous regions like Abathçodu, these sorts of displays were unpopular.

"The slanted ground and the wind, you see," Vüqar had explained over mugs of kumis, idly pulling at his mustache.

Akram then smiled ghoulishly and pantomimed something falling and crushing a person. To this he added an imitation scream under his breath.

Vüqar nodded intently, flourishing a hand toward Akram in emphasis.

But as Abathçodu grew over the last century or so, as the school drew in Quru from the rest of the kingdom, some had in them the steppe-born need to make and admire statues. An artist named Alfia had been the first to build one from hay, depicting an old, pre-Tetrarchic Quru king. The statue proved to be very popular, and so, after it was blown down the mountain, to the great confusion of the town below, Alfia built another. Embracing her material's transitory nature, she chose to portray a much less dignified subject: this statue was a self-portrait, showing Alfia bent over in an awkward position as she wove hay. I only know of it from contemporary descriptions, as the figure didn't last long—although there are many sketches in the library of her later works.

Alfia died less than a decade before I came to Abathçodu, and she was still beloved and venerated for having begun a local tradition that saw the city positively dotted with statuary. Just about every empty spot sported a figure crafted from temporary materials that would not cause too much harm if they became unmoored. Many were by known artists (like Doctor Eldor's husband, Big Rüstem), featured historical personalities, and were unveiled with dedication ceremonies; others appeared quietly in the night, depicting subjects of lesser grandeur, such as a favorite of mine: *Alimjun the Feckless Grocer, Ejecting Me from Her Store, as Rendered in Twigs and Curtains.*

Once, about a month into my stay, I was caught by a small gust of wind that sent me stumbling into a statue. It fell, its plaster cracked, and the head of the depicted laundress careened off a cliff, twirling wildly. I was mortified. But then everyone around me cheered and clapped. Vüqar explained to me that the destruction of an Abathçodu statue was as much a part of the art as anything else.

Naturally, this whole trend got me thinking about traditions that use effigies or dolls as stand-ins for those who are to be cursed or blessed. It's supposed to be a popular method far south in the Bandit States, with some scattered adherents in Masovska, but unheard of in Quruscan or further north. I began to absentmindedly compose the volume I would write for the Loashti Cultural Exchange Authority, which would entirely justify my choice to make this research trip to the Tetrarchia. How naïve that feels, looking back now.

The Library of Abathçodu had much on such dolls, although, upon further reading, it appeared this method was fading from use due to its, well, ineffectiveness. Curses mostly work through imitation, and it seems a doll is too dissimilar from its subject, which can move and think and react. It fascinated me nonetheless, and I made assiduous notes in my Commonplace Book on this, and on many other rituals and magics. In those library shelves I found the worldliness that the city itself lacked, as I immersed myself in every language I could read (which are quite a few, I must say).

The library had begun as the personal collection of some petty local prince in the days before Quruscan became its own nation, let alone part of the Tetrarchia. At that time, Abathçodu, the prince's capital, had been all yurts, although Vüqar told me this had already been but a vestige of nomadism. The prince loved to collect books and scrolls, despite reportedly not being much of a reader, and he began to create a library within the series of great, fur-carpeted yurts that made up his palace.

When Abathçodu was taken from him, his collection was left untouched, and his Library Officials became the city's librarians. Over the years, the library expanded into more yurts, and wooden buildings as well, until it sprawled throughout the streets like stalls on a market day. It twisted and turned, following its own strange logic, sometimes completely encircling the generational homes of families with no connection to the library or the school. To study in the Library of Abathçodu was to move throughout the city, dodging laughing children and men coming back from the hunt. Half the year, up in the mountains, the air was so dry that the yurts and buildings could be left open all day long, allowing in sunlight and the sounds of the street, while leaving the texts in good condition. Somehow, despite the seemingly haphazard nature of the place, the librarians always kept a watchful eye on what was taken, or damaged, and by whom.

The only reason that I, a Loashti, was able to peruse this magnificent library was due to the so-called Blossoming of good feeling between our nations. Or, if not *good* feeling, then comfortable acceptance and some cultural exchange.

Why did the Tetrarchia suddenly turn so favorably toward us? If our spies knew the answer, that knowledge was not disseminated to the masses. For centuries, the Tetrarchia had treated us as the great threat looming in the north, waiting to swoop down and . . . well, honestly, I haven't the faintest idea what we were expected to swoop down and do. If Loasht had truly wanted to conquer the place, I suspect our armies and guns could have done so.

But what would the Grand Suzerain have wanted with the Tetrarchia? It would have been an expensive place to conquer, an unruly place to govern, and then our southern neighbors would have been the Bandit States, which were even more vicious and sectarian.

The Tetrarchia, however, needed a common enemy in order to convince itself it was not a fragmented homunculus of a country. (I call it this with *love*.) As far as I knew, the Loashti government and its Grand Suzerain were more than happy to let this young country of "squabbling children" to the south have its way, so long as it did not bother them.

When the Tetrarchia troubled our borders—particularly in places like the ziggurat city of Galiag—our rebukes were swift and violent, but those rebukes were never followed up with conquest.

Such was the way of our countries until, mysteriously, the strongest anti-Loasht voices to our south—specifically, the nationalistic and isolationist factions in Rotfelsen, that most insular kingdom of the Tetrarchia—seemed to simply vanish. Overnight. Again, the reasons for this were never made clear to the normal citizens of Loasht, if even our leaders knew them. (Strangely enough, *I* would soon learn something of what had so altered Rotfelsen.) But a year later, the Blossoming officially began.

This meant Loasht now had a Cultural Exchange Authority, and that I was among its first applicants for a meager dispensation to study in the Tetrarchia. Did I overstate the usefulness of what my travels would teach me? *Of course* I did, but that had always been the way of my career.

Nonetheless, it was an exciting opportunity, as Loasht's libraries had suffered from centuries of our on-again, off-again war with what some termed "the occult," meaning any ritual that the one using the term did not like. At many points in our history, anything deemed "occult" was considered both unforgivably evil and entirely ineffective.

You see, Loasht, despite its varied peoples, was always terrible at ambiguity in certain things. There was right and wrong; there was true and false; there were exactly Eighty-Three gods; and you could practice your own culture so long as it did not conflict with the Grand Suzerain's will.

In my life to this point, the slow pendulum of Loashti policy and opinion had swung away from hatred of the "occult," and toward embarrassment at the past's purges and angry mobs. Magic was still considered, at least in academic spaces, to be categorically false, but not evil, which was why I'd been able to have a career at all. Curses, my specialty, are like any other rituals—for the most part—and have such a low success rate that I could easily claim, and sometimes believed, they were as ineffective as everyone else assumed. (I don't believe so now, and by the time you've finished reading this, I hope you won't either.)

But in the fractious, superstitious Tetrarchia? Ah! There they had "sorcery," "witchcraft," and a hundred other overlapping terms to describe harmful magics, alongside many more that did not assign moral values at all, such as "wizardry" or "psychicry." This was because, refreshingly, their many belief systems—countless gods, all with clashing desires and domains—left plenty of room for the unknown. Those people could have a beautiful flexibility in what they thought possible.

This meant the Tetrarchia's jumbled and forgotten libraries housed many volumes that Loasht had burned, in an orderly manner, centuries before my birth. For all my home nation's pride in its millennia of knowledge, the children nipping at our heels had caught the bits and pieces we wrongfully discarded.

When I Left Yekunde

"Must you look so happy to leave me?" asked my spouse, Silver Petals Alight on Sand, on the day I left Loasht.

"You know I'm not happy to leave *you*," I laughed. "And what's more, I am both happy and terrified."

We stood outside the doorway of our home: a squat little thatch-roofed stone building that was older even than Loasht's dominion over our lands, abutting the larger and slightly newer house where Silver's parents still lived. I had already shared my goodbyes with all three of them, but I could hear Silver's other father puttering in his garden.

Silver looked down at me and smiled sadly from their round face. They reached out a large, soft hand to stroke my hair—only just long enough for someone to grab it—which they did, playfully.

"Terrified?" they echoed. "Of those barbarians?"

"Now, that isn't nice."

"They call *themselves* that!" Silver replied, letting go of my hair and batting my shoulder lightly. "At their rulers' conference: the 'Council of Barbarians.'"

"Well," I offered, "its real name is actually 'The Divine Monarchic Council of Pure Blessed Blood for the—'"

"I don't care, Radiant. The Council of Barbarians, which only this year deigned to receive our ambassadors."

"'Our'?" I raised an eyebrow. "Are we sending Zobiski ambassadors now?"

"Perhaps soon we will," said Silver, with a shrug. "Our great-grandparents' generation would be dumbfounded at the simple fact that we have official papers now, which say 'Zobiski' and—"

"And have their own color, yes," I laughed. "We've come so far. And yet our great-grandparents' ancestors would be shocked at how they had to suffer!" I shrugged. "It's a cycle, but the Grand Suzerain's rule keeps it from going too far."

"In either direction," Silver sighed.

"Oh, certainly. But you see, Silver Petals Alight on Sand," I liked saying their full name in Zobiski, when I had the time; it was so beautifully sibilant, "that's why the Tetrarchia's prejudice will be novel! They won't fear me for being Zobiski; they'll fear me for being Loashti. Imagine being mistaken for Loashti!"

"We are Loashti."

"You know what I mean!" I grinned, and they couldn't help smiling back. "Anyway, the Tetrarchic peoples call themselves barbarians ironically."

Silver snorted.

"I love you too," I said. "And I love your meanness."

"So long as it's never aimed at you, my little weakling."

"I couldn't survive it."

They kissed me then, crushing me to them, as was their way: making me feel small and slight and helpless, almost squeezing the breath from me. Their strong arms, almost never covered in Yekunde's heat, were wreathed with tattoos of human footprints, in the shape of an old Zobiski prayer-dance that was seldom performed anymore as it was deemed to be "occult" and "atavistic." The fronds of our door rustled pleasantly.

"I'll miss your face," they said, lips inches from mine.

"Still?" I couldn't help replying. "It isn't quite so pleasing anymore."

"Stop that."

"It's just a—"

Silver broke our embrace. "*Stop that*."

"But—"

They gave me a look. Of course, I continued nonetheless.

"But I used to be *beautiful*," I said.

They held the bridge of their nose between their thumb and forefinger, eyes closed. "I do not want this to be our last conversation before you leave."

"But—"

"Please, Radiant."

I stopped. In the following silence, I looked over their shoulder at the heavy trees bordering the distant swamp. At the western end, I could just barely see where the mire opened up into the mouth of the south-flowing Lanreas River; where the great river boats of dark wood and lightly faded reed were stationed, tied casually to the shore but held fast by the mud of the swamp, as still as if they sat on land.

"This is all hard enough," said Silver, "with you leaving for at least a year, and everyone going on about whether or not this 'Blossoming' is viable. And not to mention Aloe Pricks a Mare upon the Mountain Bluff, and everything *he* is whipping up. And then for you to keep harping on about—"

"I know," I said. "Silver, I stopped."

They looked at me for a long time, silently. We weren't silent often. I studied Silver as I waited for them to find—or not find—whatever they were looking for. Personally, I was just marveling at how beautiful their plump face still was: warm, brown skin they'd never chosen to tattoo, still perfect and soft, with the lightest dusting of fuzz above the upper lip that had been there almost as long as I'd known them. Mesmerizing. Particularly when compared to the unfortunate crags and dents that I felt were accosting my face in middle age, leaving nothing to be proud of but my stubbornly high cheekbones.

Yes, I took Silver's heartfelt silence as a chance to indulge in exactly what they had forbidden me from saying aloud. To wonder why they, or anybody, would want to be around someone who could no longer use beauty to offset his tiresome nature.

We made our goodbyes. And as I walked away, out of our small community in Yekunde and away from my spouse, I called back over my shoulder:

"Don't sleep with anyone I wouldn't!"

They shouted back, "I will!"

Chapter Two

When Everything Went Wrong in Abathçodu

One afternoon during Abathçodu's mid-spring, I was sitting in the yurt that I rented from Alimjun the grocer, right behind her shop. Despite the statue depicting her, I had not (yet) found her to be at all feckless. Spring up there was still cold, to me, and I was wrapped in a beautiful Quru blanket of prismatic colors woven in a swirling pattern—I did not even have the Yekunde clothing I had come with anymore, as I'd sold them all to a collector of "oddities." Sitting there, I could smell the earthy fresh vegetables and pungently fermented hot peppers that sat in buckets at Alimjun's store.

I was bent over a beaten copy of *The Miraculous Adventure of Aigerim*, a rather silly old romance set mostly around the border of Quruscan and Skydašiai, back when they were separate countries. According to other sources I had read, this fanciful story contained scenes of magic that were very instructive as to how curses and blessings were carried out in the area a few hundred years ago. I was flipping through page after page of weeping maidens, tyrannical fathers, five-day sword fights, and many other things that would tell me quite a bit, were I studying Tetrarchic ideas of family, gender, history, or escape. But I was looking for the magic bits—and real magic, not the kind allowing characters to fly through the air or see for a thousand miles. And certainly not the great beast whose "flatulent death throes" created a gorge supposedly known "to this very day" as "The Thrashing, Bone-White Tail."

When I found a useful bit, I would copy it into the current volume of my Commonplace Book, which I'd kept since late childhood, and in which I jotted down quotations I came across in my reading, often with commentary, and small reminisces of my life. In my absence from Loasht, Silver became the keeper of its volumes, save for the three most recent, which I had brought with me to Quruscan.

> *Mindaugas the Sorcerer cackled with great malice as he watched his underlings carry out his orders. One henchwoman, a sad and gnarled old thing, was dressed as a mockery of Fair Aigerim herself, in a tattered headscarf of faded forest green. Mindaugas' second-in-command, the nefarious Romualdas, was swathed in wooden armor, painted silver in imitation of Aigerim's great love, Sukhrab, the Knight of the Moon. The two twisted doppelgängers spun in circles, at Mindaugas' insistence, to further muddle their minds and allow them to become mere vessels, able to dictate the actions of the True Great Lovers. In addition, Evil Mindaugas wafted toward them the smoke from his fetid mixture of—*

This is what I was copying down when I heard excited speech outside my yurt, in a different tenor than the constant, pleasant chatter of the grocery. That normal background of small talk had been interrupted by near silence and a series of harsh whispers—a sudden drop in volume as jarring and abrupt as any loud noise would have been.

I could not help straining for a moment to listen; who would not? I'm glad I did, as they were not hiding their words half so well as they thought.

"*You* should do it, Alimjun," someone was whispering.

"Me? Why *me?*" Alimjun's voice cracked out of its whisper for a moment. "Why must *I* when you are all right here?"

I wondered how many "you all" was but did not yet realize how relevant this was to me.

Another voice replied to Alimjun, this one too low-pitched for me to make out.

"That's right," said another whisper. "Because you have been sheltering him."

"Sheltering? Renting out to him, you mean."

I sat up.

"Aiding and abetting."

"He's on your land. In your old yurt."

More voices I couldn't understand.

"No. *Renting*. Have you gone mad?"

"Perhaps we all did, to allow him here. Some communal madness."

"Yes, yes! Like the Teneszca Dancing Hysteria."

"Mad or no, he's paid me, and *you're* here for him. You never said anything about 'colored papers' when he arrived, so I certainly never looked for them or . . . or noted their hue! *You* go get him."

I had thought, for a moment, that Alimjun was defending me, but she had only been defending her right to not "go get" me.

I heard no more after this, because, before I had even thought about it, I threw on a coat and bolted out the door of my yurt. I carried with me only the volume of my Commonplace Book that I had been filling with *Aigerim* pabulum, because it had not occurred to me to put it down. The pen I had been using lay on the floor of the yurt, staining Alimjun's rug.

I was at least three streets away before I fully realized what had happened, and I did not know whether I'd been seen or heard in my escape—whether I was being followed. I had stopped thinking and simply followed deep-seated Zobiski tradition and memory, passed down by our grandparents in terrified whispers.

I had never needed to run from enraged and whipped-up Loashti neighbors who were convinced that the Zobiski in their midst were practicing "blood magic" (which categorically does not exist). In my parents' generation, only a few had personal memories of fleeing mobs. But cultural memory is long in Loasht, for everyone. At various times, the Zobiski were seen as incorrigibly, dangerously "occult" people, even though our traditions simply involved a little more dancing, a different sort of chanting, and symbolic sacrifices a shade closer to the real thing. So when Loashti public opinion moved in certain directions, we were often on the wrong side of it.

It was this Zobiski history that had me stumbling through the streets of Abathçodu, trying desperately to not look like myself, as though I did not have tight curls, which had now grown three or four inches out from my scalp, and obviously ornamental tattoos. I tried to walk as fast as possible without looking like I was trying to escape anything. The spring sun was shining brilliantly that day, reflecting off the wetness of the streets, coaxing up flowers between the flagstones and making the gold threads of my Quru coat glimmer. I covered the markings on my hands and neck as much as possible, but was almost certainly, clearly, the "foreigner," because who else would be so fully covered in spring? Most Abathçodu citizens already had their coats open in this weather.

And I was cold even for me, with my teeth chattering and my fingers numb. Where was I even *going*, I wondered. I suppose many people would have gone to the authorities for protection, but Zobiski memory told me the authorities were *never* my friends. I hated myself, at the time, for my inability to go ask for help, to "save" myself. But I still refused to do so.

I stepped wrongly on my way up a steep hill lined with scent shops and began to tumble backward. I was self-possessed enough to not cry out and so spun silently back down the way I'd come. My quiet fall ended when I slammed bodily into a statue.

This must have been the loudest statue ever erected in Abathçodu: it was made of dried, crackly twigs hung with tens upon tens of little bells. I tumbled right through it, breaking it apart with much noise, until I lay in the center of its remains, with a great rock in my back and a small crowd of Quru faces looking down at me.

None of them cheered this time.

Then, in the sea of faces, I picked out Akram's. I called to him and tried to reach out toward him, but I was tangled in the twigs of the broken statue, and I could hardly move. With each try, the bells jingled about me. Everyone stared silently, so my weak cries of "Akram! Manti Dumpling Akram!" accompanied by the ringing, were the only sounds beside the wind, which further disturbed the bells.

Finally, Akram smiled and made his way toward me, quietly mollifying those he was walking past. He patted an old lady's hand and said something reassuring to her that I did not catch, before bending over to help me up. I gained my feet to more crackling and ringing, and the noises only sped up as he vigorously cleared the remains off of me.

"Why did no one cheer?" I whimpered.

"Eh?" asked Akram, still smiling at the crowd.

I realized I had said this in Zobiski and so repeated it in Cölluknit.

Akram patted my back. "Let's discuss it later, friend." His voice did not sound as though he was smiling, even though he was.

Akram walked me through the crowd, telling the people, "It's fine! It's fine. I'll handle it! Nothing to worry about!" as he continued patting my back. I coughed and looked sheepish.

"Was that a special statue?" I gulped once we were out of the crowd.

"We both know you're smarter than that," he replied. "You are trying to will that to be the case. To convince yourself."

I said nothing. He was right, of course.

"But you're too smart to outsmart yourself that easily," he continued. "Yet *not* smart enough, it seems, to avoid speaking Loashti in public just now. Don't do that again."

I opened my mouth to tell him I'd been speaking Zobiski, not Loashti Bureaucratic, but decided this wasn't the time for a pedantic correction.

Akram took me back to our favorite bar, a small wooden place on a winding little street. He had taken me there the day we met, and since then, he and I, often with Crybaby Vüqar and others, had spent many nights trading drinks and stories. I still thought of it as partly *my* bar, which was both sad and so very presumptuous of me. I still, right now, can remember the place well enough to navigate it with my eyes closed, avoiding the torches and the strange half-wall, winding toward our regular table. That table was situated so we were always in view, allowing Akram and his friends to reap the social capital of being seen with the talk of the town. This day, however, he led me to a different table: smaller and mostly hidden in the back. He sat me down and told me not to move—his smile still on his face, but fading.

I sat for a moment and began to worry that I was being set up for something, but just as I readied myself to run, Akram returned. He had a mug of kumis for himself and a brandy for me.

"You have an adventurous palate," he said, "but I think right now you could use something more familiar to you than our drinks. And stronger."

I nodded numbly and took a drink. It was not a particularly Loashti brandy, but it burned like what I was used to, and that was enough. I realized that even here in the warm bar, in spring, under my coat, I was shivering. Questions filled my head, but I just stared at Akram silently, imploringly.

He sighed, slowly turning his mug with one callused hand and laying the other across the top of the table. Finally, he looked up at me.

"This is a real mess, friend," he sighed.

"*What* is?"

"You know."

"I certainly do not, Akram."

He blew out a long breath. "But you're Loashti."

"Yes, Akram, we've been over that."

"So you must've heard about the Council."

"Of Barbarians?"

"*Don't*"—he slammed his hand on the table, then seemed apologetic as he finished his thought—"call us that. If you please."

"I'm sorry, Akram, it's just what—" He was glaring, so I cut myself off and started over. "Did it just take place? Did something happen?"

"Of course it did, friend. It's spring, isn't it? And yes, 'something' happened. How can you not know?"

"Akram," I pleaded, "I'm the same man you've known these past seasons. I spend all my time studying old books. Anything I learn about the world outside, any news, comes from *you*."

That made him stop and think a moment. I took another drink.

"I suppose that's true," he sighed, before intently fixing his eyes on mine. "Honestly, no one in town knows the specifics. By the time outside news gets to Loudmouth Zhyldyz, and she runs up here from Boloida to tell us, it's always a garble." He shrugged and tried another smile, which I weakly returned.

"Well, what did she say?"

Akram looked up at the ceiling, putting a callused finger to his chin. "Something like, 'The Loashti delegation told the Council that those whose identification papers are pink, sky blue, mottled orange, and . . .'

I think, chartreuse? 'Are trouble.'" He chewed his lip. "Now, how a normal person is supposed to know chartreuse from another green is—"

"Trouble? Trouble how?"

"I rather hoped you could enlighten me, friend."

"I am just a scholar, and not a very important one. No one sends me . . . sends me *new policies* by bird, smoke, or . . . or *magic mind power*. I certainly don't know what the Grand Suzerain—"

"Don't say his name so loud."

"I didn't say his *name*."

"And stop doing that," he snapped. "Always correcting. I am trying to help you."

I finished my drink, and Akram beckoned someone over to refill it. The attendant did a very good job of not looking at me; even though I knew his name was Granny's Favorite Dren, and just last month he had told me all about that same granny's declining health. Akram and I drank in silence for some time.

"Understand," said Akram, finally, "that this is all very confusing for us. Why, we've never had papers that say we're so-and-so from such-and-such, and we certainly can't read your Loashti ones. But yours *are* pink, yes? I recall you showing them to me."

"Yes." It hardly seemed worth lying about that now. "I think, Akram, that it's all much more confusing for me than it is for you."

"Oh, I don't know. You're Loashti, after all."

"Am I? If my papers are invalid, perhaps I'm not."

"Well then, that may be the problem!" He clapped his hands together, as though we had solved everything.

I looked into my drink. "Akram, am I in trouble because I am Loashti? Or because I'm not Loashti anymore?"

"Trouble? No one's in trouble, friend. But folks are scared, you see. You must understand, in Abathçodu, we've always been scared of . . . your home."

"Yes, the Tetrarchia—"

"I only know from Abathçodu," he cut in. "We were happy to have the Blossoming, happy to talk with you, to try not being scared. But even when you were here, being your charming self—"

(Even in the midst of all this, I felt myself preen a little, deep down.)

"—many were scared of what you might be up to. Of what you might *be*. Of how you might think of us. Be *studying* us."

"I wasn't studying you!" I wondered whether this was entirely true. Perhaps I had been, a bit. Idly. "And what do you mean about what I might be?"

"I don't know!" Akram seemed to be getting testy now. "Some kind of a . . . I don't know, Loashti sorcerer!"

"Sorcerer?!" I knew I should not have argued, should not have raised my voice in indignation, but I couldn't help myself. "I'm a scholar! And Loasht is even more irrational about supposed 'sorcerers' than the Tetrarchia."

"Don't call us irrational!"

Cowed, I moistened my lips and continued in a lower voice. "Loasht isn't the den of dark magics and sorcery that people here seem to think it is. Quite the opposite. Why, belief in magic is much more common here than it is up there."

Akram shut his eyes and tried to swallow his anger. "Please, I'm only trying to explain the mindset of the average mountain Quru. Is that also the mindset of your average Tetrarchic citizen? I cannot say."

I sighed for a long time and must have started on yet another drink. I was trying to digest all of this, and to marshal my thoughts.

"You know, Akram," I managed after some time, "many of those Loashti you're so scared of don't much like me because—"

"I know." He rolled his eyes. "You are Zerbenzi or—"

"Zobiski."

"—what have you."

"The Tetrarchia is not the only place with a divided populace, Akram."

"So you've told me."

"If you are scared of Loasht," I offered, "then perhaps—"

"I didn't say that *I'm* scared of anything. But, among some, there may be a feeling that you're . . . well, so wrong that even Loasht doesn't want you."

"Wrong *how?*"

"Loasht has always been a mystery to us."

"But—!"

"Radiant!" He hit the table again. Akram rarely used my name, and in Cöllüknit there was a harshness to it. "I tell you again that I am trying to help you. People are scared, and *one* nice man is not enough to wipe away centuries of overwhelming fear expressed in hushed voices."

We were quiet again for a long time. I finished another drink, which Dren immediately refilled at a gesture from Akram. I felt I'd had enough, but I appreciated his care for me.

"Thank you," I said at last, "for the drinks, and for trying to make sense of all this. I know you mean to help me, and I don't wish to be difficult."

He smiled and leaned in closer. "You aren't being difficult, Radiant. You're confused. I understand."

I nodded. "I just wish I knew exactly what was said at the Council about my papers. And why."

"Well then," he said, putting both hands on the table, as if to stand. "Why don't we go see the city Headwoman, yes? She'll certainly have a better idea about all of this, and can likely protect you."

And just like that, I felt all of my gratitude, all of my esteem for Akram, and what little comfort he had helped me feel, drain away. I realized, then, that I had been allowing the perceived warmth of both the brandy and Akram's friendship to permeate me, to let me feel just a touch safer, as though things were under control.

Surely, Akram must have thought, an appeal to the local authorities would have sounded good to me. Even if I *was* then held in a cell, or in a nice room, it would be for my safety, would it not?

But Akram had not considered that Zobiski memory I have mentioned. "Go see the Headwoman" may as well have been "walk into prison, where you will be killed, and your land given to your killers." This had not happened in my lifetime, but it was endlessly impressed upon me by my elders.

Trust the state only when the state trusts you was a well-known Zobiski aphorism.

A cold fear cut through me, filled me, and though it was terrible, a part of it was also gratifying. It blew icicles onto my warm tipsiness, banishing it entirely and bringing me to the present with great clarity. And, whether or not this was *fair*, I now saw that Manti Dumpling Akram was not my friend. Not anymore. He had been once; why, he had gone so far as to tell me his family name! But even if he still thought of himself as my friend, even if he truly believed my best and safest choice was to turn myself in, I knew better. No matter how he saw our relationship, he was now only a danger to me. An enemy to be avoided.

I did not know what had happened in Loasht, or at the Council of Barbarians; how, or if, I had been outlawed, but it hardly mattered. I was not safe in Abathçodu.

I set down my mug and cleared my throat. I was not sure how I would use this new understanding. I was not a great liar; I liked to think it was my honesty and straightforwardness that had endeared me to Akram and the others in the first place, aided perhaps by the remnants of a faded beauty.

"Yes. Yes," I finally managed. "Maybe you're right."

"I am," said Akram. "You'll see."

I nodded, because I could not bring myself to even pretend to agree more than that. (Had Kalyna yet entered my life, she would have been aghast at my inability to manipulate this man.)

Akram stood and looked down at me, smiling. The attendant, Dren, who had been dutifully refilling my mug, was also standing by our table, looking down at me. He was not smiling. I gulped audibly. My throat was so dry I almost took a little more to drink, but I could not count on being scared into sobriety a second time.

I fixed my eyes on Akram's thick midsection and hoped that he wouldn't know I was purposefully avoiding eye contact.

"May I," I croaked, "stop by my yurt and get a few of my things first?"

There was silence for a moment, and I could not bring myself to look up and see how this was received. My hope was that it was a reasonable enough request, and that they would now think I was resigned to some degree of imprisonment.

"Of course," said Akram. From his voice, I could tell he was still smiling. "I will go with you."

"No, thank you. That's—that's—that's not necessary."

"But I want to keep you safe," he said. "Safe from the unreasoning fear carrying away some of our good neighbors."

So he did not trust me and wanted to keep me in his sight. Or he did not trust his neighbors. Or, even worse, he *did* trust them to string me up.

I looked up at Akram, finally. It was amazing how quickly I had stripped that face of anything resembling friendliness or affection—much quicker than he could have, I'm sure. He was, after all, still trying to be friendly.

"So," I said, "you are afraid my presence will force them to make mistakes? Are they not full humans, possessed of a will of their own?"

His smile faltered. "What did I say about your endless corrections, Radiant? Come, let's go to your yurt."

I stood. My knees were shaking. "Are you worried I'll run?"

"Perhaps."

"Akram, where would I run to?" Though I *did* intend to run, I meant this question. I had no answer. Perhaps I hoped he did.

But all I could see was an enemy unnerved at such a naked show of fear and anguish.

"Come now, friend." He put a hand on my shoulder. "Let's not make a scene. It was embarrassing enough when you fell down out there. You know we don't love great, ah, *outpourings*."

I nodded and walked out into the street. My eyes burned. In fact, my body was heating up: cold fear was being replaced by something else, although I knew not what. Dren did not follow us, at least. Out in the empty little side street, it was just Akram and me. It had already gotten dark.

"Now," he said, "let's go get some of your things. Don't worry about your library books; I can return them for you."

Akram was my enemy now, but the way he said this last part made it clear he didn't know it; he really did feel he was doing me a great kindness. To him, in my hour of need, his role as my friend, and as a reasonable resident of Abathçodu, was to help me turn myself in and keep me from incurring library fines. I looked in his eyes and saw a genuine feeling of care.

So I hit him. It was all I could think to do. I had not hit anyone since I was a child, and I mostly threw myself awkwardly at Akram and flailed wildly for his face. I doubt I hurt him much, but I did knock him over. (He had had a few drinks himself.) Akram sat on the ground and stared up at me with a look of stunned betrayal.

"Radiant!" he yelled. I don't know if it was imploring or angry, if he wanted me to be sensible, or if he had been convinced that all Loashti were indeed evil. Whatever his feelings, I ran from them.

Soon after, I wondered whether doing what Akram wanted would have been the better choice. If turning myself in and accepting mild imprisonment would have been perfectly safe and uneventful. But for all that I loved (and still love) Abathçodu, I could not be sure that I wouldn't be accused of something impossible and executed. Even beyond that, having it decided for me, and being forced to put my life in the hands of the authorities, felt unfair and insulting.

So I ran, although I did not know where to. Not back to Alimjun's store and my yurt, though I could not bear the thought of leaving my Commonplace Book volumes behind.

At some point, as I ran aimlessly, I began to be chased. I still don't know if Akram raised the alarm, or if he still considered himself too much of a "friend" to do so. But soon enough, disparate groups of people were looking for me and shouting. I didn't understand what they were shouting, and this is likely for the best.

Abathçodu, like most Quru mountain cities, did not have a real guard or garrison: just its citizens stepping up when needed. This lack of guards had been one reason I chose the place—it felt safer to me. And perhaps it still was, when compared to the capital and other great steppe cities, or the border-fortress cities in the mountains through which I had initially passed.

So it was groups of concerned citizens that hunted me through the streets as I felt my chest ache and my breath grow short. I am not someone who has spent much of his life running or otherwise exerting himself. What's more, I no longer recognized the streets I ran through, as the city I had known by heart became a dark, harrowing maze.

I heard, "Over there!" repeated many times, from different directions, followed by boots thudding toward me. I looked behind me and felt tears sting my face, obscuring my view so that all I saw was an indistinct mass of people.

As I looked back, I came to a jerking stop when something crashed into the front of my right shoulder. It was the strong hand of someone standing before me.

"Hey," said a gruff voice. "Hold still."

I turned and saw a cloaked figure taller than me. Between the darkness and my tears, I couldn't see the face. I began to try thrashing out of its grip.

"Stop that," the figure said, gripping me tighter. I realized that the street beyond this person was empty. But pursuers were still barreling down behind me.

I thrashed again, hoping to get behind this tall person.

"I said, stop that!" They sighed. Then: "Get behind me."

Smoothly, as though rather than a struggling man I was a chair on casters, I was simply placed behind the figure. I heard a sword drawn from its sheath.

I decided then that perhaps I should not keep running but stay behind the tall person with the sword. I was entirely out of breath, anyway. I wiped the tears from my eyes.

There was yelling when the pursuers—some five people, but mostly unarmed—encountered my savior. One of them lunged forward, and was repelled by a cut raking, not too deeply, across the right arm and chest. Some more words were yelled, and then the concerned citizens ran off for more help.

I knew then who my savior was before they turned to face me. Her easy violence, lanky height, and uneven straw-colored hair in the moonlight made her unmistakable. This was the sellsword who had seen my way to Abathçodu the previous summer. A Rotfelsenisch woman named Dagmar Sorga.

She sheathed her sword and stood staring at me for a moment. Then she slapped my face, but not hard.

"Hey, smart boy. Get moving, will you?"

Excerpt from *My Wondrous Travels, the Second Part: Outside Loasht* by the famed Loashti merchant Dust in the Air Is Not a Cloud

There is simply no reason to visit the Tetrarchia for one who is not a merchant, or a dragoman escorting a merchant. Its wonders—such as the great rock of Rotfelsen and the congested forests of Masovska, home to a temple even older than Loasht—are so <u>normal</u> to the locals that they never think to treat them as attractions. They are such a simple group of peoples that they fail to understand how strange their lives and homes are.

What's more, for a merchant such as myself, there is hardly ever a reason to go beyond Skydašiai. I had hoped that in visiting the other three Tetrarchic kingdoms, I would find stranger textiles and produce, new dyes or spices. But perhaps the Tetrarchia's only great accomplishment is how seamless and easy trade is <u>within</u> its borders. In this one way, perhaps, Loasht could even learn from the Tetrarchia. (Loasht is, of course, much larger.) Anything interesting that can be bought in the Tetrarchia can be bought in Skydašiai: at a slight markup, yes, but you will save much by avoiding travel through inhospitable lands inhabited by unhelpful people.

Honored Reader, you may take it from me, who has traveled to all of the farthest places: there is simply no reason to visit Rotfelsen, Masovska, or Quruscan.

Chapter Three

How I Left Abathçodu, with the Help of Farbex the Good Donkey

"Get moving where?" I asked breathlessly as Dagmar began to push me down the street, away from my pursuers. My pursuers who had been my neighbors for nearly a year.

"I don't know," she said. "Away. You're the smart boy." Her Cöllüknit was halting but did the job.

"Why—?" I took a deep breath and tried again. "Why are you here? I'm glad to see you, of course, but it's been three seasons."

She moved to the next intersection, looked down every street, and then seemed to pick the left turn at random.

"Thought you could use some help," she said. Then she stopped so abruptly that I bumped into her. She rounded on me. "You *can* pay?"

I blinked. "I . . . What will you do if I can't? *Un*-save me? Throw me back to them?"

"No. No. But we will go our separate ways."

My mouth went dry. I must have looked very strange, standing in the middle of the street, slowly licking my lips as I stared fervently at nothing.

"I can pay," I finally said. "If we can get my things."

Dagmar looked thoughtful for a moment, tapping a long finger against the side of her nose.

"Do you . . . erm," she began. "Do you speak Rotfelsenisch?"

I shook my head and then offered, "I can *read* it decently."

Dagmar groaned and stared off into space, as though she would see the words she needed there. She spat some sort of Rotfelsenisch oath or insult. There was still shouting in the distance, and it sounded as though the chorus was growing.

"Do you have," she began again, "anywhere safe you can wait? A friend or, ah, ally?"

I thought about this, as the voices clamoring for me got louder. Dagmar did not seem particularly worried, which I took as proof that we were, for now, safe. I felt like a child relieved that an adult was now here to fix everything, even though she was younger than me.

My one-time friend, Manti Dumpling Akram, was of course right out. Certainly, I could hope that my terrified flight had shaken his resolve—perhaps even shaken his trust in the fairness of authority—but I was not about to turn right around and ask for his kind of "help."

"Think faster, smart boy," urged Dagmar, as she grabbed me by the collar of my jacket and dragged me around a few corners, into an empty yurt. We were at the base of a hill covered in yurts, like friendly little mushrooms, right where the wooden buildings ended in this part of town. Dagmar deposited me onto a stranger's bedroll.

"What would you have done if someone was home?" I asked, feeling surprisingly mild about everything.

"No one is," she replied, standing by the entrance. "Lucky them."

Would the librarians help me? I had become familiar with a number of them, and perhaps those who spent all day buried in old texts would better understand the historical context of my situation. *Or*, as the guardians of the Library of Abathçodu's system, integrity, and order, they would prefer that things go back to the way they had always been. Either way, I had never spoken much with any of them outside of searching for books. That was the way of the library.

"Find the Loashti!" came a voice from outside. It sounded like the person yelling was running right past us and up the hill.

Dagmar grumbled something at me in Rotfelsenisch, which I

assumed meant "hurry up" or similar. At some point, she had silently drawn her sword.

I remembered the temporary, and clandestinely placed, statue I had seen some months ago—*Alimjun the Feckless Grocer, Ejecting Me from Her Store, as Rendered in Twigs and Curtains*—and wished I'd known the name of its sculptor. Perhaps that person would have hidden me, purely out of spite, as Alimjun was my landlady.

"Maybe Doctor Eldor?" I finally asked.

"Sure," Dagmar hissed.

"Do doctors in the Tetrarchia have any . . . *code* about how they help people? The dictates of which can, sometimes, supersede the government's wishes?"

Dagmar's passable Cöllüknit broke down at that question, so she stared at me as though I had babbled hidden oaths in the Words of the Gods. Backward.

"Let's try Doctor Eldor," I sighed.

"Sure," she repeated. Then she peered out of the yurt and beckoned to me.

The bottom of the hill was quiet now, and I did not even hear yelling in the distance. Had they given up? Had the whole city been roused against me, or just a small, angry aberration? Perhaps there were even competing groups, and Akram and Vüqar were leading a faction that wanted to keep me "safe" in official custody.

Whatever the case, I felt safest with Dagmar and her sword. She was not bothered by my being Loashti, because she hardly ever seemed bothered at all.

I managed to get my bearings and lead us to Doctor Eldor's without incident. The streets were mostly quiet now, which, given the bustling school and its merry students, was worrying. It was dark, but not that late yet. Dagmar flattened herself against the wall of the doctor's wooden house, and I knocked on the door.

Doctor Eldor opened the door slowly, cautiously, with warm candlelight radiating from behind her. She was a stout, gray woman who always looked inquisitive. When she saw me, she stopped opening the door and left it halfway.

"Is it an emergency?" she asked. "Did they hurt you?"

This moment of seemingly genuine worry, even if it was purely professional, made tears come to my eyes for the second time that night. I very pathetically wiped them away on my sleeve.

"Not yet," I whimpered. "Will you let me hide here?" My voice cracked. "Just—just for a little while?"

Eldor only hesitated a moment, but in that time, I fancied I saw a thousand calculations and emotions cross her eyes. Then she opened the door fully.

"Come in. It isn't illegal to harbor you yet. Just frowned upon."

I rushed in, and Dagmar appeared behind me, like a looming death spirit with her sword a pale glint angling out of her cloak. She followed me in before Eldor could fully react.

"Who is that?" she asked, as Dagmar kicked the door closed.

"My protector," I said.

Eldor nodded at the bare blade. "And that is for . . . ?"

"You, had you turned him down," said Dagmar, as she sheathed her sword. It did not sound like a threat, just a fact of life.

Eldor, in the most classic Quru fashion, asked no further probing questions. She led us through the small front room of her home, which was where she treated patients, complete with a small couch and a number of strange instruments.

Off to the side of the doctor's office, there was an open door into the workshop of her husband, Big Rüstem, where we could see piles of hay and cane, plaster heads for temporary statues that had not yet been constructed, and small models no more than a foot high. Dagmar craned her neck for a closer look into the artist's domain.

Meanwhile, Doctor Eldor took us into a different, smaller back room, which contained a low table, with sitting pillows on the floor; a multicolored lamp hanging from the ceiling; and wall shelving stacked high with jars. She closed the door and sat on a pillow, and I joined her nearby. Dagmar put her left boot on the face of the table, leaning forward, resting her left elbow on her knee and idly dangling her hand. That this was extremely uncouth could be read in the slight curl of Eldor's lip.

I could now see Dagmar's face fully in the light from above, refracted through red, green, blue, and yellow glass. The sellsword looked just as I remembered from the previous summer: a lean, pale face, with brown eyes searching suspiciously even while she seemed unbelievably calm. She was less sunburned than she had been, and I think she had a new scar: a nick below her jaw.

"Only one exit," she said.

"Either you trust me, or you do not," said Eldor, looking up at her. "In here, if anyone comes to the door, they will not see you. If Rüstem's workshop door was closed, it would make them suspicious."

"I," replied Dagmar, shrugging, "am just being observant."

The Rotfelsenisch woman leaned down and elbowed me in a way that was meant to be chummy. I went stiff and nearly screamed in fear. Dagmar gingerly removed her hand and stood up straight.

"So, smart boy," she said, "where is your . . . um . . ."

"Things?" I offered.

". . . money," she finished, at the same time.

I stared down at my knees, took a deep breath, and tried again to be still.

"No . . ." I gulped, then tried again, closing my eyes. "No money if you don't get my books." It was not courage—only the thought that going through all of this *and* losing my Commonplace Book volumes would be too great a calamity.

"Yes, yes, I'll get your *things*. I just forgot the"—she spat out a Rotfelsenisch oath—"Cölluknit word for 'things.' Why must such a simple word have six syllables?"

Doctor Eldor opened her mouth to answer, but I shook my head at her, and she decided against it.

I, with Eldor's assistance, tried to give Dagmar directions to my rented yurt behind Alimjun's shop. When she didn't understand, we rearranged some jars on the table into a quick, makeshift map, which she grasped instantly.

"And when you smell fermented peppers," added Eldor, "head toward the scent."

"Why didn't you *start* with that?" sighed Dagmar.

She finally removed her foot from the table and then shook herself out of her cloak. Underneath, Dagmar was wearing thick leather trousers and a blue, billowy blouse, with a number of small red feathers sewn onto it. The specks of red rippled as she rolled up her sleeves. Dagmar's arms were long, wiry, muscular, and absolutely etched with scars: nearly as covered as mine were with tattoos. Some of those scars were still red, and the doctor widened her eyes at them.

"You should take your cloak," I said. "It gets cold up here at night." It was a stupid thing to say.

"Cute," replied Dagmar. Then she was gone.

After a few minutes, I felt I had to do something, so I got up to inspect Doctor Eldor's jars. She watched me quietly, and seemingly dispassionately, from her seat on the floor.

"Are you a doctor of some kind?" she finally asked, as I gazed at a jar of dried mushrooms. "Or a scholar of healing? I would be very disappointed if *now* I learned that you had been a fellow doctor, or whatever the Loashti version is, and we had not discussed it."

"No, no. I'm not. May I smell these mushrooms?"

"Yes, but don't take in too much vapor."

"I am a scholar," I continued, "of folklore and—ooh, what a smell!—rituals, and the like." Now was certainly not the time to say that I studied curses. "Many of these mushrooms are used in ceremonies I have studied."

I could positively hear Doctor Eldor raise a suspicious eyebrow at this.

"Loashti sorcery?" she asked.

"Why would I study that in the Tetrarchia, Doctor?"

She made a vague noise of labored assent, which turned into a long throat clearing.

"Well," she said, "that is why people here fear you. Loashti sorcery."

"Meaning what, exactly?"

"I don't really know," she admitted readily. "I think that if my neighbors out there did know what that meant, they might not fear you so much."

"*Our* neighbors," I muttered, because I could not help myself.

"What was that?" she asked. I don't know if she actually didn't hear me or was politely giving me a chance to rethink what I'd said.

"Loasht," I began slowly, "is much more virulent about stamping out what it considers to be 'sorcery' than the Tetrarchia has ever been."

She made a thoughtful, but not at all assenting, grunt. I went back to fawning over her collection in an attempt to stop worrying about my predicament.

I got the feeling that, regardless of my area of study, or my origin, mine was simply a personality that Eldor would never have liked: chatty, fanciful, and argumentative. And yet, she was protecting me while Akram, who did like me, had not. He may have thought he was, but that was beside the point.

I next browsed the doctor's collection of preserved cacti, and we had a nice, long silence, until she said, "They are not bad people, you know."

"Who?" I asked. I still faced the jars but no longer saw them.

"The people here," she said. "In Abathçodu."

"I am sure some of them are bad, and some of them are not bad," I replied. I did not turn to face her, but scrupulously inspected labels. "Just like anywhere."

"You know what I mean."

"You mean, the people who were chasing me through your streets—"

"Yes."

"—because of some faraway change in policy—"

"Yes."

"—that no one here can fully articulate—"

"Yes!"

I had never heard her yell before, so I quenched whatever I had meant to say next. I took a deep breath instead.

"They're scared," she said.

I wanted to tell her that *I* was scared. That I was alone in a foreign place, hunted by those with the luxury to be "scared" in packs. To chase down and overpower the unimportant, isolated, powerless scholar who "scared" them so. But I said none of that. Instead, I walked back over to the table, sat down on a pillow, and looked at her.

"All right," I said. "They're good people. They're just scared. What do you wish me to *do* with that knowledge?"

"Just—don't judge them too harshly."

"I hardly see how my judgments of them will matter."

"I respect you," said Doctor Eldor. "You are clearly learned, and it must have taken great courage to come study here in the first place."

I sucked my teeth audibly.

"And so," she continued, "I wish you to have a little mercy in your consideration of my neighbors."

At least ten possible responses came to my mind, but I imagined each one would have made Doctor Eldor angry, sad, or more argumentative. I wanted her to keep sheltering me, but I could not bring myself to concede that I was in any place to have *mercy*.

She continued: "I would simply hate to think that you, or anyone, was viewing them unfairly. They are not hateful, violent people, deep down."

I was about to say that their "deep down" had nothing to do with me. Thankfully, Dagmar returned before I got myself kicked out of the good doctor's home.

My mercenary savior now *sat on* the small table, with her dirty boots on the floor. (She almost stepped on a sitting pillow, but I saved it.) Her sword was sheathed, her elbows rested on her thighs, and she was sweating and breathing hard. In front of her, on the floor, sat two of my packs.

"I grabbed all I could." She winked. "I hope it was the right yurt."

It was. Inside were some Quru clothes, most of my money and valuables, every volume (*Thank the Eighty-Three!*) of my Commonplace Book not back in Loasht, and a few of the other books I had brought with me. Not all, but I wasn't going to be picky: my own volumes contained everything I'd recorded of my research thus far, alongside anything else that caught my eye. Dagmar had not brought, however, any of my glass bottles or dried gourds, which contained what I used to keep my skin and hair as soft and beautiful as was possible in this dry climate. (The typical Quru hair texture is so different from mine that they sold nothing up there that would be helpful to me.)

Also in the packs were a few library books, as of course Dagmar had not taken the time to pore over what was mine and what was borrowed before throwing things in the bag. These I left with Eldor to return.

"And please do," I added. "I won't have it said that I stole your books, besides."

Doctor Eldor nodded sagely.

As I handed her the last one, *The Miraculous Adventure of Aigerim*, Eldor stopped just short of taking it. I looked down and saw a splatter of fresh blood on the cover. The doctor looked up at Dagmar.

"What?" asked the sellsword.

"They are just *scared*," Eldor repeated, as though Dagmar had been present for our conversation. Or as though I directly controlled her.

Dagmar grinned. "They are now."

Eldor trained a withering look on me.

I readied myself to leave, and Eldor insisted I keep the stained copy of *The Miraculous Adventure of Aigerim*. I didn't want to waste space on a light, romantic adventure—which was, crucially, not light *to carry*—but I was beginning to wonder what might set the doctor off and cause her to throw us to her neighbors. I like to think that she was too good a person to do such a thing, but I had no way of knowing for sure.

"So," said Dagmar, "how do we get you out of town?"

"I . . ." I gaped. "I thought you had a plan?"

"I don't know the city," she said. "And I'm not much of a planner."

"It's still dark," said Doctor Eldor. "Maybe you can sneak out?"

"Someone will be watching the borders," said Dagmar.

"Abathçodu doesn't really have set borders," I added.

"Well," the sellsword replied, "*someone* will be *somewhere*. And I can't cut through everyone."

Eldor's eyes widened, and her jaw clenched. Dagmar did not seem to notice.

"There must be a way we can sneak out," muttered Dagmar. "What are those . . . uh, silly sculptures all over the place?"

"You mean the statues my husband makes," said Eldor.

"Yes, exactly! Those daft things of sticks or mud or hay that break, or go tumbling down the mountain, if you so much as look at them."

Eldor pressed her lips together angrily. I must admit, in that moment, I felt more of a kindred spirit with the doctor, and with the city that was persecuting me, than I did with my brutish, indelicate savior. There is a lot to consider there, another day.

"Maybe we can do something with them," said Dagmar. She mumbled for a bit in Rotfelsenisch and then added in Cöllüknit: "What would that one do?"

At the time, I did not know who "that one" was, or even their gender, thanks to Cöllüknit's single, universal pronoun.

"Doc," asked Dagmar, "which cliffs offer the softest landing?"

"Well . . ." began Doctor Eldor.

"Wait . . ." I begged.

"You know," Dagmar continued, "with a lot of, um . . ." She mimed something unintelligible. "With a lot of little bumps rather than a long drop. Preferably with some nice thickets as a cushion."

"A cushion?" I asked.

"But not too soft!" added Dagmar. "Some sharp bits would be good. Bits that catch and cut down on the . . . the, ah . . ." She mimed some more.

"Momentum?" offered Eldor.

Dagmar nodded and looked relieved.

According to Dagmar, what "that one," whoever they were, would have done was mad, senseless, and dangerous. But it was also the only idea that anyone offered.

And so it was that Doctor Eldor, Big Rüstem, and their "large assistant" (Dagmar in a cloak and hood) trudged through Abathçodu carrying a new work of the artist's. This statue was made of hay and held together by the hoops and planks of an old barrel: it depicted Farbex the Good Donkey, a popular character beloved for his jolly rotundity. Big Rüstem spent the whole way grumbling that anyone who got a good look would be disgusted at how bad a job he had done—but of course, this was because he had thrown Farbex together at the last minute, with myself bundled inside the friendly animal's straw guts.

What a terrifying ordeal this was. I was encased in a prison weak and pliable enough that I fancied I could be seen and heard, but stiff enough that I could not move. The beloved Farbex had been chosen to give me lots of padding, but the reason I needed such was particularly ghastly.

From what I heard on the way, many residents of Abathçodu did in fact see Big Rüstem's statue of Farbex, but no one saw it very well. They were all quite busy looking for the Loashti sorcerer.

After some particularly harsh and violent words about me from a passerby, I heard Dagmar whisper, so quietly that I'm sure no one else could hear her: "Don't cry now." There was no harshness or judgment in it—simply a warning.

It must have looked like she was speaking into merry Farbex's much-celebrated rump, and *that* image did stifle my tears.

Once the statue of the Good Donkey was placed in its spot, Doctor Eldor's large, clumsy assistant bumped it.

"Oops," said the large, clumsy assistant.

All was spinning and falling, bouncing and cutting, terror and pain. Finally, I lay curled up in my hay prison, not even attempting to free myself. Hours later, I was wrenched out of whatever thicket I had ultimately landed in, and then Dagmar eviscerated poor Farbex, freeing me.

"No more lazing about," she said, throwing down my bag. "Is anything broken?"

"I don't know," I said as I tried to stand. It took three attempts, but I managed. I was bruised and shaken, with my clothes torn, and my skin lacerated all over. Certainly, neither of my arms felt as though they were quite correctly fitting in their sockets, but they could move, at least.

"You seem whole." Dagmar clapped her hands loudly and grinned. "Looks like the burrs and spines of the Quru stinkbrush did their work!"

"At least I was in there so long I can't smell it anymore," I sighed.

"How lucky!"

"Oh yes."

"Because you smell like shit!"

"Yes."

"Well. Let's go, smart boy!"

"Where?"

"Away. Then we figure out the rest."

I nodded numbly, for I was numb all over, and followed Dagmar down the steep rocks. It was morning now, and Quruscan's springtime sun was just peeking over the mountains in pink lines. I could smell the flowers around us, and even hear chirping and movement nearby. There was no path here, just gnarled beige trees, low gray brush, and blooms of every color I could possibly imagine. When I looked behind me, the cliff face above was angled such that I could not even see Abathçodu.

"So, how did you know to come save me?" I finally asked, after we'd traveled for perhaps an hour.

Dagmar, walking in front of me and cleaving the brush with a long dagger, grunted back, "I saw that things are going bad for some Loashti. Remembered I dropped you there." She shrugged. "Thought you might need help."

"Going bad how? I still hardly know myself."

"What I heard was that Loashti with papers colored . . ." She took a moment to grasp for the words, snapping the fingers of her free hand as though it would help. "Loashti with papers colored pink, robin's egg blue, orange marble, or lime are no longer Loashti. Ex-Loashti." Dagmar kicked over some sort of small dirt mound that must've been a creature's home. "I knew some people here would take this chance to . . . oh . . . you know . . ."

"Act upon their worst impulses?"

"Yes! I think. My Cölluknit is still not . . . good."

"Wait. How did you know my papers are pink?"

"Went through your . . . your . . . *things* while you slept."

"Of course."

"'Things,'" she muttered. "What a word to make so . . ."

Dagmar stopped moving for a second and turned back to look at me. Her expression seemed almost . . . plaintive.

"Smart boy, do you speak Skydašiavos?"

"I do."

"Oh! Thank the gods!" she shouted in that language. "I have *much more* of this than Cölluknit."

Quite pleased, Dagmar went back to cutting our way through the brush.

"I should have asked you that months ago, when we first met," she said, partly to herself. "Been more inquisitive. That's what she would have told me to do."

I did not ask who "she" was.

"Anyway," Dagmar continued, "I came to find you because I know it's easy to make Tetrarchic folks turn on Loashti. Some of us, anyway, and I should know: I'm from Rotfelsen, and most Rots don't like *anybody*."

"Is the whole Tetrarchia now hostile to me?"

"You'd have to ask the whole Tetrarchia." She looked back at me over her shoulder and winked. "Not everyone is as reasonable and tolerant as I."

"What a pity," I murmured in Zobiski.

To her credit, Dagmar did not demand to know what I had just said in my native tongue. Whenever I would speak in that, or Loashti Bureaucratic, she acted as though I had said nothing. I did the same when she let Rotfelsenisch words hack their way through her throat.

Dagmar seemed to hold no great animus toward Loasht, or indeed anybody. She was evenhanded and nonplussed with everyone—and also willing to kill everyone. (Or most everyone.)

"Do things in the Tetrarchia," I asked, "usually change so suddenly after every Council of . . . well . . ."

"Barbarians? Say it if you mean to say it." She cut her way through another thicket. "But no. I've guarded Prince Friedhelm at . . . five or six Councils? I've lost track. Usually nothing happened that would . . . that would . . ."

"That would change day-to-day life?" I offered.

"Yes, exactly. Until the last one I attended. Since then, things have been much more . . . interesting."

"Was that last year? When the Blossoming started?"

"No, no. Year before."

I nodded as though this explained much to me, and we trudged in silence for some time.

"I don't want to scare you off," I finally said, "but you *do* know I have less money than when you last went through my belongings, yes? Those were savings. I've been studying in Abathçodu, not doing paid work."

"Well, I *last* went through your things when I retrieved them last night." She laughed. "How much have you spent since then?" She then muttered, "Things. Things. *Things.* Two syllables; much better in Skydašiavos."

"It's only one in Zobiski," I offered.

"My head won't hold another language." Dagmar destroyed a bush that puffed out dust as some sort of attempt at defense, causing her to cough. "Anyway, you can at least pay me all fifty of your remaining silver abazi when we part. Work has been slow lately—not many blood debts or duels in Quruscan. They are not the most martial of people."

"I know, that's why I came here." I laughed sadly. "I thought it would be *safe.*"

It was true: Quruscan's security lay in the difficulty of crossing its mountains and steppes, not in an ever-present army or an armed populace.

"Well," replied Dagmar. "It's been too safe for me. I don't know why I've stayed."

She finally cut our way to a path and cried out in joy, before spitting loudly on the ground. The path was small and winding, but it was something. We began walking side by side.

"No," she sighed under her breath. "I know why I've stayed." She sounded disgusted with herself.

"Why?"

Dagmar's back straightened, and her eyes widened.

"Did I use Skydašiavos?" she asked.

"You did."

"Huh."

"You don't have to tell me why you stayed."

"I know I don't," she grumbled. Then a long sigh. "Because of a person."

"I see."

We were quiet for some time as we moved downhill along the path. Dagmar kept looking around to see if we were being followed, or were anticipated, but we seemed to be alone. I mostly tried to not think about how hungry I was becoming.

"Do we know where we're going?" I asked eventually.

"Rather," she said. "We're looking for zip lines to the steppe. Down there we'll find a place that may contain a person I know."

"The same person you . . . ?"

"Yes."

"You don't sound like you really want to find this person."

"I don't know," she said, stopping and turning toward me. "But did you *like* falling down the cliff in a roll of hay?"

"Of course I did not."

"Well, that was the best *I* could do. I told you I am not a planner. I am a stabber. But I cannot stab your way back to Loasht. You do want to get back to Loasht, don't you?"

I hadn't even considered it. I had been so caught up in escaping Abathçodu.

"I don't know," I said. "If I'm no longer Loashti, can I even go back?"

As this occurred to me, I was overwhelmed with a feeling of impossibility, of the insurmountable.

And what of my family in Loasht? Were all Zobiski now exiled, or was something different happening to them? Something better? Something worse? I could not imagine I'd be allowed back into the country, but I also had to know what was happening in Yekunde, and I could think of no way to do that from the mountains of Quruscan.

"I assume," I said, "that the guards at the border will take one look at my papers and—"

"That's why we sneak you in," said Dagmar.

I moaned and realized how parched my throat was. I would die here in the Tetrarchia, hunted and despised. I would never again see the lands of my forebears, who had been forced to become part of Loasht, and whose descendants were now, it seemed, being forced to sever themselves from its embrace.

"I suppose I have to go back," I said. "See if this is all some bureaucratic *mistake* the Academy can fix for me."

It seemed unlikely, but once a teacher or researcher was fully in the embrace of the Loashti Academy, that body did what it could to protect them. It could at least be a safe place for a few days as I found out what had happened.

"And if it's not some mistake," I continued, "I will have to find my family and . . . figure out what all we can do next."

"So, that's a yes to getting back into Loasht?"

"I suppose?" I croaked.

"Then you need someone wilier than I," said Dagmar. "I know what I am, Smart Boy." Even in Skydašiavos, she continued saying that last phrase in Cöllüknit, as though it was now my name. "I'm a blunt thing to be pointed at whoever needs killing," she continued. "You need a planner, like I said. Someone who is, you know, tricksy like. Erm . . ." She added something else in Rotfelsenisch, before saying, "A cutthroat, understand?"

"Don't *you* cut throats?"

"Well, yes!" She threw up her hands, angry at her difficulty in communicating her ideas to me. (And not, thankfully, angry *at* me.) "But you need someone . . . someone *cutthroat* in the way they do things. The way they use things. And use people."

"No scruples?"

"Yes."

"A scheming manipulator?"

"Exactly!" She gestured broadly toward me. "Thank you!"

I nodded to show her I understood, although I was confused. And worried.

"What you need," she said, "is that reason I stayed in Quruscan so long. She'll figure this out!"

"Oh. Good."

"Yes, yes," Dagmar continued, beaming at me. "Not a scruple on that one. Not the ghost of the father of a scruple!"

I stared down at the path and felt as though I would faint.

Excerpt from *The Miraculous Adventure of Aigerim*

It was not the great love between Fair Aigerim and her brave Sukhrab, Knight of the Moon, that broke them free from Mindaugas the Sorcerer's foul curse. Even the greatest love of all past ages, and of all ages yet to come—Which is, Treasured Reader, exactly what the two of them shared!—could not have done such a thing. No matter the strength of a heart's desire, no one person, not even steadfast Aigerim herself, has willpower beyond what a single human being can demonstrate.

You see, Mindaugas, for all of his dastardliness, had help. Everyone within his Dread Fortress was in utter thrall to the sorcerer, who had led them to believe that everything he did, and everything he wanted, was in each of their own best interests. So when the entire population of the Dread Fortress reinforced his curse with all of their combined willpower, not even our heroine and her knightly love could save themselves. Not while the thralls chanted in unison and watched two of the sorcerer's underlings, acting as twisted imitations of Aigerim and Sukhrab, begin to beat and berate each other.

And when they did so—Woe of all Woes!—the true Aigerim and Sukhrab began to do the same.

(The next three pages describe exactly how, and how badly, they beat one another, which, despite the flowery style, is uncomfortable to read.—R)

The historic battle between a bewitched Aigerim and Sukhrab, spilt into the very throne room of Skydašiai, where the King and Queen cried out to them to stop.

"You have been fighting for three days!" wailed the King. "Even as I am in awe of your great prowess, so too am I in mourning for your love, and for our fair country, across which your battle has been waged!"

Upon hearing this, the Queen, who was herself familiar with sorcery, understood what had to be done. For, as the Attentive Reader will remember, she had been apprenticed to Mindaugas before being saved by Aigerim's own mother!

"They are ensorcelled!" shouted the Queen. "Let the very country come to their aid!"

The word went out, and messenger birds were sent to every part of Skydašiai, North and South, bearing the message: "PRAY FOR AIGERIM AND SUKHRAB TO LOVE ONE ANOTHER."

(The fight continues for a fourth day. It becomes quite unpleasant.—R)

And then, on that fourth day, once everyone in Skydašiai had received the news, the combined power of their earnest prayers, to whichever god each person chose, overcame even the power of Mindaugas. With all of that willpower, the spell was reversed, and Aigerim and Sukhrab found themselves in control of the bodies of Mindaugas' two minions.

Brave Sukhrab was disoriented and did not know what to do, but quick and clever Aigerim understood what was happening immediately. In one sweeping motion, the body of the gnarled old hag representing Aigerim snatched the dull sword from nefarious Romualdas, who had been acting the part of Sukhrab, and drove that sword, blunt as it was, into the chest of Mindaugas.

(A lot about how painful and difficult this particular stabbing was, and then details of the Dread Fortress crumbling, crushing everyone inside, so on and so forth.—R)

"Aigerim!" cried the King, as tears flowed from his eyes. "You have defeated Mindaugas and saved Skydašiai!"

Aigerim, breathing heavily, bruised and bloody, grinned and shook her bouncing locks.

"No, Your Highness. Skydašiai has saved me!"

(Twenty pages of wedding details and children's names.—R)

Chapter Four

Once More, Dagmar Sorga's Escape Plan Involved Plummeting

A few days after my escape from Abathçodu, Dagmar decided she could safely enter the next mountain town, and I asked to accompany her.

"You can come into town if you wish to be murdered," she said, looking at me as though I was stupid. "You are clearly a Loashti, and they will probably want to look at your papers right away, especially since you are bruised and bedraggled. When they find out you're an outcast alien—"

"I am not an *alien*," I bristled.

She shrugged and ignored this, which was the right choice. I knew how silly it had sounded the moment it left my lips.

Besides, Dagmar was correct. Down in the steppes, out of the mountains, Quruscan supposedly got more cosmopolitan, and when we got there, I was promised, Dagmar would let me enter buildings again.

In the meantime, she left me on the outskirts of each mountain town—in the brush or the trees or among the head-high red poppies lit delicately at night by iridescent moonblossoms—and told me to wait.

Hours later, she'd return with supplies, and sometimes information. The supplies from one town included a bedroll for me and a small tent, which made my long waits much easier. She also brought food: mutton cooked in maple; angry, lean mountain bird meat somehow massaged and spiced until it tasted lovely; and pickled fruits and vegetables of every kind one could imagine.

Sometimes there would be proof of a fight on her: a bruise, a torn sleeve, some blood (not hers).

"I hope you're not stealing any of this," I said. "I'm sure the people in these towns need it too."

She raised an intrigued eyebrow. "No, no. If I was *stealing*, we'd be eating better."

"But this is amazing," I muttered in Zobiski between bites.

"Sometimes I just attract trouble." She shrugged. "Must be something about me," she added, grinning. I *thought* she had been missing that tooth near the back as long as I had known her, but it stood out just then. Was it in fact newly gone?

As for information, it turned out there had been Loashti in the second town we reached.

"They cut them both up yesterday," Dagmar told me upon returning in the evening. "Their papers are proudly on display in the Headman's office—only one was an alien."

I suddenly didn't want my delicious mutton anymore. It tasted rancid.

"Won't that bring them trouble? Loasht and the Tetrarchia are still on good terms."

"We're far from the world up here, Smart Boy," she reminded me. "I suppose they can get in trouble if the right people learn of it . . . but then the Headman will blame the Loashti for their own deaths. That'll probably be the end of it."

I looked down at my half-eaten meat and had a sudden, visceral wish for the Tetrarchia to have the sort of power and control that Loasht did—for the full force of a state to come down on this little town. But such a sentiment was against Zobiski nature, as I interpreted it, and I soon felt guilty.

At the third village, Dagmar returned to me smiling broadly.

"They've had news from Abathçodu and are looking for you," she said.

"Then why are you so happy?"

"Well, I also heard about the person we're looking for!"

"And who is she, exactly?" I asked. "A friend? An enemy? Lover? Family member?"

"None of those. Not anymore," she replied, her smile melting away.

"But she can help me?"

"I hope so. According to these folks, she's plying her trade down in a steppe city."

"What trade?"

"Wily cutthroat, as I told you. Fixer of problems. Creator of bigger problems." She frowned. "Don't get your hopes up, Smart Boy."

"Don't get my hopes up about *what*?"

"I don't know." She put a hand on my shoulder and squeezed. "Just don't."

After a few days, we came to the Selju Cliffs, where the mountain's west side abruptly ended in a series of outcroppings. It was an arresting view, which I'd never seen before: the normally uneven rocks of the mountain, full of brush and angular trees, suddenly smoothing out into a great, barren wedge. Beyond this wedge were shorter mountains, dotted with towns and cities, roads and forests. Even further, one could see the vast steppes of Quruscan stretching out into the distance.

Near the cliff edge was a small enclosure, protecting the top of a zip line from the elements. Dagmar sauntered up to the edge, under the enclosure, and slammed her hand against the zip line's metal carriage a few times to ensure its sturdiness. These conveyances were only ever big enough for three people at most, and really only consisted of a rectangular metal frame connected to a pulley.

"This could get us down to the steppe very quickly."

"But?" I asked.

Dagmar smirked and pointed directly downward. Carefully, slowly, I peeked over the edge. Below us, perhaps a hundred feet down, was another outcropping, with its own zip line. Off to the south, I saw yet another.

"More zip lines." I shrugged. "What about them?"

"I told you the last village was keeping an eye out for you. Yet no one's waiting for us here, or at any of the zip lines we can see. I think that's on purpose." She stepped back from the cliff and shook the metal carriage again. "I will bet money they are waiting at the bottom of each."

"I'm already paying you," I replied.

"*I'd* wait at the bottom," she continued. "Where we'd sail right into their open arms, with nowhere to run."

"So . . . we go down long, winding paths? Or scale the cliffs?" The very idea of so much climbing made me feel exhausted and hopeless.

"Or we drop off partway," she added. "Dangerous, but fast."

"Is . . . that what you recommend?"

Dagmar looked thoughtful.

"Yes." She grabbed me around the waist and heaved me toward the zip line.

"Wait—!" I cried.

Our little metal cage raced downward at such a speed that I had to shout to be heard over the rushing wind. I did a lot of shouting.

"You don't *know* where we'll drop?!" I cried.

"I'll know it when I see it!" Dagmar yelled back, unbothered. She was bent forward over the front of the carriage, watching the low mountain rush by below us.

"*When you see it?!*"

She nodded, smiling. The carriage clattered around us, and the thick rope above spun by with a whirr.

I looked back at where we'd come from, at the Selju Cliffs speeding away behind us, and swore I saw a great set of sharp teeth coming for us. I almost screamed, before realizing they weren't moving. What I was seeing embedded in the sheer cliff were the wide jawbones of a dead creature, around which the mountain had perhaps congealed. That made its remains old even by Loashti standards. A creature large enough to fit those jaws would not have been much smaller than the mountain itself. I was relieved when we passed over the peak of the next, much smaller, mountain, and the teeth were hidden from view.

We continued downward, and I sat on the floor and gripped the sides of the carriage so tightly that my hands were going numb. Whenever I looked down at the ground, I fancied I saw things moving about below us: wolves, lizards, or those Quru bears that are covered in alternating maroon and cream stripes.

"I don't see anything yet!" Dagmar called back to me. "It's all rocks! Nothing soft!"

"We're in the Quru mountains! They aren't usually soft!"

She nodded as though this made perfect sense, but did not seem to care about my anger.

We sped farther, and the steppe began to come into view.

"Oh, look!" She pointed. "They're definitely waiting for us!"

I craned myself up enough to look. In the distance, I saw where the bare rocks of the mountain turned into grass and sparse trees—where the zip line would end, at the top of a small foothill. A group of ten or so people were gathered there.

"I've got a new idea!" called Dagmar.

I began to pray. But I couldn't bring myself to close my eyes.

Dagmar stretched out her legs, wedging her feet between the bars in the sides of the carriage, to brace herself and reach up higher. Her head was just a few inches below the pulley now, almost touching the whirring, speeding rope. She drew a thick-bladed dagger from her belt, then twisted back to look at me again.

"They don't seem to have guns!" she said, grinning. "Just swords and spears. Brace yourself!"

I was already braced—there was little else to do. Dagmar turned back to the pulley and seemed to wait for something. I saw her head swivel up to the pulley, then down toward the grassy foothill. Up, down, up, and down again.

We drew close enough that I began to hear small snatches of whatever the people waiting for us were yelling. With both hands, Dagmar jammed the point of the dagger into the bottom of the pulley, where the rope came out. She threw herself so hard into the motion that I thought she'd tumble forward, out of the carriage.

We slowed very slightly, for a moment. Dagmar pulled her feet in and fell to the metal floor next to me. We lurched forward, and the rope creaked as it was pulled against the dagger's blade. Then it snapped loudly as it was cut through.

I did look away then, and we careened forward, toward the shouting beneath us. I saw Dagmar, curled into a ball, grinning. I closed my eyes.

There was a crunch and a scream as we landed with a jolt, which was not as bad as I'd expected. Yes, I felt as if my bones were grinding against each other inside me, but none of them broke.

Our momentum hadn't stopped, and the metal box tore its way down the foothill. I opened my eyes to see grass and rocks spewing up in front of us. Dagmar sat up to look in front of, and then behind, us. She laughed. I hazarded a glimpse: back where the zip line should have deposited us stood a group of armed men looking very confused.

They disappeared from view as we continued down the foothill. We slid, bumped, finally slowed, and then stopped in the high grasses of the Quru steppe. Dagmar hopped out.

"We'd better get moving," she said.

Eyes wide, mouth agape, I nodded and reached a leg out of the carriage. I was so shaken that it took me a moment to realize I was stepping on something soft and uneven. I looked down and saw it was a human hand. I fell the rest of the way out of the carriage.

"What . . . ?" I cried.

Dagmar reached in to pull out our bags, unbothered by the man crushed and mangled beneath our metal box.

"He cushioned the fall," she said. "Nice of him. Probably helped us go down the hill too."

I felt sick.

"Like a sled," she said. Dagmar hoisted our bags and looked at me quizzically. "Do you have sleds in Loasht, Smart Boy?"

I simply pulled myself to my feet and began to run through the tall grasses. Dagmar followed and, in her kind way, said nothing of the fact that I'd left her with all of the bags. She knew well enough how little it would've taken to bowl me over just then.

The steppe grasses here were brilliantly green, covered with dew at all times of day, and taller than I—even Dagmar only had to duck her head slightly to be out of view. The sellsword led me through zigzags, twists, and circles, seemingly at random, and showed me how to avoid disturbing the swaying green strands more than necessary. Dagmar never once looked back at me, but must have been listening carefully, because every time I slowed, she did the same, ensuring I didn't lose sight of her.

When the sun began to set, she decided we were safe, and we stopped. This gave me a chance to actually look at the sky, which, out here, felt *too big*. It was as though the purple and orange of sunset was bleeding into everything, ready to swallow me whole. Dagmar cried out, staring and pointing at the sunset, and for a moment, I thought she was having similar feelings.

"So that way's west!" she said instead. "We went around so many times I wasn't sure anymore. Tomorrow, we head southwest, toward a city I know." She dropped the bags. "And tomorrow, you will carry your own bags."

The steppe in front of us seemed as endless as the sky above. Looking at it, I could not imagine that there were cities anywhere—only grasses stretching out in all directions, sometimes punctured by small copses of wind-gnarled trees. Personally, I had preferred the look of the mountains.

"A city? Out here?"

"Oh, there are many cities out here, if you know where to look. Great big ones that dominate the landscape, and nicely hidden ones where everyone minds their own business. Our cutthroat should be in Desgol, which is the second kind."

For two days, we waded through miles of grasses that were, at their lowest, waist-high for me. Sometimes, with no humanity in sight, we would come across statues hidden in the grasses. One, of a man with a sword, scared the life out of me until I realized it was stone. We navigated by the sun and the few copses of trees, as Dagmar refused to cut down any grasses.

"That will leave a trail," she explained. "I don't think we're being followed, but the folks around here don't like too many extra trails."

At dusk, the bugs got so bad that we spent two nights crammed into the small tent that had, in the mountains, only fit me. It was awful. Dagmar's limbs were so blasted long that neither of us could get comfortable. We spent those nights tangled up together, but not in a fun way—it was brutally clear that neither of us was the other's type.

It was still spring, and I could not understand how the afternoons and nights were so cold, yet the mornings made me sweat constantly.

Chapter Five

When I Met Kalyna Aljosanovna

After those two uncomfortable nights, we made it to Desgol, where I hoped I would be able to speak to and touch people who were not Dagmar Sorga.

My mercenary had not been lying about whole cities being hidden. Desgol officially existed: it had a Headman, a small council, taxes, and signs along a road that pointed the way to the city. But that road wound and split in strange ways; the signs were often hidden by tall grass; the taxes were often ignored; and the Headman and council mostly spent their meetings at a tavern. Desgol existed, but it was hard to find if one did not know where to look. From afar, the place appeared as an especially tall grouping of grass, behind which was a big rock and another copse of trees.

However, if one were to part the grasses, find the signs, and reach Desgol, one would enter a bustling little city. Smaller than Abathçodu, yes, but big enough. More of its people were openly armed than anywhere I had previously seen in Quruscan, which was interesting. This seemed to excite Dagmar, conceptually.

The buildings were mostly squat, round, wooden houses with wooden roofs insulated by layer upon layer of steppe hay. Aside from those, there were a number of two-story buildings which seemed to clash with the rest of the city. Instead of nice round shapes, reminiscent of yurts and ponds, these were hard-edged and rectangular, of wood that had been lacquered until it was almost black. There were a few old statues throughout, which were mostly ignored, with none of the joy in art of Abathçodu. At the far end from where we entered, a rock loomed as tall as any of the squat houses, and much wider. Quite imposing, if not for the children playing atop it, slapping each other, and falling laughing onto soft dirt below.

I'm sure that if I had visited Desgol early in my time in Quruscan, I would have thought it some lawless bandits' nest hidden from the world. Having, by this time, a better understanding of the kingdom and its ways, I knew the city to simply be Quruscan's culture of Minding One's Own Business taken to its natural conclusion. Or *a* natural conclusion. Despites its small size, Desgol was much less strictly Quru than most places in the mountains. People from all lands known to the Tetrarchia were here, so long as they appreciated a bit of privacy and kept to themselves. As a social person who enjoys learning and discussing new things, I would not have picked Desgol as a destination—but as a fugitive alien, it seemed perfect.

"Don't get too comfortable," muttered Dagmar, as though she had read my mind. "They still get news here."

"Of course, but can I at least go get a drink and be around people?" I muttered back. "I haven't been under a roof in ages."

We found that one of the great, rectangular, two-story buildings was in fact a tavern, with a few rooms to let on the second floor. It was early evening, and the place was quite crowded and raucous. I could hear a great many languages, although none were Loashti. The closest was the version of Skydašiavos spoken in the wind-bludgeoned border city of Galiag, which was liberally peppered with Loashti words.

On the whole, most non-Quru in the tavern stuck to their own kind, and after we got two plum wines, Dagmar found a small group of her fellow haggard-looking Rots. They eyed me warily, and I took myself away, to let my mercenary catch up with her peers in their hoarse language.

I wandered through the tavern unsure of what I should do, or even what I wanted to do. I was simply happy to be around people again—happy even when they jostled me. I felt giddy. I hadn't gotten a good night's sleep since leaving Abathçodu, which may explain why I, a fugitive Loashti, did what I next did. But I was so lonely and had not been possessed of a clear thought in weeks.

I saw a man sitting alone at a table and decided that we could both use some company. It didn't hurt that I found him attractive, but this seemed more like an added benefit to socializing with him. I truly had no goal beyond that.

I said hello and asked if I could sit, and he smiled and said that he wished I would. His name was Sofron, and he looked like no one I had ever seen before. This was apparently because he was Quru, but from a family that was mostly Masovskan. I had never met a Masovskan before—he was not pink like Dagmar, but sallow, in an intense sort of way. He was tall and broadly built, but his pallor made him look sickly to me. This supposed sickliness made his handsome face more interesting, and attractive, in my eyes than it would have been otherwise. Still, I really just wanted someone to talk to.

I chose to be careful, for once, and when he asked my name, I panicked and said it was Akram.

"Well, all right, Akram," he said. He eyed my tattooed face but asked no further questions.

"Are you from Desgol?" I asked, leaning forward just a bit over the table.

"Oh yes," said Sofron. "My whole life. I think about leaving often."

"Why? It seems a nice, quiet place."

"Well, that's one problem with it." He laughed and sat back in his chair, allowing me to see more of his barrel-chested shape. Sofron looked like he could crush me, which I liked.

"But also," he continued, "there are people here I have known my whole life—since I was a baby—who still call me 'the Masovskan.'" He made a face. "I would love to leave this place, but it's what I know best."

"I'm *very* familiar with that feeling," I replied.

Sofron laughed knowingly, likely because I was clearly not a Quru named Akram. But I laughed with him anyway.

"So," I continued, "since you're a local, maybe you can tell me why some buildings here are square and lacquered, and some are—"

He began to laugh. But not at me. At least, not too much.

"No, no, I'm serious," I said, laughing too. "I just don't understand it!"

"Of course!" He smiled broadly. "I just love that I can now impress you with the most basic knowledge."

"Well then," I said, sitting back and crossing my arms. "Go on. Impress me."

He blinked a few times, a bit surprised. "Well, it's not *that* impressive, really. Wood is hard to come by out here, that's all. Those little copses of trees are protected. Kind of. 'Holy' might be a better word. Kind of holy."

"What is 'kind of holy'?"

"I mean . . ." He stammered slightly now. "No one thinks a god lives there, but we all know we're not supposed to touch them. A single copse can have creatures that don't live anywhere else in Quruscan, preying upon even smaller creatures that also exist nowhere else. Or so the old-timers say."

"So the houses that are here . . . ?"

"Have all been as you see them for a long time. And these two-stories: even longer."

"How much longer?"

He shrugged.

"Well," I said, finishing my drink, "I'm hardly impressed then, am I?"

I smiled to show I didn't really mean it, and it was only in this moment that I realized I was flirting, although I wasn't sure why. Perhaps I was starved for attention. In my travels so far, I had stayed entirely chaste, even to the point of curbing innocent speech that could be misconstrued. But now . . . Well, I was on the run anyway, wasn't I?

That this encouraged me, rather than leading me to worry I was being tricked or found out, shows how truly past rational thought I was.

"Would you like another drink?" asked Sofron.

"I haven't decided."

He smiled and leaned closer, both elbows on the table, his face not far from mine. "Is your mother named Tahirović?"

I must have looked absolutely perplexed. He laughed and moved up off the table, sitting back again and watching me.

"All right, 'Akram,' you aren't even remotely Quru, are you?"

I smiled sheepishly and shook my head.

He sat still for a moment, studying my face. Then, finally: "I wasn't asking about your actual mother, you know."

I nodded. "I guessed that much." It was only then that I remembered I had not properly bathed in days. Had not treated my skin or hair.

Nonetheless, Sofron said, "I was asking whether you'd like to . . ." and nodded toward the door, indicating leaving the tavern. He did not elaborate beyond that.

I nodded again. We both knew what we were discussing, just as we both knew to not say it out loud. Partly for safety, and partly because it was simply how things were done. Lightly conspiratorial.

"I know a place," he continued. "Quru tend to not care what happens in their midst so long as they don't *see* it. And the lake is also 'kind of holy,' so it's usually deserted."

"You don't even know me," I said. I leaned forward myself, now. "Does this feel *safe* to you?"

"No," he said.

And *that* is when Dagmar clapped her long-fingered pink hand onto my shoulder and said, "We're leaving."

She dragged me bodily out of the tavern, with my packs, and I was too embarrassed to even look at Sofron. To see whether he was put out, disgusted, laughing, or frustrated. I was simply pulled from the tavern like a flower caught in the wind.

"Now look," I said as I struggled to shoulder my packs, while Dagmar marched me through Desgol, "maybe it wasn't smart of me to talk to anyone, but I was just trying to have a little fun after so long. I'm sure it seems strange to you, coming from Rotfelsen, that two men might—"

"What *are* you talking about, Smart Boy?"

"Well, just that I was—"

"I don't care what you were doing," she said. "I found my person. Come on."

"But I was just—"

"Don't care." She pushed me a little. "You don't have enough money for me to watch you every second. Honestly, I'm not sure she will even help you now. You're almost out."

I felt very small, just then.

Dagmar dragged me, in point of fact, to exactly the place Sofron had suggested we go. There was a lake on the other side of the great rock behind Desgol. The rock protected the lake from most of the city's noise and refuse, allowing for a source of fresh water and the occasional fish. The lake was wide and shallow, stretching out quite far and shimmering in the moonlight. Shimmering *beyond* the moonlight, in fact, as closer inspection showed that tiny creatures in the water were, themselves, blinking a white light.

A copse of trees, untouched for centuries, bent around the edges of the lake, growing up out of surprisingly short grass. But I saw no one— only trees and water washed in silver.

"Who *is* this 'person,' anyway?" I finally asked. "Why don't you tell me anything?"

Dagmar stared at the water as we began to walk along the lake's edge.

"I am not," she finally said, "good at, erm . . . feelings. Even in Rotfelsenisch."

"Oh. I thought there was something terrible you were leading me into."

Dagmar shrugged. "Maybe. This is someone who saved my life, and who I have, ugh," she almost spat, "*feelings* for. But then . . . hm."

"Yes?"

"The feelings. They weren't always . . ."

After a pause, I offered, "Reciprocated?"

Dagmar stopped dead in her tracks. For a long moment, I thought I had struck the right idea so perfectly that it amazed her. Then I saw how uncomprehendingly blank that pale face was in the moonlight.

I defined "reciprocated," and she looked thoughtful.

"That's not exactly it," she finally said. "Maybe."

"Well, you did call her 'wily,'" I offered. "Manipulative."

"Able to talk anyone into, or out of, anything."

"Except," I ventured, "she didn't talk you into staying with her, did she?"

Dagmar blinked a few times, watching the glowing lake.

"Yet here I am, Smart Boy," she said.

We walked in silence then. The lake was larger than it looked, but once we had gotten to the far side from the great rock—with as much distance from the city as possible while still in its official environs— Dagmar stopped and pointed at the ground.

"Idiot," she said. "I almost stepped on her."

Lying half on top of a blanket and half in the grass, with her head on a bundle of some kind, was a woman. She looked quite normal to me: not some big, pale Rot like Dagmar, but a brown woman of average size with long dark hair in loose curls. She was asleep, not snoring but clearly drooling a little. She wore rough trousers and a blouse, huddled beneath a wool jacket of burnt orange—a color the moonlight did not quite know how to bend around properly. Spread out on the blanket next to her was a small repast: a hunk of an aged cheese on its paper wrapper, a cut-up apple that had turned brown, a pile of dried fruit hued in brilliant yellows and oranges, and an end of brown bread. It looked as though she had made a decent dent in it, but there was quite a bit left, and I worried that bugs would colonize it, or had already.

Dagmar sighed. "Wake up, Kalyna." She pushed the smaller woman with her boot.

The woman in the grass moaned and reached vaguely for a bush next to her. Without even trying, Dagmar got there first, and plucked a sword and small farming sickle out of it. She crouched, holding them both in one hand, just a foot above the sleeping woman, who groped groggily at where the weapons had been.

"It's me, Kalyna," said Dagmar.

She was speaking Skydašiavos, and the other woman responded in the same, even as she seemed mostly asleep.

"If it's *you*," muttered the woman, eyes still closed, "why aren't you down here with me?" She lazily thwacked the grass next to her.

"Because it's been eight months," said Dagmar.

Kalyna Aljosanovna swore an oath in a language that I now suspect was Masovskani and sat up. Dagmar stood slowly, still holding up Kalyna's weapons. Continuing to swear, the smaller woman began to grope her way to her feet. Then she glanced down at her food, swore louder this time, and began to frantically wrap it back up, brushing away insects. I felt that I was quite doomed.

"Dagmar, what kept you?" asked Kalyna in Skydašiavos. She was now wide awake and leaning against a tree, staring intently up at Dagmar. I may as well have not existed.

"I'm not sure what you mean," replied the sellsword.

Dagmar had relinquished the sword and sickle now, and they were each tucked into Kalyna Aljosanovna's belt as she leaned back with her arms crossed, and her bright wool jacket hung over her shoulders.

"I just thought you'd come find me sooner," Kalyna smiled, just slightly. But in that smile, I saw the barest sliver of what must have been an overwhelming, and stifling, personality.

Dagmar could not help smiling back, a bit, in response, even as she said, "Find you? Why? For what?"

"The reasons would be up to you, wouldn't they?" replied Kalyna.

Dagmar seemed to be *flustered*, which I had never seen before. She stammered as Kalyna stepped forward and took Dagmar's hands in hers: the gesture looked friendly, companionate, almost familial.

"I needed *time*, Kalyna," said Dagmar. "I probably still do."

"Time? Whatever for?"

"For?!" Dagmar then swore angrily in Rotfelsenisch, but did not pull her hands out of Kalyna's. "Whatever for?" she repeated. "Kalyna, you . . . you . . ." She pulled her hands free, nodded toward me, and said, "I'm here for him, anyway. He needs your help."

Kalyna furrowed her brow and turned her head to look at me for what felt like the first time. While regarding me, she dramatically—purposefully, I now realize—shook out her loose curls.

"I don't think I've had the honor," she said to me.

I gave my name in Skydašiavos.

"Radiant Basket of Rainbow Shells," Kalyna said back to me, but in Loashti Bureaucratic. She smiled and quirked her eyebrows, enjoying my surprise at her mastery of the language.

"He needs to get back," said Dagmar. "To Loasht."

"Back?" asked Kalyna. "I don't see why you'd need me for that. The border is—" She stopped herself and cocked her head to the side, regarding me with a look of deep, seemingly genuine, sympathy, albeit with an ironic edge. "Oh, I see." She then switched to Zobiski: "Your name is really *Radiant*, yes?"

I nodded. I felt a wave of relief after days and days in the mountains with the sturdy, but limited, Dagmar Sorga; not to mention almost a year in the intellectual, but provincial, Abathçodu. Here was someone so worldly, so *cosmopolitan*, that she knew what I was not from a piece of paper but from perhaps my accent, my features, my manner, my tattoos, or something else. Knew but did not judge.

"My Zobiski is . . . weak," she said. "How do you say your full name?"

I told her.

"Radiant Basket of Rainbow Shells." Kalyna seemed to savor every syllable, to appreciate how beautiful my name is in that language. "You wish to escape this barbarous cesspit," she continued in my language, "back to your land of broad fronds and lazy crocodiles."

"I would not call it a cesspit. But yes."

Kalyna rolled the idea around in her head.

"This sounds difficult," she said in Skydašiavos, to Dagmar.

"Your kind of difficult," replied Dagmar. "Tricksy like." She shrugged. "I can't—"

"Stab your way, yes." Kalyna fixed her dark eyes on me again. She was a bit taller than me, with slightly broader shoulders. "I'd like to help. But I'm quite busy."

"With *what*?" asked Dagmar. I could hear her disdain.

Kalyna smiled broadly, and even though it was trained on Dagmar, I could not help smiling too, as though we were both in on some great joke. Her teeth were brilliantly white.

"With doing nothing, Dagmar. I think I've earned that."

"People like you and me, we don't just stop . . . doing," grumbled Dagmar.

"Perhaps we aren't as alike as you think."

Dagmar's nostrils flared.

"I have money!" I choked out. "Some back in Loasht too!"

"You see, Kalyna, he can pay."

Kalyna sighed. "Radiant, I am so sorry about your predicament. But for the first time in my life, I'm not in desperate need of funds."

"I'll be killed if I stay!" I cried.

"Loasht may well kill you when you arrive," Kalyna replied.

I put my face into my hands, pressing hard on my closed eyes as though it would somehow change things. I exhaled loudly, trying to speak.

"Kalyna," grumbled Dagmar, "you didn't have to—"

"I know," I interrupted. "Believe me, I know. But my family is there." I looked up at her. "What's more, I . . . I know Loashti hatred better than I know Tetrarchic fear. In a way, it feels safer."

"Well," murmured Kalyna, "I can certainly understand *that*."

"*Please*," I begged.

She looked at me in a new way, then. Every part of her face smiled, every element of her being seemed to be saying that I was the only other person in the world—that she cared about nothing so much as she cared about my predicament. She did not meet my gaze so much as engulf it.

"I'm sorry, Radiant," she said. "Someone else will have to help you. I've done enough."

Excerpt from the Loashti volume *Knaves, Ruffians, Sorcerers, and Charlatans: A Guide* by A Phoenix Manacled Beneath the Mountain Cries That It Is Not Permitted to Die

You see, the difference between a charlatan and a sorcerer is actually quite small. They are, in essence, the same thing. They both look at the world, choose something in it that is not true, and then say and demonstrate that untruth until you believe it; until they believe it; until the very world bends around them to make it true.

In short, my Most Illustrious Prince who has granted me the opportunity to produce this work for your edification: Never trust anybody. Least of all me.

(Phoenix, if that was her real name, famously vanished after completing this volume and was never heard from again.—R)

Chapter Six

When I Started to Understand What
Kalyna Aljosanovna Was

Kalyna Aljosanovna insisted on walking back to Desgol proper with us.

"Let's talk through your predicament, Radiant," she said, clicking her tongue thoughtfully. "That, at least, I can do for you, and may even enjoy!"

I felt heartened by this, even though she was offering so very little. Perhaps I would grab onto any hope, just then; perhaps I was just relieved to have someone new to talk to about it all.

"Well," I began, walking beside her, as Dagmar hung behind, "do you know anything about *why* my papers are suddenly invalid? About what happened in Loasht?"

I did not bother to say, *After all, you're so very worldly*, but I thought it, and I'm sure she heard it in my voice.

"I'm sorry to tell you," said Kalyna, "but nowadays I try to know as little about politics as possible. I've had enough of *that* to last a lifetime."

Dagmar let out a gruff laugh that seemed knowing, conspiratorial, and accusatory all at once.

"You've *done enough* and you've *had enough*," she grumbled. "But when *I* have had enough . . ." She trailed off, waiting to be argued with. Kalyna did not take her up on it.

"But what little have you heard?" I pressed. "Any clarification would be welcome! I still know so little of what happened, of . . . well, what *I am* now. Am I still Loashti? Am I a stateless alien?"

"All I know," replied Kalyna, "is that the Loashti delegation came once more to the Council of Barbarians." She shrugged. "I think I heard that a Loashti dignitary gave a speech about curbing unsavory elements in Loasht and abroad—elements that were the 'real' reason for the Tetrarchia's age-old fears of our neighbor."

I felt a numb terror inside of me. As if what I'd just heard was both too big and terrible to be possible, and too obvious and inevitable for me not to have already known it. How deep into Loasht had Aloe's poisonous ideas seeped? What dizzying new heights had my old colleague reached?

"That's much more than I'd heard," I managed to say. "Thank you."

"I thought you weren't paying attention to politics," said Dagmar.

Kalyna grinned. "Well, Dagmar, I was not personally responsible for this Council of Barbarians taking place. I think that's quite uninvolved, for me."

Dagmar sucked her teeth loudly. I furrowed my brow and walked a little faster to get a better look at Kalyna's face.

"What do you mean 'personally responsible'?" I asked.

"She wasn't," grunted Dagmar.

"Another time," said Kalyna. She acted as though Dagmar's comment hadn't happened and waved away my curiosity like one would a silly question from a child.

"Beyond what I've just told you," Kalyna continued, to me, "I'm sure I only know what you do: that, in Quruscan at least, Loashti with papers of certain colors are in trouble. From my last time in Loasht, I happen to know the Zobiski's are pink."

"I still don't know what could have changed so quickly," I murmured. Even with Aloe and his followers terrorizing people, Loasht did not alter itself overnight. And *overnight* to Loasht was decades, if not centuries—while other countries rose and fell.

"But Loasht has a new government, doesn't it?" asked Kalyna.

I stopped walking and stared at the small, round houses of Desgol. There was a very long pause as I tried to make sense of what I had just heard.

Finally, I managed: "What do you mean, a new government?"

"You hadn't heard? The Grand Suzerain died, oh, four or five months ago. There's been a new one since."

There were, essentially, three reasons why learning this shocked me.

1. This was the first I'd heard of it. I suppose the movements of internal Loashti politics didn't matter much to the average people of the Tetrarchia, so long as it didn't change their lives.
2. A new Grand Suzerain *didn't* normally change the lives of Tetrarchic citizens, nor even of Loashti. All leaders throughout Loasht bowed to the Grand Suzerain—they did not get to bicker and skirmish and make deals like Tetrarchic monarchs—but the goals of the Grand Suzerain and his government shifted only gradually.
3. The Grand Suzerain at the time I left had been younger than I.

Had I still been in Loasht, I would have learned at least the official version of whatever happened to the old Grand Suzerain, far from the truth as that might be. Out here in the Great Homunculus of the Tetrarchia (they even called it an "experiment"!), I knew no more than what Kalyna told me.

Of course, if I'd been in Loasht when the old Grand Suzerain died, I would also have been there as things turned worse for the Zobiski. I thought, for a moment, about Silver, and my community in Yekunde, and then stopped myself. It was all too terrible to contemplate.

We got back to the tavern in Desgol quite late, when its common room was emptier. I did not see Sofron anywhere, which was disappointing. Kalyna smiled at the large man behind the bar, who greeted her by name.

The group of Rots Dagmar had found earlier were still there, six of them taking up two tables. They had the look of men who would continue drinking even later into the night, possibly to escape something. One smiled and waved at Dagmar, who waved back and said something in Rotfelsenisch. The others glared quietly over their drinks, and I tried to remember if that was how they had looked earlier in the night. Was this simply their way, or was there suspicion in their eyes? A threat?

As we started up the stairs to the second floor, Dagmar leaned over to Kalyna and said quietly, "Ex-Purples, by the way."

Kalyna nodded thoughtfully.

"What does that mean?" I asked.

"Rotfelsen politics," replied Kalyna, as though this explained everything. "They have strange ideas there."

"I'm *right here*," said Dagmar.

"Am I wrong?"

"Well, no."

Kalyna turned partly toward Dagmar, walking sideways up the stairs. I trailed behind them both and fought the urge to glance back at the Rotfelsenisch men in the tavern.

"Papa will be delighted to see you, Dagmar."

The sellsword beamed with what seemed to be, since finding Kalyna, her first smile that had not been coerced.

"It's been some time," said Dagmar. "How is he without his mother?"

"The Villain of His Life, you mean," corrected Kalyna, as we came to the top of the stairs.

Dagmar snorted. "Of your life, but not—"

"*You* didn't know her that long."

I saw Dagmar's shoulders tighten, but she didn't respond.

The stairs, the railing, and the landing were all of the same dark, lacquered wood. It was nothing like Yekunde or Abathçodu, and yet something about it felt . . . homey. We walked toward a similarly dark door, until Kalyna put out a hand to stop me. Gently.

"I'm sorry, Radiant, but right now it will worsen my father's health to meet new people." She clicked her tongue. "No matter how much he *thinks* he'd like to."

"I won't say a word," I replied. All I wanted was to put down my heavy packs. To sit for a moment. To sleep if I could.

Kalyna shook her head. "Even being in the room will pain him."

"How?" I asked.

If Kalyna found this irritating, she hid it marvelously. "Trust me," she said.

"Perhaps Aljosa can see something helpful about Smart Boy," Dagmar offered.

"Not worth it," replied Kalyna. "Radiant, my room is next door." She pointed. "Wait in there, if you please."

I nodded. I realized I was scared of being left alone, but Kalyna and Dagmar seemed so supremely confident and comfortable (even if Dagmar's confidence had been truly shaken by Kalyna, somehow), that I was too embarrassed to voice my fear. I walked into the next room.

"And please sit at the *far* end," Kalyna added from the door, in Zobiski. "I know it's an odd request." She pointed to a small, red velvet couch pressed against the wall farthest from her father's room.

I couldn't help feeling this was some sort of caution around supposed Loashti magics—as though my very presence would poison her ailing father. Did she know more about the official reasons for why Zobiski, and others, were alienated from Loasht?

Something of this must have shown on my face, because she added, "My father's mind is troubled. He loves to be around people, yet even proximity to others can hurt him—particularly to others who may be heading into, ah, difficult situations."

I must have looked quite confused. But I didn't want to argue, given the circumstances.

It occurred to me that I might be in some sort of trap, but I couldn't quite figure out the *why* of it. Kalyna seemed interested in my plight only in a vague, theoretical sense, and if Dagmar had wanted to abandon me to my fate, or sell me out, she would have by now.

Also, I was very tired. So I mercifully dropped my packs and sat on the couch. If I had to run from these two, where would I even go?

"Thank you for understanding," said Kalyna, closing the door behind her.

I sat on that couch for what felt like hours, but was probably no more than fifteen minutes, perhaps taking Kalyna's request too much to heart. Once seated, I did not move, lounge, rustle, or even breathe too deeply. Whatever her reasons for restricting my movement, she had made me believe they were clear to her, that she was doing me a service by her kind request, and that she would somehow *know* if I disobeyed.

Thankfully, for a time, I was distracted by Kalyna's room itself. The walls were of the same dark, lacquered wood as everything else, but brightening it up were silk drapes of orange, turquoise, and gray, and a marvelous number of colored glass beads everywhere. There were sitting pillows covering most of the floor, like a sea of multicolored textile prints depicting flowers, farmers, abominations, and most anything else you could imagine. The bed against the far wall from me was unremarkable and clearly property of the tavern.

In front of the couch where I sat was the only other piece of furniture: a low, but long, golden (or at least gold-plated) table. Atop this table were a copper bowl of water next to a matching smaller copper bowl of sand; a Loashti-style incense burner shaped like a rhinoceros' head, meant to leak smoke through the eyes; a wooden carving of a chicken covered in a thousand little holes, each holding a real chicken feather; three decks of cards of entirely different sizes; and finally, an old, wooden tobacco pipe sitting in a circle of dried flowers.

Who *was* the person who stayed here? She had a number of ritual objects, certainly, but none that were cohesive within any traditions I was aware of. The room's colorful—possibly garish—nature brought to mind the design of a carnival tent. Why had Dagmar thought Kalyna could help me?

Unfortunately, once I was done poring over all of that, I was forced to think clearly for the first time since leaving Abathçodu. I had passed many hours sitting alone in the mountains' wilderness while Dagmar got us food, but there had always been noise, bugs, danger. Now I was alone, it was quiet, and the utter incongruity of Kalyna's quarters had slapped me about the face, pulling me into clarity.

I did not know *exactly* where we were on a map, but if we had come down out of the mountains and were still in Quruscan, then we were farther from Loasht than where we'd started. I was alone— entirely alone—in what may as well have been the blasted center of the Tetrarchia. Alone in the room of some . . . carnival mystagogue who was supposed to save me, but seemed uninterested. I began to run through the unspeakable names of Loasht's Eighty-Three gods in my head, desperately fumbling for what I might have done to displease every single one of them.

Then the door was wrenched open, and I felt my heart seize up— but it was only Dagmar. She stomped into the room, nearly making me jump, looked me in the eyes, and *growled* something in Rotfelsenisch. Dagmar always seemed so composed in every situation, but now she radiated rage.

I stared, mortified, until she realized I had not understood her.

Dagmar smiled weakly, tromped over, and much to my surprise, slumped onto the couch next to me. I assumed we'd had enough time together in close quarters to last a lifetime. In the most Dagmar-like fashion, she stretched one long leg over the armrest, and I heard the wood creak.

"That woman," she said. "That's all I was saying just now. No one else has ever . . . what's the Skydaš version? Crawled in behind my eyeballs?" She looked at me.

I shrugged. "I don't know the idioms."

"Well, she really gets in behind my gods-damned eyeballs. Roots around in my brain. Picks and prods. If someone else made me feel that way, feel a tenth of that . . . type of way, I'd kill them."

"But," I couldn't help myself, even though I knew this was imprudent, "it doesn't take much for you to kill someone, does it?"

"That depends," she replied. "And the people you can't kill can *really* get on your nerves."

I wondered if I was always so easily bothered by others because I couldn't imagine killing anybody. What a dark thought. I decided to move back to the original point.

"What did she do?" I asked. "Just now, I mean."

"A thousand little things! Told me I was part of her family but treated me like a pet. Said I *abandoned* her when she needed me, while refusing to understand why I was driven away. Assumed I'd spent the past eight months in Quruscan just to be closer to her, waiting to run back to her. And that makes my blood rise, because *it may well be true*. I gave up my commission for that woman!"

She slammed a large fist against the couch cushion, and its frame groaned from the force. I felt it shake. I knew Dagmar wouldn't hurt me, but this sort of angry outburst was too familiar to me, and I froze up. Even though she wasn't looking at me, somehow she knew I'd reacted, because she hung her head sheepishly.

"Sorry," she muttered. "And now, she digs at me with polite, veiled little asides during what should have been a pleasant reunion. In front of Aljosa, no less!" Her voice was rising again. "As though I would not want to spend some time with him for myself and not only . . . not only *through her.* I love him too, in my way."

I ventured: "And do you also love her?"

There was a long silence.

"I suppose," she said at last. "I didn't at first—we were just having fun. But people change. My feelings changed. She changed too." Dagmar sighed and sank into the couch, leaning her head back and staring at the ceiling. Her dark blonde hair was mostly tied in a little knot at the back of her head. "Or maybe she was always like that, and I just got close enough to notice."

"Do you think she loved you before, and doesn't now?"

"I wish I knew," she sighed. "I thought she would want to help you. Thought she and I would get you to your family in Loasht, and it would be like old times. Maybe then I'd be able to figure out what she felt. Or . . ."

Dagmar coughed, then looked down at the table, at the pipe surrounded by dried flowers.

"Or at least," she muttered, "I could pretend it was old times again for a little while."

She grunted and shifted out of her lazy positioning, sitting forward, elbows on her thighs, as though about to leave.

"Maybe," she said, "I should go back to Rotfelsen. See if Lenz or the mad prince will take me back."

Suddenly, any care I had for Dagmar's personal problems drained away.

"But what about me?" I blurted.

She blinked and turned to look at me, surprised by my outburst.

"Well," she said, "you might be safe to stay in Desgol. I don't even need you to pay me much, just whatever you have—"

"I'm very sorry about your romantic frustrations," I said, probably sounding more facetious than intended, "but I won't survive being alone in a hostile country!" I threw out a hand, gesturing fervently at nothing in particular. "Stranded in this wilderness, imagining terrors visited upon my family, while I am hunted by superstitious *barbarians*, abandoned here by a lovesick . . ." I trailed off, stuttering, looking for the word.

"Lovesick what?" asked Dagmar. Her voice was even, her face was still, and her eyes were narrowed.

"I don't know," I sighed.

"Yes, you do," she said. "Lovesick what?"

"Do you two *mind*?" asked Kalyna.

I jumped in place. Dagmar turned her head slowly to the door, but I think even she was surprised. Kalyna was standing in the doorway, looking only slightly annoyed.

"Papa needs to sleep, so please keep quiet."

"How much did you hear?" asked Dagmar.

"I came in at 'superstitious barbarians.'"

"I'm sorry." I swallowed hard. "I didn't mean . . ."

"Yes, you did," said Dagmar. She turned to look at me, and she was smiling now. She even winked.

Kalyna walked in and shut the door, leaning against it.

"I'm certainly not insulted," she said. "Just close the door next time."

I opened my mouth to apologize.

"And I understand your worries, Radiant," she added, cutting me off. "Better than you realize."

She looked up at the ceiling, muttered something in Masovskani, and then let out a long sigh. Her eyes snapped back to me, and she smiled wearily.

"Which is why I will help you get to Loasht and find out what has happened to your family."

Something that had been coiled inside me seemed to unspool. I felt a glimmer of hope. I still didn't entirely understand why Dagmar thought this cutthroat could help me, but she must have meant it. Dagmar did and said very little that she did not mean. Besides, if Kalyna helped me, then surely so would the lovesick sellsword who had stayed in Quruscan for months waiting for her.

"Wonderful!" said Dagmar. She stood up, looked down at me, and clapped a large, callused hand on my shoulders. "Now you won't need me, Smart Boy!"

My hope was instantly doused.

"Wait!" I cried.

Dagmar smiled. "Of course. You're right, Smart Boy. There's the money. Well, I have taken you half of the way; half of what you had when I found you sounds reasonable."

My hands shook as I drew out my purse—a beautiful little striped, velvet thing I'd bought in Abathçodu—causing my remaining coins to jangle loudly. I had not counted what sort of dent food and supplies had put in the fifty silver abazi I'd had when our flight began.

"But then," added Dagmar, "I like you. Let's say twenty abazi, yes?"

I nodded and began tremblingly counting out coins.

"Please, please don't leave me," I begged.

"Why? You have Kalyna now."

I wanted to scream that I didn't *know* this other woman. Hadn't Dagmar *wanted* to spend time with Kalyna? Hadn't she, perhaps, only helped me because she saw a way to pretend it was like "old times"? None of these things, however, seemed appropriate to say in Kalyna's presence. Instead, I put twenty silver coins into Dagmar's callused hand.

"Thank you," she said, pocketing the coins and giving my shoulder another hard pat, followed by a tight squeeze. "You'll be just fine. Really. Kalyna may get in behind *my* eyeballs, but that's only because she can get behind everyone's! You'll see. If anyone can get you across that border, it's her."

Dagmar turned to leave, and Kalyna looked at me quizzically, mouthing, *Get behind what?*

I shrugged at her and shook my head.

Dagmar made for the door, against which Kalyna was still leaning. The smaller woman inhaled, as if about to speak.

If this Kalyna was so good at manipulation, I allowed myself to hope that she would find a way to convince Dagmar to stay.

"I'm sorry about earlier, in front of Papa," said Kalyna. "I didn't know what I was saying."

"You always know what you are saying."

"I always *act like* I know what I am saying. But it had been a while, and I—"

"From the moment you got used to me, you began to pick at me! As soon as I stopped being just . . . just a *novelty* to you!"

"Now, Dagmar, that's not fair—"

"It doesn't matter," said Dagmar. "Can I leave? Or must I break the door, and you, to do so?"

Kalyna sighed and stepped away from the door.

"Look," she said. "Go your own way in the morning, but at least let me give you a place to stay without paying. You can sleep in my room—"

Dagmar began to protest. Loudly.

"Both of you!" Kalyna interrupted. "And I will sleep in Papa's. You won't have to deal with me."

"Smart Boy?" Dagmar turned to look back at me.

I felt overwhelmed. My future was murky and unknowable. A wily cutthroat said she'd take me home, where my family was perhaps already dead. Even the smallest possible choice presented to me felt impossible to make. So, instead of making a choice, I just said how I felt.

"I!" I yelled. "Have never been more tired in my life! And I don't know what I can even afford right now!" Then I pulled my feet up onto Kalyna's couch, lay sideways, and turned my back to them.

I heard Dagmar chuckle and say, "Fine."

If anything was said next, I didn't hear it, because I was asleep.

I dreamed of angry mobs, just as I had every time I slept well enough to dream since Abathçodu. But this time the yelling was closer, more insistent, more realistically muffled, and in a language I didn't understand. The sound that actually woke me was of Dagmar launching herself out of Kalyna's bed, buckling on her sword, and moving across the room all at once, knocking over Kalyna's small copper bowl of sand.

"What?" I muttered.

"I don't know," she snapped. "Grab your bags and go quietly out the back. My bags too."

Dagmar vanished into the hallway, leaving the door open. That was when I realized there were people yelling downstairs in the tavern, and not only in my dream.

I began to gather up my bags, and Dagmar's as well, with numb fingers, desperate to move faster than my tired body could manage. We had not really unpacked, but there were a few coats and hats to gather up.

Blasting up the stairs and through the open door were the sounds of tables and chairs being knocked and skidded about, while men yelled in guttural Rotfelsenisch. The only word they said that I knew was "Loashti."

I tried to gather our things much faster, but my hands would not stop trembling. The Zobiski memory pounded through my every vein.

I heard the sounds of bodies colliding and a voice that seemed to be Kalyna's crying out in pain. Then the crunch of something—I hoped wood—and more Rotfelsenisch shouts as, I think, Dagmar arrived among them. The fighting began to sound more frantic. Some large, heavy piece of furniture shrieked and fell.

Kalyna yelled something in Rotfelsenisch. The only words I understood were "Dagmar" and the word for "don't."

I threw my packs onto my shoulder and strained to lift Dagmar's as well. They were all so heavy, I could barely have carried them even if I hadn't been tired and sore. I waddled out onto the landing with as much urgency as was possible, desperately looking for the back door.

Even as the fight raged on below, I found myself possessed by an ugly, stupid urge to sneak a look at Kalyna's father, Aljosa, while she was occupied. I think I would have, if his door had not been closed.

Downstairs, a new group of thudding footsteps and yells joined the tumult, but these were in Cölläknit.

Cautiously and laboriously, I crept to the edge of the landing, peeking carefully over the railing for a look at what was going on below.

At least I did not see the angry mobs of Abathçodu, nor the shouting Loashti followers of Aloe Pricks a Mare upon the Mountain Bluff. What I saw was a brawl: broken furniture, an overturned cabinet; a group of angry, drunken Rots who seemed mostly intent on Kalyna; Dagmar swatting one of those men aside and catching another in a headlock; the Quru tavern keepers yelling at the damned Rots to stop already.

"Outside! Outside! Outside!" boomed one tall Quru man with a luxurious mustache as he swung a broom handle over his head.

Two of the Rotfelsenisch men were on the floor, unmoving. One's head was in a puddle of blood, soaking into his crushed hat and blond hair.

A Rot who was still up began to draw his sword, but he had exposed no more than a few inches of the blade before Kalyna yelled something in their tongue and stomped on his foot. Before he could react, Dagmar gripped Kalyna's hip with a strong hand and slid her backward, stepping forward to take her place—in the same motion, Dagmar grabbed the man's hand and slammed it down, resheathing his sword. When the hilt clacked into place, there was a small splash of blood, and he howled as he curled into a ball on the floor. I did not see if he lost a finger.

Dagmar's left hand was still on Kalyna's hip when she reached for her own sword. Kalyna moved closer, against Dagmar's back, and put a hand on the taller woman's shoulder. Kalyna said something, and Dagmar left her hand on the hilt, but did not draw.

The remaining three Rots in fighting condition were now mostly backing away from the Quru man swinging the broom handle. He continued to yell, "Outside!" as though it was a knight's war cry from *The Miraculous Adventure of Aigerim*. Or, indeed, a spell of some kind, chanted until it became reality.

"Smart Boy!" roared Dagmar.

My gaze snapped to her. Dagmar was standing in the center of the tavern, breathing hard, ready to draw her sword, with her left arm still twisted back to protect Kalyna behind her. She did not seem to have broken a sweat, unlike Kalyna, who was pressed against her back, panting.

"Kitchen!" Dagmar ordered.

I nodded numbly, and then Kalyna and Dagmar were gone.

I began moving toward the stairs as quickly as I could, while carrying all of Dagmar's and my things. It was pathetic to see, I'm sure, but no one was watching me. The three remaining Rots had indeed gone outside, and the Quru man with the broom was standing imperiously in the doorway. Of the Rotfelsenisch men on the floor, two weren't moving, and I did not want to get close enough to see whether they were breathing. The third clutched his bleeding hand and did not seem to notice me. The tavern workers didn't care about me in the slightest.

I hobbled back through the kitchen (it smelled *wonderful*, but I never did get to eat there) and emerged behind the tavern, where Kalyna and Dagmar were standing in the shadow of the next building. I was breathing much harder than either of them.

"Can you believe her, Smart Boy? Her pack was just sitting by the kitchen exit. Like she knew." Dagmar was smiling as she said it.

"Like I can *seeeeeeee the future!*" retorted Kalyna, wiggling her fingers. "Or like I was ready, in case those men got belligerent." She was also smiling, despite the blood around her mouth. "This has everything I'll need for this little jaunt."

"But," I began, panting, "how did you know that those men would be the ones to come after me? I fancy I see angry mobs everywhere."

"They weren't after you, Radiant," said Kalyna. "They were after me."

"But they said 'Loashti,'" I whispered.

"Rots always seem to think I look Loashti."

Dagmar chuckled and took her bags from me, which was a relief. An even greater relief was that, for now, she seemed to be leaving town with us. I worried that if I asked whether Dagmar had changed her mind about accompanying us, she would then *un*-change it.

Just past the border of Desgol, with the tall grasses of the steppe in front of us, we slowed our pace slightly. Dagmar was still with us.

It was then that I realized exactly how tired, scared, and sore I was. My body did not want to move, and I felt like I could not catch my breath. Each step was an ordeal. And yet, I had learned something so confounding that its great glare blocked out even my exhaustion. I ignored the pain and sped up, so as to walk next to Kalyna and look at her face. Squinting and studying it in the dawn light that was just beginning to cut through the clouds.

"You look *Loashti*?" I asked, stupefied. "I don't see it."

"I do," said Dagmar. "But I always thought it was cute." She winked at Kalyna.

We walked for some hours through the high grasses of the Quruscan steppe. I kept waiting for Dagmar to leave, but she did not. As the spring sun moved high into the sky, we came to a little copse of trees at which I positively insisted we rest.

"I have hardly slept in days. If I go on like this, I will do something stupid and die, and you will not get paid."

I felt like some sort of spoiled prince throwing this threat at them, but Kalyna and Dagmar actually seemed to think it a good idea.

The copse was no wider than a five-minute walk from end to end, and its trees were pleasantly tilted and gnarled by the wind, causing them to be shorter than the surrounding grasses, so it was quite well hidden. As it was a spring day, we had no need to light a fire: it was cold in the shade, but heavenly in the sunlight.

I settled down in a sort of divot in the roots of one tree, my back against its surprisingly smooth bark, half sitting and half lying down. I gazed absentmindedly at a nearby shallow pool of water no wider than a yard, and at the multicolored bugs that flitted about its edges.

Once I caught my breath, I was not able to sleep just yet, no matter how tired I was. Too many things were running through my mind.

"Why did those Rots in Desgol want to kill you?" I finally asked Kalyna, in Skydašiavos.

Dagmar, who had stretched out on a bedroll laid over grass and dirt, exhaled loudly. "I think I'll go to sleep now." She then put her hands behind her head and immediately did so.

"Some mess in Rotfelsen a few years ago," replied Kalyna. She was sitting against another tree, a few feet from me, with her legs crossed. She darted her eyes to Dagmar, then back to me, and smiled. "Let's switch to Loashti," she said in Loashti Bureaucratic. "It will let Dagmar sleep—be less distracting."

Sitting just a few feet away, stationary, and lit by natural sunlight, Kalyna was quite striking—and not just because a bruise was beginning to form around her left eye. There was a small scar on her upper lip, and her deep-set dark eyes seemed to be learning the workings of everything she saw. Her hair was mostly black, but with the copper tint of a Central Loashti (not I), which I suppose could explain the Rots seeing her as such. But her facial structure was unlike anything in Loasht; aquiline might be the word.

I felt myself liking Kalyna.

"What kind of mess?" I asked.

She laughed. "Politics, assassinations, unrest. Those men think me responsible for the death of their beloved leader, even though I did not touch him."

"But were you responsible?"

She nodded. "Yes. And proud of it. He was an ass and a tyrant, and a well-protected one to boot." Kalyna allowed herself a smug grin.

"But aren't you . . . ugh, *Eighty-Three*, I shouldn't ask this. The last thing I want in the world is for us to go back to Desgol."

"Go on."

"Aren't you worried about your father? If they hate you so much, might they hurt him? Or might someone else mistake *him* for Loashti?"

She shook her head. "The Rots don't know about him, and only Rots ever think we look Loashti. But Little Bolat and Smiling Zhuldyzem and the others working at the tavern know my father well. They even like him! I've paid them quite a lot to look after him: keep him fed and well groomed, listen to his ramblings, and a thousand other things that he needs. A thousand things, each one solely my responsibility for years upon years." She let out a long, contented sigh. "I love him, but I'm happy I can finally pay others to do some of it."

I had a feeling she was trying to make me curious about other parts of her life, to get me away from my original question. I am not so easily swayed.

"But how can you be sure he's safe? Those Rotfelsenisch men learned of your presence *somehow*. They must have been suspicious when they saw us come back to the tavern. They could easily have seen the room you went into."

"No, no. They didn't."

"You don't know that! Maybe they have been hunting you down! What if they spent days asking around about—"

"Radiant," she interrupted, looking me in the eye. "They knew who I was, because I told them."

"You . . . told them?"

"Specifically," she continued, "I packed what I would need for this trip, left it by the back exit, came into the common room, got their attention, and then told them exactly how their beloved leader died." She smiled languidly up at the blue spring sky. "Actually, I embellished a little."

I opened my mouth to speak, but I could not form a response. I simply sat there.

Kalyna's smile dropped a bit, but she continued to look entirely calm, gazing off into the distance. Then she addressed what my next step was to be before I even conceived it.

"If you tell Dagmar," she said, "then she won't come with us. Meaning you and I will be as good as dead." Kalyna cleared her throat. "Which is"—a yawn—"exactly why I started that fight in the first place. She was going to leave us to our fates, *again*, but I can't very well get you safely to Loasht if we're killed along the way."

"Why . . . ?" I stammered.

"I know, I know, I wasn't going to help you. But I do feel for you, and I realized that Dagmar was going to leave you to your own devices."

Had she realized, I wondered, or had she been listening to our conversation at the tavern before she interrupted it?

"I thought," Kalyna continued, "that I could tempt her into helping you with my presence, but she still decided to leave. So . . ." She shrugged slowly and then gestured to her bruise.

"Wasn't it . . . painful?" I asked.

"Very."

"How could you invite that sort of violence on yourself? Weren't you worried they'd break something, or kill you?"

She turned her head to the side, showing me her angular profile. "Does this nose look like it's been broken?"

"I don't know. Maybe. It *is* bent."

"That is its natural shape," she laughed, "which has been retained over decades of beatings." She turned back to face my general direction but still looked up at the sky. "In my family, I had to learn quickly which blows I could take and which I could not. Naturally, sometimes things can get out of hand, but everything carries risk."

"Your father beat you that much?"

"Gods, no! Papa would never hurt me. And Grandmother was too smart to break anything. The family business simply attracted that kind of attention."

I was about to ask about this "family business," but again thought Kalyna was using my curiosity to steer the conversation away from where it had begun.

"And Dagmar?" I managed, shaking my head. "That was a terrible thing to do to someone who cares about you."

"Yes." Kalyna did not seem glib: her smile melted away, and she sounded as though she meant what she said. "But so is abandoning them to die. Or abandoning them right when their grandmother is *dying*—no matter how terrible the old woman is." She sighed and finally looked directly into my eyes. "Besides, in the past, it was always *Dagmar* who would instigate a little violence to bring us back together."

"Fine. Why tell me all this?"

"Because *you* ask a lot of questions. You were already on your way to figuring out something was off." Her smile returned. "Also because, now that I am dedicated to helping you, I want you to understand how far into deception I will go for you, Radiant."

"And what will this deception cost me?"

Kalyna raised her hands, palms upward, in front of her, as though presenting me with something. Then she smiled brightly.

"Nothing, Radiant."

"Why?" I'm sure I looked skeptical. "Do you also want to trick Dagmar into thinking it's 'the old days'?"

"Not at all. But I . . ." She breathed in deeply, as though she was about to make a great confession. "I want Dagmar to feel useful. And believe it or not, I truly do want to help you—some things about your plight are very familiar to me. And, well, I truly am not desperate for money anymore." She laughed. "It sounds so outlandish to say."

"I'm not sure I believe you."

"That's fair." Kalyna closed her eyes. "Sleep well."

I sighed very loudly and pressed my head back against the tree trunk, looking up at its fluttering, deep green leaves. Then, I admit, I *did* sleep well.

Chapter Seven

How We Left Quruscan, Soggily

After a nice, deep morning's sleep, Kalyna, Dagmar, and I began walking through the steppe. We didn't yet know that this would be our last clear and sunny day in Quruscan.

"Tonight I'll decide exactly where we should go," Kalyna told us. "For now, vaguely northward and away from Desgol will do."

She then began to ask me a lot of questions: about myself, my history, and my problems. She made me feel as though no one in the world found me more interesting than she did. Including Silver.

"And who is waiting for you back home, Radiant?" she asked in Skydašiavos. "Who will we find and rescue?"

She sounded so confident when she said it, that I believed we would rescue them. The cold fear at imagining what might be happening in Loasht was warmed and diluted, for now.

"I have a spouse," I said, "and their family, and many friends, and lovers."

"A spouse *and* lovers?" laughed Dagmar, who was walking a bit ahead of us. "Smart Boy, I didn't know you had it in you!"

I felt myself flush, rather proudly.

"Parents still living?" asked Kalyna.

"Yes, but we don't get along."

"I see," said Kalyna. "What possessed you to leave Loasht in the first place? I mean, I love the Tetrarchia . . . but I also hate it."

"I feel much the same about Loasht," I replied. "But I came here to study."

"Oh?" Kalyna's eyes seemed to light up, and her smile got wider. "What are you studying?"

Dagmar, ahead of us, visibly drooped, as though she knew she would find my answer boring.

Kalyna's interest in me was so captivating that I didn't think to lie: "The history and methods of humans putting curses on one another. You know, harmful magic."

Kalyna stopped, then, right in her tracks. I continued another step or two without noticing and so walked right into Dagmar, who had also stopped, and was looking back at us. The sun was warm on my back, while grasses up to my chest swayed in the wind.

I had gone too far. I knew it immediately. It had been foolish to be so forthright. The people of this land still thought of Loasht as some evil warren of sorcerers, and a worldly Tetrarchic citizen was still a Tetrarchic citizen. I winced, expecting Kalyna and Dagmar to leave me stranded in the middle of the steppe. Hoping for that, even, rather than that they kill me.

"Curses," said Kalyna, feeling the word in her mouth. She looked intently at the sellsword. "Dagmar."

"Yes, Kalyna?" Dagmar sounded unhappy.

"You have been on the run—"

"Yes."

"—from angry mobs—"

"Yes."

"—with—"

"Yes! Apparently with a sorcerer! It does seem that way!"

"And you didn't—?"

"No," Dagmar sighed. She sounded annoyed, mostly with herself. "No, I didn't ask him to blight crops or strike a Headman with gout or force a mob to fight one another."

"Dagmar, you have been traveling with a sorcerer and doing nothing with him." Kalyna shook her head in disbelief, smiling.

Dagmar shrugged. "How was I to know Smart Boy's a—"

"I'm not a sorcerer," I muttered.

"How was I to know Smart Boy's a wizard?"

I wanted to protest again, but she continued.

"I thought he was studying something like history, or etiquette, or, I don't know, tattoos."

"Whyever didn't you ask?" replied Kalyna.

"*Whyever* would I? I expected the answer to be boring."

"And you'd be right!" I added, as quickly as possible. "Please don't get ahead of yourselves. I'm not a sorcerer, or a . . . wizard. I'm a *scholar*. To do any of what you described would take a lot of time, assistance, knowledge, and ingredients, and even *then* it still likely wouldn't work!"

Kalyna cocked her head to the side and looked visibly confused. "Really? You can't just . . . concentrate, and the magic comes to you?"

"Absolutely not."

"Hmmm." She put a hand on her hip and pivoted to one side, furrowing her brow and looking off into the distance, before returning her gaze to me. "Do you have to concentrate to *keep* the magic from coming to you? Assailing you?"

"What? No. Not at all."

"You aren't some sort of Magic Man?" Dagmar added.

"No, no. Magic is . . ." I snapped my fingers, looking for the right words. I'd read and thought about the subject so much that it was difficult knowing where to start. "Magic is just a ritual like any other, that anyone can attempt. It isn't guaranteed to 'work' any more than praying is."

"You see?" said Dagmar. "Boring." She began walking again. "And useless."

"Dagmar," asked Kalyna, "would it kill you to ask questions?"

"*Not* asking questions was my greatest virtue in the army. It's how I became trusted enough to start guarding you."

"So then," Kalyna asked me, as we began walking again, "how *does* magic work?"

"Why? Do you wish to learn it?"

"She wishes," muttered Dagmar, "to learn how she can best use you."

"Well," I replied, "very little, I expect."

"Humor me," said Kalyna.

I wondered whether this knowledge was actually part of her *price* for helping me, in lieu of money. Well, that was fine with me: curses are difficult to do, and I like talking about them (even now).

"How much time do you have?" I asked. "I've spent decades studying 'how magic works.'"

Instead of recoiling from this answer, Kalyna sucked her teeth thoughtfully.

"Let's try an hour," she said.

"Oh! Really? I'm no lecturer, but I'll do my best!"

"And perhaps," she began in Skydašiavos, before switching midsentence to Loashti Bureaucratic, "this will be easier for you to discuss it in."

"How do you do that?" I asked instead, in the same. "Do you even mean to?"

"Habit from my own family—we would change languages constantly without a thought." She shrugged and looked at me intently as we walked. "But anyway. *Magic*, Radiant."

"Well, essentially, spells and curses are more of a state of mind than they are clear actions with proven consequences."

"Sounds like an awfully loose discipline to study."

I smiled, I hope, charmingly. "That is why I'm not an architect."

Kalyna graced me with a chuckle in answer. We each had our own ways of drawing people in.

"Magic," I continued, "is about ritual, intent, and imitation. You need all the pieces in place, but you also need to *feel* that you are affecting the world. Which can, of course, convince you afterward that you *have* affected the world, even if you didn't." I threw up my hands. "My academic work was often torn between attempts to prove its power and attempts to prove its falseness."

"Which would you prefer?"

I thought about that for a moment. "Depends on the day. And the curse. And how angry I am."

"Does that mean that if I went through the motions of something I could not do, I don't know, *hard enough*, it might start working for real? If I believed it?"

"Oh no, absolutely not! You would need to effect all sorts of intentional, purposeful incantations, rituals, and likely concoctions. It does not happen by mistake, and never lasts for long."

She looked thoughtful.

"Curses are different, though," I added. "They can, theoretically, happen more organically, which is why they're so fascinating. If you were imitative in the other direction, you might be able to negatively affect the person you were imitating."

Kalyna's pace slowed, and there suddenly came to be more tall grass between us than there had been. Perhaps this was on purpose.

"I could curse someone I imitate?" she asked quietly. "Even someone I loved?"

I wasn't sure what fear I'd touched in her, but I found myself stumbling to assuage it anyway.

"No, no, I don't think so! And it's all theory anyway. Curses are normally—insofar as anything about them is normal—carried out through imitation, ritual, drugs, and lots of help. Even then, they can still fizzle out and do nothing."

"I see." She seemed to sour on methods, for the moment, and quickly switched to a different aspect: "Why do you study something so imprecise?"

"Well, for one thing, it's hard to be *constantly wrong* about something imprecise." I grinned, and she smiled back weakly. "But, originally, I chose to study harmful magics in order to prove that, by comparison, there was nothing inherently evil, nor even particularly 'magical,' in historic Zobiski practices."

"To redeem your people in Loasht's gaze."

"And to redeem them in their own," I replied. "Many in my own community don't much like that one of the few Zobiski visible at the Academy studies something so 'backward.'" I wondered again what was happening in Yekunde—perhaps they had been right. "They worry I'm giving those who hate us false examples of our evil; or, even worse, some think I'm giving them *true* examples—that in the past, our people were base and savage."

"And that Loasht 'civilized' you?" asked Kalyna, with an arched eyebrow.

I nodded. It was a revelation to have someone grasp these currents of Loashti conflict and distrust so quickly, which made me feel I could be honest with her.

"Truthfully," I said, "I don't *only* work to prove that our old ways are harmless."

"Of course." She grinned. "What's a little harm, here and there?"

When the evening came, I learned how the Quru steppes could main-
tain all those charming little shallow pools: torrential spring rains rolling
across the expansive sky. We saw the dark and unending clouds coming
toward us for hours, but there was no escaping them. Soon enough, we
were caught in a downpour where every drop seemed bigger than the last.

"We'd better find a place to try sleeping," sighed Dagmar. "Kalyna,
you didn't pack a tent, did you?"

"I thought you had one."

"We do," sighed Dagmar. "It's very small."

Dagmar pitched the little tent by herself, insisting we would only
get in the way. Kalyna graciously allowed this but smirked at me.

The tent was erected beneath the largest tree in the copse, which
would offer only the slightest protection. What's more, this spot sat
uncomfortably between two shallow, but widening, pools. Still, it was
the best we could do, particularly as Dagmar was quickly losing light
by which to see.

The three of us spent a truly miserable night packed into that tent
on top of each other. The skins of the tent had been decently oiled to
resist water as much as possible, as all Quru tents are, but a person still
got very wet when pressed right up against the side. Since there was
only comfortably room for one, we were *all* pressed up against the sides.
I suppose we got less wet than we would have outside of the tent, but it
certainly didn't feel that way.

"So," said Dagmar eventually, in the dark, speaking over louder and
louder rain, "what's your plan then?" She made some sort of gesture we
couldn't see and accidentally rubbed my face with her clammy hand.

"For getting out of the rain?" asked Kalyna, rearranging her legs and
kneeing my ribs.

"No, there's nothing for *that*," replied Dagmar. "How are you getting
into Loasht with Smart Boy here?"

"Dagmar," I sighed, "I *am* older than you."

"What's that got to do with anything?" she replied.

I turned over and inadvertently elbowed Dagmar in the back.

"I don't know yet," said Kalyna, answering the initial question. "Or
rather, I don't know *which plan* yet. Too many possibilities, and we don't

yet know the situation at the borders. I will have to think it over as we travel."

Dagmar made a dissatisfied grunt.

"If you must know," continued Kalyna, "I have four distinct plans right now, but they depend on what we find."

"And can you *tell us* these plans?" asked Dagmar. I couldn't see her, but she was clearly beginning to remember why she hadn't wanted to come with us. The rain wasn't helping.

"You know very well I'd rather not," said Kalyna, sounding quite unbothered by everything. "Because you probably won't like them. Or they may seem ridiculous out of context."

I could hear Dagmar's irritation. Feel it in the way she shifted (and hit me with her shoulder). So I tried, desperately, to lighten the mood.

"Well, if you want *ridiculous*, you should hear how we left Abathçodu!" I offered. "I never will forget Farbex the Good Donkey." I tried to laugh.

The only sound after my forced laugh was the rain positively hammering our tent and the ground outside. Dagmar did, at least, seem to become less tense; we were pressed so close together that I could feel her relax slightly.

"Do we at least know which way we're going?" I asked.

"Oh yes, of course!" Kalyna answered. "To the Skydašian border, naturally."

"Naturally," Dagmar echoed.

"It's much wider and more accessible than Quruscan's," Kalyna continued. "Better guarded, of course, and there's the Tail to deal with."

"The Tail?" I asked.

"The Thrashing, Bone-White Tail of Galiag," Dagmar clarified.

"That's real?" I replied. "I read about it in a ridiculous old romance and assumed . . ."

"Well, it's not really anyone's *tail*," explained Dagmar. "But it's a real gorge full of howling and burning winds."

"Once we're at the Skydašian border," Kalyna continued, "I can begin to narrow down my plans. I'm better at sweet-talking officials than I am at scrambling over deadly Quru mountain paths."

"My home is actually closer to Skydašiai than Quruscan anyway," I said.

"Even better!" Kalyna clapped her hands, which was very loud in that small space. "Easy enough for us to get you to your home then!"

"Kalyna, might Skydašiai be any safer for me to move around in than Quruscan?" I asked.

"Now there's a thought," said Kalyna. "Certainly, they'll have a different attitude—they're a rather nosey people, which could be a problem. The Skydašians have the Tetrarchia's longest and most in-volved history of fighting your native country, which has made them less unreasonably scared of Loashti people, but perhaps more, you know, *reasonably* scared. On the other hand, they also have the most experience trading with Loasht."

"If Skydašians are so familiar with my home," I began, "would more of them be able to tell I was Zobiski?"

Kalyna shrugged, which I felt but did not see. "Possibly. But will ideas spreading over the border predispose Skydašians to believe what Loasht is spreading about your people? Or will they be more likely to see you as, now, the enemy of their enemy? And how has Skydašiai—particularly its North Shore—changed as the Blossoming has continued to, well, bloom?"

"Smart Boy here was hoping you'd *answer* questions, not ask more of them."

"I'm sorry, Radiant," said Kalyna. Even in that small, cramped tent, pelted with rain, her voice was sonorous and intimate—I believed that she was sorry.

I nodded, which no one saw, and then muffled a sob, which they must have both heard. I think Dagmar actually tried to put a hand on my shoulder, but, crammed together in the dark, it came across more as a punch to the throat.

Kalyna, Dagmar, and I trudged through the soaked Quru steppes for *two weeks*. The rain simply did not stop. Or, at least, never for more than a half hour. We spent night after night pressed together in that little tent, except for when Dagmar decided she'd rather sleep outside in the rain. I began to feel that I would never be dry.

Kalyna did not complain of discomfort. She complained of her hair looking lank and flat, of her clothes being ruined, of our food being de-stroyed, of our chances against venomous marsh snakes, but never about how she felt. Dagmar punctuated long stretches of tense silence with bouts of all-encompassing complaints: about her feet, about her joints, about her crevices, about how she did not want to look at either of us ever again. In such company, I did not complain at all (except now, to you), because I was terrified of driving my companions away. Instead, I spent a lot of time trying to mollify Dagmar when she threatened to leave.

"My sword cannot save you fools from drowning in your sleep!" she yelled one day.

"Of course it can," said Kalyna. "With a quick death."

"You should be so lucky."

"Dagmar, where would you even go?"

"Anywhere! Away! To go lie in a ditch!"

"Look! Look!" I called, voice cracking. "There's a village!"

This was the first of a few villages we passed through during that rainy, soggy, terrible trudge. Even when we would sleep for a night in a tavern, I never felt fully dry. Their roofs were perfectly sound, but the rainwater felt as though it had permeated me deeply and permanently. Like it clung about us, sneaking inside on our backs.

Kalyna paid our way when needed, insisting that I could reimburse her back in Loasht, although I never saw her write the prices down. Sometimes I'd ask her what the "family business" was that filled our purses, but she always evaded the question—seemed, even, to enjoy finding new ways to evade the question.

Not that I had any deep need to understand where her coin came from, just then. I was simply happy it existed. After all, upon reaching my home, the rest of my silver would go to Dagmar, as well as: "A few gold, Smart Boy. Depends on how difficult the journey, and what you have available to you. If you must run from your home, I won't leave you with nothing!"

She had said this quietly in a warm tavern, while Kalyna was in front of us, making arrangements for the night. "Although she might," added Dagmar, nodding toward the other woman. "Her tastes have gotten expensive."

The following day, we got an unexpected windfall when some townsfolk decided to take me to the Headman, or kill me, or what have you. Dagmar dissuaded them forcefully. She left them with their lives but not their coin, which she cheerfully used to buy dried meat for the next stretch of our journey.

Sometimes, I found myself perversely hoping we would be accosted again, just so that I would owe less money by the end of this. Would I have to sell all my possessions to pay these two and, most likely, somehow escape Yekunde with my family? All of Silver's possessions, and their parents'? By the Eighty-Three, would I have to go ask *my* parents for money?

That trek is a blur of rain and mud and complaints. I think my mind has rejected most of the memories. I fancied that Dagmar was always on the cusp of leaving us and remained only through momentum. Or, perhaps, through just how pathetic and helpless I was. The only way I knew to mark time or distance was by watching the steppe grasses slowly shrink, getting shorter and shorter by the day, until they almost resembled normal grass.

During that trip, the memory of Kalyna's initial deception back in Desgol, of the lives she had endangered (or taken), sat numbly at the base of my skull. It buzzed about my head like a gnat, always just out of sight, reminding me of my growing complicity. Every day I didn't tell Dagmar dug me deeper into the lie. Every time the mercenary beat or cut or scared away a threat—which was quite often, given my features and tattoos—I was actively benefitting from my passive omission.

But then, wasn't Kalyna drawing me deeper into her lies *for my own sake?* I began to find that initial lie, and the possibility of further deceptions I did not see, as comforting. I was in good hands. Was her ability to deceive on my part any less morally justified than Dagmar's easy violence? I began to feel so safe with these two that even the Zobiski memory became but a quiet nagging.

Yes, a voice in my head told me, *everyone else* is indeed *waiting for the chance to turn on you, ruin you, drag you to their masters in exchange for scraps. But Kalyna will trick them all, or Dagmar will kill them all.*

What's more, through it all, whenever there was the energy or inclination for conversation, Kalyna remained a smart and engaging person to be around. She could even draw Dagmar out, now and then, and I began to see how the tall swordswoman had fallen for the cutthroat in the first place. Who else had ever shown such genuine interest in the thoughts, feelings, and opinions of a Dagmar Sorga? (Not I, I must admit.)

Then one day, one blessed day, the rains began to lessen. The grasses were, by that point, only up to my ankles, and I had already been relishing the town that had appeared in the distance. There, I might at least approach dryness for the first time in days. I hardly cared whether

Dagmar would have to bloody some fools who wanted to turn me in—drudgery and numb discomfort had killed most of my sympathy.

Until the downpour fully stopped. The sun shone through, and we saw no more bloated clouds on the horizon ahead of us. Suddenly, I wanted to hug everyone in that town when I got there, even if they hated me.

None of us said a word for the next few minutes, so terrified were we of breaking the spell. Finally, it was Kalyna who cheered and began to caper in the sunlight. It seemed the freest I'd ever seen her, devoid of artifice or control. (In hindsight, I wonder if it was purposefully calculated to convey exactly that.)

So, with the sun finally shining, we strode into the bustling little town like we owned the place. Or perhaps like local heroes returned from war. I am sure we looked like wet rats.

Somewhere in all that rain and tall grass, we had apparently crossed an invisible line and were now in Skydašiai. It occurred to me that I should have felt something other than relief at being out of the rain. I had, after all, spent almost a year living in Quruscan, and I now expected never to return. It seemed to me I should have been having grand, complex, mournful feelings, but had instead simply skipped over them.

This first Skydašian town seemed no different, to me, than the last Quru one had, and I wouldn't have known we'd crossed a border if we hadn't stopped by a changing bank, where the money of one Tetrarchic kingdom could be exchanged for another, for a fee. It seemed absolutely ridiculous to me that the Tetrarchia's four little governments couldn't be bothered to decide on one unified currency. Loasht's countless princes and margraves and obas and beys and arkas and so forth had all been forced to use the same coins for at least five thousand years.

We handed our Quru coins—silver abazi and copper puli, because the Quru didn't like using gold coins—to a pale South Shore Skydašian clerk. In return, we received a small stack of Skydašian kudais, bronze-colored slips of paper which seemed awfully flimsy to me.

As we walked out of the changing bank, Dagmar knocked a fist against its outer wall and asked, "You think the Gustavus brats own this one?"

"Maybe," said Kalyna. "Who knows? I lost track of all that."

"Got lazy, you mean." Dagmar let out a melancholy sigh, but her tone was light.

The clear sky had put us all in a better mood, and Dagmar into a reminiscing one. Kalyna left the shade of the bank to stand in the sunlight, basking in it.

"Who are they?" I asked.

"Rich horse-fuckers," said Dagmar. "Upon whom we *planned* to take revenge."

"What even was the point, Dagmar?" sighed Kalyna. "It took months of hard work to get to Klemens, and the other two are still quite alive and much richer than we'd ever be from robbing them."

"You also took Bernard's little finger."

"I can't very well spend that." Kalyna closed her eyes and turned her face up toward the sun. "I hardly remember why I hated them."

"I think," said Dagmar, "you have come to care so little about other people that you can't even be bothered to hate those who deserve it."

"That may well be," replied Kalyna. She opened her eyes and laughed. "Maybe without Grandmother around modeling the most perfect hatred, I've forgotten how."

"You probably shouldn't speak of the dead that way," said Dagmar.

I saw Kalyna's smile, and body, tighten slightly, but she seemed to let whatever it was go. We began walking to the nearest market, as Dagmar made a series of uncomfortable noises in her throat.

"How did your grandmother die?" I asked.

Kalyna looked blank for a moment, and then she began to laugh. She put a hand on my shoulder to steady herself.

"The thing about it is," she struggled to say through laughter, "I don't know! She couldn't . . . she couldn't bear the *indignity* of anyone seeing her die, so one day she just . . . walked out into the steppe and never came back."

Dagmar began to laugh as well. "She might still be out there!" she added.

"Oh yes!" Kalyna hiccupped. "Just walking angrily, hands on her hips!"

After two more days of travel, I finally began to feel dry. What's more, now that we could see the sun, I knew in what direction we were heading, and it made sense with the vague map of the Tetrarchia I had in my head. We had been traveling westward; here in Skydašiai, and past the mountains entirely, we turned north toward the port city of Žalikwen.

From there, Kalyna assured me, we would be able to cross the Skydaš Sea, which bisected the kingdom.

North Shore and South Shore, as Skydašiai's halves are called, are officially on different continents. I don't know the full history, but North Shore and South Shore used to house entirely distinct peoples, who have long since all become Skydašian. Many people in the farthest south still look like their sallow, lank-haired, robustly built ancestors; while many in the farthest north have the dark complexions, tight curls, and slim musculature of their own ancestors. But most Skydašians are somewhere in the middle, literally and figuratively.

South Shore Skydašiai was a verdant, sunny place that supplied much of the Tetrarchia's produce and grains. According to the locals, South Shore fed the Tetrarchia, while North Shore protected it.

I wish I'd seen more of South Shore Skydašiai, but I spent most of that time hidden from view. Kalyna bought a rickety cart and a sturdy old horse, which we used to cut northward as quickly as we could. "Cheaper and more private than a tavern," she said, so we slept in the cart, and I kept my head down whenever people were around.

Kalyna and Dagmar's relationship had improved with the weather, but still fell into an awkward rhythm of laughter and reminiscing followed by uncomfortable quiet. It seemed to be one-sided on both sides: Dagmar feeling an unrequited love, and Kalyna feeling an unrequited friendship. But both feelings could be disguised as camaraderie, for now.

Through the slats in the side of the cart, I got glimpses of colorful clothing, often in leaf prints of green, orange, yellow, or brown, sometimes accompanied by jewelry and beads. From my hiding place, I heard a number of different local opinions on Loasht, the Blossoming, and "ex-Loashti" like me, but the people voicing them usually sounded resigned, almost fatalistic. They had lived in the shadow of Loasht for so long that it was simply a fact of life for them. (Perhaps they would have reacted differently if they'd known I was there.)

When I was not hiding, I got to enjoy the beauty and fragrance of Skydašiai's miles and miles of fruit trees. I also finally got to improve my own beauty and fragrance, as Kalyna allowed me the use of her oils and lotions and so forth. She handled her own upkeep in a brisk and matter-of-fact way, as though she didn't even realize she was doing it.

"My family's business has always relied on our presentation," she explained as she rubbed something lightly into the bags of her eyes, unbothered by the jumping cart. "I've been doing this since I was old enough to reliably use my hands." She still did not explain what that "family business" was.

I almost began to feel presentable again, although I still mourned the many (*many*) bottles and gourds of ointments, unguents, and cocoa butters that Dagmar had not thought to pack for me in Abathçodu.

Upon reaching the Skydaš Sea, and the small, breezy port city of Žalikwen, I realized it had become summer without my realizing it. The sun was warm on my back, and I could almost forget, for a split second, how uncertain and dangerous the world had become for me, my family, and my community.

The sea itself was a brilliant, shimmering band of blue like nothing I had ever seen. North Shore Skydašiai was *just* visible in the distance, and off to the west, the little sea emptied out into the great ocean. Not only was the sun high in the sky, but the Skydaš Sea seemed soak up all the beautifully bright colors of Skydašian clothing and buildings. The houses closest to the sea were mostly painted in pink, which reflected brilliantly off the water.

Žalikwen shimmered as we approached it, made of bright colors and sunlight. Light and pale pinks, blues, yellows, and greens, dotted with a deep, luminous orange.

"Hmm," grumbled Kalyna. "That's bad."

"What? It's beautiful here!" I replied.

"I have a contact who may be able to get us across the sea, but we'd have to get to the docks to find him." She pointed. "The Skydaš Sea has been open and free to all passengers since before Skydašiai became one people, centuries before the Tetrarchia began. But today, the docks are overrun with soldiers."

I blinked. I did not think I saw soldiers. Then I realized that the deep orange peppering the city—contrasting with the bright bursts of architecture and sea, darker but also somehow shining—was the color of a uniform.

All at once, Zobiski memory (and indigestion) roiled into my guts, the same way it had when the mob came for me in Abathçodu. The same way it had five years earlier, on the day Aloe Pricks a Mare upon the Mountain Bluff returned to Yekunde.

When Aloe Pricks a Mare upon the Mountain Bluff Left Yekunde

For most of my life, the thought of leaving my home to visit the cobbled-together Tetrarchia had not been even a dream, a desire, or a possibility. After all, it was important to me that a Zobiski presence remained in Yekunde.

That city had originally been Zobiski land, but its conquest by Loasht, followed by millennia of the Grand Suzerain's rule, had dispersed my people. Sometimes in order to weaken us, Zobiski were forced from Yekunde into internal exile; other times, droves of my people left for opportunities in parts of Loasht whose denizens may not have learned to hate them. In my time, there were satellite Zobiski communities near Yekunde, but the community within the city itself had shrunk and shrunk and shrunk.

Despite our size, I'd lived a happy life there, and so, like many around my age, I had only a vague notion that things could turn—a feeling that our neighbors disliked us deep down in their hearts. I, and those who thought like me, often wondered if this was simply paranoia. Others of my generation saw themselves as fully Loashti, and felt certain their own children would be safer and better treated than we were. The Zobiski memory I have described was only a dull thrum in the background of my life.

Five years before I met Kalyna Aljosanovna, Aloe Pricks a Mare upon the Mountain Bluff returned to Yekunde, and that dull thrum became acute.

For much of my adulthood, Aloe and I had both worked as faculty scholars at the Yekunde branch of the Loashti Academy. I did not consider him a friend, but was friendly toward him: after all, we both researched the history and traditions of sorcery, albeit for different reasons. We would loan each other books, smile whenever we passed one another, and chat about our research at meals. We also engaged in quite a few spirited late-night debates under the influence of palm brandy or bhang paste; debates that I thought were in good faith. Aloe struck me as intense and inflexible, but so were many of my fellow scholars. (I always fancied this would improve if they slept around more, but that was likely a personal bias.)

He was a man of about my size and age, who had a bright smile when he was relaxing but always looked entirely serious when engaged in courses or study. Despite the lack of copper tones in his closely cut hair, his family was originally from Talverag, which was much closer to the geographic, and administrative, center of Loasht than Yekunde was. He seemed to find some great importance in this, and our debates were often about family history, in some sense or another, which should have been a clue to what the future held.

But then, looking back with what I know now, I may be grasping for meanings that weren't there.

About seven years before I was ejected from Abathçodu, Aloe left Yekunde to pursue studies at another branch of the Academy, and I attended his going-away dinner. Twenty of us sat outside, talking and laughing on one of those summer nights where the humidity becomes pleasantly buoyant, as though you are relaxing inside of a cloud. We circled the Academy's beautiful old table, which was cut lengthwise from a tree, with bark still at its edges but its surface smoothed to a shine. We ate, drank, and snuck bits of a nutty bhang paste into everything, floating down the winding rhetorical roads that scholars and teachers do when they get to enjoy themselves. The torches around us flared the slight blue-green of a flame alchemically treated (although the Tetrarchia might call it "enchanted" or "ensorcelled") to ward off insects.

More than once, someone would point out into the dark and distant swamp, swearing they saw a crocodile. Then everyone would laugh.

"The flames won't keep *them* away!" someone called out.

"We'd better get louder and scare them!" replied Aloe, pounding the table. "More drinks!"

We toasted, we laughed, we made a little light fun of Aloe, and he got even more talkative than usual. For all of his seriousness, he was a man who loved to be the center of attention, which was something I could understand.

Feeling emboldened by the general air of play, I said, "And to think he is leaving all of this"—I motioned to the table and the surroundings—"to go . . . what? Research that oafish ancestor of his!"

There was muted laughter, but some were clearly wondering if I'd gone too far. Aloe stood up and moved unsteadily toward where I was sitting, and the laughter quieted entirely. Because I'd had a decent amount of bhang—my head was quite high up in the stars at this point—the few seconds it took him to get to me felt like an eternity. He leaned down and put an arm around my shoulder. Then he laughed uproariously.

"You always keep me on my toes, Radiant!" He grinned and shook me affectionately.

I shrugged, smiling lazily. Others began to laugh again.

"More than anyone else," Aloe continued, "you, Radiant, are always able to surprise me! To head me off at the pass. Your mind"—he put his fingers playfully in my hair, assuming a familiarity that I did not interrogate at the time, and shook my head lightly—"is always moving!"

"My mind is only 'moving,' Aloe," I laughed, "because you are shaking it!"

He slowly disengaged his fingers but didn't seem particularly chastened, which was fine with me, just then. He had taken my joke in the spirit with which it had been given, and so in that moment, Aloe was my friend. I turned my head slowly, languidly, up toward him.

"And what was so surprising, Aloe? I've criticized that last Minister Investigator who *graced your line* before."

"As have I, Radiant, as have I!" he replied. "But it was the word 'oafish.'" He giggled to himself and rested his forearm on my shoulder. Then he lifted the other hand, one finger out, as though trying to make a point. "Do you . . . I say, Radiant, do you know how my ancestor—Fragrances was his name, everyone, by the way. Radiant, do you know how he died?" He giggled some more.

I shook my head. No matter how much I had imbibed, I knew better than to say that I hoped Fragrances had died at the hands of those he'd so brutally oppressed.

"He was, well, he was gored." Aloe affected a mock seriousness. "Terribly. By a cassowary." Then he grinned. "Which he was trying to train into a fearsome mount!" He burst out laughing at the image of his forebear attempting to ride an angry, murderous bird.

There was much more laughter, from myself as well. I don't know whether I actually found this funny or was simply relieved. Perhaps I was tickled by the thought of a man whose memory still haunted my people dying such a stupid death.

"So 'oafish' is quite appropriate!" Aloe added once his laughter had died down, and he could breathe again.

"It is!" I replied, nodding slowly. "I had no idea. Why, every Zobiski I know would be gratified to hear"—I began to slow down as I realized Aloe's smile was disappearing—"about the undignified demise of one of our chief . . ." I was too far from the world to stop myself from finishing the sentence and muttered, ". . . tormentors."

"Now, Radiant"—Aloe patted my shoulder and then gripped it tightly—"this is all a matter of public record for those of us with access to those records." He motioned to the surrounding scholars. "But I don't know that it should be shared with, well, with everyone. You understand."

I was suddenly very much reminded that I was the only Zobiski at the table.

"But Aloe," I tried, "you must understand that—"

"That Fragrances is seen, by your people, as having been a vicious person. Yes, I know, Radiant. We've discussed it before."

"That, too, is a matter of record."

I immediately regretted saying it; I regretted having ever brought up Fragrances in the first place. I did not want to be dragged back down to the ground and into this silly disagreement, but I had crossed the line from friendly jibes into something that bothered Aloe. It *was* his party, after all.

"But Radiant," he said, sounding (as always) as though he truly wanted to convince me, "you must understand that he . . . that I . . ." Aloe grasped for words—after all, he was no more sober than I was.

I reached up and patted his hand. "Aloe, the way that I—the way that we—see him doesn't need to reflect on you. So he was vicious? My father was vicious."

I immediately felt guilty for throwing my father to the table as a sort of sacrifice. (And *sacrificing* was one of the many things Zobiski had once done that got them branded as "occult.") It felt wrong, in such company, to expose any Zobiski as imperfect. But then, I had always used the divulging of (carefully chosen) secrets and deeply personal feelings to gain trust and protect myself.

Thankfully, my friend and colleague, Casaba Melon Water Soothes at Noontime, saw my discomfort and immediately gave an excessive account of how her father had beaten her in childhood. It made everyone very uncomfortable, but it took the attention off me and showed that such behavior was not, somehow, Zobiski. She did this on purpose, because she was a great friend.

I then largely dropped out of the discussion and gazed off into the distance. I think that for a moment, I actually did see, in the distance, the vague outline of one of our upright crocodiles loping through the darkness on its two legs like a stooping mockery of a human. I suddenly imagined the thing dashing into our midst, biting and tearing into us— even though they weren't known to *dash*, or to attack large groups. I didn't point the creature out to anyone and soon it disappeared.

Neither did I tell anyone at the Academy that I found myself relieved to see Aloe go, because I was ashamed of the feeling. I was not the only one who found him frustrating at times, and I don't know that he had much in the way of close friends. I did not hate or even strongly dislike him, and so it felt unnecessarily mean to admit my relief to others behind his back—to admit that I looked forward to fewer awkward exchanges in my life.

When I returned home that night, Silver understood the truth of his departure better than I did.

"Good riddance," they said. "I hope he falls in a ditch, breaks both legs, and gets carted back here on a manure cart."

"Now, he may not be the most tactful person," I replied, "but that's a little harsh."

"Is it? Didn't you tell me he's going up to Talverag to justify his family history?"

"To study it, Silver Petals Alight on Sand. He's a smart man; justification may not be his conclusion."

"Is he smart, Radiant, or does he just read a lot?"

I didn't have an answer to that, so I said, "Well, I can tell you one thing he's read . . ."

I then told them about how Fragrances had died by cassowary. You had better believe I would go on to tell *every Zobiski I knew*.

Looking back now, I wish Aloe had stayed in Yekunde to irritate me forever. There he could have toiled away in the obscurity of our great libraries and perhaps not become, well, what he *became*. That celebratory dinner of seven years ago feels so recent that I fancy I can reach out and change it: convince him to stay and stop so much unpleasantness.

Chapter Eight

The Žalikwen Salon, and the People I Met There

The port city of Žalikwen, on the Skydaš Sea, was absolutely teeming with soldiers. They were everywhere, in their light, linen uniforms of deep orange, gathered up in the straps of their spare leather armor. I was told that they threw on voluminous capes of white fur when it got cold.

"Officially," Kalyna told me, "the orange is meant to mirror that of the dart frog, which can be quite deadly. Historically, I have read that orange dye was very expensive wherever the North Shore Skydašians originally came from, and so it was a show of power." She smirked and rolled her eyes. "Skydašians often call them the 'Yams.'"

I am no expert on blades, but these *Yams* all carried swords quite different from Kalyna and Dagmar's, which were thin, long, and flexible. The swords that glimmered in the sunlight by the hundreds were just as straight, but shorter and wider.

More worrying, every last Yam carried a long gun with a wheellock firing mechanism. On these I was a bit more knowledgeable, because a well-rounded Loashti education always included some healthy gloating over our country's superiority in firearms. I did not realize the Tetrarchia *had* wheellocks yet: the plans must have been shared with them as part of the Blossoming, as an act of good will. (Loasht's army had, of course, moved from the wheellock mechanism to the much superior flintlock years ago.)

"Did . . . did *every single* Yam have a gun last time we were here?" mumbled Dagmar.

"I don't think so," replied Kalyna. "But the Skydašian army always had the most firearms in the Tetrarchia."

I stared at the soldiers who seemed to stand guard at every intersection, roam every street, sit laughing in the windows of every restaurant, and congregate around the docks conducting inspections. The Quru people, like the Loashti, largely lived their daily lives without soldiers in their midst, and so it was utterly jarring to see them suddenly everywhere. I felt a numbing bleakness move through me, killing any hope. How had I been stupid enough to think I would ever see Silver again? Why had I thought a lovesick sellsword and an inscrutable cutthroat could get me there?

"Not to worry," said Kalyna. "I'll still find a way to my contact, I promise you. If they're checking Loashti papers at the docks, it will be a messy process—no Tetrarchic kingdom has identification papers, after all."

"The Yams are probably sick to death of it all then," added Dagmar. "Enforcing unclear, slapped-together rules and such." She grinned at me. "Of course, whether that means they'll be lenient or cruel will depend on the person, and the moment."

Was I meant to smile back? I'm sure I just looked worried.

We stopped our cart at a nondescript corner on the outskirts of the city where we did not, immediately, see any nearby soldiers. As always, Kalyna and I climbed down, while Dagmar jumped out dramatically. The first order of business was for Kalyna to sweet-talk someone into buying our cart and horse, because they could not very well cross the sea with us.

"You two make yourself scarce," she said. "We'll meet as near to the docks as we can get before being checked by soldiers. Dagmar knows which dock."

"Do I?" asked Dagmar.

"You do."

Dagmar rolled her eyes. "Is your 'contact' Liudvikas?"

"Naturally."

By this time, whenever Kalyna and Dagmar would reference "the old days," I simply let it pass over me. There was too much history between these two.

"Let's see," said Dagmar. "A blue dock. East-ish?"

Kalyna nodded idly as she patted the horse that had brought us here, seeming to study its mane. The creature made a little grunt at her, and she scratched it behind the ear. It occurred to me that she had held the reins through most of our trip—I certainly couldn't be trusted to do so—and I wondered if she would miss the stumpy old thing.

"Who's Liudvikas?" I asked. "Trustworthy?"

"Certainly!" replied Kalyna. "Those Bari listen to no masters; or at least, they don't listen very hard. And Liudvikas and I have known each other for years. He likes me."

"Bari?" I asked.

"The Barge People," explained Dagmar. "They control the back-and-forth of the Skydaš Sea. Like a trade guild, but . . . more. They live out on the boats."

"They spend more time on land than people think," corrected Kalyna between coos at the horse. "They aren't Rots; they know when a living situation is unnatural."

Dagmar glared. But, I think, playfully.

"I'll see what I can learn about the soldiers filling the docks," said Kalyna. "The Skydaš Sea has always been seen as a sort of . . . sacred conduit between our land masses. Even to those who do not worship the sea's god, if the Skydaš Sea isn't free to cross, is instead treated like a *border*, then it rather complicates Skydašiai's standing as a unified kingdom, and the Tetrarchia's as a country." She began to lead the horse away. "Someone will want to tell me more: the inviolate doesn't get *violated* without a lot of gossip."

Kalyna waved over her shoulder at us as she walked off with the horse and cart. Dagmar and I took up our packs beneath the hot summer sun, and a pleasing breeze came off the water.

"Hood up, Smart Boy," said Dagmar.

"But—"

"People here may very well suspect that a face full of tattoos, with your hair, which has now grown out a bit, will mean a Zobiski."

"Other people from Yekunde have tattoos, and—"

"Well, then you can stop and explain it to everyone we pass."

Grumbling, I put on the heavy hood, which made the summer day much less pleasant.

"Now," said the swordswoman, "where should we hide?"

I gulped. I did not like having to make decisions just then. "A tavern?" I offered.

"Don't be stupid. These aren't Quru. They'll ask you a *lot* of questions."

"Do they have a library here?"

Dagmar let out a long, heavy sigh. "Probably," she said, clearly disappointed.

Žalikwen did in fact have a library—a beautiful one, in fact—but it took us some time to find. It turns out that a tall, squinting Rot unenthusiastically mumbling, "Where is your"—a deep sigh—"library?" doesn't always make people receptive.

Once we got there, the Žalikwen Library was an enormous, octagonal wooden building painted a beautiful lilac, although the paint on the wall facing the sea had faded considerably. Its façade said "LIBRARY" in each of the four languages of the Tetrarchia.

We entered through the building's great door, with its triangular arch, and I was greeted by something I did not expect in a library: noise. Not the fleeting sounds of a surrounding city, like in Abathçodu's winding, partially outdoor, library, but the noise of a public house or restaurant. Conversation, laughter, the clattering of mugs and plates. The Skydašians were, I'd noticed, generally a louder people than the Quru in most contexts, but in a *library*, this still seemed excessive.

"I thought it would be quiet," muttered Dagmar in Cöllüknit. "This is as bad as a tavern. Let's go."

"Wouldn't it draw more suspicion if I walked in, hooded in summertime, looked around, and then immediately walked out?" I countered. "There must be a quiet corner somewhere."

Dagmar grunted assent.

The library had three stories of books, wreathed with catwalks and landings, and a great expanse of shelves that stretched before us. The noise came from our left, where the shelves were interrupted by tables and chairs, around which were a number of people talking excitedly. They gesticulated with their mugs, dragged screeching tables across the floor to be closer to one another, spilled into the stacks, and excitedly enjoyed tarts and *coffee*.

O wondrous coffee. I realized I had been smelling it upon entering, without fully registering why the library felt so divinely welcoming.

I had not had coffee since I left home. I had greatly enjoyed exploring Quru food and drink, much of which was sublime, but I'd missed coffee. At first, I missed it actively; later it became a passive emptiness. I love Quru teas very much, but they are simply different. South Shore Skydašiai also preferred tea, but we were now close enough to the continent of my home that these people were drinking coffee.

"Dagmar," I muttered urgently, "I don't want to draw attention to myself, so if you go get me a coffee, I will love you forever."

"Why, Smart Boy," she gasped, "you mean you don't already?"

Blessed Dagmar Sorga then winked at me before walking up to the bar.

I crept in among the closest shelves, set our bags on the floor, and watched her go have small, pleasant interactions with strangers as she moved up to the bar. I felt a deep jealousy. I missed casual chat.

I also watched the locals at their little tables, enjoying each other's company, and, I fancied, discussing weighty and fascinating ideas. What a people, I thought, to make space for camaraderie and discussion even in their library. I felt desperate to join them but knew I should not.

Sea breeze blew in through the large and expertly angled windows, but I was still sweltering in my hood. A hot coffee would not help, yet when Dagmar returned with a red earthenware mug, I took it gladly. She ushered me deeper into the stacks, motioning with a plate matching the mug, on which sat a tart of some kind. I sniffed my coffee as we walked.

"We're allowed to bring these with us," she said. "But if we stain the books, we're in big trouble."

"The coffee-woman tell you that while she was making eyes at you?"

"Yes!" replied Dagmar with a grin. She took a bite of the tart and then continued speaking with a full mouth. "Did the, 'Oh, I'm just a big, dumb Rot' thing. Usually works."

"So you *aren't* just a big, dumb Rot?"

Dagmar glared at me, swallowed, and laughed. "I like it when you get bolder, Smart Boy. Yes, mostly. I'm no big actor like Kalyna, but I can play my base nature up or down a bit when needed, like anyone."

"I should get better at that."

"You should." She leaned against a shelf and continued eating.

"Did you learn anything about what's going on here?"

"Not yet," she said while swallowing a bit of her tart. "All I've heard is a bunch of smart people like you talking nonsense. The men behind me in line were arguing over the best way to end all war. Forever." She snickered at the thought.

"Through what methods?"

"War, of course. One said that a government would *only* have to conquer the entire known world, but do so with the 'right intent,' to ensure eternal peace."

"He doesn't sound very smart."

She nodded. "The other insisted that the only way to end war was to create a weapon so powerful and brutal that kings and queens would realize it must never be unleashed." Dagmar took another bite and continued with her mouth quite full. "He then described this weapon in a lot of detail. The line was slow."

"My apologies. Thank you again."

She smiled.

I looked down at my coffee. I had not dared a sip yet; I had only been savoring the scent. I hadn't wanted the first sip to be while walking, talking, or being otherwise engaged. It was served without sugar or milk here—dark brown, like the deep earth or Silver's forearms. I took a sip, and it was, indeed, heavenly. I closed my eyes and smiled.

"It feels as though I am already back home," I said.

Then I heard someone yell, "Loashti!"

I froze. I did not want to turn and look at where the voice had come from, lest I reveal myself.

Dagmar, leaning against a shelf and facing me, blinked languidly and took another bite of her tart. But the hand that held her little plate tightened.

"You there! The hooded Loashti in the stacks!" cried the voice from behind me, out where the tables and refreshments were. The other conversations began to quiet down.

Dagmar nodded to me almost imperceptibly. She slowly set the remaining half of her tart onto the plate and smiled. "This should crack a skull if thrown hard enough," she whispered through her smile, raising the plate slightly.

I turned around.

A smiling, narrow-faced Skydašian man was beckoning me toward him and a number of others. These people were all looking up from their coffees, their tarts, or the oval green leaves they were chewing, to watch me. Those at unrelated tables were now regarding me as well.

What could I do? I smiled back.

"Come talk to us!" said the man.

Dagmar whispered, "Go on. Charm them, Smart Boy."

Bolstered by this (I am easy), I walked out from the cozy, narrow, supposedly hidden stacks, and into the open area full of people and chatter. Those who were not sitting with the man who'd called me over had already lost interest in me. As I approached, I pulled back my hood, which hardly seemed necessary now.

The smiling man waving to me looked rather young, and was wirier than I would have expected of one with such a loud voice. He had large, expressive eyes beneath dark hair that bounced down both sides of his head in tight, well-oiled ringlets. He wore a sort of close-cut silk robe of blue, dotted with pink flower print, and a necklace of shining, multicolored beads that hung over his chest. As I sat, I made sure to position myself so that I could still see Dagmar, who was watching the man across from me intently.

The man's name was Vidmantas. I gave my own and was pleasantly surprised to learn that everyone in this group already knew how Loashti names worked. We were close to my home indeed, not just geographically, but culturally—so close that I could feel Loasht's presence, rather than just the locals' fears of Loasht.

I sipped my coffee and allowed myself to smile warmly at my new conversation partners. I swore I could *feel* the wrinkles gathering about my eyes. Hear them, even. How long could I continue to coast on looks?

Vidmantas and his companions told me I'd stumbled into the weekly Žalikwen Salon, when the library forsook its rules about quiet and order to allow discussions, speeches, debates, and songs. Being at the meeting place between the two continents meant that there were always new ideas coming through the salon. New songs too: one began wafting from a nearby table where a woman was playing a tall, stringed instrument and singing plaintively about an old Skydašian princess.

"You're just in time," said Vidmantas, "to weigh in on my debate with Žydrė here." He flourished toward a woman at my right.

In contrast with Vidmantas' lush, almost hedonistic, curls, Žydrė's hair was pulled tightly to her scalp in complex braids that must have taken a lot of work. Her small but powerfully built body was wrapped in a dress of plain tan linen, with a bright red sash wrapped many times around her waist. She was holding a stalk of oblong green leaves in one hand, and when I looked at her, she stopped chewing and looked surprised.

"Vidmantas," she growled from one side of her mouth, which seemed to be full, "is trying to embarrass me. Please look the other way so I can spit without being crass."

I obliged, of course. Vidmantas shrugged.

"I suppose you weren't ready to defend your position," he said to her in a way that I think was playful. I hoped very much that she also saw it that way.

"Radiant," he continued, turning to me, "we'd love to have a Loashti perspective." He smiled with light mischief. "Or, at least, I would."

"Oh? A Loashti perspective on what?" I kept my smile but could not help worrying their topic was how best to murder me, or something along those lines.

"Ways of organizing a society," said Vidmantas.

In the distance, I saw Dagmar roll her eyes. Sure that I was in no danger, she stopped looking ready to throw the plate and instead finished her tart.

"Pleased to meet you," said Žydrė, whose mouth was no longer full. "And I apologize for *Vidmantas'* rudeness. Those leaves had just reached their end."

"Leaves?" I turned back to her.

"Khat leaves." She lifted the leafy twig in her hand, twirling it slightly. "You chew them and get, you know, twisted up a bit. Chatty. Like coffee, but more so."

Žydrė held the twig out to me questioningly, but I demurred. My first coffee in almost a year would twist me up plenty.

"So," I said, "ways of organizing a society? That's . . . broad."

"Vidmantas is being grandiose," said Žydrė. "We're discussing a specific society. A new one. That *works*."

Vidmantas rolled his eyes.

"Works for whom?" I asked. "If you want the 'Loashti perspective,' as if such a singular thing could possibly exist, it would be that Loasht is absolutely a society that works, which is why it's lasted so long. But it was never intended to work *for me*."

I realized this was getting very close to admitting my recent change in status and so pivoted: "It works first of all for the Grand Suzerain, then for the noble classes of Central Loasht, *then* for everyone in Central Loasht, and then for the thousands of different kinds of leaders throughout the rest of the country."

"And you're none of those?" asked a quiet voice behind me.

I laughed and shook my head, turning to see a small Skydašian man watching me intently.

"Most Loashti aren't," I said. "It's . . . hard to convey just how big Loasht actually is. Even I have trouble visualizing it."

"Well, the Tetrarchia," Vidmantas began, leaning forward, "doesn't really work for *anyone*, does it?" His eyes positively glimmered with the excitement of dancing on the edge of sedition. "Are even our monarchs happy with it? They're always bickering."

"They prefer it to constant war," said Žydrė. "On that *one* thing, I agree with them."

She was also leaning forward now, as though excited to be in both conspiracy and vehement disagreement with Vidmantas. Žydrė had an appealingly weather-beaten face, beautiful in the way it was lightly cracked.

"So, Žydrė," I asked, "what's your 'new' society, and whom does it work for? I assume it's a theoretical one."

She turned her chair toward me with a loud creak. "Oh no, it's quite real."

Vidmantas guffawed derisively.

"Loashti," said Žydrė.

"Radiant," I corrected.

"Radiant," she continued, "I'm here to propose a world in which every person is cared for, and none are left behind."

"Propose?" I asked. "I thought you said—"

"*Thank* you," interrupted Vidmantas.

"—that it wasn't theoretical?"

"Up north," Žydrė began, her eyes wide as she began chewing another khat leaf, "I live in a community that is demonstrating how a decent, caring, fulfilling society can operate. The Lanreas River Guild—"

"It's *not* a guild," mumbled Vidmantas.

Žydrė smiled condescendingly, as though she'd heard Vidmantas say this many times.

"The Lanreas River *Guild*," she repeated, "is the model that . . ."

She stopped herself to shoot Vidmantas a look. He smiled and raised his hands, silently promising he would not interrupt this time.

"The model," Žydrė continued, "that the rest of humanity will follow, provided we demonstrate it correctly."

Vidmantas looked at me with a sort of *You see what I'm dealing with here?* face.

"And then," said Žydrė, "we will someday have a world in which kings and queens and nobles and suzerains don't get so far ahead of everyone else. How does that sound to you, Radiant?"

Even to me, a seemingly exiled Zobiski, the idea almost didn't make sense. Loasht had perhaps a thousand different cultures and laws within it, but even the most radical Loashti still understood that the Grand Suzerain was, simply, meant to be *better* than the rest of us. It wasn't done to think otherwise—or at least, not to suggest so.

Besides, it was the Grand Suzerain's laws and protections that had shielded my people, at least to some degree, over the centuries. I wondered again what could have changed. I even still hoped it might all be some cruel mistake.

I couldn't quite help thinking of what Žydrė had said about the khat leaves "twisting her up." Over the years, I had been told of many "new" ways of seeing the world by people wide-eyed from one substance or another. I had certainly been that person, now and then. But on the other hand, she did claim that some version of her perfect society already existed.

"I suppose such a world sounds nice," I said. "If it could ever exist."

"And if it exists at all," Vidmantas cut in, "it does so only in a small, out-of-the-way place."

"And how much good are you doing here in the big city?" asked Žydrė.

Vidmantas shrugged. "I just think that creating your own little society—"

"Is the only way to get anything done."

"—ignores the reality of *where we are*," Vidmantas finished. "Your charlatan leader has, in a genius way, masqueraded selfishness for charity. Convinced you that hiding away and only helping your own will somehow redeem the world! And while you and the other utopians wait for the lords to peacefully give up their lands and profits and powers, the rest of us will continue living as King Alinafe's *blessed* subjects."

"You have no great love for your king?" I asked.

"Kings don't require love, just obedience," he replied. "But their officials can be petitioned. The guilds keep us safe, protecting one another. Our guilds—*proper* guilds, that is, with the paperwork to prove it—elect our burgomasters, who in turn appoint our voivodes, who speak directly to the King, avoiding most of the nobility. They can advocate for us."

"Can," said Žydrė, "but don't. And the voivodes are *also* nobility."

"I said 'most,'" muttered Vidmantas.

"Just visit Lanreas, Vidmantas," said Žydrė. "Visit once." She clasped her hands together. "I will even say please. If you will just visit once, with an open mind, afterward you can criticize Lanreas all you like. Please."

Vidmantas' ironic smile disappeared, and he suddenly looked touched, understanding.

"But Žydrė," he said, "I already criticize it all I like."

Žydrė growled irritably and leaned back in her chair.

"Radiant," murmured the small man behind me, who had barely spoken, "do the Loashti petition the Grand Suzerain?"

"No," I replied. "We don't engage in any such petitions. And your name was . . . ?"

"Ifeanyas," he said, looking at the floor. "Sorry."

Ifeanyas wore a fraying green robe and pale linen trousers, and his tightly curled dark hair was cut very close to his skull. He seemed very much to want to be involved in the conversation one moment and then to not be perceived the next.

"Well, Ifeanyas," I said, "no matter how one's local Loashti government works—and there are hundreds of ways in which it can—only a fool would expect their complaints or requests to reach the Grand Suzerain. And only an even bigger fool would expect those complaints to be addressed."

Ifeanyas, who had eventually looked back up at me as I was talking, now knitted his brows with great intensity.

"But the Tetrarchia is *different*," said Vidmantas. "We are newer and more flexible."

"The 'Tetrarchic Experiment,'" Ifeanyas chimed in, nodding.

"Precisely," Vidmantas continued. "We have the space here to try new things, change our way of life."

Žydrė sighed and slumped back in her chair. "Vidmantas, you keep making my point for me. That is exactly what we're doing!"

"But what you and your little cult leader are playing at isn't sustainable."

Žydrė sat forward now. "How do you know if you've never seen the place?"

"Nothing is sustainable," added Ifeanyas.

I considered pointing out how generally unchanged Loasht had been for millennia but decided against it. (Besides, the Blossoming had been a change, as was my exile. But then, how much did either effect most Loashti?)

"I've heard," Ifeanyas continued, looking down as if he were embarrassed to be offering us information, "that there are places in the Bandit States where the government changes with the seasons." He looked up from the floor, and his round face broke into a warm smile. "Not because of wars or coups, I mean," he added quickly. "On purpose, like."

Ifeanyas paused, but it seemed neither Žydrė nor Vidmantas were interested in interrupting him the way they did one another.

"When it's time for the harvest," he continued, "the leaders simply *stop* being leaders and follow the same rules as everyone else: listening to the head farmers. Then, in their frozen southern winters, everyone sequesters and listens to no one but their own family."

"Well," said Vidmantas, "they do a lot of strange things in the Bandit States."

"But it sounds better to me," replied Ifeanyas. "More honest."

"What if you hate your family?" I asked.

Ifeanyas shrugged. "Maybe you can find another?"

This was when the salon ended abruptly, as a troop of soldiers burst into the library.

When Aloe Pricks a Mare upon the Mountain Bluff Returned to Yekunde

As I have mentioned, Aloe Pricks a Mare upon the Mountain Bluff left Yekunde for Talverag: a much more important city, and his ancestral home. Long ago, it had been from Talverag that the Ministry of Curse-Breaking had signed purge orders, because the Grand Suzerain in the August and Unchanging City of Loasht was too lofty to concern himself with "occult elements." Many times throughout history, Talverag had sent that ministry's functionaries throughout the country to curb—or terrorize—many Zobiski, some Kubatri, various other subject peoples, and countless individuals for worshipping, alchemizing, cursing, blessing, or speaking incorrectly.

Eventually, opinions would change, or the Ministry would be seen as going "too far," and so it would disappear for a century or two before being dredged back up. Its resurrections always came with a new name for its agents: Witch Inspectors, Sorcerer Cleavers, Scribes of the Breaking of Spells, and so forth. Aloe's family, once upon a time, had birthed a few generations of the most recent iteration, Minister Investigators of Atavism. His ancestor Fragrances, who was gored by a cassowary, had been the last one of these.

Of the many debates I had with him (which, again, I took for light rhetorical exercises), not one had included any claims that the Ministry of Curse-Breaking had been *correct* when it was in power. When we knew each other, no one would have said such a thing at the Academy. Rather, he continued to insist that his ancestors from the Ministry's last period of ascendance had been good for Loasht in other ways: yes, they may have gone too far in their treatment of the Zobiski, or of other healers and mystics, but they were also strengthening communities and rooting out harmful practices. Sometimes even saving people (for example, my people) from themselves.

He had remained stuck on this point: that his forebears must have been at least partly virtuous. Held it to himself like a charm until, well, I suppose it overtook everything else.

Around a year after Aloe left Yekunde, we began to hear about him again. After Talverag, he had gone to quite a few of Loasht's central margravates, trying to convince their leaders that a Minister Investigator would be a useful functionary to employ. He had removed "of Atavism" from the title, I suppose to show that he was enlightened, although the function of the role was the same as it had always been.

He was laughed out of many places, and back in Yekunde, we laughed as well. Ah! Intense and self-serious Aloe had once again run up against people who saw him for the fusty little academic that he was!

Until he found a margrave mired in enough scandal to listen to him. All it took was one leader in need of someone else to blame his poor governance on. I don't even remember where exactly this was—I suppose eventually it had to happen somewhere.

So, when Aloe returned to Yekunde two years after he had left, he did so with a new title and a small group of armed followers. You must understand that weaponry was never a common sight on Loashti streets, and that soldiers did not roam the country enforcing petty laws. The state's own sense of long-held and unquestionable authority mostly ruled the populace from afar.

Whether Aloe's little army was an official piece of the Loashti military, a group of officials who happened to be armed, or some little "hunting club" was left purposefully murky. But whatever they were, they marched back south through Loasht, and then through the streets of my home, yelling and laughing, sometimes breaking things. There were not that many of them, really, and they didn't hurt anyone in Yekunde. But, of course, all the Zobiski stayed inside during their little parades, so we did not know what would have happened if they'd caught any of us out in public.

When they swarmed through our streets, I suddenly felt that I had some vague inkling of what my great-grandparents had once experienced, huddling in their homes and contemplating flight. Now I also knew how many of my neighbors had never cared for my kind, if not outright hated us: there they were, cheering or excitedly discussing Aloe's reappearance. Then I thought of people throughout Loasht in whom he had already been instilling this fear, while I had blithely ridiculed his attempts to dredge up a defunct title.

Aloe gave some talks at the Academy that I did not attend, and he accepted an award for his new research at a ceremony I also avoided. He stayed in Yekunde for a week, and at the end of that time, he threw a party to which he explicitly invited everyone who had been at his earlier farewell—including me. I accepted the invitation in hopes of proving to myself, and others, that really nothing was wrong.

This night was quite different from the last time I'd seen him. It was indoors, in a great hall of the Academy, and though there was a bit of alcohol, no one was greatly indulging. Certainly, no one made fun of Aloe. Or of anybody, for that matter. I would say the conversation was more self-consciously "academic," but much less interesting, than it had been at his previous farewell. Certainly, no one spoke about their parents, although Aloe did discuss his oh-so-important ancestor Fragrances. (I kept feeling the urge to mention cassowaries but restrained myself.) I was, for the most part, relieved that his little army was nowhere to be seen that night.

"Radiant Basket of Rainbow Shells!" he called from across the long table. "It's good to see you again. I missed our conversations these two years!"

I smiled and nodded. I could not bring myself to lie and say that I felt the same, so I said, "I'm gratified. What about them did you miss?"

Aloe grinned that bright smile of his. "Everything about them, Radiant! You're a wonderful thinker, you know."

I murmured a thank you.

"Have you considered," he continued, "working for the Ministry?"

I wanted to laugh. The newly revived Ministry of *Curse-Breaking*? Aloe had blandly renamed this iteration the "Ministry of Investigations," but it pursued the same goals it always had.

"I must say I haven't," I replied. "I'm quite busy here, after all." I did not ask how in the world he expected a *Zobiski* to work in the same Ministry that had justified the slaughter of our ancestors.

"That's a shame," he said with a sigh. "It's quite different than what you expect, I'm sure." He seemed genuinely put out.

I made some muttered apology, and we didn't speak again that night. At the time, I took this exchange as a good sign. Perhaps he really was intent on making an entirely new Ministry of Investigations.

When Aloe finally left, some laughed at the ridiculous spectacle he had made, some worried for the future, some hoped for his return. Many simply marveled at how "well-behaved" his little army had been.

Chapter Nine

Concerning the Barge People, or Bari

The moment that Skydašian soldiers swarmed into the library, I dashed away into the stacks, upending tables and chairs.

"Dagmar! Dagmar? Are you here?" I whispered harshly as I ran between the shelves. "*Please*, Dagmar!"

I heard commotion, yelling, sounds of earthenware breaking. I looked desperately for Dagmar. Then I felt a strong hand on my shoulder, but it was not hers.

Where the salon had been there were now some ten people whose hands were being tied behind their backs. I was quickly thrown among them, alongside Vidmantas and Ifeanyas, but I did not see Žydrė.

"...and a Loashti," one of the soldiers was saying to his commander, a square man who stood out because he had a bigger hat and did not carry a gun.

"What is the meaning of this?" someone yelled.

My wrists were bound painfully behind me.

"Arrests," answered the commander. "A lot of treachery going on in here."

"You know as well as I do that it's just talk," said Vidmantas. I had expected him to be angry and blustery, but he sounded sad. Resigned. "You used to come to the salons, Gintaras."

"Oh," said the commander. "You really caught me there, Vidmantas. Guess I'll let you go."

We were dragged out of the library.

I seemed to be the only Loashti among the prisoners. Had these people all been arrested because of me? Had someone in the library recognized me as Zobiski and alerted the authorities? The soldiers did not tell us why any of this was happening, nor where we were going. We were simply kicked and jostled down the incline of Žalikwen, toward the sea—through those streets of brightly painted houses.

There were some fifteen soldiers surrounding the ten of us, and I slowly began to realize that out here, in bright daylight, Dagmar could not save me. There were limits to even her powers.

The people of Žalikwen watched us curiously as we were forced down toward the docks. Many of them seemed dismayed by what was happening, but that didn't mean they were particularly interested in speaking out on our behalf. We were then brought through a cordon of soldiers and right up to the sea itself.

Žalikwen's docks were so beautiful that I forgot my predicament for a moment. They were wooden squares, like any others, but each was painted a bright color, I suppose to easily delineate them. The dock in front of us was a sort of mauve, and moving from it to the east I saw docks in red-orange, bright green, deep blue, and more. These colors reflected off the waters, and far across the sea, I could just make out the opposite side's rainbow of docks. Between the two shores, in the distance, floated a number of barges, which seemed to sport glittering, metallic filigrees. Many sat still, while others were pulled along by oars: they were low boats, without sails. One, with gold trim, was quite close. It was a stunning view.

Then the butt of a gun was slammed into the back of my legs, and I was forced painfully to my knees, as were the rest of the prisoners from the salon. The wood of the mauve dock was quite hard, and my knees radiated pain. I heard some of the others cry out, as I looked up across the sea, to the far shore. It felt like we were *so close* to my home. But instead, I was here, kneeling with prisoners as soldiers pointed their long guns at us.

"Are they going to kill us right here?" someone murmured.

I suspect many had been thinking it, but once it was articulated, I could feel a greater fear slide through us all and begin to bubble out. Those near me began to fidget, whimper, or breathe heavily.

"In the middle of the city?" exclaimed Vidmantas. I could not tell whether he didn't believe it, or was hoping to speak its impossibility into being. "This has never happened before."

There was silence for a moment, and then Ifeanyas muttered, "They've never set up checkpoints at the sea before, either."

Vidmantas moaned assent. "They've never raided the salon before," he sighed.

I stared at the mauve wood beneath me and began to mutter prayers. Moving from one god to the next. Anyone I thought could help me.

"We broke up your salon," said Gintaras, the commander who'd arrested us, "because of you, Vidmantas. A lot of treasonous talk these days." He frowned in a mockery of disappointment. "You must've known this would happen eventually."

I blinked. They weren't here for me? Not here to stamp out the Loashti that even Loasht didn't want? I admit I felt an immediate, overwhelming, urge to tell them of Vidmantas' comments about their king, the urge to throw him to them for my safety. I don't feel guilty for thinking this; we often look to our own safety first. The test is what we actually do after that first thought.

I said nothing, of course. No halfway decent Zobiski is an informer. None of the other prisoners said anything either.

A crowd of Žalikwen's citizens kept trying to look past the cordon of soldiers but were turned away. They would not see us if we were shot, but they would certainly hear it.

There were other nonuniformed Skydašians on this side of the soldiers: small groups of parents and children. They did not wear the customary robes, only faded shirts and trousers, and some with their hair tied up in kerchiefs. The soldiers were shooing them over to the next dock (red-orange), but not out into the city at large.

My throat went dry. I could not keep my breath. This wasn't right. Kalyna and Dagmar were supposed to protect me. I was so close. (So

close to *what*, I did not think about just then.) I began to cry. I felt
Vidmantas' eyes on me, watching me fail at strangling my sobs.

"Look," he said, "at least let the Loashti go. He couldn't very well
speak treason against a country that's not his, could he? Do you want to
cause an incident while the Blossoming is still—?"

A soldier hit him. Hard, with the butt of their gun. I heard a dull
thud, and Vidmantas let out an undignified wail. Not that I, sniffling as
I was, faulted anyone for being undignified.

"Let the soldiers worry about 'incidents,'" said Gintaras. "We'll deal
with the bureaucracy of arresting a Loashti national. If we have to." He
then pointed at me.

A soldier began riffling through the pouch at my waist. Why he
needed to shove my head, hurt my neck, and punch my stomach to do
this, I don't know. Then I heard my papers rustling in his hands.

"Pink, sir!" he yelled into my ear.

Gintaras smiled. "Ah! No bureaucracy necessary then. This man isn't
Loashti, and he certainly isn't from the Tetrarchia. Stateless." He re-
garded me for a moment, then shrugged. "Let's do our allies a favor.
Shoot him."

The soldier behind me stood, giving my head one more shove for
good measure. I heard his gun lifted in his hands. Felt the cold steel
against the base of my skull.

I just cried more. I did not want to die here. I did not want to haunt
this foreign land and these *boring* soldiers. Spending twenty or thirty
years as a rage-filled phantom watching wretched, *stultifying* Gintaras
go about his empty life was a sickening thought.

"What, by the gods, do you think you're doing?!" shouted someone
nearby, punctuated by the sound and vibration of boots clacking onto
the wooden dock.

I looked up and saw that the barge with gold trim that had been
nearest to us was now docked. Up close, its "gold" was just wood covered in flaking gold paint. At the front of the barge, also painted gold,
was carved the image of a sinuous god holding a barge in one hand and
some sort of antennaed predatory fish in the other.

Standing just in front of that god, on the mauve dock, was a
woman dressed like the families I had seen nearby: faded shirt and
trousers, with a kerchief tying up her hair. But she also wore a bright

red-and-gold sash across her chest, perhaps denoting authority. She certainly had a commanding presence, evidenced by all the soldiers looking up from us and their guns to see what she would do next.

She was also, it seemed to me, Kalyna Aljosanovna.

I felt a flutter of safety, of relief, at her appearance. I knew, intellectually, that Kalyna's very presence was not enough to save me from a horde of armed soldiers, but I felt that my fate was now in *her* hands, not mine, whether I escaped or died.

"Ma'am," said Gintaras. He looked at her for a moment and then corrected himself: "Captain. What we think we're doing is our job. *On land.*"

"Maybe you are," replied Kalyna. "But you're on *Bari* docks, where *Bari* children play." She pointed to the families on the nearby red-orange docks, in their faded clothes. The children looked back, little hands to their mouths and eyes suitably (exaggeratedly?) wide.

"Captain," said Gintaras, "we are only saving you the space of one more prisoner to transport."

"Meaning you plan to shoot a Loashti. With a *gun*." She was speaking Skydašiavos in an accent I'd never heard before: the words positively loped and rolled out of her mouth.

"What do you care?"

"What do I . . . ?" Kalyna strode along the dock, up to the commander. "You are," she began as though she was speaking to a child, "threatening a *Loashti*"—she slapped one hand against another, slowly emphasizing each word—"with a"—she mimed pulling a trigger—"*gun*." Then she glared silently, waiting for him to catch her blindingly obvious meaning.

"Would you rather we cut his throat?" asked Gintaras.

"I would!" she cried.

My heart sank.

"You absolute block of wood," she continued.

"Now see here, *Captain*," growled Gintaras, "you Barge People get a lot of leniency, but this is—"

"You Yams get a lot of leniency," she interrupted, grinning, "but I am hearing that you'd prefer to *swim* across the sea."

Gintaras looked very much like he wanted to throw her down right next to me. I did not understand what stopped him.

"Don't you worry, big man," she continued, waving dismissively at him. "Officers don't swim. Your poor soldiers will lug you across."

Gintaras took a deep breath, pinched the bridge of his nose, and asked, "What is this all about, Captain?"

"Where do guns come from?" asked Kalyna.

"These were made in—"

"No, idiot, where do they *come from*? Where do the schematics and gunpowder come from?"

There was a long pause, as Gintaras clearly did not want to say the answer.

"Loasht," said one of his soldiers, finally.

Kalyna snapped her fingers and pointed at that soldier, favoring him with her brilliant smile.

"At least one of you has some sense," she said. "Don't you know that the designs Loasht sends here, as well as their gunpowders, are enchanted?"

Gintaras laughed. "Ridiculous."

"Ridiculous?" she echoed, bending forward, hands on her hips. "Why? Because you're too dense to know it? Why else would they let us have such dangerous weapons?"

Kalyna walked closer to me as she spoke and then pushed at my head with the next few words, as though I was a thing, not a person. The same way the soldier who had been about to kill me had done.

"Because they know the guns won't work against Loashti," she finished.

"Skydašiai has fought Loasht in the past," said Gintaras.

"When?" asked Kalyna. "And when did you start using guns? Loasht only started giving them to us a hundred years ago."

"Selling them."

"So they make a profit *and* prepare us for their invasion."

Gintaras sucked his teeth loudly. "Galiag, *Captain*, has fought them more recently than that."

"Galiag," said Kalyna. She tapped her chin and made a show of walking slowly, thoughtfully. "Galiag. Galiag." She repeated. "That's a good point, Commander. Galiag is the one up north with the ziggurats and the hot winds, isn't it?"

Gintaras smiled sourly and nodded.

"The hot winds," mused Kalyna, "that fill the air constantly with debris, jamming guns and making them useless." She spun to face him, with an eyebrow raised. "You thought I wouldn't know that, Commander, because I live on the sea. But I also know that only *our* guns jam in Galiag, not the Loashti's."

Gintaras threw up his hands. "Then let's test your theory and shoot him! We can sort this out right now."

I heard a click behind me. It took all my strength to not cry out Kalyna's name.

"And my beautiful deck will be blown to pieces!" she yelled. "Who knows what kind of blast will come about?"

Gintaras shook his head. "This is nonsense."

"Is it?" murmured one of his soldiers.

"*I* certainly don't know how these things work," said another, the gun clacking in his hand as he motioned with it.

"You said they wouldn't *work* on a Loashti," growled Gintaras. "What's this about a blast?"

Kalyna shrugged angrily. "There are a lot of ways a gun can *not* work. Is backfiring or exploding never heard of?"

"I was told in training," one of the soldiers began to murmur to another, "that once—"

"He's not even Loashti anymore!"

"And I'm sure the *guns* understand that. Fool."

"Fine!" yelled Gintaras. "You're wasting my time. Take these traitors aboard, and we'll get them to the Goddess' Guts and sorted out."

"Aboard *our* barge?" Kalyna cried. "Oh no. No, no, no. Not with you waving those guns at him. I absolutely refuse."

I looked harder at her and began to wonder if this person was even Kalyna. She had not spared me a glance and did not seem to be driving at all toward saving me. Did she perhaps have a double, or a twin?

Gintaras sighed. "Our guns will work on *you*, Captain, and I am tired of standing around here." He pointed, and some of his soldiers aimed their long guns at her.

"But the—"

"If there are consequences, I will deal with them," he said.

Kalyna (or whoever she was) grumbled as she turned toward the barge. She yelled something in a Skydašiavos patois that I couldn't understand, and then the Barge People allowed the soldiers to herd us onboard.

The prisoners and I were shoved belowdecks, down a narrow staircase, with our hands still tied, all as the Yams shouted at us in that small, crowded space. One poor soul cried out as they were shoved down those stairs headfirst.

The underbelly of the barge somehow felt cavernous. It was full of freight, but also beds, hammocks, loose clothes and food, and entire families living their lives. Children ran about yelling, parents looked bored as they held those same children up to open portholes to relieve themselves, and no one batted an eye at the arrival of ten prisoners, nor the fifteen armed soldiers who were guarding us.

The prisoner who'd tumbled down the stairs was dragged to her feet and told to walk, even as she asked if her leg was broken. I felt guilty for being too scared to speak up for her, and I doubt I was the only one. Forcing her to get up and walk was doubly cruel, because we were led only a few feet over before the Yams threw us down to the wooden floor. We were made to sit up, in that we were kicked and prodded until we did so.

The soldiers took their seats on nearby crates and, with shocking speed, transitioned from actively cruel to impossibly bored. Because our hands were tied, their long guns were set against the crates as well—it seemed the Yams were tired of carrying the heavy things. Gintaras paced back and forth, irritated. In front of us, we saw the families and life of the Bari, while behind us and the staircase was a sea of boxes and sacks and hanging nets stretching off into the dark. There didn't even seem to be portholes back there.

We traveled along the Skydaš Sea for some time. None of the prisoners spoke, but the Bari became quite talkative. More than once, groups of children would approach with seemingly endless questions in that Bari patois, which the bewildered soldiers hardly understood. The adults too would sometimes show curiosity, although never about us. The soldiers were constantly getting up, craning their necks to hear Bari who were approaching them, or pressing their hands to their foreheads as they tried to quiet five or six children.

Once, Ifeanyas made the mistake of smiling at a Bari child. He was kicked over by a seated guard, who did so without breaking the stride of her conversation with a companion. It was almost impressive.

"Why can't we have our own blasted boats here?" she griped. "We have warships out on the *real* ocean."

"Not to mention the Goddess' Guts," added another Yam.

I looked questioningly at Vidmantas. He shook his head and sighed.

"Winds here aren't strong enough for sails," said a third.

"But," began the one who'd kicked Ifeanyas, "can't we just—"

"Make our own rowboats?" A laugh. "Are you new? A southern provincial?"

". . . Maybe."

"Every time we try, our rowers defect to the Barge People. Then the deserters are protected from punishment, because, according to some ancient contract, they've now *become* Barge People."

"The Barge People control the Skydaš Sea," someone groused. "Always have. A nation within a nation within a nation. You'll get used to it."

"Maybe I should join them," muttered another Yam.

A few soldiers then jostled each other playfully. The Bari children giggled. I felt lost.

"When it hits," someone hissed in my ear, "run upstairs."

I began to turn my head.

"Don't look," hissed the voice.

I did anyway.

Dagmar, crouched between the crates behind us, with a hood covering her blonde hair, winked at me. A soldier pointed at us and stood up, about to yell. I felt my bonds being cut.

Before I could think, the entire boat lurched as though it had, well, *hit* something. The other prisoners were caught off guard, but since we were all sitting on the floor, the worst anyone did was roll over a little. The long, iron-like fingers of Dagmar Sorga gripped my shoulder, keeping me up.

The soldiers, on the other hand, *all* fell over. Tumbling off their feet or their crates, some going head over heels, like the man who'd seen Dagmar. At least one Yam had his leg crushed by the crate he'd been sitting on. The Bari barely stumbled. Dagmar found all of this very funny.

Dagmar did not need to tell me twice. I bolted up and ran for the stairs. A soldier began to yell, and from the sound of it, I believe Dagmar kicked him. I heard many sets of footsteps coming up behind me and hoped they belonged to Dagmar and the other prisoners. But I did not turn to look.

I burst up onto the deck, back into the sunlight, and beheld a surprisingly quiet scene. Up here, the Bari stood, or sat, doing nothing as their barge pressed up against another, which had silver paint. The rowers' arms were crossed. No one seemed angry about the collision: instead, some on our barge were chatting amiably with those on the other.

Kalyna, also, was on the other boat. Her hair was free, and she was waving furiously to me to follow her.

I ran to the edge of the barge and looked down at the space between the two. Bright blue water flickered there, but there were darker depths beneath. I thought I could *probably* jump that far, but the barges were rocking, and the gap kept changing its width.

"Go on, Smart Boy!"

The shouting from below began to get louder and closer.

Vidmantas, Ifeanyas, and a few others appeared in my periphery, following close behind us. Dagmar had already cut Vidmantas' bonds, and he cried out before taking a long running jump from one barge to the next. He made it, hitting the deck hard and rolling. Kalyna looked down at him and sucked her teeth, then glared across the water at Dagmar, who shrugged.

"Go!" yelled Dagmar.

I still dithered a bit at the edge, staring down at the water and trying to drum up the courage. It wasn't until I looked back and saw Gintaras' hat appear at the staircase that I finally jumped.

I sailed. I felt shockingly unmoored from the world. But I did not jump far enough. I began to realize (slowly, or so it felt) that I would not make the deck of the other barge.

I began to flail wildly for the edge. I managed to get a hand onto the lip of the barge but felt my own weight wrench down against my hand and shoulder. There was no way I'd be able to pull myself up.

Dagmar's boots landed next to my hand as I felt my grip failing, and she caught my wrist. She strained a bit but seemed to have no doubt she could lift me bodily to the deck. My arm ached, but up I went.

For a brief moment, I saw what must have attracted Kalyna to a Dagmar Sorga. The strength and confidence as she saved me, and the feeling that I was in good hands, was intoxicating.

We both fell to the deck. Kalyna yelled something, and the barge began to move. The Bari had all begun shouting as soon as Gintaras appeared on deck, acting as though they were angry and surprised at the collision between their barges.

Ifeanyas was just barely ahead of the soldiers, his arms still tied behind him. Face stern, he made a mad dash and leapt with no hesitation. His small body twisted through the air, the composure left his face for what seemed to be wide-eyed fear, his arms pulled up against their bonds as his legs wound in the air, almost as though he was running.

Incredibly, Ifeanyas made it to our barge, but without free hands to break or steer his fall. Dagmar moved to cushion him, and the two went down, rolling across the deck.

I then saw more of our fellow prisoners standing at the edge of the other barge, watching us leave, full of yearning, sadness, and anger. They had not been fast or foolhardy enough to make the leap while bound, as Ifeanyas had.

(Later, I learned some of their names from Vidmantas, and I still carry them in my memory, as I do the looks on their faces as they saw escape slip away. Repeating them all here would feel like a limp paean to my own guilt, but they are recorded in my Commonplace Book.)

Gintaras and his soldiers were now fully on deck and pointing at us, screaming. The Bari on the oars shook their head, giving some reason or another for why they couldn't pursue.

Gintaras growled and grabbed a long gun from one his men, pointing it at me. Other soldiers began to follow his lead, albeit more hesitantly. I began the movement of throwing myself to the deck but felt as though I was doing so in a swamp. I could never avoid his shot.

There was a crack, a burst of flame, and a puff of smoke. Then an aureole of blood.

Gintaras dropped the gun and fell to the deck. Half of his head was gone.

"Don't shoot at a Loashti, idiots!" cried Kalyna at the top of her lungs.

The other soldiers, who had been aiming for me, stopped and stared down at their commanding officer's corpse. They stood around him, glancing at us, then back at him, as we floated out of their range.

Kalyna crossed the deck of the barge toward Dagmar and me, laughing.

"Did you mean to blow his head apart?" she asked.

"I just stuffed some things in the barrels while they were distracted by the Bari," replied Dagmar. "Had no idea what exactly would happen."

"So," I gulped, "all that about the guns not working on a Loashti . . ."

"Nonsense, of course," said Kalyna. "Didn't you know that?"

"I feel like I don't know anything anymore," I sighed. "Are you a . . . Bari captain?"

Kalyna snorted. "I just borrowed the sash from a friend. Don't be daft."

Our boat moved through the water toward the North Shore, powered by rowers who seemed entirely unbothered by their recent brush with angry soldiers. Dagmar began pacing around Kalyna and me, doing stretches of some kind.

Vidmantas approached us, with Ifeanyas just behind him. The taller man was trying to force a smile, and failing, while the smaller one winced with every movement.

"Thank you," said Vidmantas.

Kalyna looked at him evenly. No smile, no frown.

"What were you arrested for?" she asked.

"Having bad ideas," Vidmantas replied.

"I don't see why," muttered Ifeanyas, rubbing his bruised hip. "We always had bad ideas before."

"I haven't a clue what changed," added Vidmantas, "but I suppose we are outlawed."

Kalyna looked thoughtful.

"Vidmantas," said Ifeanyas, "we should go to Žydrė's community, shouldn't we? I can't think of anything better."

Vidmantas let out a long, irritated breath. "I can't either, but I don't trust her people."

"Do you trust her?" asked the smaller man.

"I . . . think so."

Ifeanyas nodded and timidly tapped Kalyna's shoulder, as though she had not been watching this whole conversation.

"The place we're going," he said, "is near the Loashti border. I hope it will be better than here, but we'll have to get around the Tail first. Are you going that way?"

Kalyna said nothing.

"We are," I replied.

Kalyna glared at me.

"What?" I cried. "I should pretend I'm not heading for the border? Who would believe that by now?!" I got louder than I intended to. "Loasht isn't safe for me, but neither is Skydašiai, clearly!"

Kalyna sighed. "Let's first cross the Sea"—she pointed vaguely northward—"and then get out of any cities. I don't want these two squealing for leniency."

Vidmantas straightened a bit at the accusation. "Madame," he said, "I was on my way to prison for saying what the government doesn't want to hear. I hope you know that I—"

"Would say *exactly* what they want to hear if they began cutting off parts of you."

Vidmantas was quiet. Dagmar looked at him and Ifeanyas, and then at Kalyna. The sellsword seemed uncharacteristically thoughtful.

A stout Bari man with his brown hair tied up walked over to us and smiled. Kalyna removed the red-and-gold sash that delineated captaincy and returned it to him. He introduced himself as Liudvikas, and he, like every Bari I spoke to, was perfectly capable of speaking Skydašiavos that I could understand, when he wanted to.

"We had other ex-Loashti aboard recently, like you," he told me. "They were promised a trip home, told it was all some misunderstanding. Then they were put in the Goddess' Guts." He pointed westward.

"And what *is* that?" I asked.

"A prison," replied Vidmantas, "in the lower decks of a warship patrolling Skydašiai's west coasts."

"The Goddess of the Summer Sun," added Ifeanyas. "That's . . . that's the name of the ship." It was the most intently I'd seen him refuse to look at anyone while speaking.

"We," continued Liudvikas, "must help the soldiers to a point. But we have decided to stop taking part in that deception."

"That's . . . well, that's good of you," said Ifeanyas.

"I didn't say we'll *stop* taking Loashti people to the Goddess' Guts," Liudvikas corrected. "Just that we won't aid the soldiers in their lie that your people are on their way home. It's not much of a difference, I know." He paused for a moment, seemed to realize something, and quickly added, "We're not taking *you* there, of course. You're Kalyna's friend!"

"And you can just tell the soldiers 'no' like that?" I asked.

Liudvikas smiled. "You know what they say—"

"'Skydašiai loses its way without the Barge People,'" said Vidmantas.

Liudvikas harrumphed. "We say it dries up and blows away without the Bari."

Vidmantas smiled accommodatingly. "That's good too."

The Bari did not take us to the city that mirrored Žalikwen, but instead a bit farther northwest, to a town called Osimwu, which had one small, neglected, and sadly unpainted dock. Supposedly, no one in Osimwu would know to look for us yet.

"We'll make it complicated for them," promised Liudvikas.

"That's very kind of you," I replied. "Won't you get in trouble?"

"The noble families all know they need us to keep Skydašiai together. We were crossing this sea before the Tetrarchia existed, before the guilds, before even Skydašiai was unified." He smiled. "We can't outright defy the army all the time, but we should be able to explain this away as a big mistake."

"And if not?"

He shrugged. "Then we're in a lot of trouble."

"You must really like Kalyna, to do this for her."

He pursed his lips thoughtfully. "I suppose I do, yes." He crossed his arms and leaned against the silver painted wood crisscrossing the barge. "My parents ferried her family back and forth many times, when Kalyna and I were but children. One time, her father gave them . . . information that saved my life."

"So," said Dagmar, who had not spoken in hours, "you risk your lives and your people's own . . ." She snapped her fingers, grasping for the term. "Their own . . ." She growled a word in Rotfelsenisch.

"Autonomy?" I offered.

"Yes, their autonomy," replied Dagmar.

Liudvikas shrugged and nodded. "You could see it that way, yes."

Kalyna was a few yards away, with one foot up on the lip of the barge, arms on the railing, watching the North Shore loom closer against the orange sunset sky.

"And you, Kalyna," said Dagmar, walking over to her, "have risked the Bari's entire way of life for Smart Boy here?" She smiled as she said it, sounding like she was in awe.

"Of course," replied Kalyna.

A Bari man was making his way up the deck, handing out crusty brown bread and mugs of a thick red wine. I gladly took some for myself.

Dagmar took two mugs and leaned against the railing, handing one to Kalyna, who took it without looking back. Dagmar faced the horizon as well.

"You always act like everybody owes you their life," she said.

"Because everybody does," replied Kalyna, turning to Dagmar and raising her cup.

Dagmar laughed and clinked her mug against Kalyna's. They both drank.

Osimwu was smaller, quieter, and hotter than Žalikwen, but otherwise quite similar. There were, however, no Yams at the dock. According to Kalyna, it was Dagmar who'd specifically insisted on Osimwu.

"Said she has a plan," Kalyna told me.

I shuddered at the thought.

Naturally, we didn't stay long. To show his trustworthiness, Vidmantas hocked his necklace of multicolored beads in order to buy us a bit more food for the road.

"It is, truly, the last thing I own," he said.

As we left the city, I began to see the difference between North and South shores. In the south, the landscape had been predominately green; here, the most visible color was a golden yellow. Farther north still, I knew it would get hotter and drier, not becoming truly humid until my long-missed home of Yekunde (which was both golden and green).

When it got dark, we came across a clearing of dry, yellow grass alongside the Lanreas River, and Dagmar decided we would bed down there for the night. Kalyna mostly looked irritated at the two new people we had picked up.

"So, what exactly is this place you think is safe?" she asked them.

"It's called the"—Vidmantas rolled his eyes—"Lanreas River Guild, although it is in no way recognized as a guild."

"Fine," she growled. "Where is it?"

"North of here, near the border, east of Kalvadoti. It's on this side of the Lanreas River, but the Tail's in the way."

"And this Tail," I began, "just so I'm clear, is The Thrashing, Bone-White Tail of Galiag?"

Ifeanyas nodded.

"It's a gorge twisting down from Galiag, right on the northeast border," said Vidmantas.

I was familiar with Galiag by reputation: a wind-blasted city of ziggurats that was sometimes Loashti and sometimes Skydašian.

"The Tail," Vidmantas continued, "cuts down through the North Shore, crossing the river, and ending just below the city of Kalvadoti. The gorge's sides aren't that high, but all of Galiag's horrid burning winds travel between those walls. The river goes through it, but we can't."

"Fine," Kalyna repeated.

"So we have to cross the river," said Vidmantas.

"No, we don't." Dagmar shook her head and smiled. "Just wait here. I have a plan."

I shuddered at the thought. All through Osimwu, and before, Dagmar had said very little, speaking only to guide us toward her "plan," and often regarding Kalyna with a sort of merry glint in her eye. I wondered whether she had found a new, more agreeable way to love Kalyna Aljosanovna.

I suppose, in a way, she had. The next morning, Dagmar Sorga was gone.

Kalyna refused to make a scene in front of our new companions. She simply shrugged and said, "I suppose her contract was up."

"Part of her plan, perhaps?" murmured Ifeanyas.

"It isn't," said Kalyna.

"Contract?" I asked as Vidmantas and Ifeanyas began to gather up what little we had.

"Yes," replied Kalyna. "The *contract*." She then held up a sheet of paper.

I furrowed my brow, and she handed it to me.

"I suppose you're mentioned in it too," she said.

Kalyna stared at me as I unfolded the paper. For a fleeting moment, I saw her eyes widen, her jaw grind, and her nose crinkle in rage. Just as quickly, her face seemed to sag in defeat before returning to its normal state.

Scrawled in very clumsy Cölluknit was the following:

> *Kalyna—I love you, but I cannot stand to be around you.*
> *Maybe I will like you more when I love you less.*
> *Smart Boy—I took the rest of your silver and that should*
> *do. You're all right.*
> *Just wait in the clearing. Trust me.*

Kalyna took it back, shoved it in her pack, and we set off. I wondered if anyone but Dagmar Sorga had ever *left* Kalyna Aljosanovna.

Chapter Ten

Our Terrifying Conveyance to the Lanreas River Guild

Kalyna, Vidmantas, Ifeanyas, and I sat by the bank of the Lanreas River, which flowed lazily south, its currents an unsettling white. This was not the white of rushing water clashing against itself; rather, it looked as though the very water was *pallid*, like death, as though made of flowing, liquid bone. This was, I gathered, some sort of sediment blown into the water further north, when it crossed The Thrashing, Bone-White Tail of Galiag.

Kalyna stared out at the water silently for some time, with one leg drawn up to her chest and the other dangling forward where the ground sloped toward the river. Vidmantas and Ifeanyas, a bit removed from us, seemed to alternate between looking at the river, looking at the trees that surrounded our clearing, and looking meaningfully at one another.

"Are you . . . planning?" I finally asked Kalyna under my breath, in Loashti Bureaucratic.

"If something comes to me, that will be lovely," she replied. "But nothing has yet, so I will trust Dagmar." She cleared her throat. "I suppose I can do that much for her."

"And," I ventured, "if her plan doesn't work . . . ?"

"Then I will feel very superior, and that's nice too."

"Do you think anyone's coming after us? I fancy every little noise is—"

"Oh, they certainly are. But probably further east." She shrugged. "Or so I'm praying."

I did not need to say out loud that if we were attacked without Dagmar to protect us, we were in a lot of trouble. I'd gathered that Kalyna could fight decently but had hardly seen it. Besides, she seemed in low spirits. Vidmantas was slim and wiry, even a touch delicate. Ifeanyas was clearly tough (and possibly fearless), but quite small. I was, well, me. No, neither I, nor the two men I met *at an intellectual salon*, were much comfort just then.

After another half hour or so, there suddenly began an intense rustling in the trees on the east end of the clearing. The branches shook vigorously, and alarmed cries from animals began to sound from within.

Kalyna bolted to her feet, facing the clearing and drawing her sword and sickle, one to each hand, but she looked more resigned than anything else. She knew as well as I that we had nowhere to hide and a river to our backs, if anyone was coming at us from the east.

Then the cause of so much commotion burst into view *above* the forest, skimming the very treetops. It was winged, but larger than any bird I had ever seen, and flying toward us. As it passed in front of the sun, it seemed to dim the orb's light, casting a shadow over the grass that was translucent at its edges, as though light bent around the creature and then fizzled away at its margins. My mouth hung open.

Kalyna's grasp on her weapons loosened. She even raised her right hand, which held the sword, in a helpless *What am I supposed to do about that?* flourish, while shaking her head.

Then, from somewhere among the bird's wings, came a voice, screaming over all the rustling and whooshing: "Hellooooo! Wait right there!"

"Is that . . . Žydrė?" asked Vidmantas.

Kalyna replaced her weapons and shrugged.

"Thanks, Dagmar," she grunted.

Once it landed in the clearing, the great and terrible bird sat and slowly . . . sagged. Its dark wings stuck out to the sides, perfectly still, while its mottled red head and sickly yellow beak bobbed, lost consistency, and folded in on themselves. Soon enough, two people became visible, as though they were riding on the back of the great shuddering, broken bird, which was not a bird. Up close, in fact, it was entirely unconvincing.

The body was a large basket painted black and gray, with a white underbelly. The black wings were, well, I suppose they *were* wings, but built more like a set of rudders. The basket hung by countless ropes beneath a large floating sphere, upon which was painted the gigantic head of a ghastly bird, whose black eyes were devoid of any feeling. The rest of the sphere was muddily transparent, like a dim window onto the sky above. The sphere was also becoming *less* buoyant by the minute, curling in on itself.

Two people were sitting in the basket: Žydrė and someone I couldn't see very well.

"What—?" I gulped out as we came closer. I was less frightened now but all the more confused. "What *is* it?"

"A balloon, of course!" yelled the person next to Žydrė, as though it were the simplest and most obvious thing in the world. Although, it was also said with great pride.

Stranger than that answer, however, was that the one who'd given it did so in Skydašiavos, but with an unmistakable Central Loashti accent.

"I must admit, Žydrė," said Vidmantas, once we were finally close enough to speak normally, "it's as impressive as you said."

Ifeanyas nodded enthusiastically.

Kalyna was not particularly enthusiastic. She stood entirely still and silent, staring at the thing's big, blank, round eyes, which listed unevenly. Each bigger than her head.

In the center of the painted basket, beneath the drunkenly weaving balloon, was a metal enclosure housing a pink-and-blue flame. It was at a low ebb, but nonetheless, its presence in a *wicker basket* felt wildly unsafe to me. Žydrė climbed out of the basket, quickly followed by a small woman who ran over to me (leaving the flame unattended!), and clapped a hand roughly to my shoulder, squeezing it awfully hard.

Shaking my shoulder in her strong little hand, she began speaking quickly in Loashti Bureaucratic: "A countenance of home! Another civilized Loashti to speak to! Among these southern types, good conversation can be rare, and I must say you have the bearing of a scholar or other—" She stopped and blinked, finally managing to slow her barreling words. "I'm sorry, have we met before?"

I studied her. She had a broad face topped with dark coppery hair cut relatively short; of looser curls than mine, yet tighter than, say, Kalyna's. She did feel familiar, but I thought that was only because she looked *so very* Central Loashti.

She let go of me and stepped back farther. Then the Loashti woman snapped her callused fingers.

"Radiant Basket of . . . something. Pearls?"

I smiled back, even as I felt lost. "Rainbow Shells," I corrected. "I'm afraid I don't . . ."

She waved a hand over her face, flourishing, as though this would make me recognize her. Clear my memory. It did not.

The Loashti looked thoughtful and then said, "I was laughed out of the Yekunde Academy branch. Only you didn't laugh quite so much as the others."

"I'm sorry," I said.

"Oh, my sweet friend, I have been laughed out of *much* better places."

"Well . . . good? I may be remembering," I lied, which felt a bit like Kalyna was rubbing off on me, "but your name was . . ." I snapped my fingers as though it was on the tip of my tongue. (It was not.)

"The Simurgh Rules Air, Wind, and Sea" was the reply. She grinned, showing a gap-toothed smile. "My parents really regretted that one, once I was an adult."

I waited for an explanation, but nothing came.

"Well, come on," she yelled in Skydašiavos, "let's get moving. We've still got some way to go. And the poor bird will fully deflate if we don't hurry!"

"Do we need to do the embarkation ritual again?" asked Žydrė.

Simurgh screwed her mouth to one side in thought. She looked up at the sky for a moment, then at the trees fluttering in the wind.

"If it was *very* windy," she explained, "I would say yes. And if it was completely still, I would *also* say yes. But conditions seem good, and seeming is the most we'll ever get. So I say we take the risk." She shrugged. "If we crash and die, I will apologize."

Kalyna threw her bag into the basket without a word, hopping in after them. She seemed relieved to no longer be within sight of the balloon's false eyes. Vidmantas, Ifeanyas, and I followed suit, and Simurgh began to stoke the fire. She sprinkled something over that pink-and-blue flame, and began to coax it under her breath in words I could not make out.

The fire suddenly became larger and pinker, singeing a bit of the dirty scarf around Simurgh's neck. She jumped back and smiled. The bird's head slowly regained its full, terrifying form. Head, neck, beak, wings, and (most alarmingly) throat sac all snapped into strong, sturdy place, filling out above our heads as though it was a living thing, gorging itself and growing its own bones.

We began to lift shakily off the ground. Simurgh continued to whisper to her flame. Cajoling it, entreating it.

"You'll like it back at the Guild," said Žydrė. "I promise."

My legs shook throughout the entire flight, and I could hardly bear to approach the edges of the basket. Vidmantas and Ifeanyas fared better, I think, because Žydrė had apparently told them about this flying balloon before—they'd had time to prepare mentally, if not physically.

Kalyna, for her part, sat on the floor of the basket staring at the wicker between her feet. She was clearly queasy, but I suspected there was more to it as well. The fast-talking cutthroat, who was so adept at sea travel that she could pass for a Bari, hadn't said a word since she'd stood in the grass staring at the huge, empty, painted eyes of the false bird.

Shaking legs or no, I was determined to stay standing. I would taste the air meant only for birds, bats, and flying serpents if it killed me. It was thrilling: like the Quru zip lines magnified by a thousand. Colorful Skydašian towns looked absolutely divine from that height, like little models of the perfect human dwellings, where nothing bad could ever happen. To the north, I saw what looked like a ribbon of hills cutting across the land. Perhaps, I thought, I could see past that to Loasht in the distance. In fact, what was to stop such a balloon from taking me home?

"I'm sorry to have left you all in the lurch back at the library," Žydrė explained. "But whenever I'm in Žalikwen, I keep one ear open for the Yams, you know."

"She is a known propagandist," laughed Vidmantas.

Žydrė smiled and nodded amiably as she leaned against the wall of the basket, unperturbed by the open air whooshing by her upper back.

"Outside the library," she continued, "I was accosted. Not by a Yam, but by a big Rot woman."

Did Kalyna laugh about this, somewhere deep in her throat, between her moans of unease?

"She asked me how I planned to escape the city," Žydrė continued, "and she was *very* convincing, so I told her: a simple disguise to get across the sea, and then Simurgh's balloon. I was surprised at how easily she accepted the reality of this wonder of ours." She tapped the basket's wall.

"A woman of discerning taste," muttered Simurgh.

I think Kalyna moan-laughed again.

"The Rot told me," said Žydrė, "that if I helped you, Radiant, she would also save my 'fancy friend.'" She nodded at Vidmantas.

He mimed flipping his curls out of his face, even as the winds made such a gesture unnecessary.

"We decided on the first clearing north of Osimwu," explained Žydrė. "When I asked how she'd save you two, she said, 'Kalyna will think of something,' and disappeared."

Žydrė then looked down at Kalyna, whose head was between her knees.

"Yes, that's her," I said with a shrug. "And she did think of something."

"Why, Žydrė," cried Vidmantas, "I didn't know you cared!"

She regarded him for a moment and then grunted, "You damn well did."

"Why does your miraculous balloon look like a deathly bird?" I asked.

"*I* wanted it to paint it as a grand and dignified flying creature," said Simurgh. "Perhaps even as, I don't know, a *simurgh*. But what do I know? I only created the thing." She rolled her eyes. "Apparently it had to be a ratty stork."

"A marabou," corrected Žydrė.

"Which is a ratty stork," Simurgh muttered to me in Loashti Bureaucratic.

I made a low rumble in my throat, meant as an entreaty to Simurgh to be more polite to our Tetrarchic hosts. I don't think she understood it.

"Adomas likes the marabou," said Žydrė, "because they are survivors who can adapt well to living among humans."

"She means that they eat human garbage," said Simurgh.

Žydrė shrugged and nodded.

Vidmantas turned to me, smiled brightly, and helpfully explained, "Adomas is their cult leader."

Žydrė turned on him.

"Who," Vidmantas added quickly, holding up his hands, "I very much hope will harbor us! A cult doesn't sound so bad to me, just now."

Kalyna moaned, which I took to be more nausea, but now I wonder.

"Well," I said to Žydrė, "it seems your propaganda has worked then. Even Vidmantas is convinced."

"Nearly a lifetime of arguing with him has made me very persuasive," she replied.

"You're welcome," said Vidmantas with a bow. "But am I *convinced*, or do I have no other options?"

"Do any of us have other options?" asked Ifeanyas in a soft voice.

There was an awkward silence for a few moments. I think I saw Žydrė open her mouth to try to reassure us of *something*, and then think better of it, at least three separate times.

Personally, I was barely thinking about Žydrė and her community at all; I was happy to not have been shot or thrown in prison, exhilarated to be far up in the air, and desperate to see Silver—to learn what was happening in my home.

I looked off to the north again, hoping I could see some evidence of Loasht out there. Instead, I began to see great colors dancing in the sky: bulbous blobs of red, yellow, blue, orange. I squinted for a better view but could not make out what they were as they weaved slowly across the bright sky.

"Everybody stop moping, and look at this!" cried Simurgh, pointing below us. I don't know whether she was purposefully trying to lighten the mood, or singularly focused on her own interests. "Here's a sight you can never see from the ground."

Of course I, shakily, looked over the side.

We were now about to pass right over the ribbon of hills that I'd seen in the distance earlier. Up close, it looked more like one very long hill or cliff: not terribly high, all things considered, but sheer. More like a natural wall, or as if the dust thrown up from an impact had stayed there, frozen in space.

"That's . . . that's the Tail," muttered Ifeanyas.

Kalyna looked up at us for a moment, in seeming confusion or concern, but quickly put her head back between her knees.

"Exactly," Simurgh replied. "The Thrashing, Bone-White Tail of Galiag, as you all call it. A gorge filled with burning-hot and concentrated winds that make it impassable."

"Yes," said Vidmantas, eyes widening. "Which is why I rather thought we'd fly *around* it."

"Why?" asked Simurgh. "Impassable on the ground, yes, but the winds travel nice and neat right down the line of the gorge—they don't go up above it."

"Are you sure?" asked Ifeanyas. He was leaning against the side of the basket, staring down intently. "No one crosses the Tail. It's death. It's always been death."

"'The pallid rent in the ground, where nothing has ever grown,'" quoted Vidmantas. "Isn't that the old poem? Then something about 'flaying little boys and girls to the bone'?"

"Fanciful nonsense," Simurgh sniffed. "Children's bones aren't so hard as adults'—it would shred those too."

Kalyna, despite her discomfort, snorted.

"My father," Ifeanyas murmured, "always ended it with 'and now it's got your nose!' and then he'd . . ." He looked around, cleared his throat, and didn't finish.

"Well," said Simurgh, "now we can go easily above it. No flaying, I promise." She then added, under her breath, in Loashti, "These people are so superstitious," and glanced at me.

I did not respond.

"I was unsure about it the first time as well," Žydrė offered, "but I promise you, it's quite safe. And fascinating. I can't imagine anyone's ever *seen* inside the Tail before, except perhaps from its ends, which are dangerous enough as it is."

And, with that, we passed over The Thrashing, Bone-White Tail of

Galiag. At first it did simply look like a strange gorge—as I described earlier, like it had been the place of a great impact. I suppose that was where the idea of it being the death throes of some great creature came from. But as we moved farther, I could actually *see* the wind down there, in a sense. Rather, I could see the same white sediment—dirt, sand, dust, I knew not what exactly—that had filled the southern part of the Lanreas River.

It streamed through the gorge, fluidly and violently. I thought that perhaps I even saw sparks against the gorge's inner edges. True to Simurgh's word, none of that wind reached us above, and we flew along as placidly as before. But what did reach us was the sound and the heat. Although it was already a sunny day, the shade of the marabou balloon and the winds up high in the air had kept us cool, but now an oppressive heat reached us, like being in an oven. I began to sweat copiously. Kalyna moaned and gurgled, putting her head farther down between her knees.

Even worse, to me, was the sound. A howling assaulted us, keening and moaning; somehow melancholic but also just, simply, *too loud*. I knew, of course, that it was the sound of the winds echoing through their enclosure. But if I had not been looking right down at the white current and feeling its heat, I would surely have thought I was passing a battlefield whose every ghost was still in pain, whose every spirit had been abandoned by their family, never prayed for or thought of again.

Simurgh thought the locals too superstitious, but I, looking right down at the cause of the heat and noise, could not shake the feeling that this was, indeed, a place of only death. Judging by their faces, Vidmantas, Ifeanyas, and even Žydrė seemed to agree. Kalyna's exact discomfort was her own, as I could not see her face.

That overwhelming sense of the very air being full of . . . of *emotion*, of unreality, seemed like what I'd read about the trances of great sages and sorcerers. Far beyond what any of my own feeble attempts at magic had produced in me. So far.

After only a few minutes that felt much longer, we exited the heat and noise, and were on the other side of the Tail.

"Unpleasant, I'll grant you." Simurgh spoke first. "But it saved us hours. And how many can say they've seen what you just saw, eh?"

I had to admit the truth of that. And now, as I write this, I am particularly glad that I'm able to share such a singular experience.

"Besides," the Loashti woman continued, "it's exactly for the purpose of seeing such inaccessible places that I designed my balloons. Not for travel." She patted a bundle strapped to her side and pulled out a telescope, intricately filigreed with green enamel depicting great, broad leaves.

"And the Guild isn't far now," said Žydrė, looking ahead. "On that strip of Skydašiai between the Tail and Loasht."

"Why doesn't Loasht just conquer us right up to the gorge?" asked Vidmantas. "Seems like a good natural border, doesn't it?"

I think he expected me to have an answer, but I certainly didn't know.

"Why would we have wanted to?" asked Simurgh.

"Loasht did rule this place, once upon a time," said Žydrė, "but wasn't interested in keeping it. Even before we showed up, I mean. Maybe even *your* people found the Tail unsettling."

"I certainly do," I replied.

"Well, it's also tough land for planting," said Vidmantas.

"Maybe that wasn't always the case?" added Ifeanyas.

"Maybe that isn't even the case *now*," said Žydrė, with a grin.

"Could we keep going north?" asked Kalyna. She was no longer looking down, but had her head up and her eyes closed.

"How do you mean?" Simurgh asked.

Kalyna took a long, deep breath. "Gods," she muttered, "I can still see the ground whirring by with my eyes closed." She took another breath, a sort of gulp. "I mean, if Radiant wanted to get back into Loasht, could we use this to bring him there?"

I admit that, by this point, I had assumed this was *exactly* what we would do.

"Well," said Simurgh, "besides the danger of being shot down—which we could perhaps lessen with modifications to the marabou and a dangerous nighttime flight—there's the fact that the army has its own balloons."

Kalyna finally opened her eyes and looked up at Simurgh, blinking uncomfortably.

"*Which* army?" she grunted.

"Skydašiai," Žydrė answered, pointing to the northern sky.

For the first time during the flight, Kalyna stood. She moved slowly and warily, gripping the edges of the basket tightly, as Žydrė pointed right at the pleasantly bulbous blobs of color I had noticed earlier.

"Nothing like mine, of course," snapped Simurgh. "No alchemy, no reading the winds, no hybridized fabrics. Simply the most basic possible bag of hot air, tethered to the ground so they don't float away—into the ether, or into Loasht." She laughed. "Pathetic. Pale imitations, only."

"And yet," said Žydrė, "they're very good for watching the border, signaling the soldiers on the ground, and, probably, shooting us out of the sky. They aren't watching Loasht, since it's our ally now. They're looking south. For aliens like you, Radiant, to stop them sneaking back into Loasht." She then added facetiously: "They're being *good neighbors*."

I looked ahead at those pleasantly bobbing balloons and the baskets beneath, full of soldiers ready to arrest or kill me. Just beyond them, almost in reach, was my home and my family.

Soon enough, flying in Simurgh's balloon gave us a seemingly all-encompassing view of the Lanreas River Guild itself, which did not even abut the river that gave it its name. At first, I only saw farmland, which was not divided into squared and regimented fields; it twisted about, running here and there, with small buildings cropping up in odd places. It rather reminded me of the Library of Abathçodu, in a way.

We drifted farther north, over a town dominated by the shadow of a sprawling, crumbling building made of turrets. Past even this was a great clearing, where our terrifyingly ugly bird landed with a jolt. I fell over in the basket, but I wasn't the only one.

"Go! Go! Go!" chided Simurgh. "I'm going to put out the fire!"

We did so, with Simurgh tumbling out after us in a most undignified manner. The sphere began to deflate, rumpling and folding with surprising speed. As the air went out of the balloon, its limited transparency and painted marabou head faded, until the basket and its wings were mostly covered by a pile of nondescript tan canvas.

"The number of times my idiot assistants have gotten trapped under the thing . . ." Simurgh grumbled to me in Loashti Bureaucratic, shaking her head.

My relief at meeting another Loashti was so strong that I felt the immediate urge to tell Simurgh to be more careful of her words. After all, at least one local spoke our language.

"You shouldn't call them idiots," I replied to Simurgh in the same language. I was very aware that Kalyna could be listening as she stood with her back to us, slowly regaining her composure.

Simurgh brushed this off. "I don't! Not in their language. These Lanreas people are too sensitive to understand that a genius *must* insult their assistants at times."

After Simurgh left for her hut at the edge of the clearing, Kalyna turned toward me with a subtle smile on her lips and her eyebrows raised knowingly. She then nodded slightly, to let me know I had done right by not revealing her skill with Loashti languages. I saw regard in her eyes and felt a little sick at how proud I was of being deceptive enough to impress her.

A group of smiling residents of the Lanreas River Guild came to greet us. They certainly didn't seem bothered by my being a Loashti alien; in fact, they didn't seem bothered by anything at all. Leading them was a large, handsome man named Yalwas: he was thickly built, tall and broad, with a bald head and a strongly shaped black-and-gray beard.

"Well, come on!" he said. "Whether you are joining us for a few nights, or you wish to stay, you're more than welcome!"

Our bags were taken, exchanged for promises that they would be waiting for us in town. I happily gave in, despite how zealously I'd guarded my Commonplace Book volumes ever since I got to the Tetrarchia. I was just so tired.

Kalyna was harder to convince, and it took a few tugs, and many pleas, for her to let go of her bag. This despite the fact that she must have still been seasick (skysick?).

"We, ah, normally don't like for anyone to walk around the Guild with weapons, either," said Yalwas.

I caught a flash of utter disdain in Kalyna's eyes, but she blinked it away in a split second.

"Humor me. Please," she said.

"Well, all right," laughed Yalwas, wagging his finger at her playfully. "But just this once, you hear!"

Kalyna nodded and smiled. "Just this once!" she echoed back to him in a chirp.

The people with our bags ran off to the southwest, while Yalwas and Žydrė led us new arrivals south toward the big, overgrown, turreted building we'd seen from the air. As soon as Yalwas turned his back to us, Kalyna performed the most withering eye roll I believe I have ever seen in my life.

It was a beautiful day. Sunny and dry, with no noise beyond the distant chatter of people and the chirping of birds and bugs off in the bushes and trees. I looked north toward where I knew Loasht sat, waiting for me to return. I could still see those Skydašian balloons bobbing along in the distance, blocking my way. How good were their telescopes? Could they watch us right now from up there?

What Little I Remembered of Meeting
The Simurgh Rules Air, Wind, and Sea

I was finally able to summon to mind a memory of when I met The Simurgh Rules Air, Wind, and Sea back in Yekunde. There may have been more about her in my Commonplace Book, but those volumes were with Silver.

Or, I hoped they were with Silver. And that they had not been burned, while Silver, and everyone else I cared about, were slaughtered. I forced myself to go back to thinking about Simurgh.

All I could remember of her were flashes of the woman talking and talking, and talking and talking. She had stood, model balloon in hand, bloviating, while many of the Yekunde academy branch's greatest minds sat at a long table and tried to listen. In the end, Simurgh did not secure the funding and space that she sought at the Yekunde branch. Just as she would not anywhere else in Loasht.

I couldn't directly recall any of what she'd actually said, but I was able to remember a conversation soon afterward. My dear friend and colleague Casaba Melon Water Soothes at Noontime was walking with me through one of Yekunde's marketplaces. We were laughing.

"I mean, she may be onto something!" I managed to say, even as I laughed at Casaba's unflattering imitation of Simurgh's speech and breakneck pace. (Truth be told, I remembered the imitation far better than I did my first meeting with the real person.)

Casaba looked very seriously at me for a moment and then laughed her loud, honking laugh.

"What do I care?" she replied, stopping to look into a shop. "Do you think *success* would make that woman less irritating?"

I sighed and shook my head, smiling, as I followed Casaba into a tailor's shop we liked to visit whenever the proprietor got in new fabrics. Like most establishments in this part of Yekunde, the first floor of the building was open to the air, with no door, and indeed with no front wall. There were oiled skins that went down at night or in a rainstorm, but that was all that protected the interiors. There were no guards, locks, or heavy doors in this part of the city. Farther from the Academy, however, there were other markets that had not been built the same way.

Casaba was tall and stately—imposing even, to those who didn't know her—but when it was only the two of us looking to beautify ourselves, she became giddy right along with me.

"A lot of our colleagues are also irritating," I offered, as we scurried about the shop, which was fragrant with incense.

"I know," she replied. "Isn't it awful?" She took a sheet of coral-dyed wool woven in a light and open fashion, with an agreeable little crisscross, and held it up to her face. "More of them should be insufferable in the ways that you and I are," she added. Then held up the fabric. "What do you think?"

"I think it would be lovely on you as a hat or a sash, but a full dress would be a bit much."

She nodded sagely.

"I just mean," I continued, "I'm not sure why we had to be quite so mean to her. Laughing at her, telling her 'no' on the spot."

"Because our colleagues are mostly miserable scholars who don't understand how people work. You only laughed because the others did, and I didn't until she'd left. Besides, I think telling her to her face, rather than making her wait for a messenger in her sad rented room, was a kindness."

"Perhaps." I looked over at some patterned green-and-yellow night shawls.

"Radiant," Casaba sighed, "you're too nice." She leaned over and kissed me on the mouth.

To be clear, Casaba and I were never lovers, and had no plans to be such. To one from the Tetrarchia (or indeed many parts of Loasht), it can be hard to comprehend, but in some parts of southern Loasht, there were many shades between "lovers" and "friends"; even friends often held hands or kissed one another. (Some saw this freeness as "Zobiski influence," but I don't know whether we can take credit or blame for it.)

"Not so nice," I said. "I certainly won't lose any sleep over how Simurgh was treated today." This was true. "I think I'm more worried about how we must have looked to her than I am about her *feelings*, if I'm being honest."

"Ah, so that's your problem. You aren't nice after all; you just don't want to look bad." She looked in the mirror. "I think . . . a hat." Then she saw my reflection. "And I wouldn't get that shawl, were I you. The green is too dark—you look best with bright colors."

I shrugged and looked somewhere else. The tailor knew well enough to leave us to it: we'd been here many times, and we always bought *plenty* if we were given our space.

"I suppose I feel a little bad for her," I added.

"Perhaps if she hadn't led with"—Casaba sped up her voice—"'Look, you all weren't my first choice either. The air is too heavy here, and the people too stupid and lazy, but we all must compromise in life. So, let's compromise!'"

"That wasn't *exactly* how she worded it."

"It's close. She did everything short of calling us bumpkins."

"Well, she didn't say anything about the Zobiski, at least."

Casaba turned and leaned down to look closer at me. "Oh, Radiant, you simple dear."

I faked offense.

"She didn't insult the Zobiski," Casaba explained, "because she was hoping proximity to *your* people would mean no one would call her bizarre plans 'occult sorcery.'"

"Of course I know that, but I still prefer she not say it." I shrugged. "I suppose I should be happy she was refused. After all, I've been trying to secure funding for years: just a stipend to travel Loasht looking for corners of scholarship that escaped the Ministry's purges. Much less than her project would cost."

"And much less likely to literally crash and burn."

"Exactly!"

Casaba sighed and looked at me. "Radiant, the Academy is more likely to spend on a thousand of Simurgh's mad schemes than it is to send you around Loasht studying curses."

"Why? I . . ." She gave me a look, but I continued. "No, no, I mean it this time. I'm allowed to be a Zobiski at the Academy, and I'm already paid to study curses. What would be the harm in letting me—?"

"They can keep an eye on you here, Radiant."

"That's silly."

"I don't mean that you're a dissident who is constantly watched," she clarified. "But think about it. Here you are just another southern Loashti, part of what makes Yekunde what it is. There are Zobiski in other places, but this is the *most Zobiski place.*"

"Because it was our land before Loasht conquered it."

"Of course. But people who tolerate, or even appreciate, your eccentricity here would find it embarrassing to have you travel to more . . ." She didn't quite have the word.

"Civilized places?"

Casaba blew out a deep breath and nodded. "You understand that *I* don't consider—"

"And would you be embarrassed to imagine me in Talverag, or the City of Loasht? Asking about curses and acting so very Zobiski, and saying that I represent the Yekunde branch of the Academy?"

Casaba caught the tailor's eye, holding up the coral fabric and nodding. Then she looked back at me.

"Honestly? Yes, I would probably feel that embarrassment, at first. But then I'd try to . . . to *un-feel* it."

I smiled, because I believed her.

Eighty-Three. Remembering this made me realize how badly I missed my friends. Since Abathçodu turned on me, I had thought mostly of Silver and their parents, but romantic and familial love are simply not enough for a person. Or at least, they are not enough for me.

Chapter Eleven

The Lanreas River Guild,
Its Parade of Oddities, and Its Leader

Yalwas and Žydrė led us downhill to the great, crumbling building that loomed above the rest of the Guild's town and farmlands. It had once been plastered in white, with blue accents, although now much of that was missing, revealing the clay bricks beneath. The closer we got, the more I saw of how overgrown it was, with great vines, bushes, and even a small tree or two snaking through windows and bursting out of broken bits of masonry. We walked into a huge gap in its high brick walls and approached a small entrance at the northern end. Trees with broad leaves in deep green swayed pleasantly between the wall and the Estate itself.

"The wall," explained Yalwas, "is from a time when Adomas needed his home to be something of a fortress." The large man chuckled.

"So your leader lives *here*?" I asked.

"Of course not!" said Žydrė. "No one lives here anymore. This monstrosity needs an army of servants to keep it clean, and the Guild has better things to do."

"Besides," added Yalwas, "Adomas would never lord it over us like that. It's not how the Guild operates."

"Yet he *does* lead you, doesn't he?" asked Vidmantas.

"Yes," said Yalwas, "but not like a king or a voivode would. Adomas' very word is not law, he does not tax or police us—he simply helps to shape and guide what we want. And if what we wanted was for him to no longer be our leader, then"—he mimed throwing a person backward over his shoulder—"he'd be gone."

"Who is 'we'?" asked Vidmantas.

"Everyone!" laughed Yalwas.

"So you all agree on *everything*?" grumbled Ifeanyas. He sucked his teeth in irritation and turned to Žydrė, throwing up his hands. "Look, I'm not as picky as Vidmantas. If this is a cult of arcane mysteries, or . . . or just another noble's farm dressed up to look like the master is your friend, that's *fine* with me. I have nowhere else to go, and I'll take what I can get." Even as he grew frustrated, and his voice was raised, something in Ifeanyas' tone remained soft. "But I would really like to know *what exactly* it is I'm getting into!"

"Ifeanyas," said Žydrė, "My—that is, *our*—duty today is to help you understand just that."

He looked up at her angrily for a moment, then seemed to deflate back to his unobtrusive self.

"Fine then," he sighed, motioning to the Estate. "Let's get on with it."

Žydrė smiled and opened a creaking door with a broken hinge. "This used to be a servants' entrance," she said. "No one lives here anymore, but the house is still useful for storing Adomas' collection and protecting it from the elements." She went through the door.

"Collection?" asked Vidmantas as he followed her. He sounded skeptical.

"You'll see!" called Žydrė from inside. "Don't you trust me?"

I heard Vidmantas make a noncommittal grunt as I followed them inside.

If the outside of the Estate was in disrepair, the inside had an overgrown lavishness. There were paintings, statues, patterned rugs, plush couches, cane chairs, ornate lamps, and who knew what else, all covered in thick patinas of dust and dirt. Some were just as they'd been left, others knocked over or broken, while bare spaces on the walls indicated even more art that was no longer there. Plants crept in everywhere they could, through windows and corners, filling holes in the ceiling, puncturing every tableau with green, red, and yellow leaves.

As we made our way through what must have been a sitting area of some kind, I inspected some of the art. The paintings were in styles from throughout the known world and seemed to be of fine brushwork (although I am no expert), but none of them were of people. They showed fields, orchards, steppes, wolves hunting in darkened forests, a family of meerkats up on their hind legs watching for danger to their (charmingly painted) young. I actually exclaimed slightly when I saw, in a river scene, what I thought was the silhouette of a human figure, far off but beginning to encroach: I had found conflict, or perhaps a theme. Upon closer inspection, it was actually the silhouette of an upright Loashti crocodile—the same type that I was told as a child would drag me away if I wasn't careful; the same type that was now tattooed upon my arms. My understanding was that Skydašian crocodiles walked on all fours. (I began to wonder if our two breeds cross-pollinated. I imagined what that mating would have looked like and suppressed a giggle.)

"Something wrong?" asked Yalwas, walking over to me. I suppose he heard me exclaim at what I thought was a human figure.

"Oh, ah, no. I was just wondering why some of them are missing." I pointed to the empty square on the wall next to the river painting, which was as dirty as everything else, but a lighter shade of dirty.

"Adomas sold off the expensive ones to help establish the Guild—for seed and equipment and the like," replied Yalwas. "He kept only those that would fetch a low price or were already damaged."

"I see." I became aware of Yalwas' body looming over mine for a moment. Purely in a friendly manner, but it got me wondering: what were the taboos in this strange little pocket culture?

"A little odd," mused Vidmantas, wandering ahead of me, "to choose a crumbling ruin as your first impression."

"It's symbolism, Vidmantas," said Žydrė. "I thought you'd appreciate that." She raised her hands to indicate all around us. "The Estate is crumbling because we no longer have noble masters here. Those who enjoy the art take some care of the art, but plants are reclaiming the brick, making the house so much more *alive* than when it was full of servants working themselves to death." She moved into a beam of sunlight that shone through a great gouge in the ceiling, closing her eyes. "The sun streams in, and it feels heavenly, doesn't it?"

"Until a loose brick falls and kills you," replied Vidmantas.

Żydrė sighed and opened her eyes. "Can you ever be happy with anything?"

"Żydrė, when have I *ever* been?"

As we made our way through the Estate, Kalyna said almost nothing. At the time, I assumed she was recovering from some combination of Dagmar's departure and her skysickness (yes, sure, I'll go with skysickness). In hindsight, I think she was allowing Vidmantas and me to ask the obvious questions and make the tactless observations, because that's exactly what we would have done with or without her input.

We were soon led to the door of a room that was entirely dark. Żydrė and Yalwas obligingly went in first, to light candles in sconces and show us that it was safe. There were four of us and two of them, and only Kalyna was armed, but she still came in last. Slowly.

This room, unlike every part of the Estate we had seen so far, looked like it had been cleaned recently. Nothing was dusty or broken, no vines had crept in, and no streams of sunlight dotted the floor. Despite the midday heat, this room was somehow cool—pleasantly so, like a summer night when the sun hides, and the humidity burbles away into nothing. In here, the clay brick of the house's walls was lined with deep green *velvet*, which made it the most opulent place I had yet seen in the Tetrarchia, in a way that was entirely different from how southern Loasht tended to show opulence.

But even in the strange and convoluted Tetrarchia, I doubted that a series of specimens in pots and under glass were the normal decorations of a plush noble's estate.

The pots contained a number of strange plants: flowers, bushes, a "tree" no taller than my knees, a vine slowly writhing along its little wooden lattice. Some of the flowers were unbelievably bright in their hues, communicating their poisonousness in the clearest possible language. One of the bushes had mottled purple and red berries, which looked hard and unpleasant to me until Żydrė popped one into her mouth.

But in the glass enclosures—I did not even understand what I was seeing under flickering candlelight. As I became more accustomed to the darkness, I saw misshapen masses in black, blue, or dark red, alongside what appeared to be small animals that had been, perhaps, mangled somehow. In some enclosures, scores of little skeletons were meticulously posed, as though they were acting out little devotional plays.

Yalwas obligingly waved a hand at the ceiling. Looking up, I saw that it was covered in the preserved bodies of yet more animals: mostly birds and fish, as though they all lived in the same sky-sea together.

Vidmantas, Ifeanyas, and I looked at all this with our eyes nearly goggling out of our heads. The two of them appeared equally repulsed by and perversely drawn to this morbid collection, although I admit that I was purely the latter. Kalyna showed only benign interest.

"Fine, then," I said. "I'll ask. What are we looking at?"

"Some of the oddities Adomas collected over the years," said Yalwas, "which he has generously put on display here, so that they can be used for instruction and contemplation."

I did rather like the sound of that "contemplation" bit. Here was a room intended, I supposed, to draw the attention of the curious. It reminded me of when I would visit the office of someone at the Academy whose area of study was wildly different from mine. I always enjoyed leafing through books on unfamiliar subjects, or seeing what was on display. But no one in the Academy had such a wide-ranging collection.

"So what's this?" I asked. "What am I meant to contemplate here?" I was standing in front of a shaft of glass that covered a lacquered wooden stand. On the stand sat a bulbous black, gray, and pink something-or-other.

"That," said Yalwas, "is a human liver."

I looked closer. I had seen doctors (and Dagmar) cut people open before, and I had seen animal livers prepared for food, but never a discrete human liver that was just, simply . . . sitting there.

"Alchemically preserved," Yalwas added. "Using compounds mixed from Adomas' own discoveries, alongside ancient techniques our North Shore ancestors brought here from wherever their original home was. The owner of this liver died before any of us were born."

"Not so well preserved," remarked Vidmantas. "All black and gray, and it seems eroded. Has it rotted?"

"Sort of," said Yalwas. "But the preservation is flawless: this is exactly what it looked like at the end of its owner's life. You see, this was the liver of a drunkard."

Now I felt a visceral disgust. The thought of this blotchy, crumbling thing still trying, and failing, to do its work inside a living person's body, sputtering and choking as it . . . well, I realized I didn't know exactly *what* the liver does, but it made me feel sick nonetheless.

"And *drink* does that?" asked Vidmantas.

"Ew," said Ifeanyas.

Yalwas nodded. "Drink does that and more. I have a whole lecture I give on the subject to visitors and new members."

Kalyna looked as though she was as rapt as the rest of us, until she caught my glance. Then she smirked and rolled her eyes.

"Well then," she asked, sounding bright and attentive, "how does the lecture go?"

"I think you've inferred most of it: corrodes the liver, breaks down the body, thins the blood, and so forth." Yalwas smiled broadly. "You're a bright group; I doubt you need to hear the whole tirade."

"I'm sure you say that to *everyone*," said Kalyna, playfully thwacking Yalwas' shoulder.

Even knowing what Kalyna was, had I not seen her irritation earlier, I would have thought her entirely entranced by Yalwas and his show. Perhaps, in a way, she was, and this made it easier for her to act that way.

Yalwas, entirely taken in, laughed and made a joke of shooing her away. "I absolutely do not! Which is not to say that most of our members can't think for themselves, but rather that you all seem particularly . . . erm . . ."

"Educated," finished Žydrė.

Ifeanyas snorted and muttered, "I most certainly am not."

"Neither am I," said Kalyna. "So excuse my ignorance, but I assume this means you fine folks of the Lanreas River Guild have outlawed drink?" She shrugged. "Seems a pity: they say grapes are one of the only things that grow well here."

Yalwas opened his mouth to respond, but Žydrė cut in ahead of him.

"Drink is not outlawed," she said. "We work toward a future in which we—and the whole world—will be happy and healthy enough to no longer lean on such things. But we know full well we aren't there yet, that we live in *this* world." She shot Vidmantas a look. "But in the meantime, it's helpful to know *what* we are risking when we partake. Why, over here"—she pointed to a smaller glass box—"are the jaws of a khat chewer. And I do love my khat leaves."

It was a disgusting sight. I had expected simply jawbones and a few yellowed teeth, but the gums were still attached, without any skin. Those gums were wet, as though still sitting in a person's mouth, and were covered in black spots and white ulcers. Ifeanyas absentmindedly put a finger in his own mouth and pressed around against his gums.

"So," said Kalyna, "is the general point of your lecture that we had better watch ourselves? Don't get too drunk, don't wreck our bodies so that we can't . . . farm or whatever?"

"No, no, that's not what I'm saying." Žydrė furrowed her brow and clicked her tongue. "I just mean, well, know what you are risking. It's central to Adomas' belief system that this kind of knowledge be shared with everyone."

Yalwas cleared his throat loudly. "That said," he quickly added, "don't make trouble. We have a harmonious community here."

"I can see that you do!" chirped Kalyna, smiling up at him.

"There's more if you want to see it," said Yalwas. "The brain of a poppy genius, perhaps? Or, over here"—he swept his hand out toward another glass case—"are lizard skeletons that have been arranged to represent the ideal community."

I, at least, gawped at the brain of a poppy genius, which was much more interesting to me than a diorama. I did not feel particularly instructed, or even contemplative, but I *was* fascinated. I had never seen the insides of human beings preserved so perfectly.

"So in the ideal community, we will all become lizards?" asked Vidmantas.

Only Yalwas thought Vidmantas *meant* this question, and he began to explain at length the meaning of Adomas' symbolism in using lizard skeletons to represent humans.

"Also," an irritated Žydrė chimed in, "Adomas had a lot of lizard skeletons around. He had to use them for something."

Yalwas did not much like this, and the two made a show of very much *not arguing* when they were definitely, actually arguing. I expected Vidmantas to be enjoying the show, but he was actually regarding Žydrė with what seemed to be sympathy.

We were led out through the Estate's grand entrance at the south end of the building. Here there were stairs, a courtyard, and the crumbled remains of the outer walls that had once guarded the building at this end. Beyond the wall, a few scattered dwellings of clay brick or wattle and daub began to appear. Farther down the hill, they coalesced into a real town, pockmarked by the uneven shadow of the Estate above.

Right outside the broken wall was a large garden cluttered with bright flowers and what I took to be tuber greens. The plants were disordered, sometimes almost on top of each other, except for the center of the garden, where a small, unpainted wattle and daub house sat surrounded by a square of flowers in careful, orderly rows. A small path cut through them to its wooden porch, which was, at this time of day, entirely in the shade of the Estate. On that porch sat an old man, waving to us.

This was Adomas. As we approached, I saw that he was hunched and brittle, but wiry in a way that suggested he had been quite sprightly once upon a time. He wore the broad-brimmed straw hat that I would see on his head whenever he was out of doors, and a loose linen robe of deep red—everyone I'd seen from Lanreas so far wore similarly simple linen garments, but only his had such an intense coloring. Adomas had a closely cut white beard, which stood out brilliantly against a light brown complexion, and his smile showed only one missing tooth; impressive at his age. His hazel eyes held a gaze as searching and comprehending as Kalyna's, if not more so. He was frail, yes, but if his mind was ailing, he betrayed none of it.

"Hello! Hello!" he called out to us in Skydašiavos. Then, seeing me, he added, "Greetings!" in Loashti Bureaucratic.

"If you'll excuse me," Yalwas said, technically to us but also to Adomas. "I have work in town."

Adomas waved absentmindedly at him, and Yalwas bobbed his head in a sort of non-bow before going down the hill. The rest of us approached Adomas' porch, where Kalyna and Vidmantas sat on two more rough wooden chairs. Ifeanyas paced slowly, while I sat on the edge of the porch, where I could also admire the old man's garden. Adomas looked up at Žydrė.

"Go on," he said.

"But . . ."

"I don't want them to feel they are being watched. Neither do *I* wish to feel that I'm being guarded or waited upon. Let me talk to them. Please." His voice had a quaver that slightly marred its natural sono-rousness, and he spoke very quickly.

Žydrė screwed her mouth to one side but nodded. She glared at Vidmantas. "*Behave.*"

"What?" he replied, raising his hands and shaking his head. "I've been nothing but charming and curious."

Žydrė took her leave.

The four of us introduced ourselves to Adomas, who described him-self to us only as a "dabbler who is fond of plants and animals, and a trusted voice to the people here."

"Please, sir," laughed Kalyna. "No false modesty. You've accom-plished something entirely singular here, and I don't just mean your collection of oddities."

"I see Yalwas gave you his lecture," Adomas chuckled. "He can be a bit zealous. He didn't light cheap liquor on fire this time, did he?"

"Oh my, no," replied Kalyna. She crossed one leg over the other and leaned an arm over the back of her chair, matching Adomas' casual tone and demeanor. "He just showed us a few specimens—impressive for a 'dabbler.'"

Adomas smiled wider. "Young woman, nothing I say is false mod-esty, because I acknowledge that when I was young, I was a great naturalist." He sat forward, looking each of us in the eyes, one after another, as he spoke. "Probably the greatest, although the very term was quite new when I started. But in the end, all that research—the collection I amassed, my robust library, my own writings—led me to-ward this project, the Lanreas River Guild. Now that it's a thriving community of some two hundred and fifty members, I am free to put-ter about in my garden and give guidance only when it is needed. A dabbler." He sat back, hands braced against his knees, looking pleased with himself.

"And give that speech often, I assume," said Vidmantas.

Thankfully, Adomas laughed. "Believe it or not, young man, I don't sit down and talk to every new person who visits the Guild the moment they arrive. But seeing as you're Žydrė's old friend, and in the company of what I take to be an exiled Loashti, I wanted to meet you."

I simply nodded, but Vidmantas looked surprised.

The old man inclined his head toward Kalyna and glanced at the pacing Ifeanyas. "But please don't misunderstand; I'm delighted to meet all of you."

"Likewise," replied Kalyna.

Ifeanyas made a vaguely deferential noise as he continued to pace. I don't know where he found the energy—the last thing I wanted to do in the world was move. It was mesmerizing, though.

"Žydrė," said Adomas, "has mentioned before that you, Vidmantas, might suspect I'm some sort of . . . What was it?"

"A cult leader," said Vidmantas.

"Precisely."

"I can't determine that yet," replied Vidmantas.

Adomas nodded. "The only real way is to spend some time with us and see for yourself. However, I would like to point out something."

"Please do," said Kalyna.

"Young woman, you referred to our Guild as 'singular.' That is true, right now, but I don't want to claim that I am the first person to ever form a community based in ideas of equity, sharing the fruits of our labors, doing away with nobility, and all that. Such groups have popped up here and there throughout history: there is always someone who realizes life would be better with less of a hierarchy. In fact, all my research and study led me to the inexorable conclusion that this was always meant to be the natural state of humanity."

"Natural state?" asked Kalyna. "Is humanity 'natural'?" She seemed entranced, leaning forward with her chin on her hand, eyes wide with interest.

"We live in the natural world, don't we?" Adomas drummed his fingers on his knee, as though his thoughts were moving faster than the words could come out of his mouth. "There are animals that build homes, animals that care for one another, that communicate, so we're hardly unique there. And most animals are built to be especially good at one thing: hunting, foraging, running, and so forth. We, too, are animals, and *communication* is simply the thing we're best at. It leads us to better understand each other and the world around us, to put together collaborative works like buildings that protect us, farms that feed us, and art that sustains us."

"So, your 'natural state' of humanity isn't . . . running around naked in the forest?" asked Vidmantas.

Adomas laughed. "Of course not! We'd die immediately. We've become warlike, but we aren't built for it—soft and slow, with blunt teeth."

"It's your Guild, isn't it?" said Kalyna. "This place."

"Not . . . not quite," the old man admitted. "Ten years ago, I thought I could drag people directly from living in the Tetrarchia into a perfect society with no hierarchy, no family, no alcohol, and so forth, but that was naïve. After all, animals adapt to their surroundings." He snapped his fingers as though he was giving a lecture at the Academy, complete with gesticulations and rhetorical questions. "Take my beloved marabou stork, which feeds off human waste. If they were suddenly deprived of *all* our garbage at once, would they starve? Put simply, the Lanreas River Guild had to be a place where people, as they are now, would actually want to live."

"I would imagine," said Kalyna, "that some of those past communities you mentioned fell apart over not living up to someone's ideas of perfection."

"Absolutely," replied Adomas. "And they were always organized around narrower ideals: the followers of a certain god would go live in the mountains, the speakers of a small offshoot language would reject their state, those escaping persecution would become a hidden army in the steppes, and so forth. We try to avoid those pitfalls. I do not tell anyone that I'm the only one who can translate the gods' will, or that they must marry in groups determined by me, or any of that nonsense." He smiled widely at Vidmantas. "I hope this makes what you'd term a 'cult' less likely to arise."

"How long did those earlier attempts last?" I asked. "The monks in the mountains, and so forth."

"Perhaps eighty years, a hundred at most," replied Adomas.

"In the Loashti view," I said, "that's the blink of an eye."

"It's pretty damned short here too," said Vidmantas. "You can't think this place will last."

Adomas sighed, as though both annoyed and impressed by a precocious child.

"I hope that we've built this place to last longer than that," he said. "Of course, it won't last forever, but my people will be happy while it's here. And my hope is that we'll inspire others, as well."

"This is all a bit theoretical for me," said Kalyna. If I hadn't known better, I would've thought she meant it. "In basic facts, Adomas, you now have on your hands a Loashti alien and three outlaws. Do you even want us to stay here?"

"I understand your concerns. Why, I was an outlaw myself, once upon a time." Adomas' eyes positively twinkled.

"You?" cried Kalyna with disbelief.

The old man nodded. "Oh yes! I spent most of my life on the run, but I am quite fully pardoned now and allowed to do what I like with the land the King has allowed me." He spread out his hands to indicate the Guild itself.

"So will we be safe here?" asked Ifeanyas. It was the first thing he'd said since we'd met Adomas.

"I hope so, young man. It feels as though things change every moment in Skydašiai these days—unless that's simply my age."

"It isn't," said Vidmantas.

"Most of our Guild members," replied Adomas, "have complicated pasts of one sort or another. I can't make any promises for the King or his Yams, but I can say that, so far, we've been unmolested. And that you are welcome to join us."

"Lovely!" said Vidmantas, who didn't sound particularly sarcastic just then. "What do we need to do to fit in here? What are the rules? You must be dying to tell us."

"I like you, young man," said Adomas. "Quite simple, really. As I'm sure you're aware, members of any guild *must* support one another: in their business, in their training, in case of starvation, and against anyone who is not part of the guild, including the government."

Vidmantas nodded.

"Our guild is the same," continued Adomas. "We look out for one another but on a larger scale. If someone is hungry, feed them. If you are hungry, eat! But don't hoard or overindulge. Approach the Guild with the desire to help where help is needed, and you'll do just fine." He sat back, looking pleased with himself. "I simply don't believe mutual support can only come through an exhaustive charter and a trade in common. Being fellow humans, working side by side, should be enough. Our entire community is a guild with no binding paperwork, nothing to keep people here other than our love for one another."

"And whatever it is that makes this place safe from the government," added Vidmantas.

"Well, I'm afraid *that* is nobility." Adomas shrugged and sighed. "My family owned this land but didn't much care about it. Even when I was an outlaw, my own nobility brought me close enough to King Alinafe to earn his favor and his pardon. Now I have the land and the freedom to use it how I like. Nobility is a worthless concept, but it still matters in the outside world, so I use it to help my community. But here, on this land, I've re-nounced it—the Lanreas River Guild is not part of the so-called Tetrarchic Experiment. Not really." He grinned. "We are a *new* experiment."

Vidmantas opened his mouth to speak.

"And yes, young man," Adomas interrupted with a wink, "I do give *that* speech quite often."

"Of course you do."

"Well!" said Kalyna, slapping her thighs and standing up. "You've given us a lot to think on, old man."

Adomas seemed tickled at being called "old man."

"But I think we need some rest," Kalyna continued.

"Of course! Head into town, and someone will help you find your lodgings."

"Who?" I asked.

"Why, anybody."

I suppose I'd expected the town to be orderly rows of houses, all in the same color, but this wasn't the case at all. Adomas' house, and the first few we saw, were unpainted, showing only the browns and tans of their building materials, and seemed to have been placed haphazardly.

As we descended into the town proper, I saw that for the most part, the members of the Lanreas River Guild had continued the Skydašian tradition of painting each home largely in a single bright color. Predominant were reds and oranges—rather than the pinks and blues near the Skydaš Sea—but the paint was often fading and chipped. It was not the drabness I expected, but neither was there the same at-tention to upkeep I'd seen in much of Skydašiai.

The houses were, generally, around the same size, but their shapes and layouts varied wildly, from round to rectangular, to narrow, to bul-bous. The lanes of the town split and twisted in order to avoid trees, bushes, gardens, and courtyards. It seemed a pleasant place in which to get a little lost.

In the village, in the middle of the day, were Guild members going about their work—sewing, cobbling, cooking, taking inventories, and more; there were many others, sometimes right next to those doing work, who were happy to lounge together under a nearby tree; two small flocks of children wreathed themselves through it all, running and yelling. General chatter in a number of different languages seemed to float atop all of it, and I saw many people who (to my untrained eye) looked Quru, Masovskan, or Rotfelsenisch, rather than purely Skydašian. It felt like a dynamic and cosmopolitan city in miniature. All the clothes I saw worn were of plain tan linen, but the cuts and styles were varied: robes, dresses, and trousers, garments that were tight or billowing, skin almost entirely covered or quite bare. Differences aside, none of the clothing seemed to be intended for adornment, but rather was light, cool, and functional.

"Very nice," I said.

Vidmantas glanced around, looking miserable. His hair had been pushed into all the wrong directions by the wind on our trip, and his silk robe was tattered and dirty. He let out a long, irritated breath. "I think they're trying too hard to be nice."

"Of course you'd say that," I replied.

Ifeanyas snickered.

"But," I continued, "I'm not sure I disagree. Niceness can hide a lot."

Vidmantas yawned loudly. "Kalyna, what do you think about these people? You've got a good head on your shoulders."

Kalyna dipped her head slightly in thanks. "I think," she said, "that this is the only place that's safe for us right now, so it hardly matters."

At this, I looked up to the north. The Skydašian army's balloons were still visible, although some were blocked out by the Estate. It was a good reminder that the Guild wasn't as separate from the rest of the world as Adomas liked to think.

"Also," Kalyna continued, "they'll hear us if we keep talking about them."

As we walked through the town, we garnered some curious looks, some waves, and a "good afternoon" or two. These people seemed entirely unfazed by our appearance in their midst.

A group of children ran by us, carrying burlap sacks and yelling at each other. One grabbed some garbage off the ground, threatened to throw it at another, and then instead dropped it into her sack.

When she looked up, she suddenly saw us and stared wide-eyed for a few moments. Then she ran over to the others, yelling and pointing at us. The children all began chattering in Skydašiavos too fast and mispronounced for me to understand as they ran off, giggling.

"Well," said Vidmantas, "I must say, they seem like normal enough children."

"But why are they collecting trash?" asked Ifeanyas. "Are they the children of people here, or orphans and foundlings?"

"I'm hungry," I said. I didn't mean to say it out loud; I simply felt it come on suddenly and couldn't help myself.

There was silence for a moment before Vidmantas said, "Me too. Something smells amazing."

So we followed the smell. It was coming from a man cooking beneath a tree with broad, green leaves. Higher up in its branches were chirping birds of some kind, while a furry, wizened-looking binturong slept on a lower branch. The man beneath the tree sat on a stool as he roasted something in a great pan over a fire; next to him was a crate of little canvas bags.

"What are you making?" I asked him before anyone could introduce themselves. "The smell is beautiful."

He laughed. "Thank you, my Loashti friend! Today it's chickpeas in a number of spices. Roasting them up until they're good and crunchy. Want a bag?" He nodded to the crate at his side.

"How much?" I asked.

"Free, of course. Take what you need! We don't use money here, although we have coffers for our dealings with the outside world. If you brought any with you, you're of course welcome to donate it, but that isn't required!" He shook the pan, and the chickpeas jumped up into the air for a moment. "One bag is suggested, but some people take more, and I don't fault them for it. Good to eat now, or good to take home and incorporate into your own cooking."

I did manage, at least, to not growl, "*Now!*" as I took a bag and began to eat.

Introductions were made, although Kalyna had to introduce me because my mouth was full. The chickpeas were spicy enough to pleasantly burn, and the crunchy-to-chewy texture was perfect. I did in fact take a second bag.

"Just don't clear me out!" laughed the man, whose name was Uzochi.

"And all you're doing today is roasting chickpeas?" asked Kalyna.

He nodded.

"Did Adomas give you this task?" she continued. "Or someone else? Yalwas, perhaps?"

"No, no. I was a cook for a public house in Kalvadoti, where I made all sorts of food. When I first came here, I prepared full meals for the Guild members, as I'd done back home. But I always hated it—too many pieces to keep track of, which forced me to remember being *screamed at* back in the public house. Nowadays, I mostly work in the fields, but when there's a surplus of something that will be good roasted up—and most things are—I like to spend a day or two doing just this. It's rewarding, easy, and entirely unnecessary." He grinned.

We thanked him and moved on. As soon as we were out of hearing range, Vidmantas muttered, "Do you think they have him out here on purpose? To show hungry new members how carefree they are?"

"I would," said Kalyna.

Someone pointed us to a long dormitory building, which was lined with two rows of beds. Our bags were there, and Kalyna and I were quite thorough in determining whether anything had been removed. There seemed to be no one beyond the four of us staying in the building at the moment.

"Everything's here," said Kalyna.

"Thank the gods," said Vidmantas, flopping onto his bed. "I'm so glad no one stole all my nothing."

Kalyna looked at him for a moment, as Vidmantas put his hands behind his head and looked up at the ceiling. Then she tossed a stack of Skydašian kudais onto his bed, next to him.

"For your beads," she said. "Although I don't know where you'll spend them."

"Well," said Vidmantas, "I didn't pawn them expecting to be paid back."

"I'm going to give the food you bought with them to the Guild for their stores. Silly to hold onto it, and I want them to think we're happy to play along."

"Aren't we?" murmured Ifeanyas, who was already on his bed and seemed half asleep.

No one replied. I began to sit on my own bed. Kalyna took off her sword and leaned it against her bed. Slowly. She looked unhappy about it and kept her sickle.

"Radiant," she said. "Come walk with me."

I was going to complain, but then I saw the look on her face and I followed.

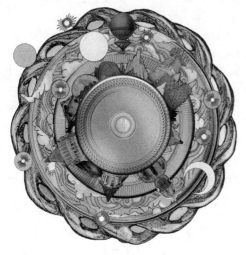

Chapter Twelve

Kalyna Aljosanovna's Opinion of the Lanreas River Guild

It was late afternoon, and northern Skydašiai's summer heat was beginning to lose its edge as Kalyna and I carried our food stores to what a helpful local had called the Meal Hall.

"I think you and Simurgh are the only Loashti," said Kalyna, in quiet Loashti Bureaucratic, "so this is still the safest tongue for us to speak right now." She grunted and hefted the bag over her shoulder. "But Skydašians this close to the border may have a familiarity with it, so keep your voice down." She grunted as she switched the bag to her other shoulder. "Radiant," she asked, "what do you think of these people so far?"

I shrugged. "They seem nice."

She snorted. "It's easy to be nice when you can't think for yourself. I have dealt with cults before, and I'm sure whatever is making them so happy is based in something . . . disagreeable."

"Vidmantas only calls them a cult to get a rise out of—"

"This has nothing to do with Vidmantas. I don't much care that they're cheery and agreeable; some people are just like that. Skydašians are often like that. What bothers me is what is underpinning it all. Any group of people brought together purely by a set of beliefs worries me."

"What about religion?"

She glared at me. "That's why we have many gods, Radiant. If my only choice was to follow, for example, the strictures of the god who dwells in darkness, I'd have been a heretic long ago." She looked around at the town again and ground her teeth. "It's not the cheeriness that bothers me, it's how *everyone* can be cheery at once. Nobody here is *annoyed* by any of Adomas' expectations?"

"Maybe the good outweighs it. After all, the abundance here of—"

"And that's another problem, isn't it? These lands—east of the river, beneath the border and above the Tail—are supposed to be dead. How are they growing so much?" She avoided a small group of chickens bobbing about in the street. "Mark my words: there is something wrong here."

"There's *something* wrong everywhere."

She glared at me. "You know what I mean; don't be dense. Either there's something very sinister buoying this place, or they're all fools." She smiled. "And if they're all fools, we can use them."

"Use them? They're trying to help us!"

"No, Radiant, they are just smiling a lot. *I* am trying to help you. So, by the gods, let me do so! It was hard enough before Dagmar left us to be *flown* in a *bird*—piloted by what I would generously term a crack-pot—to a cult's heretic temple on the frontier. But we're here now, and it may turn out to be a blessing. Let me do my job."

I wanted to disagree more vehemently—to be allowed to trust and like the people around me. But Kalyna seemed to have a response for everything, and I had to admit she knew what she was doing far better than I did.

I tried to remind myself of how people in Yekunde, and people in Abathçodu, had been *nice* right up until they decided they hated me. Why, I wondered, didn't the Zobiski memory that told me to distrust authority extend to Adomas? Not yet, anyway. I suppose what I'd seen so far felt closer to how a community ran and governed itself, rather than how it was governed by a strong, outside figure. Whatever the case, I decided it was best to trust Kalyna.

I sighed and nodded, asking, "Use them how?"

"I'm still considering that," she said. "I've got two plans simmering at the moment, but I'll need to learn more about this place first." She clicked her tongue thoughtfully. "Simurgh's balloon is more sophisti-cated than what the Yams are using," she muttered. "Perhaps we can sell the secrets to the army for safe passage. Either army."

"Or, rather than betraying our hosts, we find a way to cross the bor-der from here."

"Of course!" She threw up her free hand in irritation. "We'll just plow their damn fields or cook their cheap food, and traipse over to the border now and then, while atrocities are committed against your family!"

"You don't need to remind me of that. I didn't mean—"

"Or until the Guild turns us in, and we're sent to the Goddess' damned Guts! They may not even have to, since I'm sure we're being watched." She pointed up at the multicolored balloons that bobbed around at the border, still in sight. "Or maybe we'll get lucky, and they'll save us some time by sacrificing a Loashti for a bountiful harvest!"

"You really think they're plotting human sacrifice?" I laughed. "That's the sort of thing Loashti children are told about the Tetrarchia to scare them."

"It is not unheard of."

We reached the Meal Hall, which was quite large and filled with row after row of long tables. Enough to seat at least a few hundred people, although no one was sitting there at that moment. Something aromatic was being cooked in the kitchen at the back.

A smiling, but sweaty and harried, woman graciously inspected our odd assortment of black bread, nuts, and dried fruits and meats.

"We'll make use of it," she said. "But keep the meat and eat it your-selves. Then please do come back for dinner in an hour or so, if you have no other plans."

Kalyna told her that we certainly had none and would be delighted to join them for dinner. She spoke so charmingly to the woman that even I was almost convinced Kalyna had been won over. Until we got outside.

"No drink. No meat. Someone here must be annoyed by that," she growled in Loashti Bureaucratic, all her smiles gone. "Let's go see the farmland—the edges of this place."

We left the village, moving farther downhill, toward the fields and vine-yards, which seemed haphazardly placed and dotted by trees. In the distance, at the edges of the Guild's lands, were more trees, swaying gently in the wind. I started on my second bag of chickpeas, and Kalyna tore off pieces of dried meat as we walked.

"Where is that thing even drawing water from?" wondered Kalyna, spitting bits of dried meat. She was pointing at a large stone well that sat perfectly between the village and the farmland.

"The . . . ground?"

She glared at me and swallowed.

"Why can't you believe that they want to help us?" I asked.

"Why do you? Weren't Abathçodu and Žalikwen enough for you?"

I took a deep breath and looked up at the sky. The clouds were beginning to turn purple.

"That's . . . that's a good question," I admitted.

"It's what I do."

"I think," I ventured, "that threats to me, and to my people, have always come from people or authorities who are deeply invested in normalcy. In keeping things 'as they are,' or going back to an imagined 'as it was.'"

"Is Adomas' 'natural state' of humanity any different?"

"It is. They are trying to move outside of the world's expectations, to upend their own assumptions. I suppose that's promising to me. I think I want to believe that they wouldn't turn me in out of baseless fear. That they're better than that. That *someone's* better than that."

Kalyna gulped down a bite and looked at me. "Radiant, you can absolutely believe that, and you may even be right. But what about when their fear no longer seems baseless? When soldiers start causing them trouble? Or the crops fail? Or one of them dies suddenly? I promise you that *then* they'll remember you were alienated from Loasht for being too 'sorcerous.'"

"So we must turn on them now, before they turn on us later?"

"'Turn' is a little harsh, but yes." She either did not realize I meant it facetiously, or she did not care. "Didn't Adomas say the Guild was held together by its members' love for one another?"

"He did," I sighed. I felt I had an idea of what was coming.

"*Love* is not *trust*, Radiant. They can smile and 'love' us now, when their lives are easy enough that it poses no challenge, but sooner or later, Skydašian soldiers will come here. When that happens, if we haven't found a way across the border yet, it will serve us well to use these people as a shield." She looked right at a group of farmers working only a few yards from us, talking and laughing and wiping their brows as they did. "Or as a distraction."

"Putting them in danger," I replied.

"They chose to harbor fugitives, Radiant. They've put *themselves* in danger. Do you still want me to help you?"

"I do. Do you still want to help me? Dagmar's gone. I know I owe you some money for our lodgings, but is it worth all this?"

Kalyna snorted out a laugh. "Radiant, you are annoying me right now, but I want to help you. Why, I'd even go so far as to say that I like you. *And* that I find this to be an interesting problem to solve."

We walked in silence for a time, as Kalyna (I assume) thought about our options, and I took in the surroundings. Though I was no farmer, I generally understood that the crop adorning much of the winding fields was sorghum, that the green plants nearby were beans, and that in the distance were small fields of poppies and vineyards of grapes. I had only the vaguest notion of what the Guild members were actually doing in those fields when they tugged at the dirt or smacked the picked sorghum with big sticks; or of what most of the implements I saw even were.

There were scattered houses around the fields, many with their own patches of entirely different plants: peppers, squash, and other colorful things. I was struck by how few livestock I saw: just a few groups of chickens; three sheep by one house, guarded by a dog that was happily rolling in the dirt; and fleeting glimpses of what seemed to be a cow cavorting far off in the trees.

"It's lucky that Adomas has his own sordid past," I said eventually, as we passed through the red-and-white sorghum fields. "I was worried when you told him you're outlawed. That was quite a gamble."

"It was no gamble. I already knew his sordid past." She shrugged and yawned. "A bit of it, anyway."

"What? How?"

"I've read about him, although I assumed he was dead by now. He's usually called a 'bandit-naturalist' and spoken of in past tense, down on the southern continent. This place is quite isolated—I wonder how many people in the Tetrarchia even know about it." She picked up a long, thin stick and began idly swiping at grass with it as we moved out of a sorghum field. "Even in the balloon, I suspected: Žydrė told us his name and spoke of his love for animals. When we saw his little collection, I had no doubt. The question then became: should I reveal that I know who he is, or no?"

I felt I was beginning to understand at least a fraction of how Kalyna operated. "So, when he was so dismissive of his past . . ."

"I decided to keep it to myself, yes. And that allowed me to appear trustworthy by telling him up front that we are wanted, which would normally be quite the admission."

"Trustworthy *and* sympathetic," I added. "Since he knows the feeling of being hunted."

She turned and grinned at me. It was the first time since crossing the Skydaš Sea that she'd trained that intense, overwhelming smile upon me. I still couldn't help smiling back.

"Why, that's it, Radiant! You're beginning to wrap your head around the game, aren't you?"

"I suppose."

She broke the stick against a tree. "Well, keep it up! If we're ever getting across that border, you'll need to get better at deception." She tossed the broken stick far into trees. "I can read people and figure out the right tactic, but I need you following my lead immediately—not wandering off to get arrested at a coffee house."

"Library. And I was with Dagmar—"

"*I know.*"

We moved toward the vineyards. The sky was beginning to turn orange.

"Do you want to . . . talk about Dagmar?"

"Why would I want to do that?"

"To unburden yourself. Do you not trust me?"

She looked at me quizzically. "What, do you think I'm scared you'll tell everyone that I have *feelings*? It's not that I don't want to discuss it with you, it's that I don't want to discuss it with anyone." She looked away, down the path ahead of her. "Don't even want to voice it, if I don't have to."

"Oh. Well, then do you—?"

"Trust you? Of course!"

I smiled.

"You'd be stupid to betray me at this point," she added. "We're entirely on our own, you and I."

I sighed. "What about Vidmantas and Ifeanyas? Can't we trust them?"

"I think we can for now. They're in as much trouble as you are, and are both outcasts to the same degree."

"Outcasts? I took Vidmantas for the scion of a rich family in a fit of youthful rebellion, who just needs to lie low until . . ."

I stopped, because she was fixing me with a very smug expression.

"What?" I asked.

"Vidmantas definitely comes from a low background," said Kalyna. "I'd say he's been through hard times, but his parents likely broke their necks and spent all their money to get him an apprenticeship. He was probably the smartest boy any teacher or master had seen in years, too—natural gifts, yes, but also desperate not to let his family down." She clicked her tongue and tapped her jaw thoughtfully. "At first I thought he was a clerk of some sort, but his hands are callused, didn't you notice? His clothing, jewelry, and hair show a great care for aesthetics and textures, so I'd guess he was assistant to an artisan of some kind. Not to mention his insistence on the sanctity of the guilds. Before he was outlawed, he probably spent day in, day out, sewing buttons for his master while he dreamed of his own outfits, and his own politics."

"You got all that just since last night?"

"Gods. Was that only *last night*?" She dipped her body slightly, as though acting out fainting from exhaustion. "Just a bit of guesswork. I could be wrong, but, well, I've met people like him before. No one is as singular as they think they are."

"Even you?"

She grinned. "No. I really am singular."

I rolled my eyes, and she snort-laughed again.

"And showing off," I added.

"Habit," she said. "You're a customer, after a fashion. I want you to know I can do what I say."

"After Žalikwen, I think I'd believe you can do anything."

I probably shouldn't have admitted that, but surprising emotional honesty has long been one of my own methods of drawing people in. Besides, what would she do with my trust and belief? Con me out of money she knew I didn't have?

"Careful," she chuckled. "You may make me believe it too."

"You sound like you already do."

"Naturally."

We turned around and began to walk back toward the town. I felt dusty and dry but also rather invigorated by the walk.

"And Ifeanyas?" I asked. "Is that unassuming man also an outcast?"

"Oh yes. I'd wager Ifeanyas is a drifter, or was recently. He's certainly been on the run and done some unsavory things. Not that *I'm* one to judge."

"I noticed he reacted to a mention of that prison—the Goddess' Guts," I offered.

"Good! Yes, exactly what I mean about being on the run. Besides . . ."

"What?"

She stopped walking and looked at me, one foot up on a small rock that she had been about to step over. She seemed strangely grand somehow, even tired and dusty in this strange place.

"Being Zobiski, this may not even have occurred to you," she explained, "but I suspect Ifeanyas was treated as a girl growing up. Possibly even treated as a woman for a time. Before, I assume, he escaped."

It took me a moment to fully understand what she even meant. Ifeanyas had what I took to be a Skydašian man's name, and had presented as such in hair, dress, and manner, so I had thought no more about it.

The genders of the Tetrarchia were, after all, much more stratified than those where I'd grown up. A Grand Suzerain only ever cared about the sex of those in his direct family line. How his myriad subjects organized their little societies didn't matter, so long as they paid their taxes, paid obeisance, and did not dip into "occult" rituals. Hence Loashti Bureaucratic (like Cöllüknit) only had one pronoun, so it could work across all of Loasht.

"Combine that with his general desire to not be noticed," Kalyna continued, "and the fact he's likely been to the Goddess' Guts, and you have a man with drifter written all over him. He feels rather like he could be part of my own family." She smiled off into the distance at this and began walking again.

"But not like your grandmother, whom you hate."

"You do pay attention, and I appreciate that. No, like those I've heard about in my family's history."

"If he reminded you of her, you'd have pushed him right back into the Skydaš Sea."

"I *knew* I liked you, Radiant!"

We walked back to the village. Kalyna, somehow, had the energy to spend the hours until dinner running around asking questions. *I* went back to our lodgings, where Vidmantas and Ifeanyas were sleeping. Their blissful ignorance looked lovely, so I got into my new bed and dreamed of marabous.

Žydrė woke us up, knowing we wouldn't want to miss dinner.

"If I feel that I could eat an entire cow," she said, "I can only imagine how hungry you all are."

"And yet," I murmured, rubbing my eyes, "Kalyna and I were given the impression that you all don't eat meat here."

"Wait, *what?*" cried Ifeanyas. He immediately went from groggy to wide awake.

"Although, I did see one cow today," I added. "Cavorting."

"Oh!" said Žydrė as we stepped out into the lanes of the village, beneath a sky now deeply orange. "You saw Lini! She was kind enough to supply the community with milk during our first tenuous year of existence. There are no bulls around to give her offspring, so she's past her milking days, but she roams free, eating grass and fertilizing the ground where she sees fit. But yes, it's true. We don't serve meat here."

"After all that," murmured Ifeanyas, "I can't even have some beef?"

"Kalyna may still have some of the dried stuff," I offered.

"It's Adomas' philosophy that eating meat makes humans violent," Žydrė explained. "But there's also pragmatic side: simply cheaper and easier to not have large herds of livestock to take care of." She looked to Vidmantas, expecting, I assume, for him to argue.

"Commendable," he said. "But I've dined with you recently in Žalikwen, and I don't recall you turning down a bit of *flesh*."

Žydrė made a face. "Please don't put it that way. And I don't eat meat here."

"How would Adomas feel about you leaving the Guild to go and eat his animal friends?"

"I think it's none of his business. We are not a priesthood, and eating meat is not a *sin*. Someday, our descendants will have moved beyond it, but for now, foregoing meat is Adomas' preference. It's also cheaper, so we're happy to abstain."

"Will everyone dine together?" asked Ifeanyas.

"No," said Žydrė, "just whoever wishes to. Some prefer to dine in their homes, alone, or with friends and family. Some never eat in the Meal Hall, some leave it up to their mood that day."

"Does anybody serve meat in their homes?" I asked.

"Not my business," Žydrė replied.

When we entered the Meal Hall, most of its tables were already full of talking, laughing, yelling humanity. Mostly I heard Skydašiavos being spoken, with a smattering of Masovskani.

"It's more crowded than usual!" said Žydrė.

"Where are we going to sit?" murmured Ifeanyas.

Žydrė looked around that sea of unfamiliar faces for a space, talking loudly to various people she knew. A group of children—possibly the same we'd seen earlier—came in and were lovingly forced to wash their hands.

"Ah!" said Žydrė. "They're back from war."

"War?" I asked.

"The only competition in our guild," she laughed. "Most children can't help wanting to *win* at something, so we form them into little armies that compete at keeping the town clean. It's a good place for those that love to be filthy too."

"Another of Adomas' ideas?" I asked.

"Actually, this one was mine," said Žydrė, swelling with pride.

"Radiant!" someone yelled in Loashti Bureaucratic.

Simurgh was sitting at an otherwise empty table, waving at me. I smiled and moved toward her through the pressing crowd. Most other tables were filling up, it seemed.

"Simurgh!" I said as I sat next to her. "Thank you for holding the table."

"Holding nothing!" she spat. "These people like to think they're accepting, but I always end up sitting alone."

"Is that because you prefer to be alone, I wonder?" asked Vidmantas as he and Ifeanyas sat across from us.

Simurgh shrugged and pointed across the room. At some point, Žydrė had stopped standing with us and sat down with some other people she knew, whom she was now talking to loudly.

It occurred to me that, Loashti or no, Simurgh might be unpopular due to her . . . difficult personality. But what I said was: "Well, you two must've spent a lot of time together in that balloon."

Simurgh shrugged in a way that suggested she would complain about whatever she wanted. Moments later, Kalyna clomped into the Meal Hall, saw us, and sat on the other side of me.

"Thanks for holding the table," said Kalyna.

Simurgh opened her mouth to argue, but dinner was served.

Dinner, in this case, was huge pots of a chunky and aromatic curry (we were warned to look out for whole cardamom pods), alongside heaping plates of steaming sorghum flatbreads. Sweating and tired, but smiling, people issued from the kitchen to slam these down onto our tables, leaving it to us to portion them out as we saw fit. Kalyna, Vidmantas, Ifeanyas, and I all helped ourselves to *quite* a lot, and no one seemed to mind.

I wanted to ask Kalyna if she'd learned anything interesting, but then I remembered I couldn't use Loashti Bureaucratic as a way to be circumspect in Simurgh's company. Kalyna understood the look in my eyes and winked, as she piled her plate high with bread.

I desperately wanted to start eating, but I noticed no one else had done so. Ifeanyas looked similarly forlorn.

"Simurgh," I murmured in Skydašiavos, "what are we waiting—"

"Let the Little Baby Suzerain have his moment first," she replied in Loashti Bureaucratic.

I blinked a few times, confused. "The . . . little baby . . . ?"

Just then, Adomas walked to the front of the Meal Hall, using a cane that he may or may not have needed, with his straw hat gone and his perfectly white and full hair on display. Simurgh smiled and rolled her eyes. I looked at Kalyna, just as she snuck some food into her mouth, and then smiled when she saw I'd caught her.

"Friends!" called Adomas, and the room fell silent.

I was relieved that he didn't address everyone with, say, *brothers and sisters*, or even worse, *my children*.

"Friends," Adomas repeated, "I am, as always, so thankful that we have survived another day flourishing, as we do, in the very mouth of the Tetrarchia, which has rejected many of us." He smiled. "And which many of us have rejected. I am thankful that we, in our refuge here, can once more dine together, just as we live, work, and rear together."

Adomas then motioned to a table near him, from which two people stood up. He introduced the Lanreas River Guild's only priests: a relaxed Skydašian man dedicated to the Tetrarchic goddess of the

Sea, and a willowy Rot woman excommunicated from the mysteries of the god who dwells in darkness. They performed a short blessing that referred to the "the gods" generally, rather than any one in particular. (Although the Skydašian did chime in once or twice about his goddess, specifically, despite how far we were from the Skydaš Sea.)

I looked to Kalyna, expecting another rolling of her eyes, knowing smirk, or secreted bit of food, but she was rapt by the priests. At the end of their blessing, she closed her eyes and mouthed what I took to be a short prayer of her own.

"Now, please, start eating," said Adomas. "I have news of the world outside for those who are interested, but I don't wish to keep you from your meal."

No one needed to be told twice, and Kalyna, Vidmantas, and Ifeanyas were all ravenous, tucking in with great intensity. Well, perhaps *I* needed to be told twice, because I was too curious about what his "news of the world" was, and how he would describe it to his followers. (I also may have filled up more than intended on roasted chickpeas.)

Throughout the Meal Hall, dishes began clattering, and bread was torn apart, but chatter stayed at a minimum. I suppose this was so Adomas could continue to address the room, which he did while walking between the tables, smiling at various people as he spoke. It was hard for me to tell who cared about what he was going on about, and who simply saw their leader's lecture as the price of their meal.

"Now, we are, of course, not of the Tetrarchia," he said with a hint of puckishness, "and neither are we part of Loasht. We are Lanreas. We are on our own, by choice and by necessity. Nonetheless, we do live in the world as it is, not as we would have it be."

"Eat up," said Simurgh, her mouth full. "He does this about once a week. Usually starts the same way."

I slowly began to tear at a piece of bread, but stayed focused on Adomas.

"No matter how we see ourselves," he said, "our community sits by the border—'on the front,' it used to be called, as though the Tetrarchia was always at war with its neighbor. And so we are affected by the movements and decisions of these two nations."

There were murmurs of agreement throughout the hall.

"But that has its benefits," continued Adomas, "now more than ever. We were put out here where we would not *bother* the powerful. Where we would, so they *thought*, be the first to go if there was an invasion. However, we now find ourselves at a . . ." He grasped for a term. "A crossroads of ideas!"

"There's no way he just thought that up," Kalyna muttered.

Simurgh smirked.

"Due to our position," Adomas continued, "and the Blossoming between these two nations, we are now among the first to learn news of Loasht." He was now standing quite near our table and looking at me.

I swallowed the one small piece of bread I'd bothered to eat so far and watched the old man intently.

"And right now," said Adomas, "the news is good! In fact, a Loashti delegation is, at this very moment, on its way to the Skydašian court. Why?" He smiled. "So they can sort out what has been a great misunderstanding, and welcome back those many Loashti who have found themselves stranded in the Tetrarchia, unable to return to their homes."

I felt a pressure begin to leave my chest. Was I honestly learning, in this strange, remote, and possibly delusional place, that soon I could actually just *go home*? Had my alienage been but a momentary lapse? A mistake?

I turned to Kalyna, and I'm sure my gaze was intense and searching. I don't know why I needed her to verify what I'd just heard, but she shrugged and mouthed the word *maybe* in Zobiski, despite being in the middle of chewing.

Most of the Guild members continued to nod with polite attention, as though what Adomas discussed was news of a far-off land. I suppose, in a way, it was.

"We know this," said Adomas, becoming visibly excited, "before anyone else in the Tetrarchia because that very delegation has stopped here, in our humble home, on its way to King Alinafe himself!" He grinned and looked around the room. "*Every Guild member* should understand what an auspicious development this is: delegates from a great nation are visiting us and recognizing our importance!"

By this point, I was almost humming with excitement. By the Eighty-Three, could this really be happening? I had not realized how terribly the weight of the last few weeks had descended upon my body and mind. It had quickly become *normal* to feel as though every joint and bone was being crushed, to have my mind in a constant fog of bleak fear. I hardly knew how to react to those sensations beginning to dissipate.

"And so," said Adomas, "we have a special guest here to speak with you." He flourished toward a table at the far end of the room, which I could hardly see.

A man at that table stood up, coming into view for those of us far away. He was about my height, and wore familiarly Loashti clothing, including a brocade cape that spoke to his governmental authority.

"May I introduce you all," said Adomas, "to the most esteemed Loashti diplomat Aloe Pricks a Mare upon the Mountain Bluff. Be as kind to him as you would to any traveler."

I had never heard Aloe's name in Skydašiavos before, so it took me a moment to understand. By the time I realized what I had heard, and who I was seeing, Aloe's eyes had found me. Remembering our last interaction, after he had returned to Yekunde with his followers, I froze. Perhaps I hoped to not be noticed if I stayed very still.

From across the room, Aloe leaned forward and narrowed his eyes, pressing his lips together tightly. Then he smiled widely and waved at me.

Excerpt from *The Confession, Under Duress,*
of the Magician —— *to the Sorcerer Cleavers*
—— *and* ——

I was sure I would die. I am still not entirely sure I did not die.

I have been sick with consumption to the edge of death; I have been assaulted, beaten, and stabbed; once they even tried to hang me.

But never before, in all my life, did I feel so close to death, to the unmaking of my flesh, to the rending of all that I have ever been, than I did on that day. Nothing bruised my soul and came closer to tearing me from my loved ones than when I, with the help of my compatriots, attempted our curse upon the Grand Suzerain himself.

Did we succeed? I will submit to any punishment, accept any torture, give you a complete list of my accomplices, but please, tell me.

Chapter Thirteen

Aloe Pricks a Mare upon the Mountain Bluff

Aloe gave a short speech, but I didn't hear it over the thrumming of blood in my ears. From what I gathered after the fact, he talked about welcoming all Loashti back home, commended the Lanreas River Guild on its efforts to escape backward modes of thinking, and did a very good job of not referring to its members as though they were citizens of the Tetrarchia. Also, his Skydašiavos was apparently "good" but "not quite so good" as mine. (I found this pleasing.)

He looked much the same as he had when I last saw him. His dark hair had a few more coils of gray in it, and his face had become a bit harder and bonier. He seemed to have gotten more muscular since he'd left the Academy, but I suppose running all over Loasht (and, apparently, the Tetrarchia) would do that to a man. His time spent in Talverag and other places showed in his trousers and shirt, which were of the boxy and firm Central Loashti style, beneath a dark cape with a glittering, multicolored trim, which spoke to his authority.

His facial tattoos—three slim, squiggly lines tattooed beneath each eye—were all that would tell a Loashti he was from the south. (So few, and only in abstract patterns, would suggest that he wasn't Zobiski: part of our "atavism" was our supposed overuse and preference for identifiable figures.) Once upon a time, those lines under his eyes had represented his "tireless nights of studying at the Academy," but now they were faded, as he must have lost either the time or the inclination to have them touched up.

All I really caught was the end: "My fine allies," he said, "I had more, but I admit I find myself flustered." His smile returned, painfully genuine amid all the statecraft. "I did not realize that one of my best friends in all the world was here with you." He gestured toward me. "If you'll excuse me."

There was scattered applause. I found that, as I watched Aloe weave toward me, I had no appetite at all.

"Well, what great news!" Vidmantas said to me from across the table, as he tore apart a piece of flatbread.

He seemed genuinely happy for me, even though he and Ifeanyas were still outlawed. I somehow felt guilt for not acting relieved, for not pretending everything was fixed.

"Radiant," muttered Kalyna, "are you all right?"

"He's overcome with emotion!" laughed Vidmantas. "To find an old Loashti friend in a place like this. Marvelous!"

Aloe moved closer, making apologies and patting a local on the back as he squeezed past a table. I looked at Simurgh, who seemed only irritated.

"He's not my friend," I whispered.

Vidmantas' face switched to concern, even as he dipped his bread into the curry and took a large bite. Ifeanyas, next to him, watched my expression for a moment before setting down his own bread.

"Then," said Ifeanyas, "we will simply have to tell him to leave you alone." He began to stand up.

That small gesture produced in me such a well of good feeling.

"No," hissed Kalyna. "Look normal, both of you."

Ifeanyas looked to me and I shrugged. He sat back down.

Aloe Pricks a Mare upon the Mountain Bluff put a hand on my shoulder. My ears and fingers were burning hot. My chest hurt. He was behind me, so I stared ahead in fear and confusion. Vidmantas and Ifeanyas did not quite manage to seem *normal*, but they did not react too much.

"Radiant!" cried Aloe.

He leaned down, standing next to me as I sat for a meal, just as he had seven years before, at his farewell party—when I thought he was leaving Yekunde forever. He felt much taller this time, as though he was looming.

I turned my head slightly, facing Kalyna. She widened her eyes at me, as though willing me to do, say, or *understand* something that she couldn't tell me just then. So I tried desperately to think of what she would have done and how she could have found the strength.

I turned to look up at Aloe and tried to force a friendly smile onto my face. I hoped it was a decent attempt.

"Why, I certainly didn't expect to see *you* here!" I choked out in Loashti Bureaucratic.

"Until very recently, I didn't expect to be here, Radiant! Why, it's my first time in the Tetrarchia at all." He turned to Simurgh and shrugged. "May I sit?" He said this in much more proper Loashti Bureaucratic than he had spoken to me.

She nodded and scooted over. Moments later, Aloe Pricks a Mare upon the Mountain Bluff—who had brought a small army to my home, who had spent years now leading a growing movement against the "occult" to every corner of Loasht—was sitting pleasantly next to me. He carefully pulled his cape to one side (the side Simurgh was on) and over into his lap, to keep anyone from tripping over it.

"You may not remember me," said Simurgh, "but we've also met before. At the Yekunde branch of the Loashti Academy."

"I'm afraid you're correct that I don't. But it's a pleasure to see you again anyway."

She fixed him with a look he did not seem to notice and then focused only on her food.

"Can I get you a plate?" I asked Aloe. It was all I could think to say.

"Oh, no!" said Aloe. "I wouldn't dream of it. Sit. Sit and eat!" He grabbed a piece of bread and took a small bite.

Vidmantas and Ifeanyas continued eating, watching us with confused expressions that I hoped could be blamed on the fact that we were speaking Loashti Bureaucratic. I tried very hard to look like I wanted to talk to Aloe and so did not turn to see how Kalyna, on my left, was reacting.

"So what brings you out here, old friend?" asked Aloe. "I haven't heard of much in the way of curses up by the border. Why, they're almost civilized here, aren't they?"

I laughed awkwardly and repeated the word, "Almost!" in a sort of terrible bark. I tried to calm myself down before continuing.

Simurgh rolled her eyes.

"Well," I began, "I was . . . I mean, I'm sure you can . . ." Deep breath in, closed my eyes, opened them again. "I was trying to get *home*, Aloe. I still don't really know what happened to turn everything sour for me, or for all of my kind."

"Well, good news, Radiant! You'll be able to come back home very soon now. We've almost got it all sorted. I can't tell everyone the details just yet. Secret diplomatic stuff, you understand."

I was baffled. Not just by this turn of events, but by this seemingly relaxed and confident version of Aloe. And by the fact that he considered me one of his "best friends."

"Really?" I asked. "And soon?"

"Oh yes!" Aloe grinned. "I say, Radiant, do you mind . . . ?" Before finishing his sentence, or waiting for my reply, he dipped a piece of his own bread into my curry. (Which, to be fair, I hadn't touched.)

"I passed through Yekunde again on the way here," he said as he chewed.

My face must have betrayed the deep, terrible dread that shot through me at that. Because he swallowed and dropped his smile.

"Oh! Oh my, Radiant, you don't think—" He looked around for a moment, and then said quietly, "Let's talk outside for a bit, my friend. Privately."

I nodded numbly.

Aloe got up off the bench, swinging his cape back out.

Kalyna jabbed me in the ribs. When I turned to look at her, she mouthed the Cöllüknit word for, "*Stall!*"

"Oh, ahhhhh . . . Aloe!" I managed to say. "I . . . I realize I haven't even had a bite yet. You go ahead, and I'll meet you." I forced another smile. "Since there's clearly nothing to worry about, let me fill my stomach, would you?"

He patted my shoulder. "You have always enjoyed the simple pleasures, Radiant. Of course. I should go talk to my host a little more anyway." He winked and nodded his head toward where Adomas sat at the far end of the room.

As soon as he'd gone, Kalyna leaned in very close and growled in Cöllüknit, "What do you think you're doing?"

I didn't know how to answer, nor what she was asking. Everyone else at the table was looking at me. I shoved some bread into my mouth, but didn't want the curry Aloe had put his finger in, no matter how good it smelled.

"Come on," said Kalyna in Skydašiavos. "Take some with you, and we'll get you some fresh air." She smiled at Simurgh. "Excitement, you know. The news is simply *too* unexpected." She then shot a look to where Aloe and Adomas were talking. To make sure we'd have at least a little time. I followed her gaze, and the two men seemed quite taken with one another.

Kalyna took me outside. It was dark now, warm but not oppressive. I swallowed the bread in my mouth and began to gasp for air, breathing quickly and painfully. Feeling lightheaded.

"Hey!" snapped Kalyna as I leaned back against the wall of the Meal Hall. "Hey! None of that."

I expected her to slap me, or shake me, but instead she put her hand on mine and held it tightly.

"Later," she said in Cöllüknit. "Feel your feelings *later*. Please."

My breathing slowed, but she still gripped my hand tightly.

"We don't have time," she continued, "for you to tell me everything that's going on here. Why instead of being overjoyed, you're clearly terrified."

I started to groan. She gripped me harder—what had been comforting became painful.

"*But*," she hissed, "I do know one thing."

I looked at her. I felt tears burning behind my eyes, my heart pounding. "What?" I murmured.

"You are doing a terrible job of acting like his friend."

"Because I'm not his friend!" I snapped back, finding anger deep in me, somewhere past confusion.

"Yes, that is very clear, Radiant, which is the problem."

"I don't understand! Does he really consider me a friend, or is it all an act? He . . . he . . . !"

"I don't think it's an act, and the why is beside the point, just now."

She loosened her grip, and her hand on mine felt pleasant again. "*Radiant*, what do you think you can possibly get out of this situation—whatever it is—if you don't lead him on a little?"

"I don't know. That feels—"

"I swear, Radiant, if you say 'wrong' right now . . ."

"But—!"

"Radiant, by—" She gulped, killing whatever word was next. "You *almost* made me name the goddess of Keçepel Mountain." She let go of my hand and glared at me. "You don't need to do anything special. You don't even need to lie, mostly. Just think of anything about him, or about what he represents, that might make you happy."

"Happy?"

She threw her hands up. "Is it good to hear Loashti spoken by a native again? With a southern accent? To see someone with tattoos as adornment? Does he dress or smell like home? Remind you of good times? Even if those times were actually at his expense? Come on, Radiant, just focus on *something* that can make you smile at him like you mean it. Anything!"

"I'll try."

"Now I need to go back in and finish dinner before people get more suspicious."

She turned and walked toward the door, then stopped and hissed, "And don't you *dare* tell him I understand Loashti, hear me?"

"Yes."

I ate flatbread quietly in the moonlight until Aloe appeared through the door. He smiled at me again, brightly, even though no one else was around to see it.

"Let's take a walk, Radiant," he said. "Interesting place they've put together here. I heard about it when we crossed the border and decided I had to see it." He rolled his eyes and nodded at the Meal Hall behind him. "I was just convincing the old man to let me walk around freely. My escorts, Loashti and Skydašian both, had to camp out at the borders of Adomas' land. But they are being fed well, for free, so they aren't complaining too much."

I tried to take Kalyna's advice. I listened to how pleasing it was to hear not just a familiar language, but specifically a southern Loashti accent: slower, luxuriating in the sounds more than the mad dash of, say, Simurgh's speech. I smiled. Then I latched onto something Aloe had said, to which I could have a genuine reaction and agreement with him.

"It's odd, isn't it," I said, "how much power this Adomas seems to have. Even the Skydašian soldiers leave him alone."

Aloe nodded and patted my back warmly as we began walking.

"Now that's the Radiant I missed," he said. "Always questioning. I suppose you were just a little nervous in there, around all of Adomas' people?"

I nodded and looked up at the dark sky in order to take a break from smiling at Aloe.

"Well, I only just got here today," I said.

"Really? Why, that's incredible! What luck we would run into each other."

"What luck, indeed."

We let the incline of the Lanreas River Guild take us down through the town. Sounds of laughter and conversation floated out from some of the houses.

"Your family are doing just fine, Radiant," said Aloe. "I certainly didn't mean to worry you."

"Oh! Well, that's good to hear." At this, too, I could smile genuinely, although it meant pushing down the worry that he was lying.

"I dropped in on them just a week or two ago, on my way here. Helped them out of a tight spot."

"Well, thank you very much for doing that."

A tight spot. Aloe had said it as simply as if he'd lent out a few coins. Contemplating all the atrocious things it could actually mean made me feel that my insides were being hollowed out. I couldn't help showing this worry on my face.

"Look, Radiant, I know some of my people can be a little . . . over-zealous at times. And *you* know that your beloved spouse can be a touch disrespectful. Silver shared some, ah, inopportune words, and a few of mine didn't show the restraint they were supposed to."

My heart began to pound again. I stared at my feet.

"But it's fine! It's all fine now!" He clapped my shoulder to make me look up at him. He was smiling ingratiatingly, as though *I* was the one with the power, and he was desperate for my approval. "I talked my people down, had a good conversation with Silver, and things got smoothed over." He shrugged. "Sometimes, the people who follow me aren't . . . Well, they just aren't bright enough to understand the difference between *people* and *ways*, if you understand."

I managed to smile again, thinking that Silver was safe (and pushing down the thought of what might've happened to them after Aloe left). It also helped to imagine what Silver must have said to Aloe and his people. I even giggled slightly at the thought.

But I could not entirely lie, so I did say, "No. No, I'm not sure I do understand."

Aloe exhaled and scratched his head thoughtfully. We continued walking downhill, and it occurred to me that, if we got to the farmland, I could probably find some sharp implement and kill him. Was I capable of such a thing, physically or emotionally? And if I was, what would happen to me, to my hosts, and to the people back home?

"Radiant, you *know* I've never had anything against the Zobiski, or any people."

Did I know this? But I nodded.

"It's the *ways* that are poisonous. The rituals, the beliefs that some backwater shaman can improve your life, the uncouth *noise*, the ritual mutilations."

Aloe was not only being insulting to the Zobiski, he was throwing in his exaggerated ideas about other "backward" peoples throughout Loasht. Every fiber of my being wanted to argue with him, to point out his leaps of logic, but I remembered how fruitless our "debates" had been, all those years ago. (What would I gain by pointing out that his own tattoos, for example, could be considered ritual mutilations? Only another argument.)

Aloe was looking at me and waiting for my response. If he truly thought himself my friend, if he *liked* me for some reason, he wouldn't expect blanket agreement, would he? But then, this was a new Aloe, different from the man I'd known. Or not so different: I think this Aloe had been inside him all along.

"Well," I said, "you can understand why that difference would be hard to parse, for some people."

"Of course!" he replied quickly. "Which was why I always wanted you to join me at the Ministry, Radiant."

"Oh. Oh yes. I do remember something of that."

A group of Guild members passed us, and they, at least, had found somewhere to have a drink. They smiled but also seemed a little surprised to see two tattooed Loashti, one of whom was in a gilded cape.

"You know, Radiant," said Aloe, "I've felt terrible for some years now."

"Oh? Why . . . why is that?"

"Well, the last time I saw you, when I suggested the Ministry for you, and you were, ah, uninterested, I was absolutely beastly to you for the rest of the night."

I thought back to when Aloe had returned to Yekunde, and the dinner he held. I remembered him making the suggestion and then simply not talking to me much the rest of the night, which had been what I *wanted*.

"I am sorry," he continued, "and I greatly respect you for traveling far for your research. I mean, *obviously*. I wouldn't have any of this"—he motioned to his own clothes—"had I not gone up to Talverag."

I wanted to laugh at this comparison. Loudly, meanly, and in his face. Of course, I did not.

Then I began to have the nagging feeling that it was my fault Aloe had become what he did. That if I hadn't *wanted* him to leave, hadn't wanted to be spared a slight awkwardness (from a person who apparently liked me!), then perhaps he never would have left. Had I been nicer to him, accepted his friendship, perhaps he wouldn't have felt the need to go on his little crusade. Had I not argued with him about his ancestor, perhaps he wouldn't have felt the need to *redeem* the man, and Aloe would have been just another Loashti who didn't bother to examine his history, blithely tolerating people like me.

Perhaps if I'd been a friend to him, he would have thought better of the Zobiski.

To shake myself out of this spiral, I imagined what Kalyna, Vidmantas, Ifeanyas, or even Dagmar would have said to such a line of reasoning: *Don't be stupid*; *Of course not*; *No*; and, *Who cares?*

Aloe was still talking: "And the offer to join me at the Ministry is still open, Radiant. I want to show everyone that what they see as a backward, hopeless Zobiski is actually an intelligent, driven, and charming Loashti."

I thought of many responses to that statement, but I knew that if I said any of them, Kalyna would stand up in the Meal Hall, run through the town to find us, and slap me in the face.

I stopped walking, took a deep breath, and allowed myself to look conflicted and confused, which I was. We were at the southern end of the town now, with the farmland stretching out ahead of us. Right against a tree, not far at all, I saw some sort of farming tool with a wooden handle and a bright, sharp-looking metal head glinting in the moonlight. It looked as though it wanted me to use it.

Aloe stopped as well and looked at me. The moon shone on his face, and I saw very real concern. Worse than that was the seeming understanding that he showed in saying nothing—in giving me the space to think things over.

"Is that," I finally managed, "a condition to being able to come back to Loasht? Working with you at the Ministry, I mean."

"Radiant!" he cried. "Why, Radiant! Of course not! What kind of man do you think I am?"

Thankfully, he was being rhetorical, so I did not have to answer. I began walking again, closer to the fields and that tree with the sharp implement.

"Never. Never in a thousand years," he continued. "I do think you should join the Ministry, of course. For yourself, for me, and for the good of your people. But I would never force you."

"So then, I can simply walk back to Loasht now?"

He smiled. He nodded. But he said, "Well, I'd wait until my diplomatic work here is done."

"Meaning?"

"Radiant, you must understand that I really have put myself in a lot of danger. I have become blessed enough to be able to speak to the Grand Suzerain himself."

"The new Grand Suzerain, as I learned recently."

"The very same! He's actually a bit lenient, as Grand Suzerains go." Aloe shrugged and laughed.

"Aloe, you must understand: I've been gone a long time. What . . . what happened to the *old* Grand Suzerain?"

"Why, he was struck with an apoplexy of some sort. From what I heard, he froze up, he babbled, and then he died."

"Aloe." I decided to allow myself a bit of conspiratorial frankness, in hopes that it would further win his confidence. "Is that the true story?"

He laughed and patted my back roughly. "People always mutter about foul play when a Grand Suzerain dies, even if he does so past ninety. But I'm afraid I never met the last one—it was his successor who was greatly interested in my projects."

"Your projects," I murmured.

"The point is, I got into the new Grand Suzerain's good graces. Whereas past Suzerains were above such things, he became deeply interested in my thoughts on atavistic, non-Loashti ways! But he is young and impetuous—he has no nuance yet—and so moved to cut people off entirely." He shrugged and smiled. "It was a silly choice, but what do you expect? A Grand Suzerain has no normal life experience after all. I've spent the last month jeopardizing my hard-won position by trying to convince him that exiling or imprisoning those who exhibit non-Loashti behaviors isn't the way."

I nodded and walked deeper into the farmlands. They were quiet and empty; I did not even see Lini the cow.

"So then," I murmured, not able to hold up the fake smile any longer, as I stared at the glinting farm tool (whatever it was), "what does that mean for returning to Loasht?"

"It means that once I've done my work here, any Loashti can return home! I suppose you could try now, but our zealous new allies are still checking for Loashti papers. So I'd recommend you wait." He grinned. "When I return home, anyone still stranded down here in the Tetrarchia can come back with me. *As a Loashti.* Not as a Zobiski, not as a shaman, not as some sorcerer or bush healer."

"I . . . What does that *mean*, Aloe?" I didn't mean to show so much confusion, possibly even irritation, but I didn't know how else to respond at this point. "Functionally, what does that mean?"

He positively lit up. He looked excited to tell me. "This was why I went through the trouble, and danger, of advocating directly with the Grand Suzerain! Because I want Loasht to be Loashti. All you, or anyone, need do is stop speaking your imperfect languages, stop carrying on with noisy and useless ceremonies, stop putting trust in things that scratch away at the very bedrock of what makes Loasht *work*." He stepped forward, putting his hand on my shoulder and looking into my eyes. He grinned. He was jubilant. "I just need you to truly become Loashti."

I blinked. My breath quickened. I looked over his shoulder at the farming tool—was it sharp enough? Had I the nerve? The image of the Skydašian commander, Gintaras, staring at me from one blank eye, with

KALYNA THE CUTTHROAT | 195

half of his head gone, appeared in my mind. Could I do something like that to someone? No matter who or why?

"Am I . . . am I not Loashti?" I gulped. I shouldn't have said this, but I couldn't help it.

"Of course you are, Radiant. Being of Zobiski origin *makes you* Loashti." He moved his hand up and held my face, cupping my cheek in his hand, like we were very close friends, or even relatives. "But origins are meant to be left behind. Like childhood. You are one of the most intelligent and gifted people I've ever known, Radiant. This Zobiski business is beneath you."

I felt tears in my eyes and couldn't help letting out the exhalation of one who is about to cry. I was angry. I was hurt. I was beginning to realize that returning to Loasht now would be as difficult as it had been a week ago, if not more so. I thought about Silver, their parents, our friends, our community, and all the Zobiski in Yekunde who weren't lucky enough to have their tormentor think he was their friend—to have him offer them a *job*.

Aloe took my tears as meaning I'd seen the truth in what he'd said. And so he comforted me. He *hugged me*.

"I'm doing this," he said quietly into my ear as he held me in his arms, "because you're proof that so many bright and capable people can come from atavistic origins, if they are only given the chance." The hug tightened. "I want to give them that chance."

"Is that the whole reason?" I muttered. His head was next to mine, his chin on my shoulder as he held me. I very weakly put my arms around him as well.

"No. I'm too selfish to only go through all this trouble for people who theoretically exist. I'm also doing this for you. I knew you were still in the Tetrarchia, and so I risked all my power and influence and threw myself upon the mercy of the Grand Suzerain in order to protect you. Give you a home to come back to, as a *full* Loashti."

"Why?"

He moved back, holding me at arm's length and looking into my eyes. "Because, Radiant, you're the best friend I've ever had. And I've missed you."

I looked at him, I saw the glinting farm tool behind him, I thought about everything that had been said.

I could not kill him. The consequences to my loved ones, and to so many strangers, would be too great. That was what I told myself, anyway. Truly, I don't think I could physically have brought myself to try it. Even to a man like Aloe. I found the thought viscerally unpleasant. Besides, my reaction to danger was always to run.

So, I pictured the face of an actual friend—a non-Zobiski one, in fact: Casaba, back in Yekunde—and managed to smile the way I would have if she had been holding me.

"I missed you too," I said. Tears in my eyes.

Chapter Fourteen

Concerning the Social Undercurrents of the Lanreas River Guild

"You look miserable," said Kalyna.

I nodded intensely. Vociferously.

Aloe Pricks a Mare upon the Mountain Bluff and I had walked back to the Meal Hall together, where Kalyna was loitering with others who were done for the night but couldn't quite bring themselves to leave one another and go to bed. She had smiled warmly, waved me over, and even made small talk with Aloe (in Skydašiavos) before taking me away. It was all a blur to me.

Kalyna had, of course, learned where people in the Lanreas River Guild actually went to imbibe mind-altering substances and spend time together late into the night, and that's where she took me. It wasn't exactly a tavern or public house, and it had no signs out front to advertise itself. The building had originally been intended as a second meal hall, constructed early on, when it was assumed that *everyone* in the Guild would want to eat communally. When it became clear that many would still rather eat in their own homes—homes that were communal in their own way, usually housing multiple families or groups of friends—this second hall instead became the Games Hall. In here, people took part in pursuits that Adomas found ignoble, but would not outlaw: games of cards, marbles, matching, and strategy were played here. Never for money, of course, but Adomas supposedly preferred pastimes that were "edifying" in some way.

Soon enough, it had also become where those who wanted to enjoy wine, poppy milk, khat, or bhang around others spent their evenings, and where coffee could be enjoyed during the day. The Guild did produce wine from its vineyards, but this was mostly for selling to nearby towns and cities, so that the community could buy what they couldn't grow. Some of the wine, however, did make its way to the Games Hall. I wondered whether its consumption there had begun as a furtive secret, before Adomas realized he couldn't just change peoples' habits overnight.

Vidmantas had, apparently, wanted to go to bed more than anything in the world, but Ifeanyas had insisted on seeing that I was all right. He was waiting in the comfortably populated Games Hall when Kalyna brought me there. She then sat me down in a corner, and as Ifeanyas went to get us drinks (I requested wine with bhang mixed in, because it had become that sort of night), she told me I looked miserable.

"Hardly my fault, given the circumstances," I replied.

"It wasn't a criticism, Radiant," admonished Kalyna. "I'm *worried* about you. What happened?"

"Well, I hate him, but I think I convinced him that I'm his friend."

Kalyna put a hand on my shoulder and favored me with one of her brilliant smiles. "I am so *proud* of you, Radiant!" She laughed. "I'm sorry, that makes me sound like I'm your father."

"My father never said anything like that to me."

She sat back. "That's sad."

"Yes."

"He hit you, didn't he? A lot?" She shook her head quickly. "Just a guess. You don't have to answer."

She was trying to distract me from my current troubles by evoking old ones, which were long past, and I allowed her to.

"He did, yes," I said.

"And your mother allowed it?"

"At best."

She nodded. "But it sounds like you removed yourself entirely from them when you could."

"I didn't see a choice," I said.

Ifeanyas returned with our drinks in rough earthenware mugs. They clacked pleasingly against the stone gameboard that made up the center of the otherwise wooden tabletop.

"I, on the other hand," said Kalyna, "continued taking care of Grandmother until the end, even though she was never loving toward me for even a moment of my life." She looked thoughtful. "Well, except one moment, when she was very confused." Kalyna chuckled. "I fantasized about abandoning her, but I never could have done so."

"'Abandon' isn't quite the word, in my case," I said. "Until I went to Quruscan, I still lived a few streets over from my parents. But I didn't visit them, and would spare them only the quickest greeting when our paths crossed."

"That . . . must have been tough?" said Ifeanyas. He looked a little bewildered by the conversation he'd entered.

I smiled at him sadly. "It was surprisingly easy. But then, I had a community and a reliable vocation that gave me the freedom to do so."

"Freedom," grunted Kalyna. "I could never even really consider leaving Grandmother behind."

"But you've left your father in Quruscan, haven't you?" I asked.

"That's different. Just for a month or two, with people I trust. And, well"—she shrugged slightly—"I suppose I've got more 'freedom' now. Money will do that."

The three of us sat in silence for a moment as I took a *long* draught of my wine mixed with bhang.

Then I gave them both the most general outlines of what Aloe had told me.

"So then," said Kalyna, looking at me intently as she leaned forward, elbow on her knee, "will you go back to Loasht?"

Ifeanyas looked incredulous. "At the cost of his—?"

"Stop," snapped Kalyna, cutting across the air with her hand. "He can make his own decision."

"I don't know," I said. "I'm Zobiski and I'm Loashti. I can't imagine leaving either of those behind." I took another long drink: I was going to make sure I slept hard that night (sleeping soundly was unimportant). "And my family is still there."

"Well," said Kalyna, "I've been trying to get you *into* Loasht, so if that's changing, you'll need to let me know."

I looked back down at my drink, holding the mug in both hands. My eyes wandered to the mysterious gameboard on which my drink sat: almost a normal board of uniform squares, but with opalescent veins threaded all through it, glinting and almost undulating in the candlelight. I took this for a feature of the stone until I realized there was something too even about those shimmering lines. I began to wonder if the lines were part of the game, in order to quiet one half of my mind, leaving the other free to grapple with the enormity of the situation my insignificant life had been thrown into.

"I just don't know," I finally said, still staring down. "I hate Aloe and what he's asking of me, but I love my home and my family." I looked up at Kalyna and Ifeanyas. "And if I decide *not* to go back, what do I do then? Stay here? Go somewhere else? What about Silver?"

"Sleep on it, Radiant," said Kalyna. "You only just got here."

Elsewhere in the Games Hall, someone was getting loud in, I think, a friendly way. Others were beginning to leave, even though it couldn't be that late yet; I suppose so they could rise early to their farm work.

"No one is stopping me from returning to Loasht anymore," I said. "So whether I do that or stay here, Kalyna, your work is done. You can go back to Quruscan and your father."

"Sleep on it," she repeated. "You may still need me, my father is fine, and"—she laughed, raising her mug—"everything here is free!"

I could think of no answer. I just continued to stare at the table.

"Ifeanyas," said Kalyna, "would you mind allowing me to talk to Radiant alone?"

"Oh! Now? I rather thought we were . . . ah . . ."

Poor Ifeanyas seemed flustered, as though he'd forgotten he couldn't always melt into the background. I'd always been most attracted to people larger than myself, but I suddenly found short Ifeanyas very handsome as he stammered and looked away. I wondered if it was just because he clearly cared for my well-being, and my upbringing had never taught me how to respond to that in a normal way.

"Ifeanyas," Kalyna said with a simile, "you now see that Radiant is shaken up, but safe, with a large decision ahead of him. If you please."

Ifeanyas apologized quietly and got up to wander through the Games Hall, drink in hand. I felt bad for him.

"You could have been kinder," I said quietly. "He just wants company and doesn't know anyone else here. I don't mind if he hears us discuss what to do next—you said we could trust him."

"I said 'for now.' And *kindness* is not my specialty, unless I want something from someone." She took a sip and tilted her head thoughtfully. "He wouldn't know it, but it shows I respect him, a little, that I don't fawn all over him."

At the other end of the Games Hall, it seemed Ifeanyas had already joined a group of people and was nodding along to a lively conversation. I hoped this meant there was a future for him here. He was now more adrift than I, wasn't he?

"I've learned a bit more about this place, if that will help you make your decision," said Kalyna with a twinkle in her eye as she sat back in her chair.

"That's wonderful," I sighed, drinking more of my own drug-laced wine. "I'm sure I'll remember it all perfectly tomorrow."

"I'm sure," she deadpanned. "So, decades ago, Adomas the noble steals specimens, hunts on royal grounds, carries out forbidden research, and generally flits around the Tetrarchia to stay ahead of the law, because he is *extremely* outlawed. He writes a number of books and pamphlets, mostly covering what he's discovered and making excuses for his crimes—insists that the people he steals from are dabblers, hoarders, or fools who don't know the importance of what they have." She laughed. "I first learned of him from a Masovskani book called *Bohdan's Botanicals*. Poor Bohdan was no fool or dabbler, and he absolutely hated Adomas. But I think Adomas has outlived him now."

I realized I had forgotten about Aloe for a moment, and also that the wine, or the bhang, or the exhaustion, was hitting my brain. I set my mug down on the table to stop myself from flying too high.

"What I've learned today," Kalyna continued, "is that all was forgiven around ten years ago, when Adomas used a tincture he'd devised to save the life of an ailing King Piliranas, father of Skydašiai's current King Alinafe." She grinned. "What a coup for a disgraced naturalist! I wonder if he poisoned the King in the first place."

"Is that what you would've done?"

"Probably! But I don't hold the lives of royalty particularly dear. I hope that doesn't offend your Loashti sensibilities."

"Not at the moment, no."

"So," she continued, after another sip, "while he couldn't be returned to his former titles, Adomas was fully pardoned and given back just this land, which his family didn't want anyway, due to it being bad for farming and next door to Loasht. The Estate was already crumbling by then."

"But the land seems quite agreeable for farming."

"Yes. I haven't figured out yet what changed that. Point is, with the land being 'distasteful,' and with the King feeling extremely generous, Adomas was able to negotiate a sort of charter that said the Yams could never set foot in his domain. He also willed the whole plot to the Guild members, collectively."

"Can he do that?"

"I don't know, he hasn't died yet. It sounds quite inviolate on the surface, but all things are tenuous. Old King Piliranas died some five years ago now, and I've picked up on at least a few worries that his son will back out of the agreement." She shrugged. "So you may be as safe here as anywhere, or you may not. Very hard to say."

I sighed and picked my mug back up, draining it. Let my head fly into the stars; I certainly didn't want to be here anymore. I knew that, sometimes, bhang could strengthen feelings of paranoia in me, but I hoped I'd fall asleep first.

Unfortunately, that was when some sort of conflict broke out. I heard yelling, some of it outside, and saw quick movement by the door of the Games Hall. I felt that fear, that paranoia, *spike* into me, impale me. My hands began to shake, and my mug slipped from my hands.

Kalyna caught it, spilling a bit from her own in the process. "Stay here," she sighed, putting both mugs on the table and standing up.

What was I even scared of? Skydašiai rounding up Loashti aliens *now* seemed unlikely. Perhaps I simply wanted the Lanreas River Guild to remain as friendly as it had appeared so far. I worried that I'd found a lovely little place, which had now been destabilized and ruined by Aloe's arrival there, even though that made no sense.

Then I suddenly felt, in my befogged mind, that I had to know what was going on. So I got up and, shakily, followed Kalyna.

A group of people crowded around the entryway to the Games Hall, murmuring angrily as Žydrė stood in the doorway, arguing with some-body who was outside. I thought I had seen Žydrė argue—thought I had seen her angry—in her many exchanges with Vidmantas, but this was different. She was at the door, pushing her head out through it, and *yelling*, her voice cracking.

Kalyna was moving through the crowd toward her, while I circled its outer edges and found Ifeanyas, who was staring at the commotion. Now I, too, could see over Žydrė's shoulder to the lane outside. She was yelling at Yalwas, the large man who had greeted us when we arrived earlier that afternoon (by the Eighty-Three, what a long day!), and had shown us around the Estate. He looked entirely calm: opening his mouth to speak, then stopping and looking irritated but patient as he waited for Žydrė to finish. I couldn't make out what she was saying as I was still pulling myself down from the stars.

"It is none of my business," Yalwas finally said, with a stern sort of look on his face, "how you all choose to poison your bodies and minds, but—"

Someone nearer to me groaned and threw up their hands. Žydrė nodded.

"*But*," Yalwas continued, "it *is* my business when it involves my son. Bring him out. He's only sixteen, and he's going home."

I saw a tall figure, head down, start to move toward the door. Žydrė threw out an arm in front of that figure.

"He's old enough to work in the fields," she growled, "so I think he's old enough to have a small drink at the end of a hard day. None of us will let him overindulge."

"Why would I trust that?"

"It's funny," said Žydrė in a quieter, icier, tone, "how you can be so sanctimonious about *some* of Adomas' teachings, but not others."

Yalwas growled and put a large hand on his hip, staring daggers at her and at anyone else he could see. Indiscriminate eye daggers everywhere. (I suppose my thoughts were still flying, just a little.)

"What teachings, pray tell, am I ignoring?" he huffed. "Adomas does not, for *some reason*, outlaw this behavior, although he does strongly discourage it. I am not here to stop your good time."

Someone in the back began to yell, and Žydrė waved an arm at them, willing them to be quiet.

"Adomas also does not, 'for *some reason*,'" she added, mockingly, "outlaw adults from feeling that they have complete dominion over their . . . their offspring. But he does strongly discourage it, doesn't he? Says that we should all raise *our* children together. Many people in here have cared for Kyautas for most of his life, haven't we?"

Voices rose in agreement, and she shushed them again.

"And we," she continued, "would rather he have a drink or two in safety, with us, than sneak too much out in the fields alone, or only with other children."

"That is not your decision," Yalwas seethed. He took a step forward, and I could really see how much larger than her he was. "A father still has some rights."

"Does he?" asked Žydrė. "More than the many other mothers and fathers in here? Does he have 'rights' purely because he *squirted the boy out*?"

Žydrė, I was realizing, had been quite restrained and friendly in her arguments with Vidmantas.

Yalwas opened his mouth, but Žydrė interrupted him: "We have separated parents and children before, when those parents proved to be tyrants."

"Tyrant?!" cried Yalwas. "I have never beaten my Kyautas, never forbidden him from—"

"It's only an example," interrupted Žydrė. "No one is looking to separate you from him."

"Then send him out to me!"

"What if he doesn't wish to go?"

"Well, then—" Yalwas' eyes suddenly widened, and he pointed inside, past Žydrė. "Wait, you! Foreigner! What did you just give my son?!"

He was pointing at Kalyna, who was seated on a bench close to the tall figure that must have been the boy, Kyautas, but far back enough that Yalwas could also see her. She was leaning forward, one hand out toward the boy. Kyautas' head had been bowed the whole time, but he somehow lowered it even more. In his hand was a mug, which he began to lower.

Kalyna sat back up straight, slowly, and turned her head to face Yalwas.

"Water," she said, calmly, but loud enough for all to hear. "With a drop of something I keep on me to aid with hangovers."

"A drop of what?" snapped the large man.

Kalyna sighed. "*Terrifying* and *foreign* ginger."

Some of the others began to murmur and giggle. I suppose, in that crowd, picking on Yalwas was an easy way to become popular.

"It can help," she shrugged. "Although, more than anything, it's an enticement to drink the water. Shall I take it back from him?"

There was silence for a moment. I only saw Žydrė's back, but her body language suggested smugness. Kalyna's showed none, only weariness.

"Drink that down, Kyautas," said Yalwas, finally.

"Why don't you apologize for insulting our guest, Yalwas?" asked Žydrė.

Yalwas grumbled somewhere in his throat.

"Well?" prodded Žydrė. "Go on! You called her a foreigner and accused her, after all."

Kalyna sighed. "Well, *now* he won't, will he?" She slapped her knees and stood creakily. "If you actually wanted him to apologize, you wouldn't have goaded him like that." Kalyna shrugged, glanced at Yalwas, then back at Žydrė. "But you preferred to use me as a bludgeon."

Žydrė stared at Kalyna, unsure of what to say. She seemed as though someone had thrown cold water on her.

"Well," Kalyna continued, "better me than Kyautas. He's had enough of that for one night, hasn't he?"

Kyautas, in a sort of reply, finished his water and handed Kalyna back the empty mug.

"Thank you, ah . . ." The boy's voice was deeper than his father's.

"My name's Kalyna," she replied, looking back at the boy and smiling broadly. "Just a few letters different from yours."

Kyautas nodded. Then he walked past her out toward his father. The two left without a word.

Everyone began to murmur and either spread back out through the Games Hall, or leave for the night. Kalyna smiled at Žydrė with utter friendliness and said goodnight, which Žydrė quietly grunted in return. I was more effusive to Žydrė, before trotting off after Kalyna.

"Obviously you wanted him to see you handing the boy the mug," I said as we walked toward our dormitory. "I've seen enough of your work to know that."

206 | ELIJAH KINCH SPECTOR

"I'm honored you've noticed."

"I assume you wanted to defuse things, give the poor, embarrassed boy a way out, and an easier morning."

She nodded.

"Knowing you, this was not out of care for the boy, so much as it was to make the locals *think* you're the type of person to care about the boy."

"Now hold on," she laughed. "I would say it was about half and half."

"But why did you decide to make both Yalwas *and* Žydrė look bad in front of everyone? Just for fun?"

"If it was for fun, I'd be bothering much more powerful people than those two, Radiant." She yawned. "They already made themselves look bad in front of everyone, but 'everyone' was too scared to say anything. I stepped in and became the blunt outsider who isn't caught up in the daft politics of this squalid fools' paradise. I assure you that many of the people who saw that exchange, and many who will hear about it tomorrow, will admire me for helping the boy, and for cutting those two bores to the quick."

"But after what Žydrė did for us . . ."

"If she believes half of what Adomas spews, she will forgive me."

"But what's the point? Why do you need these people to admire you?"

She stopped. We were right outside our dormitory building, and though we were speaking in Loashti Bureaucratic, she still lowered her voice. Perhaps it was so she wouldn't wake anyone inside.

"Because you haven't decided exactly what you—and, therefore, we—are going to do next, have you? Always good to build up a little social capital, just in case."

Sure enough, the next morning I awoke to Žydrė apologizing to Kalyna.

"You were absolutely right," Žydrė was saying as I blinked and re-membered where I was, "I was using you as a . . . bludgeon to bother Yalwas. It was unfair of me, and I'm sorry."

Nicely folded bundles of undyed linen clothes had been left for each of us newcomers in what were, at least vaguely, our sizes. Kalyna was al-ready fully dressed in one such pair of billowing trousers, but had paired it with a fading purple blouse that must have come from her bag, and the same pair of boots that she'd worn every day I'd known her. She was standing, leaning back against her bed, with her arms crossed and her face noncommittal, listening to Žydrė.

Vidmantas and Ifeanyas seemed to have only been awake a minute or two longer than me, and were both still in their beds. Each one was sitting up and watching what was happening, blinking the sleep from their eyes. Ifeanyas had on a sort of long linen shirt he was using as a nightgown. Vidmantas' hair was a mess, with his beautiful ringlets crushed in every direction. But stripped to the waist, I must say he was well shaped: almost delicate, as I used to be.

"Why, Žydrė," laughed Vidmantas, "I've never heard you apologize before!"

"Because when I'm talking to *you*, I'm always right," she snapped.

Vidmantas smiled and raised his eyebrows at Ifeanyas and me.

"What *did* you all get up to last night?" he asked.

"I'll tell you later," said Ifeanyas.

Kalyna, meanwhile, had reacted to none of this and, indeed, said nothing. She continued to look at Žydrė with an expression of appraisal.

"And," Žydrė continued, "I'm sorry that—" She stopped, seemed thoughtful for a moment, and then shook her head. "No. No, I shouldn't apologize for what Yalwas said to you. I am not him, and that would mean nothing."

Kalyna didn't change her expression but nodded slightly. She let the silence draw out until Žydrė felt the need to speak again.

"I hope you understand," Žydrė dutifully continued, "that yes, I'd had a few drinks—"

Kalyna made the slightest shrug and nod.

"—but that wasn't really why I acted that way. Not completely."

Kalyna cocked her head to the side, smiled very slightly, and finally spoke: "Of course, Žydrė. After all, *I* am not Yalwas."

Žydrė smiled widely in response. "Of course. Of course. But you weren't here for the larger context. That man has been making my life difficult for so long. It wasn't entirely about Kyautas either, although I did not say anything I didn't mean."

"I assumed as much," replied Kalyna. "But what is that context?"

Still on my back, with the covers pulled up to my neck, I looked around and began to wonder where I was supposed to change.

The Tetrarchia was, in my experience, prudish about a lot of things. But then, I'd spent most of my time in Quruscan and knew little of Skydašian mores. Not to mention, of course, that the Lanreas River Guild strove to be culturally separate from Skydašiai, to some extent.

Žydrė took a deep breath and rolled her eyes. "Yalwas and I have, really, never gotten along. But in the past few months, I've felt as though he is always picking at me. So perhaps I chose that opportunity to, you know, pick back."

"Never, you say?" Kalyna finally uncrossed her arms and now seemed more interested in what Žydrė was saying. "Different interpretations of Adomas' teachings, perhaps?"

"Oh yes, from the start." Žydrė waved her hand as though she were saying something blitheringly obvious. "And you must understand, Yalwas and I have both been with Adomas *from the start.*" Feeling more comfortable now, Žydrė began to walk idly around the large, mostly empty dormitory as she spoke. "You see, we were both working here when Adomas had his epiphany about humanity's natural state, and when he turned his old family home into what it has become. Yalwas"—she rolled her eyes—"was one of Adomas' assistants in his studies. *I* worked the fields."

"You worked the fields for Adomas before he stopped acting like a lord?"

Žydrė nodded. "I was young, with no trade, and had to leave Žalikwen in a hurry. I ended up here, and I'm glad I did."

"Didn't that ever make you, I don't know, resent Adomas?" Kalyna now seemed to be fully engaged in the conversation, leaning forward and following Žydrė with her eyes, as the other woman walked about the room. If I didn't know better, I would have seen Kalyna as supplicant—almost desperate.

Žydrė stopped pacing for a moment and looked up at the ceiling. "You know," she said, "yes. At first. When he began talking to us about all of his big ideas, I found it annoying and presumptuous."

"He must have gone from ordering you about one day, to suddenly being your 'friend' the next."

"Well, *that* was back when he wanted us all to be 'brothers and sisters.'" She laughed at the memory of it. "But, over time, I came to realize he meant what he said."

"And Yalwas?" asked Kalyna.

"Yalwas was right behind Adomas from the beginning. He had been hired from some nearby town while Adomas was on his way here. He was formally educated and has less experience of the world. I think sometimes he still doesn't understand why Adomas doesn't force us all to live 'perfectly.'"

"I see." Kalyna plopped down loudly onto her bed, scratching her chin. "So, he may think he has more *right* to Adomas' ideas than you do."

"Well, that's stupid," Žydrė sneered. "Adomas' *ideas* weren't meant for people like Yalwas. They were meant for those like me, who've toiled in the fields."

"You don't exactly come from a line of farmers, Žydrė," Vidmantas chimed in.

"Vidmantas, the adults are speaking," snapped Žydrė.

"She's only five years older than me," Vidmantas mumbled to the rest of us.

"But," said Kalyna, almost to herself, "I can see why Yalwas might think he has . . . primacy." Then she looked up at Žydrė. "Has Adomas been sickly lately?"

"Sickly? No, not at all. He's old of course, but . . ." Žydrė stopped and then sat down on the bed opposite Kalyna's, leaning forward. "Do you mean to suggest Yalwas is looking ahead to when Adomas is . . . ?"

"Dead, yes." Kalyna crossed one leg over the other. "I wouldn't be surprised if he wants to take Adomas' place when the old man finally . . . you know. So he may see you as his competition."

Žydrė laughed. "Me?"

"Well, of course! Who else would be a challenge to him?" Kalyna grinned. "Has taking over leadership after Adomas really not occurred to you?"

"I must say, it hasn't," Žydrė replied, wide-eyed.

At about this time, I decided I needed to get out of bed, no matter the taboos of this place and whatever conversations were happening around me. I had undergarments on, at least (in fact, they were the only piece of Loashti clothing I still possessed), so I simply stood up.

Vidmantas made a whistling, impressed noise, and at first, I must say, I felt quite complimented, until I realized what he was reacting to.

"By the gods, Radiant, I didn't know your tattoos were so intricate!" he cried. "Incredible."

"Oh. Well. Yes," I mumbled. (Although I did flex, just a little. The long road with Kalyna and Dagmar had filled me out pleasingly.) "I mean, thank you! Not that I drew them, of course."

"But I assume you picked them," said Ifeanyas. "Are those men with crocodile heads?"

"I . . . no. Where I'm from, we have a variety of crocodile that walks, you know, upright. Mostly upright, sort of stooped. I'm sure Adomas can tell you more than I can."

"Terrifying," Vidmantas laughed. "Why did you want those on your arms?"

"That's . . . both very complicated and very simple."

I got dressed, and no one seemed scandalized. I put on billowy trousers and a blouse of undyed, but soft and comfortable, linen. Vidmantas did the same. He tore off a large strip of silk from the tattered remains of his old robe and wrapped it around his disordered hair until it was mostly covered. Ifeanyas got up as well and began to do some stretches.

"Well," said Kalyna, "I suppose Radiant had better see his Loashti friend off, yes?"

Žydrė nodded. I realized what Kalyna meant and suddenly wanted to get back into bed.

Žydrė exchanged some parting words with Kalyna—as well as a strong pat on the shoulder—and left. Kalyna immediately turned to me.

"No," she said.

"No, what?"

"You *are* going to go out there and say goodbye to Aloe," she ordered.

I slumped back onto my bed. "Haven't I done *enough?*"

Kalyna walked over and stood above me, glaring down. She seemed to take up the whole room.

"No, you haven't," she replied. "You don't even understand the *beginning* of doing enough."

I must have looked mystified.

"What's going on?" asked Vidmantas.

Kalyna turned to him. Ifeanyas immediately jumped in before she said anything.

"Later," said Ifeanyas. "Later. Later."

Kalyna looked back at me, hands on her hips. "Radiant," she said, "I swear by every god—by your Eighty-Three, and the thousand more we have here in the Tetrarchia—that no matter *what* you choose to do next, it will be made easier by ensuring Aloe thinks of you as a friend. Whether you decide to go back, stay here, or do something else entirely, taking a few *scant uncomfortable minutes* out of your life to smile at Aloe and wish him well will help you immeasurably someday. It may save your life. And that of your family."

I shook my head. I looked down. "I just can't."

Kalyna Aljosanovna slapped me. Hard.

There was silence for a moment.

"Now hold on," said Vidmantas, stepping toward Kalyna. "I don't know what's going on here but—"

"You certainly don't," said Kalyna.

I looked up at her, and I think I was crying—willing her to see how much anguish I was feeling.

She saw it. And she slapped me again. I cried out that time.

"Stop that!" shouted Vidmantas.

Ifeanyas grabbed Kalyna's wrist, although he looked unsure of whether he'd be strong enough to stop her.

"I may barely understand what's happening here," he said. "But don't hit him again."

"Not even to save his life?" she spat.

"Does it look like it's helping?" cried Vidmantas.

I was sitting quietly, staring at the floor, quivering.

Kalyna was silent for a moment. Then I heard her breathe out slowly, and when she next spoke, her voice was lower, calmer.

"No, it isn't helping," she said. "Look, Radiant, I know it hurts. I know it's hard. Believe me, I do." Looking up at her, I saw what seemed to be real pain, frustration, and worry come into her face. "But you, and likely your family, will be so much better off this way. Do you understand me?"

I nodded.

She turned to Ifeanyas and patted his hand lightly. "I won't hit him again."

Ifeanyas narrowed his eyes and nodded once, sharply. Before he could let go, she slid her hand easily out of his, perhaps to let him know she could have done so at any time. Ifeanyas continued to look hard at her as he began wiggling into trousers under his nightshirt.

Kalyna stepped back, looked at me, smiled, and pointed to the door.

"Now go make that worthless sack of shit love you."

It was midmorning, and Aloe was making his goodbyes in Skydašiavos to a small throng of people. His escorting soldiers were still waiting politely outside of the Lanreas River Guild, and so he made a good show of being trusting and trustworthy, a man of the people. Except, of course, for the glittering cape he still wore, which was brilliant in the sunlight.

Before he saw me, I murmured a little Zobiski incantation to myself: "May he amount to no more than this." Then I spat on the ground.

You see, this is often how sorcery works, or doesn't work. Did I actually place a light curse on him and slightly diminish his confidence and standing in the world, allowing me to have some advantage in our upcoming interaction? Or had I simply convinced myself that I was above him, for a moment? Did it matter?

Aloe's face lit up as I walked closer. Even with his cape, he did not seem quite as imposing in the daylight as he had the night before. Like myself, he was shorter than most of the people around us.

"Ah, Radiant!" he called to me in Loashti Bureaucratic. "So good to see you before I leave. Of course, you'll be back home soon enough. I'm on my way to see that it's done."

I forced myself, for a moment, to believe that this was true: to believe I would be able to go home easily very soon. Specifically, to a home that I recognized and which would be safe for me. This got me to smile. Then I gave Aloe Pricks a Mare upon the Mountain Bluff a big, tight hug.

"Safe travels," I said as I hoped he would be eaten by wolves.

He patted my back heartily before breaking the hug. "And to you as well, soon enough!"

Then he stepped back and looked at the other people around him and spoke loudly in Skydašiavos: "Lanreas! Thank you for watching over my friend, while so many in the Tetrarchia have been cruel to him. It warms my heart."

He turned in a circle slowly, making sure that all present heard his voice, and that almost everyone had him look them right in the eye for at least a moment.

"What a wonderful place you've built here, and on such strong ideals. Your Guild, like my own movement back home, is looking ahead to a better future, free of the constraints of backward, ingrained thinking.

Know that I appreciate our similarities, and that I will be back on my return trip to Loasht."

There was a general murmuring of approval.

"As soon as I can, Radiant!" he said in Loashti Bureaucratic.

I wiped a tear of despair but smiled as though it was one of happiness.

Aloe waved goodbye and began to walk way. Then I had a thought, and I called out to him.

"Aloe!"

He turned back. "Yes?"

"I'd be *delighted* to join you at the Ministry!"

He grinned broadly and left with an actual spring in his step.

I didn't yet know where I was going to go, or what I would do, but I knew one thing for certain: that outburst had been a lie. I would never join the Ministry. But I'd done what Kalyna told me to do: I'd made him love me.

My Trysts with The Fog Flees When the Phoenix Flaps Its Wings

The Fog Flees When the Phoenix Flaps Its Wings always complained about his parents not naming him The Phoenix Flaps Its Wings to Send the Fog Running, or something similar. He resented everyone referring to him as Fog, rather than as Phoenix.

"But Fog is a sweeter name," I told him once, when he was complaining about this as we lay together, naked and sweating, on the floor of his office at the Academy (because it was larger than mine). "If you were called Phoenix, I might have been too intimidated to proposition you."

"We both know you wouldn't be," he said, lying on his back and looking up at nothing. It was too dark for me to see his face, so I wasn't sure how exactly he meant that (admittedly true) statement.

I remained draped over his much larger frame and chattered a bit, trying to get his mind off his name, which was perfectly fine, and wondering whether he was done for the night. This was how it went with Fog: a lot of excitingly flirtatious and frank discussions building up to a fun time together, followed by the reminder that, on any other topic of conversation, we always spoke *past* one another.

Silver often asked me, "How can you keep fucking someone you can't hold a conversation with?" They were never jealous, but they sometimes didn't understand my tastes. This was because Silver had an unending supply of love, while I possessed a bottomless need to be desired.

Fog was only a few years older than me and in an entirely unrelated field of study (something related to crop cycles, I think it was?), so I didn't see how a tryst here and there could be much trouble. Until, eventually, I decided the irritations outweighed the pleasures. We'd had some very fun times, but I simply felt the two of us were too ill-attuned to continue. I *thought* I communicated this well, and kindly, but he clearly disagreed.

You must understand: Just because Yekunde didn't have the taboos of the Tetrarchic kingdoms, that doesn't mean it didn't have any of its own. Loasht's long history of many different peoples all attempting—to different degrees in different epochs—to become Loashti enough, or to not become too Loashti, meant that we really had a thousand different intertwining systems of mores. Many of these had been forgotten or foresworn, but remained as a palimpsest, scratched in deep somewhere beneath our daily lives.

All of which is to say that Fog, who had never before made any emotional request of me, suddenly felt I was duty-bound to sit still and listen to him shout. Having me end our dalliance meant that he could now tell me *everything* he did not like about me, and everything he felt I'd done wrong, in order to show that he was at fault for nothing. As though I cared at all about *fault*.

So I began to come in for a harangue whenever I would see Fog in the hallways and courtyards and even libraries of the Yekunde branch of the academy—the location only affected his volume. It was terrible. He never physically threatened me, but he was quite large, and when a man of that size continues to corner you and tell you how he hates you, you begin to wonder what else he might do. Or at least I did. It came to such a point that I would hide in Casaba's office whenever possible. She tried, more than once, to talk Fog down, but he wasn't interested.

Soon enough, nearly every evening, Silver would say, "This is too much. I'm going in with you."

I would beg them not to, worrying that any argument, or the simple act of putting their body between Fog's and mine, would be seen as violence, as Zobiski "savagery."

One day, when I was shaking uncontrollably on my way through the halls, I saw Fog moving toward me with great purpose. I ran for the first door I recognized: the office of Aloe Pricks a Mare upon the Mountain Bluff. We'd only known each other for a year, but had already gotten into one drunken, late-night debate, and become (so I thought) mildly friendly.

"Why, Radiant! What brings you here?" asked Aloe, as he looked up from whatever he'd been studying. "Are you all right?"

I pressed my back to his wall, breathing heavily. Wincing in preparation for, I was sure, some great violence to be done upon his door.

"Just, just let me stay here a few minutes," I stammered. "Fog is out there and he—"

"Oh?" Aloe stood up, walking around the desk to me. "What about him? I thought you two, you know, got on?"

"Not anymore."

"Well," Aloe replied mildly, "that's a shame."

And that was when the pounding started. I fell to the floor, knees to my chest, shaking. Aloe heard some of the obscene and insulting things Fog was saying through the door and furrowed his brow in consternation, looking down at me. I stared back at him but did nothing else. The violent sound of Fog's fists against the door continued.

I almost shouted, *No!* when Aloe opened his door. From where I was, Fog seemed to truly tower over Aloe, who gazed up at him calmly. Was Aloe brave, I wondered, or had he never really been in danger before?

"Why are you beating at my door like a savage?" he asked Fog. "I heard you the first time, but I was busy. Is there a problem?"

"*I'm* not the savage here, Aloe, it's the little Zobiski slut who—"

Aloe slapped Fog in the face.

"And yet," he said, "you're the one making a fool of yourself in the very halls of the Academy."

"I—!"

Aloe slapped him again.

"And based on what?" Aloe continued, absolutely calm. "Outmoded beliefs as backward as anything a 'Zobiski slut' has ever done?"

"Outmoded—!"

Another slap. (In my memory, Aloe had to get up on his toes to slap Fog, but that probably wasn't the case.)

"A thousand years ago," said Aloe, "Central Loashti believed that only men could end a relationship. Radiant is, of course, also a man, but you probably consider yourself *more of one*, don't you?"

Fog looked like he wanted to say something, but had begun to realize he should perhaps watch himself around a Central Loashti from a good, and old, family. Aloe narrowed his eyes and waited, nodding when the larger man stayed silent.

"Your mother's Lilikri, isn't she?" Aloe continued. "On her mother's side?"

Fog didn't answer.

"She is," continued Aloe. "Until a few hundred years ago, Lilikri people privileged the rights of the"—he cleared his throat—"penetrator, didn't they?"

"I don't know," said Fog.

"Of course you don't. These and a thousand base urges and ancient superstitions course through you with no context, no thought at all." Aloe cocked his head to the side. "Aren't you ashamed of yourself?"

"I'm sorry," said Fog.

"Say it to him."

Fog bit his lips and stooped toward me in contrition, but simmering rage danced in his eyes. He opened his mouth to apologize.

Aloe slapped him *again*.

"I am not stupid," said Aloe. "And you are not subtle. Apologize and mean it, or leave and disgrace yourself."

Fog did the latter, turning on his heel and disappearing.

Aloe helped me up, shaking his head and smiling. "You see, Radiant, you simply must stand up to people like that."

In that moment, I was just so relieved that I only smiled and nodded. Thanking him profusely and thinking nothing of why his approach had worked, or the things he had said, until much later.

Over the next few days, it became clear Fog had ended his campaign against me. Whether Aloe had any further words with him, I don't know; I never saw much of Fog around the Academy after that, and I was happy for it.

In hindsight, I wonder if this was the beginning of Aloe considering himself to be my good friend, or if that misconception had already taken root and was why he defended me. I'm not sure which answer I like less.

Chapter Fifteen

How I Came Upon an Outlandish Plan

As soon as the small crowd that had formed around Aloe dispersed, Kalyna came up to me, smiled, and put a hand on my shoulder.

"Good job, Radiant," she said. "And I'm sorry about earlier. But I needed to get through to you how important—"

"I know." I stood in silence for a moment, looking at her: the smile, the evident sincerity, the comforting hand on my shoulder. Then I added, "I don't know that I accept your apology."

She nodded and removed her hand. "That's fair. But you did well, nonetheless. Your promise to work with him at the Ministry was particularly inspired. It's what I would've done!"

I clicked my tongue thoughtfully. "I think that in making that promise, I have only put myself in more danger."

"Why's that?"

"Because it was a lie, of course. And now if I do go back to Loasht, I will either have to live up to it or risk Aloe's wrath."

Kalyna put her hands on her hips and cocked her head to the side, looking puzzled.

"What do you mean, if you go back?" she asked.

"Well, I still haven't decided."

"Can you live the rest of your life as Aloe's *best friend of Zobiski origin?*"

"Well, I . . ." I stopped and glared at her. "Didn't you just say last night that I had to make my own decision?"

"I did. And you have."

"What—?"

"You made the decision while you were talking to Aloe; I saw it on your face. And you cemented it by making that false promise. You may not have realized it yet, but I promise you, it's the truth."

Was it? I put my head in my hands and tried to think, tried to figure out what exactly I was feeling. Was Kalyna that good at reading me? Or was she manipulating me to stay and making me think it was my idea? But then, why would it matter to her, ultimately, what I decided?

"If you don't want to help me anymore," I said, "you can just stop. You don't need to convince me it's what I want."

"That's not it at all. Your bones know you aren't going back—your sinews and tendons and guts. They've all already made the decision. It's just your brain, which is too smart for its own good, that's holding out."

"Perhaps."

Did I feel it in my bones? I was certainly feeling something deeply. The thought of returning to Loasht, which had been my goal, felt curdled now.

"Just try saying it out loud," she said. "Saying it and imagining it."

"If I . . . don't go back to Loasht, will that mean you're done helping me?"

"Gods, no! I'll bring Silver to you first. They *are* the reason you won't admit you don't want to go back, aren't they?"

"Perhaps," I said again. "You really think you can get them out of Loasht?"

"Of course I can."

She sounded so sure of herself, it was almost unnerving.

"What *exactly* did you and Dagmar do in Rotfelsen?" I asked.

"Killed some people, saved some people." Kalyna shrugged. "I admit she did more of the killing, but I think it's fair to say I did all the saving."

It was hard not to be swayed by her confidence, I must admit.

"Anyway," she said, "extracting Silver *and* their parents, yes? I think that could be done." She smiled darkly. "Not your parents, I assume."

I didn't answer her. I did not want to be around my parents, but neither did I want them to die, or be imprisoned, or face . . . whatever Aloe had planned that would make us "more" Loashti. Not because they were my parents, but simply because they were, also, Zobiski. Part of the dwindling Zobiski community that had stayed stubbornly in our ancestral Yekunde. Certainly, having Silver and their parents here with me would strengthen my desire to never return, but would that be enough? What about my community? I couldn't very well ask Kalyna to save every Zobiski in Yekunde. Could I?

Just a scant few days earlier, finding a way home had been my aim, and it had felt *possible*. But what now? What was happening to Silver in this moment? Or their parents? Was Casaba, my old friend, defending the Zobiski in her midst or turning a blind eye? What could I possibly do to help them? What could I do to help myself? Was I being a selfish coward if I did not go back? What could I possibly do if I did? I thought of my home, and I thought of Aloe, and then I knew.

"Damn it," I sighed. "You're right. I can't go back. Not to Loasht as it is now. Maybe someday, but not now."

"You've made the right choice." Kalyna stretched her arms upward, groaning with the movement. "It seems your family is safe for the time being, so I'll keep ingratiating myself with these people and figure out how they can be made useful to us."

She left, and I stood in the middle of the village, staring at nothing. I had done it. I had successfully lied to Kalyna Aljosanovna. I even felt a little thrill run through me, a warmth and a clarity. Was this how she felt all the time?

Granted, it had been a lie of omission, but I was still proud of myself. It was true I wouldn't go back to Yekunde, but accepting that fact had caused a great rupture in my conception of what was possible and what was not. Greater even than Kalyna, with all her confidence, had intended.

If I was to stay, Silver needed to be here. So did their parents. So did Silver's friends and lovers. So did mine. My parents too. And if my parents got to be saved, shouldn't everyone else?

Kalyna would simply have to bring every Zobiski in Yekunde to the Lanreas River Guild.

Unsurprisingly, I was quite delirious when I hit upon my plan, and I stayed so for the next few days. I floated through them in a daze of questions. How to do it? How to convince her? How to stop worrying that I might have gone mad and accept that I had definitely done so?

The knowledge that I would not return to Loasht began to bear down upon me. How could I survive not seeing the swamps and the buildings, and the scholars and the lazy crocodiles of Yekunde? How much of all that could I live without? What about the people I loved and liked who were not Zobiski? Even if we did this impossible thing, what about all of the Zobiski who had been forced out of Yekunde over the centuries? To its surrounding areas, and to the rest of Loasht? What of all the other peoples, across Loasht, whom we could not help?

The faces of those from the Žalikwen Salon who didn't make it to our boat often flashed through my mind as I wrestled with these question. Those people were, surely, now in the Goddess' Guts, while I had food, company, and the freedom to consider my next ridiculous and asinine move.

Ifeanyas quickly and easily threw himself into the life of the Lanreas River Guild. He seemed to enjoy working in the fields. Or, more accurately, he enjoyed the feeling of being *done* working in the fields for the day.

"Bone tired," he explained to me in the Meal Hall, "with no mind or body left over for constant, debilitating worry. No lord taking most of what we grow, so there's no frustration and anger at the end of it." He giggled to himself. "Well, for me anyway. For now, while it's new."

"Were you in constant, debilitating worry before?" I managed to ask, as my own thoughts were overrun with much the same.

"Oh my, yes! And, well, you see? I'm tired and content enough that I don't mind telling you that." He laughed and pounded the table, then seemed meekly surprised at just how loud and jarring it had been. "Perhaps I'm not so carefree just yet," he allowed, "but regardless, I have a delicious meal ahead of me, followed by a pleasant night in the Games Hall, and then deep, unbothered sleep."

"That does sound lovely. I can't say I've had the same." I felt that my eyes were burning from lack of restful sleep. "But how do you feel about the Guild's beliefs? Adomas' . . . experiment within an experiment?"

Ifeanyas leaned forward, lowering his voice and taking me into his confidence. "Radiant, I hate to admit this, but just now? I couldn't care less." He looked around, perhaps to make sure Vidmantas, Žydrė, or other deep thinkers weren't nearby. "I'm sure the philosophies buttressing this place have something to do with why I find it so agreeable, but my day-to-day concerns are such that I haven't the space for contemplation." He grinned furtively. "It's *glorious*."

I wondered how many others at the Guild felt similarly to Ifeanyas—felt that whatever Adomas' philosophy, they'd found a place to eat well, busy themselves, and be safe from the Yams (or whomever else). I didn't feel particularly safe, but I *did* feel guilty about how much better things were for me here than they probably were for many.

In contrast, Vidmantas did a great amount of talking about the Guild's beliefs and philosophies: sometimes criticizing, sometimes questioning, and sometimes seeming genuinely impressed. He and Žydrė still sparred, of course, but it was even clearer now that they were indeed friends; each one's strong opinions and propensity to argue formed and strengthened in the crucible of their combative relationship.

"Žydrė practically lived in my home when we were children," Vidmantas said to me one night in the Games Hall when he was quite drunk and unusually sentimental. "Her home was . . . bad, even before the fire wiped it out and made her an orphan. So, being a bit older than me, she helped my beleaguered parents raise me, and, in return, I shared with her what I was learning from the *prestigious* education that was running my parents ragged."

"Really? Even as a child you saw it as something you were doing 'in return'?"

"Ha! No, of course not. I just wanted someone else to talk to about it. And argue with, yes, I'll say it before you do." He took another sip, and then his smile faded slowly. "Don't tell her I said it, but I was devastated when she left Žalikwen. She was nearing twenty, and I was in the middle teens, and if you think we fight *now*"—a distant smile—"you should have seen us at that age."

I smiled as well. I remembered friends I'd argued with at that age, although none with whom I'd still been close a decade later. But then, close or no, what was happening to them *now*?

"But," he sighed, "Žydrė got into some trouble. Nothing too exciting: just another young, tradeless orphan trying to get by and running afoul of the wrong people in the process. A familiar story. For a year or two, I somehow convinced myself that she had left because of me." He laughed. "When I admitted that the next time I saw her, she was *merciless*."

Vidmantas, too, found work at the Guild that agreed with him. After a loud, and public, tirade about how sad and "functional" the Guild's clothes were, he began to "improve" them. First, he spent a day talking to the various farmers and artisans already in residence, learning what they had that could be used for dyes. Soon enough, Guild members were sporting linen clothes in purple, green, red, and so much else. He dyed them under an awning at the back of our dormitory building, and Guild members even brought him their extant clothes to be made more colorful.

"What?" he said to Žydrė one day, as he dyed someone's trousers a dusty pink. "Just because I'm a great thinker, I can't also like pretty things?" His hair was still tied up in the silk remains of his old robe. "As a matter of fact, they help me think."

"Who said you're a great thinker?" she retorted. "This just proves you've always been a dilettante." Her own dress was still undyed.

"First of all," said Vidmantas, "this *was* my trade, so I am only a dilettante if the same can be said of you when you plow the fields." He shrugged as he hung up the pink trousers to dry. "And what's more, I'm in high demand, aren't I? Why, I'd say I'm necessary to the community's well-being."

"Vidmantas, one thing you have never been is necessary."

"Is that so?" He stood up, moving to a hanging dark blue shirt, on which he began to stencil abstract golden designs with a small brush. "Then why did you bring me here, I wonder?"

"Certainly not to waste your time daubing these—"

"Providing people with nice things makes them happier," he interrupted, "which gives them one more reason to stay here." Vidmantas showed an unusual serenity, which seemed to antagonize Žydrė further.

"I have to admit," I spoke up, "that a focus on aesthetics makes *me* want to stay." Then, acting as though the idea had just occurred to me, I added, "If the Guild would have me, and my family, of course." It was the first time I'd mentioned the possibility of my family coming here, and I wanted to gauge how welcome more Loashti than just Simurgh and I would even be.

"Of course you'd all be welcome," said Žydrė, seemingly without thinking about it. "It's Vidmantas I'm not sure about."

"What good is the freedom of living apart from the world," he replied, "if we can't do so beautifully? It helps people know they are individuals, with taste, rather than mindless followers doing whatever Adomas thinks is best." He grinned and winked at her, adding in a mock whisper: "Even if they really *are*."

"Do you really think that?"

"I'm still not sure." He shrugged. "But this is where I have to stay, so I'm making the best of it. I have some ideas to make our clothes stronger as well, less likely to tear in those places strained by our work."

"*Our* work, you mean. *You* seem to only be sitting around making things pretty."

"I am following in the tradition of Uzochi and his delicious chickpeas. Isn't that part of Adomas' vision? That not everyone need break their backs under the hot sun? That some of us can do supposedly useless things?"

"But you *only* do useless things."

"You are beginning to sound like Yalwas," he replied. "Against drink, against meat, against anything that deviates from our 'natural state.'"

"Don't . . ." Žydrė seemed too frustrated to get the words out. She tried again: "Don't compare me to Yalwas and his followers. I want Lanreas to be pleasant to live in. I want us to draw people in, show people the beauty in living like this, so that our children's children can someday live in the natural state."

"And yet," Vidmantas added, "this shirt I'm decorating is for Yalwas. So he can appreciate beauty."

"He is only moderate where it suits him," she growled. "And *you* aggravate me."

He smiled at her. "I love you too."

Kalyna, for her part, spent those days at least acting as though she was useful to the community. She helped out a bit with farming (really, she just carried heavy things without complaining) and cooking, mostly in order to talk to more Guild members. She also spent time around those making and repairing clothes, shoes, tools, and whatever else, asking them questions about their work while making herself likeable, and learning how they felt about the Guild and Adomas.

However, her first and most loyal followers were the roving bands of children who worked to keep the Guild clean. She had no especial experience with children, but she was good with people, and that is, after all, what children are. She turned out to have a great aptitude for holding their interest, because she could come up with more and more baroque goals for their ongoing competition. She was also an expert at lighting up their imaginations by adding all sorts of pomp and circumstance to their work, and making them feel like conquering heroes.

"Red Company!" she called out one morning, addressing the children standing at attention in the otherwise quiet, northern end of the town. "Your charge is to bring me nails that have been dropped and forgotten on the ground where they're building that new house."

They all saluted her and shouted, "Yes, ma'am!"

"But if you swipe any nails from the builders to pad out your numbers," she added, leaning forward and tapping her temple, "I will *know*." She widened her eyes, and the children giggled in feigned—I think?—fear of her powers.

Kalyna went on to give each of her five "companies" different refuse to collect, told them she would decide the winner based on complex math ("Because a peach pit and a nail aren't the same thing, are they?"), and told the Blue Company Captain to take that pot off her head.

"Bring that back to the Meal Hall. But *clean it* first!"

"Yes, ma'am!"

The soldiers were dismissed with a crisp salute, and off they went, laughing and pushing.

"Some are orphans, some have parents here," she told me as she watched the children disperse. "But all understand more of what the adults are feeling than adults like to realize."

I burned to tell her of my mad plan, but I didn't dare yet. It was too outlandish, and I was still working out how to sell her on it.

"And what are the adults feeling?" I asked instead.

"Many different things, naturally, but if I were to generalize, I would say there are three main ways of thinking here. Those like Yalwas, who believe all of Adomas' nonsense and think we should already be in our 'natural state.'" She stuck out her tongue distastefully. "Then there are those like Žydrė, who *also* believe all of his nonsense but understand that one can't move from the Tetrarchia to Utopia all at once—interestingly enough, Adomas seems to think this way. And finally, those who simply like being somewhere they can be themselves and don't need money to survive."

"Like Ifeanyas."

"Yes, but no one is treating him like a leader. There's already a power struggle over who will run the place after Adomas drops dead."

"But didn't Žydrė say she hadn't considered—" I stopped myself. "Ah. She was lying."

"Oh, yes. She's hungry for it. But, of course, no one wants to admit that Adomas is old and may die soon, and *certainly* no one wants to intimate that the place needs a leader to function. Adomas is just supposed to be a 'guide' for the Guild's early years. According to his beliefs, they're not really supposed to have a leader at all."

"No leader is . . . hard to imagine. Until recently, I would have considered a leaderless place to be much more dangerous for people like me. Loasht's laws were not always fair to the Zobiski, or other such peoples, but there *were* laws, and the Grand Suzerain's authority often kept us from being entirely wiped out."

"But now?"

"Well, now the Grand Suzerain listens to Aloe. Perhaps no leader is better."

Kalyna made a doubtful noise in her throat. "I don't trust most leaders," she said, "but I don't particularly trust what people will do without one either."

She went on to tell me that her opening gambit—stepping between Yalwas and Žydrė, making them both look a little ridiculous—had worked out quite well. Kalyna had become relatively popular among the crowd that frequented the Games Hall, and word of Yalwas angrily calling her a "foreigner" had traveled quite quickly. No one over ten years old had been born at the Lanreas River Guild, and so most knew the feeling of arriving there as an outsider hoping for a better life. That a newcomer had been harshly denigrated as a "foreigner" was, apparently, quite distasteful.

Although, I did wonder how those same people might view my own foreignness. After all, Kalyna was still from the Tetrarchia.

That Yalwas had never apologized to Kalyna, while Žydrė seemed to get on fine with her, had also been noticed by many people. As had the fact that Kalyna had taken to, and improved upon, Žydrė's scheme for setting the children to cleaning the Guild.

My first three nights at Lanreas, I lay awake in my bed agonizing over every terrible thing that could be happening in Loasht. Even if Kalyna could, somehow, save my entire community, could she also make the Guild welcoming to us? And if I was willing to try for something so impossible, how could I be so callous as to not try to rescue even more? Then I would worry that my restlessness in bed was waking up the others in the dormitory and spend an hour or two mad at myself for that.

The days were spent in much the same way. I would wander the grounds, talk to people, obsess over what I was to do next, and worry that I was being useless. Žydrė kept calling Vidmantas "useless," after all, and he was doing much more than me. (Of course, I knew this was due to their specific relationship, but I still *felt* that she was also accusing me.)

On my third day, I attempted to be useful to the cooks in the Meal Hall by chopping food, something I used to do quite quickly and skillfully at home. (I was a good cook too. Often, as a child, I had to make my own meals out of necessity.) But thanks to a lack of sleep, my hands shook so badly that a man felt the need to grab my wrists and force the knife out of my fingers—everyone had been too distracted to cook, too busy watching me with wide-eyed horror, waiting for a finger to be lost.

I felt useless. Worthless. Constantly occupied with my thoughts, to an exhausting degree, but also bored. As I wandered aimlessly after my Meal Hall adventure, I came to two conclusions.

First of all, I simply had to decide that Kalyna *would* agree to my ludicrous plan, and that with her help, it *would* work. There was no other way to move forward. Besides, she had fought to save lives back in Rotfelsen. Surely rescuing an entire *community* would be an order of magnitude larger than what she'd already achieved. That might just appeal to her ego.

Secondly, I absolutely needed to find something I could do that would actually help the Guild, so that they would be quicker to accept more of my kind.

Before breakfast on the fourth day, Kalyna and I were alone in the dormitory. She was seated, looking in a half-body mirror she had found somewhere, and rubbing cocoa butter into her skin. The smell made me think of my home, and I began to pace away from her to avoid it.

From a few feet away, I said, "If this is to be the place where I stay, I have to make myself useful to these people."

"No, you don't," replied Kalyna, putting a little oil on her fingers as she looked at me in the mirror. "Look at Vidmantas, myself, or Uzochi, the chickpea man."

"But I'm Loashti. Do you honestly think people look at Uzochi and me the same way?"

". . . No." She began lightly massaging the oil into her hair. "No, I suppose they don't."

"Simurgh is allowed to stay here, but she is certainly teaching them about rubber and alchemy."

"Rubber? Is her balloon not just canvas with an alchemical paint job?"

She watched me in her mirror as I shook my head. "The Yams' balloons are plain canvas; I assure you, Simurgh's is something else. I'm no expert, but I think she's shown them how to extract rubber from their poppies and make a canvas-rubber hybrid."

"Meaning?"

"Simurgh goes so far as to show them Loashti alchemical secrets. I may need to be similarly useful if I want to stay."

"Simurgh is also a *difficult* personality." Kalyna fluffed her hair and raised an eyebrow at my reflection. "Whereas you, Radiant, can be quite agreeable."

I grinned. "'Quite'? High praise."

She snorted. "Don't get full of yourself now. So what will you offer? Curses?"

"That seems ill-advised. But Adomas must have quite the library somewhere, and research is really the only thing I'm good at. That, and my beauty, are all I have to offer."

She began to root around for something else in her bag. "I can't tell if you're joking or not."

"Neither can I."

"I doubt the old man will let you use his library, lest you discover what he's really up to." Kalyna pulled out a small tin of charcoal powder, shaking some out onto a white rag. "But *if* he does, what will you research? Other than, of course, what he and his people are really up to."

"I was hoping you'd tell me, after your days of learning about the place."

Kalyna sighed and took in my reflection in her mirror. I was a mess: eyes bloodshot, hair buoyantly uneven, on the verge of tears. She then focused on herself and pulled back her lips in order to vigorously rub her teeth with the powdered rag as she thought. I sat on my bed and looked at the floor in silence, just hoping she would come up with something.

"Rddddint!"

Kalyna's mouth was still full of charcoal powder, but she was smiling awkwardly, and her eyes were lit up. She snapped the fingers of her free hand, tried to talk, and then waved at me to wait, as though I was going anywhere. She rinsed her mouth out with water from a metal cup, which she then spat into, and turned toward me with a grin. Her teeth were pristine white, as always.

"Radiant, I think I am about to be brilliant."

"*Please do*," I begged.

"The Lanreas River Guild is, now, teetering on the edge of finally being self-sustainable, although they still must lean on their reserves of money, most of which came from Adomas, to buy a lot of things. What's more, the amount of work that must be done to keep the farm going is exhausting, and certainly leads to some grumbling—as well as to grumbling about, well, those of us who don't work in the farm much, or at all."

"This was *exactly* what I was worried about, remember?"

"Yes, yes." She waved a hand at me. "But, you see, farming, the way they do it here, the way that most 'civilized'"—she rolled her eyes—"peoples do, with big fields and laborers filling their days, is not the only way. Large fields that produce a few things, but hopefully in surplus, are wonderful if you're a lord with complete dominion over your land, making money off the backs of your commoners. But Adomas isn't that anymore. Or, at least, so he claims.

"But, Radiant, there are many places in the world where farming was, or even still is, done differently. Where instead of clearing out an area and planting nice, neat rows, they carefully choose and lay out plants that will complement one another. Often, to outsiders, it can look as though this carefully cultivated land is wildly untouched. But those farms, or gardens, or whatever you'd like to call them, can feed more people with less work than what we're used to, if the land can support them."

"I've seen nothing like that in Loasht. But I suppose that makes sense—no Grand Suzerain would want his communities to be able to feed themselves independently."

"Exactly! But you may have seen motley patches in the Quru mountains that were more intentional than you realized. Also look to

Rotfelsenisch cave gardens, and some small corners of Masovska, especially before it became one kingdom."

"Incredible! What should I be looking for in those places? What plants? And complementing each other how?"

"I have no idea!" she laughed. "I'm not a farmer. That's what you're going to find out. But I'm sure it's in Adomas' books, just as I'm sure that being a noble from the Tetrarchia's great kingdom of 'traditional' agriculture means that such an arrangement hasn't occurred to him."

"But won't it take time for whatever I find to bear fruit?" I frowned. "Metaphorically and, ah, literally."

"Perhaps, but we can promise everyone less work for more food, and we'll tell them how it will be done. Simurgh hasn't shared more than that, and they tolerate her even though she's an ass!"

I admit her excitement was infectious. And in what she was suggesting, I saw not just a chance for Silver and myself, but also a broad topic into which I could sink my energy. In a way, it was not that far outside of my normal area of study: so much of magic comes down to its material ingredients, the ways in which they affect the world, and how the people using them *think* they affect the world. And, of course, if Lanreas' yields could be greatly improved, then bringing a few *hundred* Loashti here might not sound so impossible.

My mind was buzzing with possibilities as I moved to step out into the morning sun.

"One more thing," said Kalyna.

I turned back to her, and she wasn't smiling anymore, wasn't excited. Her voice was quiet too, and she was staring at her own unmoving reflection in the mirror.

"If you do get to look through Adomas' books," she said, "there is something else you can look for. Just for me."

"Name it!" I nodded much too enthusiastically.

"If the old naturalist has anything concerning subterranean creatures—things that live in the deep, in the bottoms of lakes and oceans, beneath mountains, that sort of thing—I would love to know about them."

"Of course. What about them?"

"Anything."

I must have looked a little confused as I left.

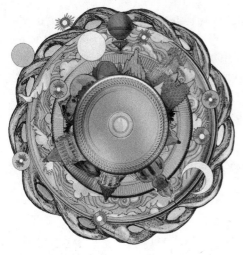

Chapter Sixteen

On Fortresses, Enticers, Sacrifices, and Ineffables

It was the first time I'd been inside Adomas' little house, which was quite spare. If the garden outside had not been larger and more orderly than anyone else's, no one would've guessed that the Guild's leader lived here.

When I asked if he had a library I could peruse, the old man's eyes twinkled, and he gestured out his window, toward the crumbling mansion where he had once lived.

"Of course!" he said. "My library is open to everyone, just as my collection is. I would tell you not to damage anything, but I doubt you ever would. May I ask why?"

"Well . . ." I gulped and shrugged, grinning awfully, I'm sure. "I'm no farmer, but I am a scholar, and I think that in your library, I may find a way to benefit this community."

Adomas put a hand on my shoulder. "I want everyone at Lanreas to find fulfilment, Radiant, whether they're here for a few short weeks or for decades. Besides, plenty in those books helped make the Guild what it is. Maybe you'll find something to make our lives even better, yes?"

I nodded. "I have some ideas, but I don't want to promise anything yet."

"And," he continued, "when you're feeling, you know, *better*, maybe you can consider teaching in our schoolroom. It's very important to me that our young are instructed in many different subjects, and you clearly have a well-rounded, and deep, Loashti education."

I did a pathetic little bow of thanks.

"Do you study anything specific that might be of interest to the children?"

I began, and then curbed, an awkward laugh, and told him I would consider teaching. I'm sure the children would have loved to learn how to curse one another.

I lugged my Commonplace Book volumes up to the Estate, planning to make it my new study. It was quite a walk to Adomas' library (over the cedar roots, right at the poppies, up the staircase *carefully*, into one of the turrets), but that was fine with me. What good is an overgrown and empty mansion if you can't wander its halls?

I happened across a child standing alone, staring up at the painting of meerkats guarding their young. Her face was stone still, eyes wide as she took in every detail, without even noticing me. I began thinking that the Guild might be a decent place to stay, now that I wouldn't return to Loasht. The people here were simply living their lives and seemed happy enough. Maybe Kalyna was right, that there was something sinister underneath, but I'd enjoyed most of my life in Yekunde, and there was *clearly* something sinister beneath all that, wasn't there?

If anyone at the Lanreas River Guild was free to use the library, it certainly seemed no one had done so in a long time. There was a thin layer of dry dirt and dust on everything, and some unfortunate colonies of bugs.

It was quite large, and its walls were lined with books and a series of catwalks spiraling upward. At the top of the turret was the library's only opening to the elements, which led into a network of carefully angled wind tunnels that replenished the room with fresh, cool air, even in summer. Inside them, a series of well-placed mirrors bathed everything in diffuse light during the day.

At one end of the library was a large table that felt more like a dais or an altar, large enough for a human to lie down on it entirely. I remembered Kalyna wondering whether the Guild members got up to human sacrifice.

Well, if they did, they hadn't done so *in here* for some time. I laid out the three broad, thick, and crinkled volumes of my Commonplace Book that I had brought to the Tetrarchia. I stared down at them: volumes 33, 34, and 35. My heart sank.

Eighty-Three. There were more than thirty volumes back in Loasht. The accumulation of my knowledge and experience through most of my life, all neatly bound and collected in a place I'd decided never to return. It's pathetic, but I suddenly felt a pang more acute than my worries for Silver. Perhaps I was shielding myself from the worst, or perhaps I am deeply self-centered. Not having access to most of my Commonplace Book wasn't losing someone close to me, it was losing myself. I had, over the years, told myself again and again: *Don't worry about remembering that. Let it disappear from your mind; you've written it down!*

I sank into the chair, which was all wood, but carved so finely as to be quite comfortable. I wanted to cry, but I didn't have the energy. So I fell asleep.

I woke as the room was darkening, so the sun must have been setting. Such was my first day of "research." I sighed deeply.

In the last bit of light, I flipped open volume 35, which I was only partway through. What was the last thing I had even written in it, I wondered? Had I added anything since leaving Abathçodu?

The volume opened easily to the last pages I'd used. More easily than normal, in fact, because there was something wedged between those pages. It was a folded piece of paper, and on its outside was scrawled in Cöl(ü)knit: "Smart Boy."

Well, of course I opened it and read it in the waning light of Adomas' library, even as I clicked my tongue at the slight ink bleed from Dagmar Sorga's heavy pen-hand onto the blank next page of my Commonplace Book.

> *You told me you read Rotfelsenisch, and it's easiest for me to write. I hope you can read this.*
> *If you need me, I plan to spend my next bit of time in*

Kalvadoti, at the Hyrax Nest. That's if you need me, not if K
does. Do not tell K about this. I don't want to see her.
    And don't let K get too full of herself. She's going somewhere
dangerous.

"Huh," I said, out loud, to no one. I wished that Dagmar had been
a little more specific about the amount of time and what "going somewhere dangerous" meant. Besides, if I needed her, how could I possibly
make it all the way to another Skydašian city without telling Kalyna?
Nonetheless, I was strangely comforted.

I got up to leave and decided my Commonplace Book volumes
could remain in the library. Who would want them? I also left the
matches I had brought in order to light lamps that, it turned out, were
empty. I would have to bring oil tomorrow.

I took a step toward the stairs, then stopped. Did I trust Kalyna to
not go through my belongings?

I turned back, wrote simply, "Kalvadoti: Hyrax Nest" in my Commonplace Book, and then used the matches to burn Dagmar's letter. In
a perverse way, I felt that Kalyna would have been happy I was learning to be more careful, even though it was in order to keep something
from her.

Then I went back to town and told everyone about how dreadfully
busy I'd been doing research all day.

Over the following days, I worked to understand the system with which
Adomas had once organized his books. The bottom floor, which held that
great desk, mostly had literature concerning animals and other natural
phenomena. Many of these published books, secret pamphlets, and haphazard piles of paper were Adomas' own writings, all of which had been
written before the Lanreas River Guild came into being. I had seen a
small shelf of books in his little hovel, but no writing implements, and I
wondered why he seemed to have simply stopped his scholarship entirely.
Adomas had never been connected to a place like the Loashti Academy;
he had only ever written and researched for the sake of his personal interest (and possibly spite), which the library attested was bottomless. What
had changed? It seemed strange to me, but perhaps I would be similarly
fed up with scholarship when I was his age.

If I got to be his age. And if I did, where would I even be? I still pictured myself as an old man in Yekunde, sitting in front of the house with Silver and watching the local children play. Perhaps, if I was very lucky, whatever was going on with Aloe and his ilk back home would blow over someday, and I would return in time for advanced age. At the rate things tended to change in Loasht, this seemed unlikely. On the other hand, the last few years, from the Blossoming onward, had been quite eventful for my home country, hadn't they?

Up in the catwalks of the library were bits of history and cultural study, which I found quite interesting. At the very top, there was a smattering of poetry and a few romances, but in a paltry number.

Making use of every possible surface for an open book—including a wooden contraption wherein a series of book-sized platforms rotated vertically between a pair of wheels—I began to look into older methods of gardening and cultivation in the Tetrarchia. The first useful piece of information I found was that in ancient Masovskan plant lore, tree onions were planted around other crops to repel weeds and pests.

I found nothing in that library to suggest a hidden, awful truth of the Lanreas River Guild. I did learn of a few strange subterranean creatures, but whenever I told Kalyna of these, she said, "No, no. *Bigger.*"

Next, I walked around the Guild, asking about every plant that was growing there, from crops to weeds. Then I began researching them in Adomas' writings, making an annotated list of each plant's functions and—is "habits" the right word? I didn't know if any of it would be helpful, but researching and writing things down in my Commonplace Book felt, at least, a little normal.

Kalyna continued to be caught up in learning the ins and outs of the Guild. These "fools," who she was sure were up to something sinister, also fascinated her. Even as she lived among them and ingratiated herself to them, she viewed them—in her conversations with me, at least—at a remove. As though she were watching a play and trying to anticipate its major plot twist, while enjoying the ridiculous characters. She certainly didn't seem to feel she was in any danger.

In my second week at the Guild, I began to synthesize our new agriculture from numerous traditions and sources. First, I made a list of the "roles" the nonhuman workers in our farms could play:

1. Fortresses, which keep out weeds and pests: tree onions (previously mentioned), elderberries, and North Shore Skydašian sorrel.
2. Enticers, which lure in the correct bugs for pollination: carrots, buckwheat, and sunflowers.
3. Sacrifices, which grow quickly to be heavily pruned and left on the ground to become mulch: beans, squash, and South Shore Skydašian artichokes.
4. Ineffables, which work in ways my sources did not understand, but nonetheless took advantage of: peanut, mandrake, and Loashti fogwort.
5. Chickens, which could break up the topsoil with their little claws and fertilize the ground with their shit.
6. Lini the cow, who was already eating weeds and heroically fertilizing the ground with her own shit.

There would be more to come, of course, as I spoke to those with the hands-on experience I lacked, but it was a start. Then, because I felt the need to show my worth as soon as possible, I made a list of things that could improve the Guild's farming right away.

For example, there were already tree onions in some members' personal gardens, and it was easy enough to dig some up and move them to more strategically chosen places, with some coaxing from Kalyna. There were also techniques being used in some personal gardens that we began planning to use throughout the Guild, such as planting herbs in a tight spiral, which allows the plants to shade one another and require relatively little water.

Learning so much more than I'd ever known about the plants around me also served to grow my understanding of magic itself. A peanut plant would improve the soil, but no one knew why—perhaps it was a process we didn't see, or perhaps people had believed it for so long that their collective will had made it so.

And could the inverse also apply? If I were conducting a particularly nasty curse, which always does take a toll on the caster, would wearing a crown of onion and elderberries protect me? (It would certainly smell confusing.)

Then, at the end of my second week, just as I was getting used to the place, everything changed when a group of Loashti arrived.

It was early evening, and as I was leaving the Estate, I heard a commotion. Usually, the only people around this far north in the Guild were a few scattered members strolling or exploring the collection, and Simurgh, whose "assistants" had recently become too fed up to work with her anymore. But that day, I heard something like a hundred people murmuring in confusion and discontent.

I quickened my pace and exited the Estate through its back door, which was the direction the sound was coming from. Through the broken walls I saw a crowd of Guild members standing around in the northmost clearing of the land, near Simurgh's balloon. They were mostly adults, in a sea of beige linen—with a few beautiful pops of color, thanks to Vidmantas. I saw Adomas, in his large straw hat, making his way through the crowd. Simurgh was at her outside drafting table and trying very hard to pretend nothing was happening.

As I moved through the crowd, some Guild members would stop what they were saying upon noticing me, which made the back of my neck prickle. At the front of the crowd was a Skydašian soldier—a Yam— in her orange uniform, which immediately made my blood start shooting and pounding through my body. I was about to hide when I saw the soldier glance at me and then immediately away, clearly not caring about my presence in the slightest. She was talking to Yalwas, whose linen shirt was now a beautiful saffron color with pale red flower prints that were awkward and uneven, which only made them more charming. Next to him were Žydrė (still in undyed linen) and Kalyna (in deep purple). Adomas was making his way toward them. I stopped near Kalyna and listened.

"Now look," Yalwas was saying, "here comes our leader now, and he will make exactly the decision I told you he would."

"Fine, fine," said the Yam. She yawned. "This whole thing is a real pain. I can't wait to be away from your creepy little cult."

"We're a *guild*, not a cult," said Žydrė. "And you aren't supposed to come onto our land."

"Well, what was I supposed to do?" laughed the Yam. "Send you a letter from a mile away? Stand at the edge and throw in rocks with messages tied to them? I came in alone and unarmed, after all." She rolled her eyes. "Besides, it isn't *your* land, is it? It's Adomas' land."

"It's all of ours," said Adomas, who had finally reached the conversation. "I gave it freely to these people. As all land should be given."

The Yam snorted. "Of course, my lord." She didn't sound very respectful, but Adomas was still a noble to her, and it seemed a foregone conclusion that she'd address him as such. "What you choose to do with your land is none of my business, and today your arrangement may just be useful."

"How so?" asked Adomas.

"Well, my lord, you see this group of some twenty Loashti souls showed up right on our very doorstep, so to speak." She shrugged. "I guess they're Loashti that the Loashti don't want? Damned if I understand it. They show up from the north, begging to leave their great, perfect, monumental home. The soldiers on the other side of the border—our counterparts, you understand—had kept them boxed up for a day or two, unsure of what to do with them." She yawned again, not covering her mouth but waving vaguely at Adomas as some sort of apology. "Finally, the Loashti soldiers are saying things like 'good riddance' and 'let them go.' So they open the little enclosure and loose the poor wretches onto us! Begging, they are, to be allowed into the Tetrarchia!"

"Well, why not?" said Adomas. "They have as much right to live happily and safely as anyone else, and if they feel they can't do so in Loasht . . ." He shrugged.

Yalwas looked back at Adomas with an expression that said he really, really, *really* wished the old man had waited until the story was finished before chiming in.

The Yam snapped her fingers and leaned forward. "I am *so* happy to hear you say that, my lord," she said. "For you see, Skydašiai is not, at this moment, accepting more of those Loashti that Loasht doesn't want. They're troublemakers, for one, and we want to keep Loasht happy, for two."

"Wouldn't Loasht be happy to have you take these people off its hands?" asked Adomas.

"Well, they don't want them there, but there are also worries about what they could do here, you know? Spread bad ideas. But then my commander—a smart man, that—had a brilliant thought." She smiled and held up both hands, as though presenting this genius truth to all of us. "'Those people down there, on Adomas' land,' he says, 'are always claiming they aren't Skydašiai, that they're entirely separate from us. So why not send these new ones to him?'" She looked at me again, holding her gaze on me, clearly with some idea of what I was. "'The old lord already has an alien Loashti or two,' he says. And, well, clearly, you're immune to their bad ideas here, perhaps due to the strength of your own . . . ideas."

"I see," said Adomas, finally. "Well, much as I feel for the wretches, I must say I don't know that we can handle this kind of an influx of new people. Particularly those who don't speak our language. How would we even teach them to work?"

"Just as I said," added Yalwas, nodding.

"So you're turning them away, then?" asked the Yam.

"I'm afraid we must," said Adomas.

I felt my heart seize in my chest. What if these people were from Yekunde? What if Silver was among them?

"Why, that's really too bad," said the Yam. "You see, we've got them right outside your land, surrounded by soldiers, of course. It'll be a shame to tell them they have to go back."

I felt the sudden urge to tear past the soldier, to run out of the Guild. To let myself be captured just for the *chance* that Silver might be out there.

"Back where?" asked Žydrė.

"Why, back to Loasht, of course. Although, naturally, Loasht won't take them either. I suppose we'll need to find a place on the border to keep them." She clapped her hands together. "Eventually, the Loashti soldiers, or our own, may simply get sick of feeding and watching them, if you know what I mean." She winked, as though she had just suggested light mischief.

I put a hand on Kalyna's shoulder and squeezed hard. She reached up, patted it gently, and then removed it.

"I feel for them," said Yalwas, "but we can't take them either."

Adomas shook his head slowly. "A lot of terrible things happen in the world. We cannot solve all of them. I'd like to help, but I don't know . . ."

"There must be something else that can be done," said Žydrė. "Didn't that Aloe fellow say that everyone would be allowed back into Loasht? Surely, they just need to be sent back, and the soldiers told that things are changing."

"Now hold on," said Kalyna. "If the problem is that they don't speak the language, that's easy enough to remedy, isn't it? We already have our own Loashti who can translate."

"But twenty is a lot to take on at once," said Yalwas. "We still have recent additions who have not found ways to make themselves *useful*, after all."

Kalyna smiled blithely, as though she had no idea she'd been insulted. "So is usefulness the only law of the Lanreas River Guild, then? The only thing that makes a life worthwhile here?"

"Of course not," snapped Adomas. Not at her, really. It almost sounded like he was angry at himself.

"Should we put it to a vote?" asked Žydrė.

"I think," said Kalyna, "that people will vote overwhelmingly against letting those Loashti in, so long as the aliens are held outside of the Guild. They are abstract this way, only mouths to feed, only *foreigners*." She glanced at Yalwas, smiled slightly, and then continued. "On the other hand, I think if you do just the same as you did with us—bring them in for at least a night, allow them a decent meal, which I'm sure they could use—the people would likely vote to keep them."

"You have only been here two weeks," said Yalwas. "What do you know of our people?"

"I know that most of *us* have been starving and destitute before, and I know that the guiding light of this place is that people help one another."

Adomas sighed loudly.

"If we let them in," said Yalwas, "we may *all* end up starving and destitute again."

"You were never destitute," Žydrė muttered.

"There simply isn't enough food!" Yalwas added, ignoring her.

"Oh, is that all?" Kalyna grinned, looking from Yalwas to Adomas.

"Is *enough food* all?" Yalwas replied.

"But didn't you know?" said Kalyna. "Radiant and I are working on that for you. Soon you'll have far more food, for far less work." She clapped me on the shoulder.

"Is *that* what you've been running around doing?" asked Yalwas. "I thought you were just trying to look busy."

"How?" asked Adomas. He sounded like he was genuinely curious.

"You know a great deal about crops, of course," said Kalyna, "but more knowledge is always better. More knowledge and more ways to manipulate that knowledge. Didn't you know that Radiant here is a *wizard*?"

I was about to protest, when Kalyna hit me so hard on the back that she knocked the breath out of me. Adomas, Yalwas, and Žydrė all eyed me incredulously. I smiled badly. Murmurs and whispers began to shoot through the crowd.

"I tell you," Kalyna continued, "there is so much more we can be doing. It will only take a bit of clever work and a touch of magic."

Adomas smacked his lips a few times, while he regarded me closely. Then he turned to the Yam, who had been yawning.

"Let them in," he said. "We'll make it work. *But*," Adomas added, raising a bony finger. "The next time people like this come to your borders, do not presume to bring them to the edges of our land in order to force our sympathy. Is that clear?"

"Of course, my lord." The Yam smirked.

"Tell your commander," Adomas continued. "I will write it out on paper and use my family's seal if I must; the seal may be gathering dust, but I know where I left it, and the mark still holds sway out in *your* Skydašiai."

The Yam seemed annoyed but stopped smiling. She nodded. "Yes, my lord."

"Fine. Fine," murmured the old man. "Let them in."

"Why, Yalwas," Kalyna positively brayed, grinning at him, "you must be *excited* to show so many people your rotted livers and lizard skulls!"

Yalwas did not, in fact, insist on leading all the new Loashti through the Estate's collection.

What the soldier had referred to as "some twenty" Loashti were in fact twenty-six. They came through the forest into the clearing in dirty clothes, with all sorts of bundles and even a few farm animals, looking at a crowd that greeted them with suspicion, or at best, confusion. I scanned them feverishly, looking from face to face, hoping to see someone I recognized as they emerged from the trees.

I knew none of them. In fact, the round caps some of them wore, as well as the paucity of tattoos, suggested they weren't from the Yekunde region at all.

Finally, I realized how cruel it was to stand silently watching them as they came into this confusing new place, so I stepped forward and yelled, "Greetings!" in Loashti Bureaucratic.

I told them that this was the Lanreas River Guild and that they were not prisoners here, but that they, like me, would be in great danger if they left. They seemed relieved, if wary.

"Is there anything you'd like me to say to them?" I asked Adomas.

He sighed, looking very put upon, but said to them, in halting and crackling Loashti Bureaucratic, "Come with us. We have food."

There were great smiles of relief, and we all walked back down to town together. Some members of the Guild ran ahead, I suppose to keep the others from being too surprised.

The informal leader of the group of Loashti was a middle-aged woman who, so far, had said very little. At first, I thought she was heavily tattooed and hoped she was Zobiski, or at least southern. Then I realized the gray lines and curlicues across her lean cheeks were painted on, perhaps with ash.

"Are any of yours from Yekunde?" I asked her, probably sounding quite desperate.

She shook her head.

"Are any of them Zobiski?"

Looking very tired, the woman with the painted face nodded and motioned behind her.

It turned out that a parent and their two teen children were Zobiski, but from farther north. I began to pepper the parent with questions in Zobiski: about what was going on back home, how bad it really was, if they'd heard anything about the Zobiski in other parts of Loasht.

The parent, whose name was The Binturong Will Eat All Things, So Why Then Shouldn't We?, shook their head and smiled weakly.

"Please, not now. Let me eat first. And feed my children. And sleep. It is a lot—none of it good."

I apologized and walked the rest of the way to the Meal Hall, listening to those Loashti who wanted to speak and thinking about what this new group meant for my (ill-conceived?) plan to have Kalyna save as many of Yekunde's Zobiski as possible. If these were well received, that would be a good sign, wouldn't it?

The new Loashti were positively ravenous. They said little during dinner beyond a chorus of "thank yous" and amazement at how delicious everything was. Some of the Guild members looked on with expressions of satisfied happiness; others with worry at the new people in their midst. I chose to take solace, and hope for my own plans, in the fact that *any* of them were happy to feed and shelter the new arrivals.

I ate quickly, as did Kalyna, and when we were both done, I signaled to her that I wanted to talk. We went outside, where the sky was now quite red, and groups of locals were walking off their own meals and talking excitedly about the day's events.

"Convincing Adomas to let them in," I said to her in Loashti Bureaucratic, "wasn't out of the goodness of your heart, I assume."

She smiled and said hello to a small group of people as we passed them. Then she replied, in Cölluknit, "Your language is suddenly not so private anymore. Besides, now it's even more important that the Guild members don't know I speak it—could lead them to think I'm some sort of . . . crypto-Loashti, sent here to clear the way for your country-people." She was talking quietly, of course, and would stop when others approached.

"I know a more private place," I replied back in the same language, and nodded toward the Estate.

We made our way northward, and I was surprised by how many people cheerily greeted Kalyna along the way. There were also some who made a point of refusing to talk to, or look at, her, but no one, it seemed, was unfamiliar with her. She had been busy.

In the library, I lit the lamps, and she whistled in awe at the size of the place.

"No wonder you've spent all your time up here," she said. She had switched to Skydašiavos, which I think she preferred to Loashti Bureaucratic.

I nodded and smiled. Seeing her in the library actually made me uncomfortable, which I hadn't expected. As though my, oh, I don't know, *sanctum* was being invaded. This was, of course, silly; these weren't even my books. Except for the Commonplace Book volumes, which were still on the large table. Had I remembered to close the one where I'd written a reminder of Dagmar's note?

"But," Kalyna continued, "it means you missed last night's sing-along." She hopped up onto the table, sitting on it with her legs dangling off.

I moved, I hope, casually toward my books and was relieved to see that while volume 35 was still open, I had filled enough subsequent pages for nothing to look conspicuous.

"Sing-along?" I asked.

"For 'enrichment,'" she replied. "Apparently, they also have dances and lectures, even plays." She shrugged. "Something every week or so, which I suppose is nice."

"Maybe it will be more often now, with more people."

"Maybe." She kicked her legs absentmindedly as she sat. "And to answer your initial question: no, I did not *entirely* keep your countrypeople from being sent back out of the goodness of my heart."

I looked up and saw that she was idly inspecting the little pile of ashes that had once been Dagmar's letter. I coughed and decided to draw her attention before she began to wonder too much. I moved back around the desk to stand in front of her.

"Then why?" I asked.

She shrugged. "For you. And out of habit. I am maneuvering to increase my power and standing here."

"Is that why you told them I'm a wizard?"

Kalyna laughed. "Was that even a lie? I suppose it would've been more honest to say 'sorcerer.'"

"I am neither, Kalyna Aljosanovna. Just a researcher."

"Of magic, which makes you a wizard or a sorcerer in their book. And mine. The curses say 'sorcerer,' but fixing their crops will say 'wizard.'"

"That's just research. There's no magic involved."

"Oh no!" cried Kalyna. "You mean that I've . . . *lied* to someone?!" She cackled. "Look, they're already suspicious of you. The only Loashti they know are you and Simurgh: both of you are off studying or experimenting most of the time."

"You *told me* to—"

"A little suspicion is fine, Radiant! And making you a *wizard* heads off the chances of them calling you a *sorcerer*. Don't worry, these people are delusional idiots."

I sighed. "You still think of them that way?"

"Of course! And hypocritical, to boot. You saw how their 'leaders' reacted to your people showing up."

"They weren't going to turn them away with relish, or with a total lack of caring: they were worried about the resources that would be taken up by so many new people." I wondered why I found myself suddenly arguing for the Guild leaders. I suppose I couldn't help being contrary.

"Radiant, don't forget that these people—Adomas, Yalwas, Žydrė— think their community's success will convince the rest of *world* to follow suit. So they can be unrealistic in their goals, their aims, and their expectations; but the wrong people show up begging for help, and now they're *pragmatists?*"

"I . . . Yes. I think you're right, and of course, I'm glad you helped them. But why, if what you want is to be liked and respected here?"

"Ah!" She brightened up. It seemed she enjoyed having an audience that could know how brilliant she was. "First of all, because there are certainly people here who would have preferred to help those in need—I wasn't lying when I said that bringing them in would arouse the sympathies of the Guild members." She rapped on the table thoughtfully. "Matter of fact, that must be why I don't trust these people. Sympathy is always conditional, and empathy even more so. Why, I've quite often used my own genuine feelings of empathy to be a better swindler. These people claim they care for everyone, but 'everyone' really only means those they can see in front of them."

"Perhaps."

"And those Guild members predisposed to care about the plight of your fellow aliens will now also be predisposed to like me. That's good, because whatever it is you want to do next, it will be helped by fostering the affection of those likely to side with the Loashti.

"Secondly," she continued, "I did it because, frankly, if more Loashti become part of this little community, then more Guild members will feel sympathy for the Loashti. It's that simple."

"Unless, of course, they start to hate the Loashti in their midst. To"—Zobiski memory burbled up—"hunt them down, round them up, and so forth. Or the different types of Loashti may not even get along with each other." I thought of Simurgh and myself.

"Well, it's a gamble, of course." She threw this line of argument off almost unthinkingly, hardly seeming to care that the lives of human beings were involved. "Would you like me to stop?"

"Of course not."

I wondered if Kalyna even *could* stop. Wondered if what was keeping her here, really, was having an all-new stage and group of players to exert her will upon. I thought of what Dagmar had said at the end of her letter to me: *Don't let K get too full of herself. She's going somewhere dangerous.* How in the world she expected me to *stop* Kalyna from getting too full of herself was something I very much wanted to know.

Kalyna continued talking. "I've worked to shore up support because doing so is the same as breathing to me. It's survival." She let out a musical laugh that was a bit haughty, but somehow also charming. "But, Radiant, I *do* need to know what exactly it is you want."

Well. Here it was then.

"To that, I have an answer," I said.

She raised an eyebrow and leaned forward, chin on her hand, one leg crossed over the other. I began to pace.

"I can't leave my family to whatever awaits them in Loasht. I must bring them here."

"Yes, an extraction." She nodded as though I'd made the decision she'd always known I would. "For Silver and their parents."

"And . . . and . . . well . . ." I began to stammer and then looked up into the darkness at the top of the library. I stamped my foot to stop myself shaking. "Not just my family. As much of my Zobiski community in Yekunde as possible. I want to try to bring them *all* here. Somewhere safe. It's a small community by now: only a few hundred, and there is still so much space on these lands. You and I can bring this Guild such mind-boggling plenty that it can support many more people and . . ." I trailed off.

Kalyna had leaned back, hands against the tabletop, bracing herself, and was staring at me hard.

"Radiant, that's a very . . . *big* goal. I daresay an impossible one. Despite what I like to pretend, I am no miracle worker. I don't know how you'd expect me to do such a thing."

"Why . . . why should only Adomas and his ilk get to have unrealistic goals, while I do not?"

She smiled at that. "Because they're fools, Radiant. Because Adomas doesn't really understand how the world can crush people. Even when he was an outlaw, he had servants."

"I know. But . . . I think we should at least aim for bringing back everyone."

"And how many is 'everyone'?"

"When I left Yekunde, my community numbered about three hundred. It . . . may now be less."

"Three hundred . . ."

"We may fall short, but how can we try for anything less?" My voice began to shake. I knew I was asking for too much, but I had to continue. "There . . . there are other Zobiski districts around Yekunde, and more Zobiski spread throughout Loasht, and I shudder to think that we can't save them as well. I'd ask you to save *everyone* Loasht views as 'unfavorable' if I thought it was possible!"

Kalyna looked as though she was about to say something but then stopped. She was quiet for a time, thinking on I know not what.

"So really," I continued, smiling weakly, "I think narrowing it down to just my community is actually quite reasonable!"

Kalyna snorted and coughed out a laugh that seemed to surprise her. "Radiant, you certainly are . . . well, I don't know what. Ridiculous, I think." She let out a long sigh and shook her head. "I have done a lot for you, for free, because I like you, I respect you, and I understand the feeling of being trapped, stateless." She slid off the table. "And also, I will admit, because I relish the feeling of having someone trust in me and my abilities, as any halfway decent trickster does. But you are trusting me too much now."

"But you can at least try. I know I can't pay you, but I've brought you to a place where you can have all your needs met for free."

"*You* brought me?"

"If I hadn't met Vidmantas in the library, then—"

"Fine. Fine."

She moved closer to me. "Radiant, you want me to save your *entire community* from imprisonment or massacre, and to make this community more welcoming to them at the same time?"

I managed to look up at her. She was very close—close enough that I could smell her hair oils—and it made me uncomfortable. But I didn't back up.

"Yes! I know you've seen hard times yourself, and I *know* that you want to help people."

Kalyna Aljosanovna closed her eyes, held the bridge of her nose between her thumb and forefinger, and breathed in and out very loudly.

"*And*," I quickly continued, "what a challenge! What an incredible accomplishment it would be! The good you did in Rotfelsen will pale in comparison to saving so many lives!"

"In comparison"—she opened her eyes—"to saving *three hundred lives?*"

"Yes!"

I had thought my arguments through in great detail, and I was sure an appeal to her vanity was my first step toward success. I was entirely wrong.

"Radiant," she said, "I am not being facetious, and neither am I exaggerating, when I tell you that *every person in the Tetrarchia* owes me their fucking life."

"What . . . ?"

"All of them!" she cried, swinging her arm out and pointing behind her, as though back there sat all four of her homeland's kingdoms. "All of them," she repeated. "Everyone who has been nice to you, or tried to kill you, or ignored you, as well as thousands upon thousands you will never meet. Each one, to the last, would be dead or swallowed up by war and violence without me. I am not being abstract, Radiant: doom was coming to our entire country, and I—Kalyna Aljosanovna—stopped it." She snapped her fingers. "Like that. Gone in an instant. And they don't even *know it.* I have done enough."

I was still trying to take in and wrap my mind around what she was saying. But I couldn't help adding, "Even if you have, that was the Tetrarchia, but these Loashti—"

"Then let a damned Loashti save them!"

"I'm trying! But I can't do it alone."

"*I did,*" she sneered.

I blinked. "Do you think Dagmar would agree with that?"

Kalyna glared at me hard. I don't know what violent thoughts were dancing through her head, but I had never seen her so angry.

"Good night," she said, before turning and leaving the library. I expected her to slam the door, but she just walked out and down the stairs, into the silence.

Chapter Seventeen

Concerning the Literal Undercurrents
of the Lanreas River Guild

I stood in the library for some time, then slumped into the chair behind the desk. The lamps went out, and I didn't relight them. I wasn't even sad or scared, I was just confused. I had known that appealing to her better nature had a low chance of success, but that was not the reasoning I expected from her. Some of her manner—and things she'd said in the past—snapped into place and made a little more sense, but they were now blotted out by even greater mystery and confusion. I found myself wondering the same thing I had when I was alone in her room back in Desgol: Who *was* this person?

I sat like that until I heard footsteps coming up the stairs toward the library. For a moment, I thought it was Kalyna returning, but they were too slow and quiet to be that woman in her boots. A light appeared near the doorway, entering the library before a figure appeared, holding a small lantern. It was Adomas.

"Radiant, are you in here?" he asked, shining the light around. He looked so small and brittle there in that great halo of light, with no broad hat to add to his size.

"Yes. Yes, I am." I got up and came around the table to him.

"Ah. I had a feeling. Treacherous old place with no lights on, though. You should be more careful."

I nodded and moved into the light. "I was thinking."

"About your new countrypeople who just arrived, I'll wager."

I chose to lie and nodded.

"I've been thinking a great deal about them too," he said. "Come with me, Radiant. I'd like to talk to you, and to show you something."

I followed him downstairs.

I had never been inside the Estate this late before: the ground floor was lit with moonlight that trickled in through its various cracks, slithering around the roots and leaves. The moon was *huge*: full, or close to it. I didn't see any other people, although there were some quiet murmurs and giggles in the distance.

"Initially," said Adomas softly, "the only reason I didn't have this place demolished was because I wanted to house my collection here, for everyone. I had no sentimental attachment to the house then—although for some reason, I do now." He shrugged. "It did not occur to me that our Guild members would sometimes come up here for"—he chuckled—"privacy. I admit that, early on, I hoped we could all be truly communal in all things. I still hope for that, in the future. The need for privacy is caused by hierarchies, taboos, and property. Or, at least, that's what I think."

I nodded. "I suppose I understand. But what about your own solitude? You live farther from everyone, and in the past, you carried out your work in secret."

"But always with assistants," he said. "Sometimes they were unknowing, sometimes accomplices, but I was almost never alone. I do take time for myself now, but I'm a relic of old noble ways; even though I created this place, I worry that my constant presence may contaminate it."

"That's quite self-possessed of you."

He laughed. "Nowadays, I'm *glad* the Estate serves a purpose, any purpose. If my people enjoy a place to fumble with each other farther from the town, then I'm happy to give it to them." His smile dropped,

and he kept moving through the hallways. "So long as they are respectful of their fellows, of course."

"And these halls have a romantic air, don't they?" I murmured. "I can
see why people would want to leave the village for something different,
now and then."

He thought that over. "I don't understand the urge, but then, I grew
up in luxury."

We passed the room that held the liver and other bits of the collection that I had seen. At a nearby broken piece of outer wall, I saw his
broad straw hat hanging on the twig of a small tree, waiting for him.

He took it in his hand and then turned left, leading me to a small,
unassuming door almost hidden beneath a stairway. Adomas turned to
me and grinned, winking. I saw, for just a moment, the dashing outlaw
he must've once been. It was entrancing. He produced a small, tar-
nished key, and unlocked the door.

"I hope," he said, "that you feel very lucky and special right now."

I couldn't tell whether he was serious or making a joke at his own
expense. Nonetheless, I must admit that I did feel both of those things.

Now, this was a locked door in what had once been the home of a famous gentleman outlaw, so I'm sure it's no surprise to learn that it led
to a passage beneath the Estate itself. The steps were perfectly even in
their carving, and the walls were paneled in wood. From what I saw in
the light of Adomas' lantern, it all looked quite well made and taken
care of, with none of the crumbling grandeur of the building above.

"Yalwas has been here," explained Adomas. "As have a few others
who were with me at the beginning, and some of their children, such as
Kyautas. It's Yalwas who insists on keeping the place clean."

"I thought children of the Guild were everybody's children."

He laughed and held up his free hand in an almost imperious gesture. "Were the world perfect, they would be."

"Does Žydrė know about this place?"

He shook his head. "No, she was in the fields at the time. Only those
who were assistants knew."

I considered pointing out how this conflicted with the beliefs on
which he'd built his community but stopped myself.

"Some things must be secret," he said as though I had spoken out loud, "for the good of everyone, so that there are no meddlers, you see."

That sounded ominous. I thought of what Kalyna had said about the Guild sacrificing Loashti for the harvest, or some such.

"But you," he added, "understand secret knowledge, don't you?"

I remembered that Kalyna had told him I was a "wizard" and sighed.

The stairs ended and became a straight hallway through what I took to be solid ground. Still wood-paneled, as though we were simply in a part of the Estate.

"What everyone knows," he said, "is that we can grow a more varied and bountiful harvest than these lands usually allow. Our people accept that this is partly due to some blessing on our plot of land, and partly to my own past study and ingenuity. The latter, at least, is correct. The former may be as well." He raised his voice a little, because a sort of howl, or whistling, began to be audible in the distance.

"They know that through my expertise," he went on, "I crossbred and carefully selected crops until we had those that could best survive out here and give us the most in return. Also true. And they feel that the Lanreas River itself probably helps us, but they don't know how."

And Kalyna had expected me to learn *new* things about our crops, which this man did not know?

The noise around us got louder, and I fancied I saw some kind of light at the end of the hallway, which was particularly confusing given that it was the middle of the night. I realized I did not know what direction we were walking in.

"Did I tell you why I named it the Lanreas River Guild? I don't remember if I did."

"No," I muttered. "I assumed it was just because the river is close by."

"Well, yes. That's part of it. The rest—well, I'll show you."

We walked in silence for some time, as the howling got louder. Even in the midst of all this mysteriousness, even as I genuinely worried about what terrible things I might learn, I couldn't help laughing to myself at how dramatic he was being in making me wait. Adomas must've truly been a mischievous and frustrating rogue in his past. Not unlike Kalyna, I'm sure. But, for better or worse, Adomas seemed to have acted out of his own principles, however strange. I thought I had been appealing to Kalyna's principles, and yet she'd said no.

There was indeed a light at the far end of the hallway, and as we got closer, it showed me another set of stairs, these going up. The quality of the light was white, like moonlight but more so. Brighter and harsher. It was unlike anything I'd seen before.

"Ah," said Adomas, at the foot of the stairs. "I haven't been here so late in some time!" He was yelling now, as the howling had gotten even louder. He put his straw hat on and ascended.

I realized that the noise reminded me very much of the awful sounds I'd heard when Simurgh's balloon crossed over The Thrashing, Bone-White Tail of Galiag. But I felt no rushing heat, no wind even: as I ascended the stairs, I moved into a pleasant night beneath the (blazingly white?) stars, with the sound of the wind roaring in my ears and the sound of rushing water somewhere under it.

I stepped out onto healthy underbrush that was brilliantly green. Far ahead of me, there was a sheer wall of rock going high into the air, and trailing off to my left and right. Behind me was another wall, and pouring in through an opening in its base was a river that ran diagonally past my right side, following the stone walls ahead of us for some way.

I strongly suspected I knew where we were, but was baffled by the comfortably cool, and still, air around me. I looked up, and my suspicions were confirmed. Above us were the moon and stars; between them and us, however, was the burning wind of The Thrashing, Bone-White Tail of Galiag. The winds were visible, because—as I had seen filling the river south of the Tail, and seen again when I floated above the gorge—they carried inside them the white sand and dirt of the city of Galiag. The silver of the moon and stars was reflected and enhanced by all that rushing detritus, until the whole interior of the gorge, as far as I could see, was lit up with a glittering, flickering, pallidly silver light.

"How?" I asked, in awe.

"What?!!" yelled Adomas, turning back to me.

"How?!!" I yelled back over the howling wind.

"Well!!" he cried. "You see—!!" Then he stopped, shook his head, and pointed down the river a bit to something I definitely didn't expect to see: a hut.

On the short walk over to the wooden hut, I saw, in that unbelievably bright light that filled the gorge, not just verdant grass and bushes, but animals. Small furry things scurried about nearby, little birds seemed perfectly content to perch in those bushes, and *larger* things that I couldn't make out slid through the waters nearby.

The building itself was a rectangular box with a door and no windows that I could see. It sat right at the edge of the river and featured some extremities I didn't understand: metal piping running down its side, with one end going into the water, and the other stretching up into the blazing, howling Galiag winds. I tried to see what was at the top of it but couldn't make it out through the refracted brightness that seemed blinding if I stared too long.

Adomas opened the door and ushered me inside. He followed me, took off his hat, and lit a lamp before closing the door, which shut out all other light.

It also shut out all other *sound*. I shook my head in disbelief, willing my ears to continue hearing what I knew was roaring by above us. I swallowed, forced a yawn, even dug into my ears with my fingers. It felt so odd.

"How?!" I yelled. Then, realizing how quiet and small this space was, I said, much quieter, "Sorry. Sorry. How?"

"How what? Which part are you asking about?" Adomas had that twinkle in his eye again.

"Well, the sound, for starters," I said.

"That's simple enough. There are mosses—in Rotfelsen and other cave places—that can absorb sound and muffle the noises of the world. The wooden walls here are really just a shell for slabs of rotrock, where a large quantity of that moss lives happily on the water from the Lanreas River, convinced, I'm sure, that it's still in the depths of Rotfelsen."

I looked around the room as the old naturalist lit more lamps. The floor, like that we had traversed underground, was shining and spotless wood. The walls were lined with bookshelves, and the space above those shelves was covered in paintings. From what I could see of the next room, it sported a bed surrounded by more bookshelves and paintings.

The room we were standing in contained a desk, two velvet-lined chairs, a few glass cases displaying more of Adomas' oddities, and a marble statue of a thickly muscled man wrestling what looked to be a hyena or a great cat—it was difficult to tell, as its thrashing and twisting had been so dutifully captured.

"In my youth," Adomas continued, "I stole into a heavily guarded Rotfelsen cave and cut away these very slabs of rotrock, in order to study the moss. To learn where its properties come from and whether they can be replicated." He shrugged. "That was unsuccessful, but when I found myself quite outlawed for a time, and discovered this wonderful little oasis, I found the perfect use for them in insulating my hideout."

"And now that old hideout is your study?" I asked, adding: "And still rather a hideout."

"It is. That statue is of me, you know." He laughed. "Although I never looked anything like that."

He smiled and eased into one of the chairs, motioning to the other. I sat, and Adomas stretched carefully, looking around his small refuge.

"I suppose I also like solitude more than I expected I would," he said. "Although, I'm often here with Yalwas or someone else." He nodded at me to demonstrate the great trust and esteem my presence here represented. "In here, I keep, you know, *different* books, as well as what I've been writing recently."

I nodded. So this was why his writings in the library stopped at ten years ago. I noted that he didn't trust the whole community with his literary output.

"Not to mention some of your art and . . . whatever these are." I waved toward a glass case next to me. Inside was a preserved piece of an animal, really just a sliver of a face: a sharp tooth longer than my arm, protruding from a piece of its wet-looking upper jaw, which was connected to a segment of eyeball that, if whole, would've been the size of my torso.

"Yes, yes. Some things are a little too valuable to have them up where anyone can damage or take them."

I said nothing.

"You think that's hypocritical of me," he noted.

"I do."

"I suppose it is. But we're all hypocrites, to some degree." He sighed. "I was raised a noble and spent much of my life putting so much importance on the building of this collection—I don't know that I can ever fully let it go. But that's all right; the community can decide what to do with it all someday." He clapped his hands together. "For now, I can't very well have everyone reading my notes." He seemed to shudder at the thought.

"But no other Guild members can have a secret lair to escape the village or store their valuables?" It was exactly the kind of question that, I think, Kalyna would have glared at me for asking. That was fine: I was angry at her, anyway.

Adomas screwed his mouth to the side. "They can have lockboxes for their own possessions, they can even keep their money if they want it—most choose not to. But I *am* their leader, and a naturalist besides. I think I deserve a place for my studies, don't you?"

"Well, yes. But I'm too new here for your ideals to have soaked in through my pores."

Adomas nodded slowly.

"Anyway," I said. "I have about a thousand questions. But it seemed you wanted to start by telling me why you named it the Lanreas River Guild. Although, seeing that you have your own private piece of the river, I think I begin to understand."

"*Our* own private piece."

"Even though most know nothing about it?"

He waved a hand at me like I was a young child being insolent. "It benefits even people who don't know about it, same as the gods' blessings benefit a baby. But this is only part of where the name came from. As you may have noticed, the river's shores—both out in the world and here inside the Tail—are home to many small communities of meerkats. They are why I named it Lanreas."

"Because of meerkats?" I vaguely remembered seeing the little creatures about when I was by the river, but they seemed an ignoble animal to choose. "They're agreeable to look at, but is 'community' the right word? I would think them more a flock, a herd, a warren. Community suggests . . ."

I trailed off as I saw how *overjoyed* he looked that, in the midst of everything, I wanted to quibble about animals. He leaned forward and clapped his hands, before rubbing them together.

"That, my dear Radiant, is exactly the point! I, too, thought dismissively of them, until I was stuck here in my hideout for months on end, with nothing to do but watch them. And I tell you, communities they are!" He pointed a bony finger at me, shaking it with each point he made. "They raise their little baby meerkats communally, you see. No tooth and claw among them, oh no. They watch each other's children, they share their food, they warn each other of danger." He sat back, looking contented. "So I thought: if these dumb little creatures can live happily together, why can't we?"

"'Happily' may be a stretch," I muttered, shaking my head. "But I suppose I'll defer to you on that. Still, why should people live like animals?"

"Why not? Plenty already do, to some degree. In fact, I realized that the people who toiled on this forgotten estate of my family's lived far more communally than I ever had. So I decided to use my resources— all the ill-gotten gains of nobility—to strengthen the love and joy of the common people."

"I don't know that I share your trust of the common people," I said. "They've risen up to terrorize my ancestors many times."

"But pushed and convinced to do so by, well, people like *my* family, who hold all the knowledge and power, and can tell them what to think!"

I was still unconvinced, and my expression must have shown that.

"Living happily together will take time, of course," he said. "But now, as our resources become strained, I feel so . . . so blessed that we have you and your occult knowledge to help us."

For once, I managed to stop myself from pushing back. Kalyna's plans, whatever they were, would apparently work better if the man thought I was some kind of wizard.

"I, of course, had to relax or change some of my original aims," he continued. "Real people are more complex than what a scholar imagines when he's shut up beneath the howling winds, visited only by his loyal assistants. But I still believe in striving for our natural state. After all, if we raise our children communally, they are less likely to be beaten or unnecessarily harangued by their parents, because the community is watching."

"Or," I countered, "the child could be beaten by more people."

He sighed and put his hand to his forehead. He looked like he wanted to apologize to me for my own history. I kept my jaw tight until, I think, he thought better of it.

"We *do* have laws, Radiant," he said instead, "and punishments. Although the worst is exile from the Guild, which we have only ever done four times."

"And did they get to take their things with them when they left?"

"Whatever they had kept. But *not* their spouse or their child, because those were not things. A spouse was welcome to follow their exiled partner if they wished." He grinned. "No one ever did."

"And I assume children of the Guild don't inherit anything from their parents."

"Of course not! Heredity would be antithetical to our ideals."

"Except," I replied, "when it comes to knowledge of this place, yes? You said that Yalwas knows and that his son Kyautas does as well."

I don't know why I was being purposefully difficult. Perhaps I wanted to show my own intelligence, or simply to prove that I would not fall under the sway of one more charismatic authority figure in my life. It certainly seemed like the wrong strategy if I wanted to convince him to allow more Loashti into his midst, which was, I reminded myself, my greater goal.

Adomas opened his mouth to respond and then stopped. He looked at me for a moment, and I wondered if he was regretting his decision to bring me here.

"You see," he began, a big smile breaking through, "this is exactly why I wanted to show you all this. I knew you'd be the type to appreciate what I'm doing here enough to question it. I hope you choose to stay with us, Radiant. You will keep me honest."

"And if I stay after you're gone, will I keep Yalwas honest?"

A laugh started somewhere in his chest and came out as a grunting cough. "Yalwas. Huh. He'd like to think so." Adomas shrugged. "I'm sure I don't know. Our hierarchy is purposefully loose, to allow for fellow feeling. I don't wish for anyone to necessarily take over as a new version of *me* when I'm gone. If I've done my job, another me won't be necessary. I am already a vestige. I had the idea and the power to make it work, but this community is quickly outgrowing me, and I love that."

He did not seem to realize that he also had a leader's self-assurance and charisma. I remembered Vidmantas at the Žalikwen Salon, saying that Žydrė's guild would fall apart the moment their "cult leader" was gone. I began to think he had been right. Especially because Adomas really did seem to mean what he said: to not want power for power's sake. No, he wanted the Lanreas River Guild to stand on its own without him, but was inadvertently leaving it unprepared for his absence.

All the more reason, I thought, to bring my Zobiski community here as soon as possible. If the place began to fracture, I wanted Loashti aliens to already be a part of it, so that they could have a voice in its future.

Adomas, still laughing at the idea of Yalwas taking over as leader of the Guild, stood up and showed me into the next room. On the way, I peered into another glass case: inside was a twisted, long-dead plant with flowers that looked somewhat like rotted meat.

Once the lamps were lit, I saw what seemed to be a bedroom. The walls were once again covered in bookshelves and art, except for the farthest, which had two paintings on both sides of what seemed to be a closed window. Against that wall was a small bed and a chamber pot.

"I sometimes nap here," said Adomas, "but I haven't spent the night in fifteen years or so. When I was hiding, I slept only here, watching the meerkats and others live their lives from this window. Since then, I've simply refused to stay too long: bad memories of feeling trapped, of being locked away from the world. It felt no different from the time I spent in prisons, except out here, I wasn't even plotting escape."

"And out here you had servants," I added.

Adomas laughed. "True, true."

He walked over to the closed window, which still let in no light or sound, and leaned against its sill.

"I assume it was the people who worked for you who built all this?"

He nodded. "Yes, those I could trust. I was a different man then, to ask so much of them." He saw me begin to open my mouth and quickly added, "No, to *demand* so much of them. Let me correct myself before you do."

I nodded. "The tunnel from your estate was already there?"

"It was, yes. Perhaps I have an ancestor to whom I owe my disdain for the law. Or perhaps the tunnel was something older, like the ones in Rotfelsen dug by ancient creatures." He grinned and nodded back toward the other room. "Creatures like that charming fellow back there. You know, those bits of jaw, tooth, and eye are the most anyone's ever seen of whatever those horrors may have been!" His eyes lit up at the thought before he got back to his point. "Anyway, I—that is, my people—paneled the tunnel in nice wood, so I would not feel like some wild man hiding out in caves."

"Did it work?"

He shrugged. "A little. They also built this house and, of course . . ."

He flourished to the window and then began to turn a small contraption. The window cover, which I assume was also of heavy, moss-covered rotrock, slid up to show us a view of the Lanreas River rushing by, glittering white and silver from the moon, stars, and howling winds above. The room was flooded with that light, and some of the noise made it in as well, although it was much more manageable than when we'd been outside.

I now also saw, much closer up, the metal piping alongside the outside of the house, running from somewhere up in the wind down into the river.

"This," Adomas began, pointing to the pipes and raising his voice over that of the wind, "is what I wanted to show you, really. The pipes collect the river water and pump it over to the Guild. Just a bit downriver, the winds go back to ground level and fill the water that moves south with sediment, but in this little pocket beneath the tumult, it's quite clear and fresh."

"Is this where the water in the well comes from?"

"It *is!*"

"I don't know much about these things, but isn't that a long way for the water to travel?"

"Yes, but you see, we have wind power, though few know it." He pointed up to the top of the piping. "The arms up there catch the immeasurably, dangerously powerful winds of Galiag, which are then used to push the water all the way to the Guild. And"—he couldn't help smirking—"not just to the well, but into a series of pipes that diffuse it out into the very ground."

I stared out at the piping, looking as closely as I could despite the blinding light. "And that's why you can grow so many crops in a place where few could."

"Exactly. Just a little secret irrigation, while most Guild members think we are either very lucky, very blessed, or very skilled."

"That must be why the farms are all downhill: just the way the water runs, isn't it?"

Adomas patted my back hard. He was surprisingly strong for his age. "That's right, Radiant. I knew you were a smart one."

"And your servants built all that. Up in the wind, beneath the river, into the ground."

He nodded. "The piping mostly runs alongside the tunnel between here and the Estate: the wood paneling covers up a lot of gashes in the stone. I had significant help from a wind power expert I hired in Galiag."

"But the building of it all, was that dangerous?"

"Yes." He nodded and looked away from me. "One man had all the skin flayed off his arm by the winds as he put up the wind wheel. Another was dragged into the river by a crocodile, and only his booted foot was found, much later, on the shore of the Skydaš Sea." He looked down at the shining wooden floor. "I don't even remember their names."

I said nothing.

"You must understand that I am trying to be a better man now, to help, rather than simply expend people. But it seems wasteful, to me, to not use what so many toiled to build."

"I suppose that makes sense," I allowed. Then I decided to move to something he'd enjoy discussing more. "What sort of crocodiles come here? You must watch them through your window."

Adomas immediately brightened. "Plenty come down here through the waters, sometimes even sun themselves on the land. The normal sort, you know."

"Meaning they walk low to the ground, on four legs? What a Tetrarchic way for you to see it."

He turned the little contraption back, and the window closed, leaving us once more in only lamplight. Then he sat on his bed and looked up at me.

"Not at all. Rather, that's a very Southern Loashti way for *you* to see it. Most crocodiles on this continent—whether in Skydašiai or most parts of Loasht—are on four feet. Where you are from is the aberration, although a *fascinating* one, I must say."

"I didn't know that," I admitted. "But I suppose it makes sense. There are stories that the crocodiles around Yekunde, which walk on two legs, hunched somewhat like a man, are the issue of Zobiski ancestors who mated with crocodiles." I couldn't fully suppress a laugh. "I haven't yet learned whether this story came from my people, or from those who meant to denigrate us."

"Whoever it was," he said, laughing with me, "is quite wrong. Your upright crocodiles aren't any smarter or more human than the four-legged ones. I assure you they are absolutely the same animal, with the only functional difference being some walk on four legs and others on two, using their front 'arms' to balance."

"That's disappointing."

"In fact, I'm sorry to tell you that your upright crocodiles are *slower* on land than their four-legged kin. They don't seem to have any benefit to walking the way they do, other than making them a useful symbol for rhetorical and religious purposes."

I looked down at my arms, where under the linen sleeves, my tattoos of upright crocodiles lurked. Those had an intelligence and menace in their eyes that the real beasts lacked.

"I hope I haven't disappointed you too terribly," he said, standing up.

"Well, you've further convinced me that there's little reason to go back to Loasht," I replied.

I watched his expression to see what he thought of this, but he only kept smiling and began to lead me back through the little house.

"So," I said, "why *did* you want to show me all this, exactly?"

"Because I know that you, like me, are a man of knowledge, who will appreciate what we're doing here. Because I'd like to offer you the opportunity to also use my study here for your research." He indicated the first room, as we passed through it, with its desk and chairs and bookshelves. "You may find something useful in my personal collection that can further help our community."

"Is that the entire reason for telling me your secrets?"

Adomas' smile faded and he said, "No."

Then he opened the door, and it became too loud to speak again.

Once we'd passed yet again beneath the blazing winds and stars, through the howling but verdant little gorge with its carefree creatures, we re-entered the passageway that led back to the Estate. Adomas walked ahead of me, carrying a lamp.

"You now understand that the Guild's success," he said, "is based on a singular machine known to but a few. The plans for it were destroyed, and it is largely kept running by my own knowledge, alongside what little Yalwas and his ilk have managed to glean from me. What's more, this machine secretly siphons water that supposedly 'belongs' to the kingdom we have officially forsaken."

"When you put it that way," I said, "it all seems quite fragile."

"Yes," he grunted. "Yes, it does. Very fragile indeed."

The sound of the wind faded further and further into silence behind us, and the tunnel now only filled with Adomas' voice. He started with a deep, pained sigh.

"The old King," he then explained, "gave me quite a free hand here, but I am not so naïve as to think that will last forever. So, you must understand why this community simply can't become a . . . camp for Loashti aliens. I want you, personally, to stay—I wouldn't have shown you all this if I did not. I really do feel for your people, but we simply can't let what happened today happen again. For one thing, it would bring too much attention on us from Skydašiai, and the government might begin to ask questions about how the Guild operates. For another, it would change the very fabric and tenor of this place. We would become a village of Loashti refugees, and the . . . you know, the culture I have tried to instill in my people would be lost. Even before the Yams, inevitably, descended upon us."

I said nothing. I stared at the back of his head, silhouetted in the light. What did he want me to say? What would Kalyna tell me to say?

Adomas continued: "I want you to understand, Radiant, because you are obviously intelligent, and I think you can do great things here. I know it will be painful, but I would hate for you to leave us in anger when we, inevitably, must turn away more of your countrypeople. That is why I wanted you to see all this, and to understand our reasoning."

"I . . . understand."

What was it about me, I wondered, that led so many people—from Manti Dumpling Akram, to Aloe Pricks a Mare upon the Mountain Bluff, to Adomas the Bandit-Naturalist—to like me *despite* what I was? To ask such inhuman understanding of me?

How Cedar Cones Pelt the Naughty Mangabey Saved My Life

I do not wish to dredge up too much of my childhood, but another bit of inhuman understanding that was often expected of me was to know whether or not my father would hit me, and why. I became vigilant and accommodating early in life, although never enough to fully curb my habit of asking uncomfortable questions. Such questions only got me a beating, say, two-thirds of the time, adding to my confusion.

This was the pattern: something I did would cause my father to hurt me, and then, as my mother cleaned me up, she would chastise me for my transgression with great sighs. Not, it seemed to me, sighs at how brutal her husband was, but at how difficult I was being. But what I've just described was the *only* pattern, so far as I could tell. Nothing else was ever clear or predictable to me.

All of which is to say that when I was perhaps eleven or twelve years old, we took a trip to a renowned temple about a day away by cart. My mother was always taking us to temples, so this one was the same as any other to me. I hated temples and therefore hated praying, because these short pilgrimages were always an ordeal. Every last one began with my father renting us a cart, only to silently seethe about it.

We spent a night at the pilgrim's rooms abutting the temple, and I suppose I threw some sort of tantrum; I don't remember about what. My father, loathe to go beyond a cuff on the ear where strangers could hear us, got so full to the brim with anger that he told us he would take the cart home himself, that night, leaving us there. This was exactly what he did.

I spent the next day sitting across the small pilgrim's room from my mother, until she had glared silently at me for so long that I ran from her. Once I got outside, into what I then considered a crisp autumn day (so, a hot summer day in Abathçodu), I wandered about, throwing rocks, thwacking sticks with other sticks, and full of emotions I could not name. Then suddenly, I knew exactly what I had to. More than anyone had ever needed to do anything in history, I needed to climb that temple—to reach its top and then, somehow, be *greater* than its god.

To be clear, this temple was a series of rounded shapes carved directly into an otherwise craggy cliff. Looking back, I can't imagine I would've survived this endeavor.

"Radiant Basket of Rainbow Shells, that's your name, isn't it?" called a trilling, almost unbearably friendly voice from somewhere below me.

It was Silver's mother, Cedar Cones Pelt the Naughty Mangabey. This was long before Silver and I would become entwined, but I vaguely knew them and their family: the Zobiski community in Yekunde was small, despite it being our ancestral homeland.

As I remember it, I was quite far up the temple rocks already, but I don't know if that's true. Childhood exaggerates.

"Yes, so?" I replied.

"Radiant," said Cedar, "would you like to come with me and—"

"No!"

"You haven't heard what we're going to do yet."

"What?" I asked, in the tone of a child clearly rolling their eyes.

"I happen to know a priest here who's become quite relaxed in his old age. If you come with me and ask him very nicely, he may allow you to whisper the river god's name into his ear."

This intrigued me. "Really? Out loud?" I yelled.

"You will have to promise him you won't do it again, though."

"Unless," I chirped, "I join his order someday."

"Yes, yes. You've got me there, Radiant. In that case, you certainly can. So why don't you come down?"

"I don't know . . ."

"He may even let you see the sanctuary . . ." she sang out.

I climbed down, falling the last few yards to be caught by Cedar. She was stronger than she looked.

We all knew the names of the Eighty-Three—we heard priests say them in prayers, read them in sacred texts, and appealed to them in our heads—but only a priest of a god's order was ever supposed to say such a name out loud. Yet Cedar's old priest had come upon a workaround: he was the river god's intermediary, and so if the name was whispered only to him, it was the same as me saying it in my head, where only the god would hear it. I stammered and wondered if the ground would open up beneath me, but when it didn't, I was exhilarated. It was the first time I felt anything other than fear or irritation at prayer.

And I was, in fact, taken to see the temple's sanctuary: a small, quiet room with a hole in the floor, through which one could see the spot where, long ago, water had burst forth out of a stone. A sanctuary must always mark a miracle, and so not all temples have them. Those that do guard them zealously, and only a priest of the temple can permit a layperson to enter.

That evening, Cedar took my mother and me back to Yekunde. When I told Silver this story many years later, it actually made them back away from our burgeoning relationship, for a time. They worried that I didn't love *them*, that I just wanted to be part of their family. The simple fact is that both were true.

I don't know if my parents ever spoke to each other about, or even remembered, that day, but for me it was monumental. It was when I first decided I would avoid them whenever I could, and I had lived up to that.

Yet now, decades later at the Lanreas River Guild, I was insisting that Kalyna save my parents as much as anyone else. Perhaps a part of me still loves them, despite everything. Or, perhaps, regardless of blood and family, I love them for being Zobiski.

Chapter Eighteen

When I Learned Just a Touch of What Was Happening Back in Loasht

It was early morning when I returned to the dormitory building, head full of everything I'd learned—and everything I'd decided—the previous day. For the record, what I wanted to do next had not changed. I wanted to bring my family, friends, and community here, no matter what Adomas said. I knew there was space for them; I knew that his artificially enhanced, and legally safe (for now), lands were the best place to bring them. We would simply need to convince him, which I could not do without Kalyna's particular gifts.

I was entirely sober, but I felt drunk when I stumbled into my dormitory, as sunlight was already beginning to peek into the sky. How did a man of Adomas' age manage? He'd been wide awake and not even winded when I'd left him at his home.

The dormitory was crowded when I entered. Every bed that had been empty was now full of Loashti aliens: it was probably the most safely they'd slept in weeks. Did Adomas plan to expel them? Or only stop more from coming? I didn't know.

Binturong, the Zobiski parent I'd met, was in bed with both of their teenaged children under their arms. I suppose there hadn't been enough beds otherwise. They all seemed too exhausted to care much.

Wearily, and slowly, I moved toward my bed. Every second that I moved closer, I expected someone else to grab me and give me a talking-to: for Kalyna to berate me, or for Binturong to decide that *now* was the time to tell me what was going on back in Loasht.

Somehow, blessedly, none of this happened. Instead, I got into my comfortable bed and lay awake. Absolutely exhausted, but unable to sleep. I wasn't even thinking through any of the things ahead of me, I was simply . . . *alert*.

This lasted until the people around me began to stir.

"There you are!" cried Ifeanyas, shaking me as though I was asleep. "We were so worried!"

I turned my head toward him so slowly that he recoiled, as though I was some sort of living dead thing.

"Good morning," I croaked. "Let's get breakfast."

And so we did. The Meal Hall was packed, more than it had been the night before, with both new Loashti and Guild members curious to see what might transpire. Ifeanyas, Vidmantas, Žydrė, and I all sat at the same table as Binturong, their children, and many others. Yalwas was at another table with Kyautas, not far away.

Everyone had started eating (breakfast was beautifully spiced rice and potatoes, with chopped-up hard-boiled eggs) when Kalyna came in and sat down at a far table. She looked almost as tired as I felt.

"When you disappeared last night," Binturong began in Zobiski, "we weren't able to speak to our new friends as much as we would have liked."

"Oh? Did Simurgh not help you?" The moment it was out of my mouth, I knew it was a stupid question.

They shook their head. "Whoever that is did not make themself known. A few of us—not I—speak a smattering of Skydašiavos, so we were able to manage a few things, but it was awkward."

"I'm sorry to hear that," I said, glaring over at Kalyna, who had, it seemed, still not let on that she spoke Loashti Bureaucratic.

"What *exactly* do these people want from us in return?" asked

Binturong. "They've given us a place to sleep and meals, and I'm deeply grateful. But there must be a reason."

They looked around the room and then back at me. Binturong was a stately type, now that they'd cleaned up a bit: almost patrician, for a Zobiski. Tall and thick, with no tattoos, and hair hidden by a wrap.

I took a very long time chewing my next bite of breakfast to think about how I would answer their question.

"Well," I finally said, "this is a community that stands apart from the rest of the Tetrarchia. They have no money and, theoretically, no hierarchies. Everyone is meant to help out and take care of one another to the best of their abilities."

"'Theoretically' and 'meant to' are interesting choices," they said.

I nodded. "I have only been here two weeks myself. I'm not yet sure where their willingness to help ends." I thought about my audience with Adomas the previous night.

Binturong nodded thoughtfully. Then they turned to another Loashti and said in Loashti Bureaucratic, "Echoes."

The middle-aged woman who'd been leading these new Loashti when they arrived looked up. Her eyes were red with exhaustion, and most of her face was painted in swirls of gray ash.

"Perhaps," said Binturong, "I should tell our hosts what we've been through."

"You don't need to do that," said the face-painted woman, whose name I took to be Echoes.

"They seem decent enough," replied Binturong. "And no decent person would turn us away after hearing the story."

I studied Binturong for a moment. To me, this seemed a wildly un-Zobiski thing to say. But then, we were scattered throughout the southern reaches of Loasht, and who was I to say that the way my community adapted and survived over the years was the same as how someone else's had? Perhaps where they were from was an easier place to be Zobiski, and so their forebears had faced less persecution; or perhaps it had once been much worse. Either one could have pointed them toward greater assimilation. (Although, clearly, not assimilated enough for Aloe.)

"Maybe," I allowed. "And I would like to hear more. But only if you feel that you can manage it."

"I think I have to. Will you translate?"

I nodded.

———————

I do not feel up to reproducing every painful detail of what Binturong told everyone—and indeed, I may have forced myself to forget much of it, for my own health. It was necessary, they felt, to get into specifics, but as I am not writing this account in order to convince *those* members of the Lanreas River Guild on *that* day, I will abbreviate.

I got everyone's attention, and, not unlike when Aloe was there two weeks previous, many listened quite intently. I translated what Binturong said as directly as I could—whether this was out of respect for them or because I knew Kalyna could hear us, I don't know.

According to Binturong, all of Loasht had been in a state of uncertainty at the unexpected death of the last Grand Suzerain. Official word was that one day he had complained of a headache, before dropping dead a few hours later. Such a death could easily have been natural causes or an assassination, and no one seemed sure of how it should be treated. Whatever the case, with the new Grand Suzerain, things quickly changed for the worse.

"This may be hard for you southerners to understand," I remember they said in Loashti Bureaucratic, which I translated to Skydašiavos, "as I know your governments and policies can change quickly, but in Loasht, those of us with little power have historically been thankful for the Grand Suzerain. You see, it's always been him, and Loasht's all-encompassing government that he represents, who kept our neighbors and local leaders from . . . exterminating us, if they so chose."

I understood what Binturong was saying, and I didn't entirely disagree, but I wondered if they were simplifying for their audience.

So, with the new Grand Suzerain, things deteriorated very quickly for anyone deemed "not Loashti enough." A number of edicts were pushed out, decreeing that all Loashti people must be truly, "culturally" Loashti. But what exactly this meant, or how it would be achieved, was left purposefully, maddeningly, vague. Where Binturong and these others were from, the people had been allowed to argue the true meaning of being "culturally" Loashti, to turn on one another, and to suggest methods of proof for about a month. Then the army had been sent in.

This was not Aloe's murky little "hunting club" that had so terrified me in Yekunde. This was the real, heavily armed, blessed by the Eighty-Three Loashti Army. I tried to convey to our audience how rare it was for us to even *see* soldiers on a day-to-day basis in Loasht. Such a thing was not normal, and to Binturong, it had felt like an invasion. (Which, I suppose, it was.)

The Loashti Army was there to enforce the new laws—laws which were, again, purposefully vague. They made arrests; they stood by during violence and theft perpetrated on those who were not "culturally" Loashti enough; they burst into schools that taught in Zobiski or other "backward" languages and beat the teachers in front of their students. Both of Binturong's spouses were killed by a mob while soldiers watched. (I felt guilty for eliding this slightly in my translation, referring to their "husband" and "best friend" instead.)

People began to be arrested in large groups, supposedly to be "taught correct ways." Others were simply forced out of one city and then the next. This had been the fate of most of our new aliens: deemed hopeless, they were made exiles from their regions, and then from any others they passed through.

Some were killed along the way, and Binturong stressed that even those who starved or died of exhaustion had been *killed*, because exile had been decreed with the hope, the expectation, that none of them would survive. And none would have, apparently, if not for the woman in gray face paint, whose full name was Echoes in the Gingko-Wreathed Valley Sound like Grandfather's Voice. She had kept the group together, kept them moving, and taught many of them how to forage.

Then, at the border, they'd been stopped by Loashti soldiers. They were ridiculed, further starved, and finally foisted onto the Yams.

Binturong held their composure through their story and thanked everyone in the Meal Hall for listening. I then chose to specify for the audience that those horrors had been at the behest of Aloe, the man who had been welcomed by the Guild just two weeks earlier, and who had *acted* like my friend. This caused a great amount of lively discussion through the rest of breakfast.

I tried to take the tenor of the room, but it was very difficult to tell how Binturong's story would be taken by those who'd heard it, or by those who would hear it secondhand. Vidmantas leaned over toward me. His hair was tied up for the morning in the remnants of his old robe. After breakfast, he would let it out and shape his curls.

"Radiant," he said, "I'm afraid I don't quite understand. I thought all the Loashti who were being kept out had been allowed back."

"We are being allowed back *if* we are supposedly Loashti enough."

"Ah, I think I see. So, what . . . what nonsense reason was given that she wasn't Loashti enough?"

"Not 'she,' if you please," I said. "In Skydašiavos, 'they' will do. And the only reason was their very existence."

"I see." Vidmantas looked thoughtful, glanced at Ifeanyas, and then back to me. "Was it *because* they're not a man or woman?"

"No, no. It's . . . Eighty-Three, how to explain." I put my forehead in my hand for a moment. When I looked up, there were a few more Guild members nearby, listening for my answer. "Do you remember when Aloe said something about 'backward, ingrained thinking'? That's how he describes people like us, with our own ways that are different from—well, not *different* from Loashti ways, because we are Loashti." I breathed out loudly. "They think we trade in the occult—that we are magical and dangerous."

"I thought all Loashti were magical," said Ifeanyas.

"What you say about the Loashti, people from Central Loasht say about us. Does that make sense?"

Silence for a moment. Then, from somewhere in the back:

"I thought you were a wizard!"

I stammered but formed no words, terrified to either confirm or deny Kalyna's story.

A hand grasped my shoulder, and I jumped.

"Whether or not Radiant's a wizard," said Kalyna, standing behind me, "none of these Loashti are. They're just normal people like any of us. Now, let's give Radiant here a rest."

There was a general murmur in the Meal Hall as I stood shakily to leave.

"Let's talk outside," said Kalyna.

"What about my rest?" I moaned.

"I'm sorry," said Kalyna. "You were absolutely right that Dagmar would have disagreed with my saying I had . . . done what I did all alone."

I was lying down beneath a large, broad tree, while Kalyna sat nearby, and we were speaking quite softly in Cölluknit. There were birds in the tree, making agreeable little noises as sunshine peeked around them. Under another tree nearby, Uzochi was roasting up something—perhaps more chickpeas. It smelled delightful. Was it intended to make a good impression on our new guests?

I was too tired for pretenses. "Is this a real apology, or one you're making for some other purpose?"

"What's the difference? I'm saying it, aren't I?"

I sighed.

"I was angry at what you were trying to pull me into, and, well, I *did* do the lion's share of the work back in Rotfelsen. I think."

I shrugged. "I'm sure I wouldn't know."

"Were I you," she said after a pause, "I would have added to Binturong's story. And I may not have tried to explain their gender—no need for greater confusion."

"I am not you," I replied.

"Clearly. And you're naïve if you think one sad story will get the whole community on your side."

"I don't, but Binturong wanted to try."

Kalyna threw herself backward into the grass. "Unfortunately," she grunted, "it may have gotten *me* on your side."

My heart jumped. "Really?!"

"Maybe. I'm thinking about it. Last night, I heard the Loashti talking to one another about what they'd been through. They thought I didn't understand them, of course."

"Well, if you'll help me, it's as good as done!"

She laughed at that, snorting and convulsing. "You are absolutely doomed if you think so," she said, sounding as though she didn't mean it. "Although I have swindled some large groups in my time . . ." She shook her head. "Nonetheless, Yalwas and his people certainly don't like me much."

"Yalwas is busy protecting his own secrets."

"Oh?"

I sat up and described what Adomas had shown and told me about the Guild and his little hideaway.

Once I'd told her all of it, I noted, "You seem disappointed there isn't a more sinister secret beneath this place."

"Perhaps. But I'm sure there's something juicy down in Adomas' *private* papers: family secrets, controversies, outlines of his heists. He was a rich scoundrel for a long time."

"Could be. There is one other piece I ought to tell you." I yawned—I'm not sure if it was uncontrollable or for effect. "In that hut, away from the world, Adomas has what he says is the most anyone's ever seen of, ah, whatever it was that, long ago, 'dug tunnels in Rotfelsen'? Is that right?"

Kalyna remained lying in the grass, but did not, or could not, hide the look of excitement and fear that wore its way across her face.

"Well," she said, "now I have to find a way down there."

She sat in silence for some time. I almost fell asleep, until she brought me out of it by asking, "Has Adomas' frank word with you dissuaded you from bringing your people here?"

"Not at all. We just have to convince him."

"Or replace him."

I stared at her.

"Just thinking out loud," she added.

"Either way," I asked, "how would we get my people here?"

"Much to my own chagrin, I've been thinking about that since last night—I couldn't help myself. The border may be easier to cross than it was a few weeks ago, thanks to your friend Aloe."

"He isn't—!"

"I know. But now those who cannot become Loashti will be leaving, and those who wish to assimilate will be coming back. That's a lot of traffic. So perhaps we could send some people into Loasht to get them."

"The way back would be more treacherous, I think. The Zobiski are a whole community; they aren't all young and able-bodied."

"Oh, I know. Are there river boats in Yekunde?"

"Certainly."

"I wonder if they could somehow steer right into Adomas' gorge," she murmured. "The Tail is supposed to be impassable, but see if you can find anything in Adomas' private writings about other ways into his gorge."

"I'll try."

"Does this new knowledge change our farming plans at all?"

"I think if anything, it will be helpful."

"Good, good. We need a name for this. Collective Garden, Guild Farming, Mutual Agriculture, or something like that."

"Not the Kalyna Aljosanovna Gardens?"

"It has a ring to it. And please start doing all your research in the daytime, so you can be back in town for the evenings, when these people socialize. They think you're strange enough as it is."

"You *did* tell them I'm a—"

"Yes, yes. Get to it. I'll think about the other pieces."

"Kalyna. Thank you."

"Don't thank me yet. It's an interesting problem to play with, but it may be impossible, or I may simply get bored after I've wrung out all the sport."

"What 'sport' is that?"

"Toying with people, making them like or dislike me. I must admit, it can be fun." She grunted and stood up, picking up her sickle and tucking it back into her belt. "I suppose Adomas is onto something: remove the desperate grasping of life, and work can be enjoyable." She grinned and winked. "Even when one's work is being a cutthroat and deceiver."

We returned to the Meal Hall, where there was much lively discussion still going on among the Guild members. The Loashti were mostly there as well, eating and drinking as much as they could.

Kalyna clapped her hands loudly, to get everyone's attention, and then turned to me.

"Radiant," she said, "be my dragoman."

I nodded.

"My Loashti friends," she began in Skydašiavos, "you've been through a lot. I want you to know that you can absolutely spend today eating, napping, meandering, or whatever might make you feel happy and rested. I will even point out to you where we play a small assortment of games here at Lanreas."

I translated and noticed she was specifically using phrasing that would translate easily and quickly into Loashti Bureaucratic. I hardly even had to think about it.

"But," she continued, "if—and I do truly mean *if*—any of you are the sort of person who would welcome a task to pass the time, who would delight in a little light work, I'll be happy to help you find something agreeable."

After I'd translated this, Kalyna looked at me, adding, "And Radiant, please do make it clear there's no unspoken *expectation* lurking in what

I've said, yes? That it really is up to them, and no one will be angry or disappointed if they sleep all day. Or all week."

She, of course, knew exactly how I'd phrased it, but I obliged.

"She does really want you to know that she means it, and I'll second that," I said. "You don't have to start working today to stay here, I promise."

"Truly?" asked a Loashti woman who seemed unconvinced. "They won't resent us? Say we're loafers who aren't, you know, appreciating their kindness?"

I shrugged. "Kalyna can't speak for everyone, of course. But that's how this place is supposed to work."

"Also tell them," Kalyna added, as though it was simply a continuation of what she'd been saying before, "that if any of our fellow Guild members have a problem with this, send them to me. I will *personally* remind them of Adomas' teachings on the point."

I did so, although I must say I stuttered a bit, distracted by what those words might suggest to the other Guild members present. Only yesterday, Kalyna had narrowly avoided having my countrypeople turned away, and now she was acting as the arbiter of the Guild's rules. Sometimes I felt I understood her thoughts and actions, and sometimes I did not at all.

"That's good," said Binturong, with a nod. "Because I won't be able to do anything besides take care of my children for some time." One of those teenage children rolled his eyes, to which they smiled and continued: "Even though, at their age, they act as though they can never be hurt."

I translated this back. Kalyna chuckled pleasantly, and a few Guild members put in knowing laughs.

Echoes, the Loashti woman with her face painted in ash, was skeptical. "Fine then," she said. "My hands are getting itchy, it's true." She demonstrated this by flexing her fingers, which I heard crack quietly. "What will they have us *do*, then? I'm no farmer or tailor."

"No, but you are a forager and leader, aren't you?" Kalyna replied, once I'd translated.

"Only when I have to be."

"What do you like to do? If you *were* a farmer and never wanted to farm again, we'd find something else for you."

I translated, and Echoes heaved a long sigh. "Aloe Pricks a Mare upon the Mountain Bluff would call me a 'shaman.'" Her upper lip twitched. "Because the *pig-fucker* doesn't know what that word means." (What I translated as "pig-fucker" was in fact a term in the Kubatri language, of middle-western Loasht, which was much more graphic about the acts supposedly being performed.)

"Well, what does it mean?" I asked. "To you, of course."

Echoes seemed to suddenly notice that I was a person, rather than a translating apparatus.

"To my understanding, a shaman is more impressive than me," she laughed. "They talk to spirits, I think? I don't really know; we don't have them where I'm from." She grumbled and drummed her fingers on the table. "The Kubatri word that Aloe says means 'shaman' does have a spiritual component: we are meant to practice our arts selflessly for our communities. But those arts themselves are really closer to alchemy than anything else."

"But of course, if they called you an alchemist," I said, "they'd have to admit your work isn't 'occult,' but just different from Central Loashti alchemy. Older, perhaps, or younger."

"Or simply . . . sideways from them, yes," she said. "Just let me pick through this childish place for anything I can, you know"—she pressed her hands together—"mix up and see what it makes. Drawing salves, abortifacients, globules you throw in the fire for a fun color—anything."

I nodded and said, in translation, only that she was an alchemist and wanted to see what could be made with the materials on hand. I fancied I saw a glint in Kalyna's eye as she considered the full possibilities of what she'd heard.

"We'll find some things you can mash together, I promise you," said Kalyna.

I translated, and Echoes mumbled in response: "Personally, I'd be overjoyed to make some more interesting colors." She indicated her face, painted in gray ash.

I was too tired to go do any research that day, yet too anxious to get my much-needed sleep, so I followed Kalyna about as her dragoman. This took very little effort on my part, because Kalyna continued to choose her words carefully, leaving me as little room as possible for interpretation. The Loashti generally kept their responses short and to the point, although they sometimes had further comments that were meant only for each other, and for me. Besides, most of them chose to continue resting, or perhaps to slowly explore the Estate or Games Hall.

Kalyna showed the few remaining Loashti around, doing so as if she had always lived at the Guild. She pointed out locations and workshops, smiled and waved to people she knew (including some, like Yalwas, who she knew would not wave back), and pointed out the well, promising that one could drink as much as one wanted, because it would never run dry. At least a few did truly want to use labor to keep their minds off uncertainty and fear—or so they told me.

One had been a serf in a Loashti polity that still allowed that sort of thing, where he had done backbreaking labor in the fields or the quarries or wherever the next week brought him. His lord had, supposedly, been practicing some sort of occultism that involved sacrificing his serfs for power, and so his entire title was dissolved. Every former serf was then questioned to see who had aided their lord's dark magics. The questions of what constituted "aid," and of how it was something a serf could willingly give, were not considered. This man had simply misunderstood the questions, and so here he was in Skydašiai, an alien. But he had always enjoyed cooking for his family (who were still back in Loasht), and after a bit of translating on my part, he was happy to sit beneath a tree and chop okra for Uzochi to fry up.

Another had been a milliner and had simply made religious head-wear for the wrong neighbors, causing their expulsion. They very quickly developed an interest in Vidmantas' work dyeing clothing, and began helping him. The two communicated through pointing and sign language, which Vidmantas thankfully found charming rather than aggravating.

Echoes, too, was interested in what Vidmantas was doing and asked a good many questions about his ingredients—this was the most difficult translating I had to do all day. At a certain point, she felt she'd learned whatever it was she wanted to know, and we moved on.

Yet another Loashti alien had enjoyed some of the work of farming in and of itself, but hated having to go to market and haggle over prices. She had simply been expelled for being the wrong kind of Kubatri. We came across Ifeanyas working tirelessly in the fields.

"She's certainly welcome to help," he said. "But I don't want her to work too hard. After all, they've all had quite the ordeal, haven't they?"

I communicated this to the Loashti, and she smiled. Apparently, she spent most of the next few days just watching Ifeanyas and the others work, learning by sight the ways in which the soil here was different from where she had grown up.

One more new arrival was what I could only translate as an "alchemist-doctor." Kalyna's confusion at the term showed that even in Loashti Bureaucratic, she hadn't fully understood it.

"Even in Loasht, some of my techniques are quite new and un-tested," the alchemist-doctor explained to me, to tell Kalyna. "My task was to find new ways of bending our existing alchemical knowledge to-ward keeping people alive." He rolled his eyes. "Even though I was only using extant, *accepted* forms of alchemy, someone decided that combin-ing some of them with the human body was somehow hubristic. Even though this was *my job*." The alchemist-doctor had the gaunt look of an evil sorcerer in an old painting, which may not have helped his case.

He seemed happy to sit with the Lanreas River Guild's own heal-ers—a rotating group of people each with a bit of herbal and medical knowledge—and help where he could.

There was also, in this new group of Loashti, a priest. She looked northern Loashti to me: powerfully built, with straight black hair and a complexion I would have called "pale" before I met Rots and Masovskans. She had been excommunicated for using an older, now noncanonical, name for the river god—the same river god whose (of-ficial) name I'd whispered to a priest when I was a child. We left her with the Guild's other two priests, the Skydašian and the Rot, to argue theology in a multitude of languages.

Soon enough, it was only Kalyna, Echoes, and myself who were walking up to Simurgh's home. I realized then that Kalyna had proba-bly planned things this way: knowing both that Echoes would do best with another Loashti eccentric, and that she would feel more secure once she saw the others were being treated well. Of course, Kalyna had also very carefully considered whom to leave the others with, choosing agreeable, welcoming people (and also Vidmantas).

So it was mid-afternoon when the three of us trudged uphill toward the clearing that housed Simurgh's precious marabou balloon, as well as her workshop. I was impressed by Echoes' energy, considering she'd spent the last few weeks being forced from her home and held in terrible conditions at the border. I hoped she wasn't pushing herself to keep up with us out of some sort of pride, although I suspected that she was.

"I can't be bothered to be your little pet dragoman if Radiant here is flagging," was the first thing Simurgh said to us, in Skydašiavos, as she stood outside over a table, inspecting plans.

"I wasn't going to ask that of you," Kalyna replied. She then smiled and walked up to Simurgh's table, leaning a hand on the other side of it. "Simurgh, you aren't returning to Loasht, are you?"

"Why would I?" growled Simurgh. "*I* came here before that silly Blossoming. No one back home wanted me around. *Me*, a Loashti as Central as any can be!"

I cleared my throat uncomfortably. Simurgh ignored it.

"I'm sure I could have gone back to Loasht at any time," she continued, "if I gave up who I am and bowed to their rules and committees."

"Simurgh," I said in Loashti Bureaucratic, so Kalyna would have to pretend she didn't understand and, therefore, might not stop me, "the rest of us are exiled for reasons much worse than our work not being funded."

"Are you?" she replied in the same. "*Are you*? You've been exiled because of your background, and all you'd have to do now is act a little less like a Zobiski. Easy. And you have a whole . . . *people* with whom you are outcast. I was *functionally* exiled because of *who I am*. Alone and singular. In a way, I'm more a Zobiski than you."

I did not even know how to respond to such nonsense. I looked at Echoes and shrugged. She shook her head. Kalyna, who was trying very hard to not react to what had been said, attempted to get us back on track.

"Simurgh," she said in Skydašiavos, "why haven't you come and said hello to any of the other former Loashti who have arrived? You seemed so happy to greet Radiant when you first met him."

"I'm very busy," grumbled Simurgh. "And when you and Radiant first showed up, I was the only Loashti here. I was lonely."

"But now you're choosing loneliness?" asked Kalyna. "Or perhaps you're angry that you no longer stand out quite so much."

Simurgh's mouth became a very small line, and she glared at Kalyna.

"I don't know what they're saying," Echoes muttered to me under her breath. "Should I leave?"

I shook my head. Kalyna, of course, betrayed nothing of having heard and understood this, but seemed to change her strategy naturally.

"More likely," she added, "you're worried that if these people don't fit in well and are expelled, you'll be expelled with them."

"And is that so outlandish a thing to expect?" cried Simurgh.

Kalyna shook her head. "No, it isn't. But all the more reason to help them become part of the Guild. Like you did so well."

Simurgh did not seem terribly convinced, but she didn't immediately disagree either.

"The Simurgh Rules Air, Wind, and Sea," said Kalyna, "please meet Echoes in the Gingko-Wreathed Valley Sound like Grandfather's Voice." She motioned to Echoes.

"She's just introduced you," I murmured to Echoes and told her Simurgh's full name.

"And what of her?" asked Simurgh, still in Skydašiavos.

"What an ass!" exclaimed Echoes in Loashti Bureaucratic, easily loud enough for Simurgh to hear.

"Excuse me?" growled Simurgh, switching to that same language. "I can understand you just fine. I can even insult you in Kubatri, if you'd like!"

"Then why do you speak their child-tongue in my presence?"

Worried, I looked to Kalyna, who seemed calm enough.

"Echoes," Kalyna began in Skydašiavos, as though, language aside, the two had not clearly been arguing, "is an alchemist who would very much enjoy having something to do, just now. Why, I believe she specializes in fire."

"She told her you're an alchemist," I murmured to Echoes. I did not add the last part, which seemed to be Kalyna purposefully blowing Echoes' mention of making fires "a fun color" out of proportion.

As a correction, Echoes used the Kubatri word that could be translated as either "alchemist" or "shaman," but really lay somewhere in between the two.

Simurgh was quiet for a moment, and the two Loashti women stared at each other from a few yards away.

"Interesting," said Simurgh, finally, in Loashti Bureaucratic. "Can you help a fire to give off excessive hot air while remaining small?"

"How 'excessive'?"

"As much as possible without roasting a human standing next to it, of course."

The two of them then descended into a level of alchemical jargon that I did not understand. After a minute or two, Kalyna and I quietly made our goodbyes.

"I'm glad that worked!" Kalyna laughed as we walked down toward the village.

"You weren't sure?"

"Simurgh's a tough one. I can't always tell what she wants." She shrugged. "Had to play that one by ear, a bit."

"I'm sorry she isn't as easy to manipulate as most people," I mumbled.

"Radiant, don't forget I'm doing this for you."

"I haven't."

We walked in silence for a few moments, then she patted me hard on the back.

"And I've got more planned," she said. "Just you wait."

At this point, I knew better than to ask what those other plans were. She would tell me when it suited her.

When we returned to the village, Adomas was holding court in the shade of a tree and against the wall of a large building in chipping teal paint. Fanning himself with his hand, the old naturalist was speaking to a small group of people that included Yalwas and his son, Kyautas. Adomas waved us over, all smiles, as though he had not told me just last night that he wanted no more of my people on his lands.

"Kalyna Aljosanovna!" he called. "I hear you've been helping our new guests get accommodated."

"I have!" she replied with a smile, also betraying nothing of what she knew. "Some have even begun working already. But I've made sure they only do so *lightly*, for now."

Kyautas also smiled. Yalwas did not.

"Well, good," said Adomas. "But I'm sure the language differences are a problem."

"We'll manage!" chirped Kalyna.

"You've seemed able to communicate with them easily enough," said Yalwas.

"All thanks to Radiant here, I assure you."

"I wonder," muttered Yalwas.

There was an uncomfortable silence for a moment, as we all tried to decide what we thought that meant and whether we should pretend we hadn't heard it. But that quiet was soon broken when Kalyna grinned broadly and stepped forward, uncomfortably close to Yalwas.

"What do you wonder, Yalwas?" she asked, before getting even more grating. "*What exactly?*"

There was such genuine mirth in her face, such a cold joy at making him uncomfortable, at forcing him into a confrontation. I don't think I'd seen such a look on her face since Gintaras, the commander of the Yams back in Žalikwen, blew his own skull apart.

"Why don't you tell us?" she added, up on her toes to put her face mere inches from his.

Yalwas, clearly flustered, backed away until he bumped into the wall of the building.

"I just wonder," he stammered, "why you are getting so close with all of the Loashti. Why you seem to be . . . to be flooding our home with them."

Somehow, Kalyna's smile got even more assured, and disconcerting, at this.

"Oh?" she replied, close enough that he could likely smell her breath. "Your home? But not theirs, of course, if they're 'flooding' it. How very Tetrarchic of you."

"Now, now," Adomas jumped in. "I think you're both being a bit unfair."

"I'm so sorry," said Kalyna, still smiling.

Adomas cleared his throat uncomfortably. "Ah, Kalyna," he asked, "what will be the subject of your lecture this evening?"

She stepped back, and her face reverted almost instantly to a more pleasant smile.

"The evils of nationalism," she replied, looking at Adomas and becoming more serious. "Something we should all be more aware of."

"Fascinating, fascinating." Adomas nodded thoughtfully. Then he snapped his fingers and looked up at me. "That reminds me, Radiant, about that Aloe character. I hope you understand that if I'd known who he was, I never would have allowed him here."

"I do. Thank you."

"I thought he was just a dignitary." The old man seemed genuinely upset at the thought. "I promise you he won't be back!"

I thanked him, and we took our leave.

"Lecture?" I asked Kalyna.

She laughed. "It makes them feel smart to have someone talk at them for a few hours now and then. I'm happy to oblige."

"And what about Yalwas?"

Kalyna snorted. "What *about* Yalwas?"

"Aren't you worried that now he'll—"

"Radiant, Yalwas is nothing. I have dealt with more powerful and formidable men in my sleep."

"But what if he's the Guild's next leader?"

She snorted and looked around the village as we passed down one of its lanes. "Then I'll continue to handle him. The only thing Yalwas is to me is entertainment."

Chapter Nineteen

On the Night Life of the Lanreas River Guild:
Kalyna Aljosanovna's Lecture

I will not reproduce Kalyna's entire lecture, as it was about an hour long. This was, apparently, shorter than most.

It turned out that the teal building outside of which Kalyna had just made Yalwas uncomfortable was the Lecture Hall. When I went inside that evening, I was treated to the largest group of Lanreas River Guild members I had yet seen in one place: row after row of benches filled with people talking and laughing, patting one another on the back, hugging, and so much more Skydašian noise and comfort. It was astounding. This may not have been all two hundred and fifty Guild members, but it was close. A few curious Loashti aliens were also there, but not many.

At the front of the Lecture Hall was a slightly raised dais with a desk and a chair on it. Given the length of the lectures, and how many of them were probably given by Adomas himself, it seemed no one expected the speaker to stand. I had expected something more like one person in the center of a circle, but I suspect Kalyna preferred to command everyone's attention this way.

Kalyna sat in the chair on the dais, while Adomas stood next to her and gave her a brief introduction. Did anyone else think this made the old man look like *her* vassal?

"I'm sure most of you already know our friend Kalyna Aljosanovna," he said, gesturing to her with his large hat. "She only joined us here at Lanreas recently, and yet she's already become a fixture of many of our lives."

I could not tell if this was a compliment or Adomas' frustration at how well Kalyna had insinuated herself into the Guild.

"But on top of occupying our children and promising to improve our crops with her wizard friend, she has also, so I'm told, traveled over much of the known world."

Kalyna smiled and nodded.

"So," he continued, "she will now favor us with a lecture on 'the evils of nationalism,' which I assume she has learned a great deal about in her travels."

She nodded again, and Adomas went to sit down in the front row, crossing one leg over the other. There was some light applause, and Kalyna leaned forward with her arms on the desk, smiling. She was dressed much more like a Lanreas River Guild member than usual, in a robe and trousers of mostly undyed linen, except for a series of purple flowers that Vidmantas must have added diagonally across the chest. She did not have her sickle, and her hair was mostly tied up in order to look, I suppose, like she needed it out of her way for manual labor. There was, of course, a carefully chosen batch of glossy and loose curls that had come untied on one side of her face.

She began by thanking Adomas and everyone present. If there was any reticence or worry in the old naturalist's words, there was none detectable in hers: she seemed genuinely pleased to be there. She made some little joke that I don't remember. It wasn't terribly funny, but her smile and laugh were, as always, infectious, and sympathetic responses rippled through the crowd.

By the Eighty-Three, she was soaking it up, wasn't she? She was overjoyed, in her element.

Kalyna began by describing how nationalism as it was currently known had been born ("of course," she added) in the depths of Rotfelsen's dark tunnels, where the Rots had "nothing to do but fixate and nobody to talk to who was not exactly like them." From here, she said, had come the idea that Rotfelsen should be its own nation, made up only of Rots, and back out of the Tetrarchia entirely.

"Wanting to leave the Tetrarchia," she added quickly, "is a perfectly worthwhile goal, of course." She then motioned, abstractly, to the Guild itself. "But the reasons and the method are important. The beauty of our Lanreas River Guild is that it is open to all sorts of people. Not so the nation those Rots would've built." She held up a finger, motioning intently with it. "At best—at *best*, I say—their separatism would have led to a number of little nations at odds with one another, like the Bandit States but more so. Realistically, however, the world those Rots wanted would be much, much worse."

Kalyna seemed to get genuinely worked up now. She bit her lip, her voice cracked, and she took a moment before continuing.

"What their nationalism ignores," she finally said, "is people like me. Those who do not fit easily into one category, for any number of reasons. To *great thinkers* like those Rots I discussed, or indeed like that man, Aloe Pricks a Mare upon the Mountain Bluff, who visited us recently, people like me simply should not exist. And I am sure we all understand where that leads."

There were murmurs that ran through the crowd. Kalyna then gave an exhaustive list of the kinds of people who might not "count" in a nationalist state. Nomads, those of mixed ancestry, those who still speak some piece of an older language, or who still practice older rituals, and so forth. She gave many examples (including using *me* as an example), and most of the audience was rapt.

I was used to lectures given at the Academy, often by bored lecturers to bored students (part of why I was happy to just be a researcher). But these people wanted to be here and wanted to listen, even if that was partly because there was little else to do. Nonetheless, Kalyna kept them interested for some time, and just when she sensed they were about to lose interest, she pivoted.

"I saw this kind of nationalism—this vicious thing—in person just two years ago, and I nearly lost my life in the process." Again, tears seemed almost ready to emerge at any time, but she held them back. It was as though she was still feeling, in the pit of her stomach, the fear of this experience. I didn't know whether this reaction was real or faked.

She had, she told us, traveled to Rotfelsen and gotten pulled into that kingdom's strange politics.

"I am expected," she said, "to keep what I'm about to tell you a secret from the citizens of the Tetrarchia. But *we are not in the Tetrarchia*." She took a deep breath. "You see, two of the most powerful men in Rotfelsen planned not only to overthrow its government, but to topple the entire Tetrarchia in the process—killing all of its leaders at the Council of Barbarians."

She paused, allowing that to sink in, and was rewarded with gasps. Kalyna then spent a good deal of time on political specifics that I didn't fully follow, but which were, I gathered, intended to convince her audience that she was telling the truth. She discussed important political figures who suddenly disappeared, well-known disturbances whose causes had remained mysterious, and the sudden lack of insular, Rotfelsenisch nationalism that had allowed the Blossoming to happen in the first place.

"And that," she said, "is because *we stopped them*."

I don't know to what extent she convinced people with her words, and to what extent she did so with the vehemence and lingering fear in her voice. I believed her, of course, but that was because suddenly a lot of things about Kalyna made more sense to me now.

"Yes, *we*," she continued, "a group of decent, normal people—but I don't say 'normal' in the way these nationalists meant it. I mean people from every corner of the Tetrarchia; people who were cooks and doctors, soldiers and soothsayers, butlers and lavatory assistants; even people whose ways of life made them unpalatable to Rotfelsenisch society. We fought, and despite all their power, somehow we won. I am honored that I got to be even a small part of it—just a little thread in a grand tapestry."

She took a moment to regain her composure. She pushed her hair out of her eyes. The room was so quiet I fancied I could hear people's breathing. Kalyna closed her eyes, pressed her palms against them, and then opened them again, looking out at the crowd.

"Those powerful men," she said, "particularly wanted to kill *me*, and do you know why? Was it because I had any power? Because I, a vagrant with no home, somehow had the means to stop them?" She laughed ironically, painfully. "Of course not. It was because, even though what runs through my veins is the blood of the people of the Tetrarchia—from every corner of the Tetrarchia—they thought that I was Loashti."

She paused again, watching the reactions, before continuing.

"And recently, I've begun to think that if that fear, that terror I felt when those men—full of their hatred and disdain—meant to kill me only for being the 'Loashti' in their midst, if those were the *worst* moments of my entire life, then what must it like to be a Loashti now? How must it feel to be exiled from one's home for not being Loashti enough, only to be too Loashti to be accepted here?"

There was a long silence, and Kalyna looked from person to person as though she expected an answer, but none came.

"I will leave you with that," she said. "And, also, with this: The nationalist line of thinking almost toppled the Tetrarchia, and a variation of it is, as we speak, destroying and displacing so many Loashti. Adomas"—she nodded her head toward the old man—"has given us here at Lanreas an incredible chance to escape the Tetrarchia's failings *without* succumbing to such ideas in the process. I suggest we take that chance and hold it for all it's worth."

Kalyna let out a long breath and seemed to be absolutely exhausted. "Thank you," she said, before putting her forehead in her hands.

There was applause, there were even cheers. There was also some grumbling and muttered imprecations that it was all a great lie. Adomas stroked his beard and looked very thoughtful. Some people clapped Kalyna on the back and complimented her, but she only ever replied with a weak smile and a nod, perhaps a word or two.

When Kalyna and I were out on our own, in the farmlands and away from any houses, hearing the low, contented noises of Lini the cow off somewhere nearby, Kalyna laughed and laughed and laughed.

"Oh, I've got them, Radiant," she said, wiping away tears that seemed as genuine as the ones she'd held back during her lecture. "I've really hooked them. Adomas too, I'll wager. He'll take some time to admit it, but he's coming around. I saw it in his eyes." She laughed some more, snorting and honking.

"So was that all a lie, then?" I asked.

"What? No! Very little of it," she said. "Always use as much of the truth as possible; it makes your emotions look real. Because they are."

"Oh. Well, I suppose Dagmar would be happy that you no longer think you did it all by yourself."

Her smile disappeared for a moment, she looked at me, and then her laughter returned even louder.

"No, no, Radiant, *that* part was a lie. It wasn't some perfect little confederation of 'normal' people; don't be daft. *I* stopped those idiots"—she pressed her hand to her chest—"with a little help from Dagmar and some other soldiers, I grant you. But I was the mastermind, and in the end, their taking me for Loashti is what I used to save us." Her smile then became a very disconcerting grin. "Their hatred wasn't so bad. I used it, and I reveled in it. What else to do, when they already think you're a monster?"

I sighed. "That . . . sounds like it was a difficult and frightening task. Should I congratulate you?"

This surprised her, and she looked up, blinking a few times in thought, hands on her hips.

"Well," she said, "I mean . . . it wouldn't hurt."

I walked up to Kalyna Aljosanovna, put my hand on her shoulder, looked her in the eye, and said, "Congratulations. Good job. You saved the Tetrarchia."

She looked like she very much wanted to make a joke, or to point out that I was being insincere, making fun of her. But I was genuine, and she could tell. No matter how much she was discounting the contributions of others, it seemed Kalyna had done some impressive, impossible thing, and that almost no one knew about it.

"I . . . Thank you," she murmured, breaking eye contact. "No one's said anything like that to me since it happened."

I gave her shoulder a squeeze and removed my hand.

"So," I asked, "was the barely repressed fear bubbling back up a lie?"

"Not really," she replied. "It just wasn't fear of those stupid men and their bad ideas." She turned and began to walk slowly in a circle. "It's like what I told you about pretending to be Aloe's friend by thinking of other things that make you happy. I knew I needed real fear in my voice to convince them, so I conjured up memories of a much, much worse thing I encountered at that time."

"And you won't—"

"Tell you what it was? No. What would be the point of that?"

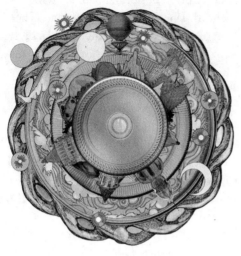

Chapter Twenty

On the Night Life of the Lanreas River Guild: The Dance

A week or so went by, and already our crop yields were improving, thanks to the immediate intervention of my Fortress plants, which meant fewer losses to pests. Bit by bit, the quantity that needed to be bought from outside lessened, as did the backbreaking labor. And if we followed my program, the hope was that it would only improve in the coming months. I was particularly pleased when I started hearing Enticers, Fortresses, and Ineffables described in regular conversation.

The new Loashti in our midst began to get at least slightly settled. Some learned bits of Skydašiavos, and even a few Guild members began saying hello back to them in Loashti Bureaucratic. No one picked up Skydašiavos as quickly as Echoes, who had already known a smattering, and now alternated her time between working with Simurgh and doing whatever she could to *recover* from working with Simurgh. For those who still struggled with the local language, it was amazing how much could be done without words when no one had to buy things, make deals, or worry about theft.

There was also much excited discussion of Kalyna's lecture in the following days: it seemed her description of normal people saving the Tetrarchia had struck a real chord. I began to see her less as, when she wasn't helping Loashti become ensconced in the Guild's daily life, more of her time was spent in the general orbits of Adomas and Žydrė. She assured me that she was slowly bringing the old naturalist around to our cause, and I thrilled at the thought.

One day, I was sitting in the library, fancifully plotting courses of escape from Yekunde to the Guild. Poring over maps, I couldn't shake the feeling that the fastest way would be to take—steal, most likely—the great river boats at Yekunde and ride them straight down the Lanreas River.

Well, straight down the river until they simply crashed into the walls of The Thrashing, Bone-White Tail of Galiag. Not that I had any idea how anyone would get even that far.

I thought again of Dagmar's note. Certainly if there was anyone who could get into Loasht and perhaps bring those people out, it was Dagmar, wasn't it? Or was I prejudiced by having been saved by her so many times before?

But, of course, Dagmar didn't speak any Loashti, and I couldn't tell Kalyna I knew where she was.

When Kalyna then appeared in the library, I nearly jumped out of my chair, sure she would somehow *know* what I had been thinking. Instead, she told me there would be a dance that evening.

"Our farms are working!" she laughed. "They've got more time for frippery."

"I'm so glad, I'll—"

"Be seen attending the dance."

I sighed. "I really don't want to."

"Why not? I thought you loved being around people, being friendly, being . . . *admired*." She winked.

I shook my head. "The more of the Guild's social life that I miss, the more scared I am of having to play catch up. Like I've missed something important, and it's too late."

"Then stop missing important things. Come to the dance."

"Why? I no longer have to carry the weight of representing all

Loashti, and who will I even dance with? This community is so small that I wonder about the gossip if I—"

"You're going. The wizard must come down from his tower sometimes."

"Fine."

I took a bit of time to pretty myself up before the dance, of course. A bit of lotion and a quick nap lessened the bags under my eyes a touch, and I chose clothes (dyed by Vidmantas, of course) in colors bright enough to be visible in the dark. My hair was now quite long, and I took some time oiling and fluffing until it was voluminous—while I tried to accept how visibly gray I had become.

Then I went to the dance and immediately knew Kalyna had been right to insist that I go.

In the center of the village, there was a firepit, beside which a group of musicians played instruments from, I think, throughout the Tetrarchia. The songs were jumpy and propulsive, with notes of melancholy, and I was told that this style was itself something of a blend. All I could say was that it sounded nothing like the quiet, but lingering, tones I had grown up with, but I liked it.

To that music, some people danced in well-choreographed lines, some flailed in pairs under flickering firelight, or found hidden dark patches to be together. Many sat and listened, or talked, or laughed on logs that had been hauled up to serve as benches around the square. I sat on one, and watched the fire and the dancers.

It was here, now—more than during the day, or at the Meal, Games, or Lecture Halls—that I began to see who the people of the Lanreas River Guild really were. There was a lot of joy among these people, many of whom had come from the margins of Tetrarchic society. They greatly appreciated the privileges that living at the Guild afforded them. In that moment, I began to give Adomas' ideas more credit than I had before.

But the Loashti view of time is not so easily shaken, and I began to wonder what would happen in another generation or two. When their children no longer carried the knowledge of how difficult life had been before the Guild. Or was that simply my own attempt at justifying the fear that Zobiski memory had burned onto my soul at a young age?

Perhaps I simply felt that every child should be made fully aware of the evil in the world when they are very young. (Perhaps I still do.)

What's more, I knew that Adomas still *ruled* these people, and that he kept secrets from them that only men like Yalwas knew. And that he, Yalwas, and even Žydrė had been ready to turn away my countrypeople when they needed help.

I suppose the deep, dark secret of the Guild, which Kalyna had been trying in vain to find, was simply that it was not perfect and was as flawed as its inhabitants. The Lanreas River Guild was just another *place*, full of *people*.

"May I sit?"

I looked up and smiled at Ifeanyas, nodding. He sat about half a foot from me on the otherwise empty bench.

"It must be nice to have more Loashti here," he said. He laughed awkwardly and shook his head. "More who aren't like that enemy of yours, I mean. Aloe, is it?"

I nodded. "Yes."

He smiled widely, and his eyes looked so bright in the firelight. "Maybe . . . maybe he fell in a ditch and died on his way south!"

I laughed and patted his hand, which was on the bench between us. "Thank you. That's very kind of you."

"Any time."

Had his hand always been this rough? I suppose I'd never touched his hands before, and now he was a farmer, after all. Ifeanyas had really filled out in his time here: his midsection had grown in a way that implied solidity, and the muscles in his arms had become thick cords from all that farm work he so enjoyed. With his sleeves rolled up right now, he looked, well, like he could *manhandle* me a bit, if he so chose. Not that sweet Ifeanyas would ever do so, I thought.

"I just . . ." he continued. "I just want you to be able to stop worrying about him, and all that. Even just for an evening. It's all so *much*, after all."

I removed my hand and took a deep breath. "It certainly is."

He drummed his fingers on the bench nervously. Was he leaning a little closer now?

"So, you should try to have some fun," he said.

"Perhaps. Have you, ah, danced yet?"

"A little!" he replied. "I really am coming to love it here. Have you?"

I shook my head.

"Would you like to?" he asked.

I grinned. "Why, Ifeanyas, are you flirting with me?" It was an easy rhythm for me to fall into: lightly teasing, mischievous, but really just joking.

Instead of continuing in the same tone, he very seriously said, "I am."

"Oh!" I was surprised, but I may have overplayed my surprise a bit. "I thought you meant some sort of . . . group dance."

"I didn't."

"Well! That's . . . that's nice to hear." I took a deep breath and looked out at the fire. "Will you let me think about it a little? As you say, I have so *much* on my mind right now."

"Of course!" He stopped leaning in toward me, which was very sweet but, I realized, not quite what I'd wanted. "If it only adds one more worry, forget it."

"It certainly isn't that," I assured him as I stood up. "I'm going to clear my head. But . . . I'll be back, one way or another."

He grinned and nodded. I realized how much I liked that smile, which had been so rare when I first met him. Even now, it was so much less *calculated* than Kalyna's. Or mine, for that matter.

I walked away from Ifeanyas in a very . . . deliberate manner, I must admit. It seemed like ages since I'd felt desirable. I suppose I had in Desgol, a little, but I'd known I looked a mess at the time—my assumption was that the man I flirted with there had just been excited for anyone new.

I walked for a bit through the square and pondered Ifeanyas, rather than Aloe or Yekunde or any of that. I felt the urge to reciprocate his attention, but worried I might be driven by a desire to please more than by actual attraction.

And yet, I'd enjoyed watching Ifeanyas become more confident at the Guild. I'd come to appreciate his taciturn nature, which usually led him to speaking carefully, unlike myself. And, well . . . now I was noticing those powerful hands and arms. (*Could* sweet Ifeanyas manhandle me?)

"Well, well, what's on *your* mind?"

I slid out of my reverie at the sound of Kalyna's voice. She was sitting on a bench with Adomas, like they were a couple of old friends. He waved me over, and I sat on his other side.

"Good to see you joining us, young man!" greeted Adomas. With both hands on the handle of his cane, he pounded the tip on the ground for emphasis.

"Young?" I laughed. "I don't think—"

"Can you still dance?"

"I haven't yet.

"But you *can* if you wish." He sighed. "I only wish I could still move like I used to."

I'd never seen Adomas so jolly before. It was disarming.

"Radiant and Ifeanyas may just skip dancing altogether," said Kalyna, waggling her eyebrows.

"Was it that obvious?" I murmured. I still wasn't sure how two men together would be seen here.

"Perhaps I'm psychic," said Kalyna.

Adomas seemed to sober slightly. "*Young man,* aren't you married?"

"I . . . I am, but you see, some peoples in Loasht, including the Zobiski, can be—"

Adomas slapped his thigh and laughed. "I know! I know! I've been around, Radiant. I'm just joking!"

I was dumbstruck by this new side of the man. Kalyna was grinning, but now that Adomas was facing me, she also gave me a nod, as if to say, *You see? I'm working on him.*

I suppose the atmosphere was intoxicating. A few people had been dropping into the Games Hall and coming back after a drink or some other imbibing, but most seemed to be soaring purely because of the pounding music and the joy that hung in the ether between them.

I looked out into the square and, past the dancers, saw that the great fire in the center was suddenly bursting into new colors: red, green, blue, orange—but a brighter, stranger orange than most fires. The smoke, too, seemed to puff up at odd intervals. On the other side of the fire pit, I saw Echoes in the Gingko-Wreathed Valley Sound like Grandfather's Voice, with the various colors reflecting off of her face, making it impossible to tell the color of the makeup covering all but her mouth. She looked extremely stern, almost like some sort of demon, glaring through that colorful flame, until I realized she was actually swaying slightly to the music.

If I felt the elation and promise of this place—the potential of what the Lanreas River Guild could really be at its best—then the man who masterminded it must have been feeling the same thing tenfold.

Adomas tapped me to draw me back into conversation. "Kalyna tells me you hope to rescue your spouse from Loasht and bring them here, is that right?"

Kalyna nodded to me again over his shoulder.

"It is, yes. I'd be so gracious if they could stay. And . . . perhaps their parents, as well." I did not mention Silver had *three* of those.

"Well, that shouldn't be a problem." Adomas smiled widely and patted my back. "So long as Ifeanyas doesn't mind!" He laughed again and then *winked* at me.

I shook my head in disbelief. I hadn't realized how tense I'd been, likely for days, until I felt my muscles begin to relax. I took what felt like my first deep breath in weeks.

"That's . . . that's incredible to hear, Adomas," I said, quite truthfully. "Thank you. I was worried that my family and friends wouldn't—"

His smile remained, but a confusion crept into his eyes. "What friends?"

"Oh. Well, I . . ." I began to stammer.

I looked to Kalyna for help. Her grin had taken on a rictus quality, her eyes were wide, and she was shaking her head.

"Well," I tried again, "that is . . . I mean . . ."

Adomas was looking at me very hard now. His smile was gone. I looked to Kalyna again, but she had nothing to offer me.

"Look," I said, "surely . . . surely living *here*, you understand the necessity of having a . . . a community? How who is 'friends' and who is 'family' can become interchangeable when . . . when . . ."

"How many friends, Radiant?"

"Well . . . I don't exactly have a full count at the moment, but—"

"No," Adomas hissed.

Kalyna put a hand on his shoulder, which he did not seem to even notice. It was as though he no longer existed down here, with us and our lowly concerns. Suddenly he was imperious—suddenly he was a noble again.

"No, Radiant," he growled. "We simply cannot become a camp for strays that Loasht doesn't want. It's beyond our capabilities."

I looked at Kalyna imploringly. She patted Adomas' shoulder comfortingly and, I think, tried to will me to be quiet.

"Is it?" I said instead. "This is already a 'camp' for those the Tetrarchia doesn't want, and last I checked, our 'capabilities' are improving. You're welcome."

"You don't understand!" Adomas stood up, eyes wide and intense, staring past me, through me. "This place, which I built with these hands"—he held them out, and both were shaking now, knobbly and *older* than they'd looked to me before, in the flickering pink light of the flame—"cannot become where Skydašiai dumps its aliens. I absolutely refuse!"

I stood up as well and opened my mouth to respond.

"I already told you this, Radiant!" Adomas interrupted. "Perhaps you nursed hope in your heart that I would change my mind, but that is hardly my business. I have been clear!"

I gulped. I wasn't sure what to say. I waited for Kalyna to jump in with some perfect gambit that would salvage everything, but she was silent.

"At this point," Adomas continued, "I begin to wonder whether *you*, or any of your countrypeople, should be allowed to stay here."

"But—"

"Good night!" Adomas stomped away, north toward his shack beneath the Estate.

I stood in place, watching him hobble away, as my guts tried to turn themselves inside out. Why had I said what I said? How could I have been so stupid? I have always spoken without thinking when I'm comfortable, but this quickly felt like the most disastrous such moment of my life.

It's terrible, but I had a moment where I blamed Binturong, Echoes, and the others for coming here. If we could have had more time to get him ready for the idea of hosting Loashti, then perhaps . . .

I shook my head violently to dispel this line of thinking.

"Come here, Radiant." Kalyna pulled me back down onto the log, next to her. The two of us stared forward at the dancers and the multicolored fire. I saw Ifeanyas milling about, trying not to look as though he was eyeing me nervously.

"You really fucked it," she finally said.

"I know."

"But the music's loud, and I don't think anyone else heard him. I can fix this."

"How?" I groaned. "It's too late. Why didn't you say anything to Adomas just now?"

"I couldn't think of anything."

"But you always—"

"Sometimes, Radiant, I can't think of anything."

I put my head between my knees, and she elbowed me hard.

"Chin up," she said. "Don't let on that anything is wrong. At least not beyond all the reasons you were already glum. I am forming a plan, and I *can* talk Adomas out of this. I'll just give him a little time to cool off first."

"How long?"

"Oh, just an hour or two. Then I'll go see him."

"How do you know it will work?" I moaned.

"I don't, really. But, in the end, it always does."

"What will you say to convince him?"

She patted my back. "You know I won't tell you that. Trust me. Have I let you down yet?"

I leaned my head back and looked at the stars, letting out a loud "hmmmmmmmmmm" sound.

"Rather," she laughed, "when I've let you down, have I ever not then, quickly, turned things back around for you?"

"I . . . suppose not."

She hugged me around the waist, pulling me close and shaking me. Her curls brushed my cheek. "*Trust me.*"

"I'll try."

"Go dance with Ifeanyas. Have fun. You deserve it. I'll handle this."

I sighed and repeated, "I'll try."

"That's the spirit. Don't worry about anything tonight, Radiant."

Kalyna stood up and walked away.

Deep in my own thoughts, I walked into the crowd of dancers. I didn't hear the music, I didn't move with other people, I just wandered aimlessly until I found myself standing in front of Ifeanyas. His smile disappeared into worry when he saw my face.

"What happened?" he asked. "Are you all right?"

"No, I'm not," I said. "Can I please kiss you instead of talking about it?"

"Oh! Of course!"

I kissed him hard, with some desperation, and let his sensory details flood my mind and push everything else out to sea. Lips slightly cracked; fingers digging into my waist; hair coiling into my grip; the (enjoyable) discomfort of arching my back a little to reach him.

Would two men kissing in the middle of a crowd bother anyone? Just then, I couldn't begin to care. The drums pounded, and the clarinets tootled, and some instruments I didn't know pulsed as well, and I simply did not want to think for a long time. If anyone judged us, they were at least quiet about it.

We danced, we murmured things to one another, I probably sighed a lot.

"You do know I'm married right?" I eventually said. "But it's not—"

He laughed. "I wasn't planning to marry you."

"You *weren't*?" I feigned insult.

Ifeanyas' face showed a moment of actual worry, and then he laughed as he realized I was joking. We kissed some more, and I touched his waist, his stomach, his hips. I don't know if we stood out; I just know there were warm bodies moving around us, and that it felt right to move with them.

Ifeanyas got on his toes and put his mouth to my ear: "Do you . . . want to go up to the Estate and distract each other for a bit?"

"Of course I do."

We parted for the moment: Ifeanyas to grab some things from where he slept, and I to swipe some vegetable oil from the Meal Hall.

Adomas' house was dark when I passed it, and I had no way of knowing whether Kalyna had already visited him or was still planning to.

Ifeanyas and I were not the only ones who had decided to make use of the Estate that night, but we *were* the only ones who thought the velvet room with the mottled gray liver would do just fine.

"When we take breaks, we can contemplate our mortality," snorted Ifeanyas. "Yalwas will be proud."

"Ifeanyas! That's so mean, for you." I didn't bother to add that I liked that; I think it was clear.

He pressed me into the plush velvet of one of the walls, and, between kisses, we had a long conversation about what each of us would enjoy doing. Then we did some of those things, took breaks, and did more. For that brief, marvelous night, I thought of nothing else: not of Loasht, or Adomas, or Kalyna, or Aloe. Some may be scandalized to know that I did not think of Silver either, but this was quite normal. I was fully occupied and did not want to do the person right in front of me such a disservice.

We ended up tired enough to simply sleep in the Estate that night, tangled up with one another on the hard floor. It was the first time I had fallen asleep with a smile on my face in a very long time.

The next morning, I was woken by Vidmantas.

"Radiant, are you in here? Someone saw you walking up— Oh!"

I blinked in the light that was trickling in through the broken ceiling, and pulled my robe up to cover Ifeanyas and myself a bit more.

"It's all right, it's all right," I moaned. I hadn't had a drop to drink last night, but I felt hungover. Exhaustion, perhaps. Also, I was much too old to go sleeping on an unadorned floor, and my neck throbbed in pain when I turned to look at Vidmantas.

"Is something wrong?" I muttered.

"I'd love to congratulate you two," said Vidmantas, "but Adomas is dead. He was found this morning in his home, with his head cracked open like a melon."

All that joy, that pleasure, that ignorance of the world, drained away in an instant.

Excerpt from *The Secret Journals of the So-Called Bandit-Naturalist Adomas Albinakas Rutorie Marijonkwo Ikennakas*

Well, I must say nephew Enyivdas' little party did not go the way I expected! But as things shook out, I made an incredible discovery.

Here I was, back on my home soil of Skydašiai, where, so far as I knew, I was in no legal trouble. After everything that happened in Masovska—the thieves' temple, the Gniezto lawsuit, the beautiful one-eyed baroness, and the trap set by the hussar Olexiy Ulyanovich—I was looking forward to a bit of peace. Time to relax, catalog my newest acquisitions, and perhaps reintroduce myself to society.

When Enyivdas invited me to his little party, I thought it would be a lovely way to begin on the latter. Besides, the poor boy is only seventeen and has been running his estates since my brother died five years ago. I thought perhaps he could use some company.

The party was fun enough in its way. The boy certainly spared no expense: he had a moat dug and filled with water, just so the guests could putter around in little boats. (I must say I felt for the poor fish who were brought in.) I spent a good deal of time in a charming two-person boat attempting to speak to a most engaging lady.

(In his secret journals, Adomas does not hesitate to name family members, enemies, nobles, and royals. But he never names lovers or potential lovers.—R)

Unfortunately, every few minutes, my nephew would float closer to us, desperate to talk to me. I feel for Enyivdas, but he is growing into quite the boor. And yet, without his boorishness, I might not have escaped.

Enyivdas had finally decided to step across from his boat into ours and, in so doing, caused us to list, and the engaging lady's drink to spill onto my lap. I assured her it was nothing and looked up to politely rebuke our young host when I saw, behind him, another little boat. In this one sat Olexiy Ulyanovich! He was surrounded by his men, who were furiously rowing the boat toward me, upsetting other guests around them.

I had assumed Olexiy's jurisdiction ended in Masovska, but I needed only a moment's glance at the stern set of his face to know that—whether judicially or extrajudicially—he was coming to drag me back to Masovska. Dead or alive, I did not stay to find out.

I apologized to the engaging lady and then made my way out of the estate by hopping from small boat to small boat. I upended many drinks and plates of food, but I hope the guests were entertained in return. I scrambled up the side of the temporary dock Enyivdas had built in his entryway, and I'm afraid I had to draw my sword and run through one of Olexiy's men who was waiting by the door.

I fled on horseback and rode for two days straight, changing horses when necessary, in the direction of the Ikennakas family's northernmost estate—that largely ignored farm for grapes and poppies. I had been cataloguing my collection there due to its proximity to the Loashti border, which it now appeared I would have to cross as soon as possible.

I arrived at the estate with Olexiy and his men only a few hours behind me—I had last seen them as dots at the far end of a great plain—and my head full of thoughts about how in the world I would decide what to take with me to Loasht and what to leave. (I wonder what the provincial servants and simple farmers thought of my sudden, haggard arrival.)

While desperately trying to pack my collection, I was running with the petrified body of a wombat in my arms and tripped on the ragged corner of a rug. The poor creature careened out of my hands, over the banister, and below into the entry hall with a great crash. I ran down to find the wombat shattered. Also broken, however, was a chunk of the wall, behind which I saw part of a tunnel leading underground.

Well, naturally I climbed into the tunnel and pulled a painting over it as best I could. I think the only reason Olexiy did not find me is that,

304 | ELIJAH KINCH SPECTOR

based on what I heard, he was mostly focused on reclaiming whatever bits of plant matter were in the estate.

"The scoundrel is on the run," he finally told his men, "and the Yams are looking for him too. No need to keep chasing. This should be enough to bring back to Bohdan."

I had worked so hard to liberate all those plants! But, in return, I've found something even better. This tunnel leads to a wondrous place on the shore of the Lanreas River and inside The Thrashing, Bone-White Tail of Galiag! Miraculously, within this one pocket of the Tail, the winds and their burning sands arc harmlessly (albeit loudly) overhead, creating a refuge hidden from the world. As I write this, my most trusted servants have begun building me a new abode there, where I'll be able to hide from the Yams *and* to secret these journals.

For years I've worried that my vanity would get me caught, but I simply couldn't bring myself to not record my exploits. Perhaps some-day, long after I've died, someone will find them and know that I was here, and what (I daresay) exciting and amazing things I did.

Chapter Twenty-One

The Interregnum

There was already a place at the Lanreas River Guild where the dead were buried. It was a clearing in the forested borders of the land: a place where Lini the cow was sleeping happily in a sunbeam when our funeral procession got there. Guild members, most of them in shock, had numbly wrapped Adomas' small body in canvas and carried it out to the clearing together, with many muttered exclamations at how light the old man was. The first argument of the day (but *far* from the last) was over whether Lini should be moved.

"What are we supposed to do?" growled Žydrė. "Dig around her?"

"Yes!" yelled Yalwas. "Do you think he'd want us to displace her? This may surprise you to learn, Žydrė, but he was *just a bit* fond of animals!"

"There's cow shit everywhere," muttered Vidmantas, who stood near Žydrė.

Meanwhile, the entire community—nearly three hundred of them, as the Loashti were there too—stood crowded among the trees, staring quietly at an argument over a cow. (Which I did not translate.)

"Maybe," said Kalyna, "she'll leave when we start the service."

"We don't *have* a service!" snapped Yalwas.

At his tone, Lini did put up her head, and her ears twitched.

"We have three priests now!" hissed Kalyna. She waved at the three of them—Skydašian, Rot, and Loashti—standing nearby. "Surely, they can give a general blessing, like they do at dinner?"

"A funeral blessing is more complicated," said the Rotfelsenisch ex-priest of the god who dwells in darkness. She was tall and willowy, and seemed to bend toward Kalyna as she spoke. "Different gods take their followers' souls to different places, after all."

"And some take their bodies!" added the Skydašian priest of the Tetrarchic goddess of the sea.

"This way," said Žydrė, "each can pray in the way they brought with them, or however they like."

"Well, that's lovely," said Kalyna, hands on her hips. "But isn't someone going to . . . *say* something?"

There was silence for a moment. Žydrė looked down at the body, wrapped in canvas, small and frail on the ground. I think Kalyna was about to give a speech herself, when she was interrupted by Žydrė erupting into loud sobs.

Kalyna was about to try again, until she realized Žydrė had burst the dam for many others, and tears began to flow all through the forest. Momentarily, Kalyna was also crying.

I studied Kalyna carefully through all of this. I wanted to trust her, but I could not shake the troubling thought that she had murdered Adomas. And, worse, that she had done so for *me*. Neither did it pass my notice that she was wearing her sickle for the first time since shedding it to give her lecture.

The mass crying finally convinced Lini to leave, although she did so very slowly. (Can a cow saunter? If so, she did.) Digging of the grave began, with shovels being passed through the community so that everyone who wished could take part. Simurgh took up the task of dragoman for the rest of the Loashti, and, to a person, each of the recently arrived aliens made at least a few gouges in the ground for Adomas. I don't know if the other Guild members viewed this as commendable, blasphemy, or a hollow gesture, but no one stopped them, at least. The Loashti, of course, did not know that the previous night, Adomas had threatened to turn them all out.

The act of digging revealed other bones and fragments of canvas throughout the dirt. At Lanreas, I learned, people were meant to be buried with little ceremony, and no grave markers were left behind. The idea was, I think, that it would be a great leveler: no expensive tombs and paupers' graves, nowhere that the living could mourn and deify a particular one of the dead; simply a return to dirt and the creatures that lived within it. This brought about the next big argument of the day, although they kept this one under their breaths.

"This will simply need to be an exception, won't it?" said Yalwas. "None of us would be here without Adomas. We've got to put up a stone or . . . or *something*."

"Is that what he would want?" muttered Žydrė.

"Perhaps," offered Kalyna, "we should think more about what all the people here want. Adomas completed so much in his life that I feel quite sure he won't be hanging about as a ghost. So what do those who remain need?"

"They *need*," Žydrė hissed, "to be reminded the precepts of this place and to not turn Adomas into a . . . a lord! Or a king!"

Kalyna clicked her tongue and leaned in closer to whisper, "They also *need*, my good Žydrė, to not simply disband to the four winds now that he's gone. Veneration has its purposes."

Žydrė looked from Kalyna to Yalwas, then at the crowd.

"Fine," she grunted. "But only to keep this stupid argument from continuing. Everyone's getting restless."

Kalyna nodded. "Look at it this way: Lini will probably desecrate the grave marker soon enough." She allowed herself a dark chuckle. "Maybe that will even be Adomas speaking to us from beyond—his ideals living on."

Adomas was buried, and a stone was placed on his grave, with promises that it would be inscribed as soon as possible. Guild members began to file back to town, although some stayed to leave flowers, say their own prayers, or quietly clean up cow shit.

Kalyna took a moment to say a few prayers under her breath. I did not; I was too caught up in watching her. Was she giving a normal prayer for the dead, or for forgiveness? I certainly couldn't tell by looking at her.

If I'm being honest, I was also disturbed by the very fact that the Lanreas River Guild buried its dead in an unmarked mass grave. To them, perhaps, this was some laudable attempt at simplicity and natural decay; to me, it was a brutal crime. How many Zobiski lay in unmarked mass graves? How many entire families and villages of my people were, over the centuries, shoved into pits by murderous neighbors who did not even give them the benefit of a stone or a prayer?

Was this an overreaction on my part? Probably! But I didn't much care.

Kalyna and I walked together back toward the village, but there were now too many Loashti around for me to feel comfortable saying what I wanted to, which was, *Did you murder Adomas?*

Instead, I asked in Cölluknit, "How did he die?"

"It seems," she replied, looking ahead as she walked, "the old man tripped as he entered his home, before lighting any lamps, and smashed his head open." Kalyna shrugged. "The sort of sad accident that happens to so many of us, and more so when we age."

I stared at her. She seemed entirely placid.

"Perhaps," Kalyna continued, under her breath, "he shouldn't have lived so far from everyone else. If he'd been *part* of the community he thought so important, someone might have found him before it was too late."

This did not help me see her as innocent, I must say.

"So what now?" I asked instead.

She nodded ahead to where Žydrė and Yalwas were walking, some distance from one another.

"We watch those two fight it out, I suppose. I think people will crowd toward the Lecture Hall." She shook her head. "I doubt our good Adomas left behind a strong succession plan. I think he rather expected to live forever—or at least four or five more years."

I couldn't look at her. I stared ahead at the various groups of people moving toward the village. Most were quiet, and when they did talk, it was some muted version of: "How did this happen?" or "What will we do?" or even "How could he do this to us?"

Sure enough, the Lecture Hall began to fill up. It was not the entire population of the Guild, but it was close, and I did notice that every Loashti was there. Soon there weren't enough chairs, and people crowded in along the walls. There was a general low murmur through-out the room, and collective anxiety was a physical presence thickening the air between us all.

At the dais stood Yalwas and Žydrė, the former leaning forward with his thick hands resting on the desk, the latter standing beside it with her arms crossed. Surrounding each of them were various others whom I recognized but didn't know well; although near Yalwas was his son Kyautas, and near Žydrė were Vidmantas and Kalyna.

Ifeanyas, sitting in the front, waved me over. He looked deeply wor-ried, and my first thought was to give him a reassuring kiss, but I wasn't sure how that would be interpreted, either by him or by the Guild at large.

I watched Kalyna. Perhaps she had killed Adomas, perhaps not; either way, what was her *plan* here? I began to worry that she didn't have one. She seemed awfully sure that she could twist anything to her advantage, and she'd laughed at the very idea of worrying about Yalwas. Perhaps she'd deemed this little affair not worth the energy of a complex plan?

What's more, if she had murdered Adomas, did that taint her enough that I should cut ties? Or would I accept that evil and move forward with what I wanted from her? If she did so to keep the secret of our plans to save my community, was it entirely my fault?

Žydrė and Yalwas both seemed hesitant to call the room to order. I fancied they each worried the other would accuse them of being too pre-sumptive. Neither did Kalyna, for once, take the initiative here, perhaps for a similar reason. Finally, it was actually Ifeanyas who stood up from where he sat next to me and slammed a fist on the back of our bench.

"Excuse me! Everyone!" he cried, accompanied by another blow against the wood.

The room quieted, and Ifeanyas seemed a little surprised it had worked, and that everyone was now looking at him. He blinked a few times, and his voice went down to the quiet register he usually used.

"I'm . . . I'm sure that those who were closest to Adomas can tell us a bit about what, you know, about what will happen next. Thank you." He sat back down quickly and then looked at me, eyes wide, with a sort of *Why did you let me do that?* expression.

I smiled. It was good, for a moment, to remember that Kalyna was not, in fact, the center of the world.

"Yes," Yalwas spoke up. "Thank you." He cleared his throat and looked at Žydrė, as though he expected her to interrupt him, but she did not.

"The good news," the large man continued, standing up straight, "is that I have always been kept abreast of Adomas'"—there was a catch in his throat—"finances and will. He did indeed, as he always promised, leave the lands of the Lanreas River Guild, and all that lies upon them, to *us*."

This did not bring quite the applause and relief that Yalwas seemed to hope for. Uncertainty seemed to persist in the room.

"Define 'us,'" said Žydrė.

"The people of the Lanreas River Guild, of course," replied Yalwas. "*All* of its people. Everyone who lives on these lands."

"How will that be enforced?" asked Vidmantas. "The Skydašian government didn't have to like what was going on here before, but they could say to themselves, 'Oh it's some eccentric noble doing what he wants with *his* land and *his* people,' but now . . ."

"We always knew," began Yalwas, "that our existence would be complicated and tenuous. Adomas himself often said he didn't know how long the Guild would last." He turned from looking at Žydrė and Vidmantas to gaze out at the rest of us. "All I can promise you is that the land *should* now belong to us."

"Including the Loashti?" called out someone behind me. It was, I think, a Masovskan accent, and they did not sound happy about sharing the land with us.

Argumentative voices began to rise throughout the hall. Moments later, after some rough translating, Loashti voices joined in, louder still. I could not bring myself to look behind me and take in the state of the crowd. Zobiski memory encroached on my mind, and then enveloped it. Adomas had wanted a community based in love and fellow feeling, and we were now seeing the limits of where that could lead these people who, despite their allegiances, were still of the Tetrarchia and not about to simply give power to the Loashti in their midst.

The Loashti, despite being alienated from their homes, were also, of course, just as much people of Loasht, and I heard quite a few comments along the lines of: "How can these children tell us what to do?" or "What right have they?" and "This was our land once!"

"Please! *Please!*" bellowed Yalwas. His voice carried above everyone's, and the room began to quiet. "One thing at a time! Adomas wished for a day when the Guild could move forward with no central leader, but he did not live long enough to get us there. So, decisions like *that* will rest in part upon whomever attempts to follow in his footsteps."

The tenor of the room changed again, and Žydrė became much more attentive.

"I will not obfuscate," the large man continued, "or pretend at modesty right now. It's no secret that I think I would be best suited to lead in Adomas' place. Although, I did hope for more time with him before I would need to accept that burden."

Žydrė did not, to her credit, roll her eyes. Although I think she largely had Vidmantas and Kalyna there so they could do so in her stead.

"I was with Adomas from the beginning of this project," said Yalwas. "I came to these lands with him, I worked alongside him as he reasoned out how our home would work, and I aided him in keeping his accounts. We have no use for money here, of course, but the coffers of the Guild, which we use to purchase supplies from the outside, have not been depleted and I think I am at least partly responsible for that."

"By that logic," Vidmantas cut in, as though making an aside directly to Yalwas, but he of course knew that the entire room could hear him, "so did everyone else here. We've all done work for which we were not directly paid, yes? That must've helped grow the coffers."

"And how much work have you done?" yelled a Quru woman near Yalwas. "We plow the fields while you make finery!"

Vidmantas didn't even have to respond, only smile and motion to Yalwas' own shirt, which was covered in abstract magenta shapes.

"This is not about who does or does not do the 'correct' type of work," said Yalwas, "or about who does, or does not, belong here."

"Except for the Loashti, it seems," said Kalyna. "We're already saving money, thanks to fewer pests in our crops, and soon enough, we'll save much more. All thanks to the agricultural *innovations* of a Loashti." She motioned to me.

"Well, we've never turned the Loashti away!" Žydrė added quickly.

"We are losing the thread," said Yalwas, gripping the bridge of his nose. "The point is, I am best suited to continue leading the Guild. I am the most familiar with Adomas' methods and holdings, because I was with him from the start."

I saw Kalyna purse her lips, about to speak, and then think better of it.

"So was I," said Žydrė. "Only *I* was in the field, doing hard work, while *you* were learning about aristocratic 'holdings' and gorging yourself in the Estate, before Adomas moved everyone out of that ruin."

The room was silent. I saw a twinkle in Kalyna's eye, the slightest tug of a smile on her lips.

"I see," said Yalwas. "So now we are going back to what sort of work is superior, to what someone was before they began living under the precepts of—"

"It was *your* choice, Yalwas!" Žydrė yelled. "You decided to use your cushy role as Adomas' assistant when he was a noble dabbler as proof that you are best suited for the position!"

I heard a few scattered gasps, and Žydrė quickly added, "He called himself a dabbler! He found his true calling when he formed the Guild! He said so!"

"Žydrė," Yalwas began, calmly now, leaning toward her, "are you putting yourself forward as a possible leader of the Lanreas River Guild? Or are you just criticizing?"

Žydrė was quiet for a moment and then nodded. "I am. I'd damn well do better than you."

Yalwas stood up straight again, smiling a bit. "Really? How so?"

"For one thing"—Kalyna cut in so smoothly that Žydrė didn't have time to form a thought or look surprised—"she wouldn't keep secrets from the rest of the Guild."

A stunned silence, and then the room began to fill with confusion and anger. The utterly pained shock on Yalwas' face was clear to everyone. Even Loashti who didn't understand what she said must have known she'd caught him unawares.

Žydrė, too, seemed surprised, and she turned to Kalyna with an inquisitive look.

"What . . . whatever do you mean?" choked Yalwas.

Groans rippled through the room.

Kalyna shrugged. "My wizard here is improving things, but before that, why was the land already surprisingly fruitful, Yalwas?"

He seemed to regain himself, perhaps thinking Kalyna didn't actually know anything but had only guessed at there being a secret.

"Luck," said Yalwas. "And Adomas' carefully chosen crops. That is nothing new. Perhaps, Kalyna Aljosanovna, you would understand that better if you ever did any work around here, rather than riling people up."

"Luck?" she echoed. "Just luck? Not a stretch of the Lanreas River flowing through an entirely habitable piece of The Thrashing, Bone-White Tail of Galiag?"

Žydrė knit her eyebrows together, and Vidmantas seemed to want to laugh at the ludicrousness of this. Yalwas said nothing and betrayed nothing, but Kyautas' eyes went wide behind him, and I could not have been the only one who saw it.

"What *are* you talking about?" Vidmantas finally asked.

"Oh, just a contraption that pumps water into our lands," said Kalyna, with a shrug and a light sort of air about her, "whose breakdown or destruction would doom the Guild, and yet Yalwas has told nobody about it. Just a pleasant little house in the supposedly inhospitable gorge, which can be reached through an underground passage behind a locked door in the Estate."

"Now hold on—!" Yalwas began.

"A door," Kalyna interrupted, "to which Yalwas has a key."

There was much yelling, among the crowd and on the dais—except for poor Kyautas, who stood stock still and stared at nothing, eyes wide. Ifeanyas turned to me with a questioning look, and I nodded. Most of the Loashti who understood what was going on, I noted, didn't take this revelation as much of anything at all. (I suppose we expected our leaders to have secrets.)

Žydrė, as surprised as anyone, had quickly reoriented herself and was demanding Yalwas say whether or not this was true, while Kalyna loudly egged her on. Yalwas was, it seemed, trying to deny it without lying outright, but he was drowned out. Vidmantas was laughing.

Finally, Kalyna hopped up onto the desk at the front of the Lecture Hall and stomped loudly with her heavy boots in a kind of jig. This managed to draw everyone's attention.

"Everyone! Please!" she cried. "Give the man a chance to answer." She looked down at Yalwas—something a man of his size was not accustomed to—and smiled with seeming benevolence. "Yalwas," said Kalyna, "is what I've described true?"

Yalwas opened his mouth.

"*Or,*" Kalyna interrupted, "will we have to go force open that door to prove your innocence." Her smile became less benevolent. "You know, the one beneath the stairs at the back of the Estate."

Yalwas let out a long breath. "It's true," he finally said. The noise of the crowd began to surge, but he yelled over it. "It was Adomas' choice to keep it a secret! For the safety of the Guild! So that no one could sabotage us or tell the Yams!"

"And if you took his place," asked Vidmantas, "would you have kept that secret as well?"

Yalwas chewed his lip and admitted, "Most likely."

The crowd erupted again. I couldn't help feeling a surge of fear at being surrounded by an angry crowd, and my hands shook purely from the noise of it all. I found Yalwas pompous, but I certainly didn't want him on the receiving end of anything like Aloe's "hunting club" or the mob in Abathçodu.

Žydrė tried to speak a few times and then looked up at Kalyna, pointing to her boots and mouthing, *Would you mind?*

Kalyna grinned, nodded, and did another loud jig on the table, before flourishing at Žydrė.

"Brothers and sisters," Žydrė began (I heard Simurgh mutter "siblings" in Loashti Bureaucratic, and I could practically hear her irritation with the Tetrarchia), "there are a lot of things to consider here. We must learn more about this contraption by the river, and we must decide about the place of the Loashti in our Guild. But before any of that, we must pick a leader. I, clearly, don't think Yalwas can be trusted to keep the Guild's best interests at heart, but I may be biased." She smiled stiffly, seeming to expect a laugh, but none came.

"You all know me," she continued, "and you know how important Adomas' teachings are to me. I truly think we can make this place a beacon to the rest of the Tetrarchia, even to Loasht and the world. I believe that when we show them how good life can be, the rest of humanity will follow suit peacefully, building communities like ours!"

There was scattered applause and some exclamations. Yalwas looked like he also wanted to give a speech but didn't have the courage.

Kalyna, still standing on the table, said, "Assuming we don't have an existing method for choosing a leader . . ." She paused for a moment and saw that no one disagreed. "What say we reconvene here at sundown? Give everyone a chance to think over what they've heard and choose the leader they think is best. Then we can vote."

There was silence for a moment, until I stood up.

"Do the Loashti get votes?" I asked.

"Of course!" replied Kalyna before anyone else could. "You're here, aren't you? You work and eat beside us."

"Now wait—" Yalwas began.

"Would you bar them from the Lecture Hall this evening?" Kalyna interrupted. "Decide their fate without even inviting them in, as though you were their Grand Suzerain?"

"Well—"

"Are they not our neighbors?" Kalyna continued. Then she added, in purposefully stilted and badly pronounced Loashti Bureaucratic: "Our Loashti neighbors!"

There was reserved applause from the Loashti and some more from certain Tetrarchic Guild members, although plenty did no such thing.

"I agree!" added Žydrė, attempting a similar volume to Kalyna. "The Loashti deserve a vote!"

I certainly remembered that Žydrė had not tried to talk Adomas out of turning down the Loashti aliens when they arrived, but of course, most people didn't know that. I suppose she was hoping to count on their votes. I began to worry very much about what would happen if all of the Loashti voted for Žydrė, but Yalwas still won: then we would surely, to a person, be expelled. Or worse. Had Kalyna considered this? Did she have a way out of it, or was she simply gambling with my people's lives?

Whatever the case, there was much yelling and grumbling, but it was decided that a vote would be cast that evening, and people slowly began to disperse.

That was, as I'm sure you can imagine, a strange and tense day. Žydrė and Yalwas spent most of it in their respective homes, as their friends and hangers-on came and went. There was much loud discussion throughout the Guild, I am told, although I heard little of it because conversation tended to stop when Loashti were near.

First, Kalyna and I visited the Estate, where a large group of people had congregated around the door to Adomas' secret passageway. Some tried the knob, others threw themselves against it, before yet others told them to stop.

"Adomas must have kept it secret for a reason," someone said. "Let's not desecrate his memory while he's still warm in the ground."

Again, though, much of this discussion stopped when they saw me.

"Radiant, why don't you leave me for a bit to talk to these fine people," suggested Kalyna. "I'll meet you in the library."

I sighed and made my way up the stairs, before slumping down at the desk.

Had the old man already been dead when I went past his house the previous night? If the official story, that he had simply tripped upon entering his home was true, then I supposed he must have been. Perhaps when I passed by, he had been still alive—even still awake—quietly dying, while no one knew.

But then of course, there was the other possibility, which had been on my mind since the moment I learned Adomas was dead. Kalyna had told me to trust her, told me that she would "fix this." Had she killed Adomas? Had she gone up there with the intention of killing him, or perhaps they'd had an argument that got out of hand?

Dagmar—*Dagmar*, of all people, who killed so easily and often—had called Kalyna a "cutthroat." What reason had I to think that murdering a stubborn old man to achieve her aims was beyond her? That such action was beyond a woman who had, apparently, fought a small *war* in order to avoid a larger one?

Worse still to contemplate was whether condoning this supposed murder was beyond *me*. At this point, I wasn't sure, so I put my head in my hands and closed my eyes. The redirected breezes cooled the library, lightly rustling pages.

Murder or no, what would happen if Kalyna's plans here (whatever they were) backfired upon the very Loashti we were hoping to protect? There was great power in angry and determined groups of people, and I worried that the Guild's sense of being exceptional from the world could be easily turned toward ugly purposes.

The power of a group, all focused on one goal, is a terrifying thing. This was part of what I had been researching, back when I had the time for my studies. Curses needed belief, and the more the better. That, alongside Zobiski memory, told me much about the horrifying power of the crowd: whether Žydrė or Yalwas, how would that crowd react when it had a new avatar through which to process its needs and desires? An avatar on shakier ground than Adomas had been, knowing that they really could lose their position if the people decided so.

Perhaps this was why so many Loashti—myself included, at times— found the strong central authority of the Grand Suzerain strangely comforting. Loasht could be monstrous, of course, but our leader would not bow to public opinion, good or bad.

Then again, I suppose Aloe found some sort of way around that, didn't he?

Eighty-Three, it was just too much. Why had I been born into such a time? Or perhaps, why hadn't I been born *more recently* into such a time, so that I would be accustomed to it? I might have preferred that to spending four decades living through the best possible years to be a Zobiski since Loasht first swept over our lands, until that comfort was crushed by sudden exile.

I laid my head on the desk and wished that I could cry, but the tears wouldn't come.

"Why so glum?"

I started when Kalyna spoke to me in Loashti Bureaucratic. I looked up, blinking.

"Adomas is dead," I replied.

"Oh, that. Well, yes, but I think we're in a good spot, all told."

She eased into a large armchair, beside which was a little desk. Open on the desk was my copy of *The Miraculous Adventure of Aigerim*, which I had been reading in bits and pieces when I needed a break from more important work. In that moment, the idea of extracting Yekunde's Zobiski population seemed about as believable as Aigerim's greatest triumphs.

"Did you kill him?" I asked.

Kalyna, who had been idly reading the open romance, looked up with her brows knitted.

"Who? Adomas?"

"Yes."

She snorted and sunk deeper into the chair. "Of course not, Radiant. Why would I do that?"

"Perhaps because he wouldn't allow more Loashti to come here and threatened to expel the rest of us. Or because he was the only person that we—" I coughed. "That *I* told about our plans."

I looked directly in her eyes, hoping that, somehow, I could catch a bit of truth in them, futile as that was. She sat in just the right spot for the soft light bounced into the library by mirrors to illuminate her face and hair.

"I mean, if that were so, would it even be the wrong choice?" she asked. "Hypothetically, if Adomas was about to expel the Loashti who are here, including yourself, leaving you all to be taken back to the border and arrested, tortured, and killed—if such was his plan, then he'd be doing as good as murdering you all, yes? So wouldn't killing him be as justified as every time Dagmar hurt someone to protect you?" She shrugged. "I know it's harder to look at, when it isn't a man coming at you with a knife, but does that make it wrong? Would it be *wrong* for you to stab Aloe in the back while he was hugging you and calling you 'friend'?"

"I don't know. I came close."

"It would be *distasteful,*" she said. "But I don't see where it would be *wrong.*"

"Is that what happened then?" I asked. "Adomas was absolutely set on expelling us?"

"Radiant, I don't know!" She slapped her thigh and leaned forward, voice echoing through the great library. "I decided it would be better to talk to him in the morning, when his temper had cooled further. I never even went to his house last night."

"But I thought you had a whole *plan* to convince him."

"Sometimes plans change."

"Killing him would also be a change in plans."

"Yes, it would." She sat back again. "Radiant Basket of Rainbow Shells, I have told you I didn't kill the man, and that is all I can do. Believe me when I say, I wanted him to agree with us, not to have to deal with his daft followers as they grab for a piddling amount of power."

"You seemed to be enjoying yourself in the Lecture Hall, dancing on the table and making Yalwas uncomfortable."

She grinned and leaned her head back, looking up at the inside of the turret above us. "What can I say? It's fun to have power over people; it's fun to outmaneuver them, and those two are just so easy."

"So the plan is to put Žydrė in charge and influence her?" I pushed my chair back and put my feet up on the desk. Perhaps I could will myself to be as relaxed as Kalyna seemed to be.

"That's the size of it, yes."

"Why didn't you tell her about Adomas' secret passage and the river and all that beforehand?"

"Because I didn't trust her not to blurt it out. You have to save things like that for the right moment."

"Didn't you worry it would also make her look . . . I don't know . . . ?"

"Stupid? These are the risks we have to take." She let out a long, pained sigh. "Truth be told, Žydrė is not quite acting like the leader I was hoping she'd be. All that excitement she had when she was telling us about the place and bickering with Vidmantas—everything I've heard about her in the salons—seems to melt away in the face of the crowd."

"If only we could capture the fire she had that night in the Games Hall, when she told off Yalwas," I muttered.

Kalyna harrumphed in agreement. "I may have chastised her too hard after that. And now it's too late to get her drunk and see how that endears her to the crowd." She shook her head. "Unfortunately, in her bid to be leader, Žydrė seems interested in being the most *qualified*—like a very good apprentice—when what she needs is to draw people in."

"Isn't it good to be qualified?"

Kalyna thought that was very funny. Her laugh wasn't even mean.

"Kings aren't qualified, but deposing them takes a lot of work. Adomas wasn't 'qualified,' he was mostly a . . . a big personality that the people of this Guild could invest with their hopes and dreams. Vidmantas wasn't wrong when he said the Guild would fall apart without Adomas."

"So you don't think Žydrė has the, I don't know, presence? Or conviction?"

Kalyna looked at me again, searching for something, although I don't know what.

"Presence, no," she said. "At least, not in front of a crowd. As for conviction, she may have too much of that. These people, *right now*, do not want to hear about being a beacon to the rest of the world; they want to know how they'll survive the next few months." She shook her head, frustration spiking into her voice. "On the morning they learn of their beloved leader's death, they won't be interested in following his beliefs so closely that they don't *mark his damned grave*."

"Perhaps she feels it's in moments like these that people should think of their ideals."

"Exactly! Which is why she needs my help to *get anywhere.*" She sighed again. "Gods, this is exhausting work you've gotten me into."

"Are you going to leave me then?"

"No. I'm staying for now because I would like to help your people and see that dead thing in Adomas' hideout. Besides"—she grinned—"it *is* fun." She stood up. "The light is starting to fade. We had better go see how the vote turns out."

"And if Yalwas wins?"

"Then we see what we can do with Yalwas."

Chapter Twenty-Two

How the Lanreas River Guild Voted by Carnival Rules

The sun was setting, and the cooler night air was flowing in, which I hoped would make people less prone to explosions of anger or violence. Unfortunately, as we approached the Lecture Hall, there was some kind of altercation taking place outside.

Kalyna ran over, while I lagged a bit behind her. I slowed even more as I realized what was happening: it seemed that a number of the Tetrarchic Guild members did not want the Loashti to enter the hall. I saw Kalyna's hand dip down toward her sickle as she ran.

The entire group of recent Loashti aliens were at the entrance to the Lecture Hall, blocked by about ten Tetrarchic people who were holding farm implements. I slowed even more. The last thing I wanted in the world, on top of everything else, was to be murdered with a rake.

Echoes was just outside the front door of the Lecture Hall, her face fully painted yellow and light brown. I didn't know what those colors signified for her, or the Kubatri, but it clearly meant something, and it *definitely* unsettled the man whose pickaxe she was grabbing and shaking as she yelled. Soon, Kalyna was also yelling and pushing herself between the two groups.

The man with the pickaxe was sturdy and muscular. He wrenched it backward, out of Echoes' hands, then threw his body forward, slamming her with his shoulder. Both sides of the crowd got louder and angrier, swirling into total incoherence. Echoes sprawled backward, seeming to cry out when she hit the hard ground, although I could not hear her. The man kept moving forward, raising the pickaxe above her, above his head. Echoes wriggled, and the man drove the pickaxe downward.

Kalyna encircled the pickaxe with her sickle's blade, redirecting and skidding down the handle until she'd sliced the man's hand. The pickaxe flew off into the air, embedding itself in a wall of Lecture Hall.

The man stood still, breathing hard, holding his hand tightly. On his face was rage, confusion, indignity, bafflement. Kalyna, who was about his height but much narrower, stood between him and Echoes' prone body, regarding him coldly. She very obviously took a moment to decide what to do next, rather than acting in the heat of the moment, as he had done.

Sickle in her right hand, Kalyna struck him hard with her left. Not a slap or a backhand, but a punch with her full weight. The man spun backward and fell to the dirt. His companions, also with dangerous-looking implements, did nothing but stare helplessly.

Kalyna, unbothered by the man's companions, turned to look at Echoes, who was still on the ground, partway to a sitting position. Echoes' right hand was behind her back, as though reaching for something.

"I'll live," said Echoes in Skydašiavos.

"What were you reaching for?" asked Kalyna in the same.

"Something I . . . keep around," replied Echoes. Her mastery of the language was halting. "To, erm, throw in the eyes. If someone is a fool."

"Leave it."

"Plan to," grunted Echoes. Then, frustrated, she looked at me and added, in Loashti Bureaucratic: "But tell her we have been through enough of this. *I* have been through enough of this. And I will happily kill, or die, to keep anyone from continuing to shit on my people." She pointed angrily at those blocking the entryway. "She definitely shouldn't expect *us* to be peaceful if we can't expect the same from *them*."

I translated, essentially word for word, into Skydašiavos. Perhaps I should have been more diplomatic in the words I chose, but I didn't think of it. Or I didn't want to.

Kalyna, face seemingly emotionless, waited for Echoes to look back at her. Once the two women had made eye contact, Kalyna nodded.

She turned to the man, who was still in the dust and holding his hand. The cut didn't seem very deep.

"What's your name?" she ordered in Skydašiavos.

"O . . . Obinnas," he stammered in reply.

"Obinnas," she said, "you are the worst kind of coward."

"Coward?!" he cried and began to sit up.

Kalyna kicked him in the ribs, and he went back down, moaning.

"These Loashti," she seethed, "have nothing, no weapons, and nowhere else to go. Whereas we"—she feinted as though to kick Obinnas again, and he cringed—"outnumber them three to one. I don't care what hell you fled to come here, Obinnas, because *now* you are the one with power, aren't you?" The edge in her voice was terrifying and, I think, not exaggerated for effect. Kalyna Aljosanovna seemed to have dispensed with theatrics, just then, and was venting blisteringly real feelings.

Obinnas said nothing, just stared up in shock.

"Were it up to me," Kalyna continued, "I would exile you from the Guild in a heartbeat for *daring* to raise a weapon against a fellow member."

It was at this point that Kalyna sighed, looked up, slowly turned her head, and realized that the Lecture Hall was full. Nearly everyone in the Guild was in there and had, until recently, been adding to the general noise and confusion. But they had quieted when the violence took place and had *all* heard everything Kalyna said.

Just inside were two more Guild members with farm tools, looking as though they had been stopping a group of others from coming outside. At the front of *that* group was Ifeanyas, and so it was very much my hope that they had wanted to help the Loashti. At the dais, in the back of the Lecture Hall, Žydrė and Yalwas were already there, also watching.

Kalyna did not seem to react to all this, although I'm sure it was a surprise, and she may have acted differently toward Obinnas had she known. Instead, she looked right into the building, so I only saw the back of her head.

"That's right," she began, projecting her voice until it felt like that of a god. "I said 'a fellow member.'" She pushed her sickle, still with a little splash of blood on its blade, back into her belt. "If this land"—she raised her arms—"is not the Tetrarchia, then these people have as much right to it as any of you. Unless, of course, you'd like to create another hierarchy." I suspect, from her voice, that she smiled bitterly.

No one replied, so she walked slowly into the Lecture Hall, ignoring Obinnas' comrades, who were still armed. Once she was a few steps in, she turned back and beckoned forward.

"Please follow," she called in purposefully clumsy Loashti Bureaucratic.

Echoes went in first. She did not ignore the armed Guild members but sneered at them. Slowly, the rest of the Loashti aliens entered as well, and I went in with them.

Inside the Lecture Hall, Ifeanyas fixed me with a very serious look and carefully revealed to me that he'd snuck a knife from somewhere. I found this both comforting and worrying.

The Loashti spread out wherever there was space and were followed by those who had been stopping them, although they left their implements outside. The hall was quite packed: it felt like everyone was on top of one another.

Kalyna walked up to the dais, and stood between Žydrė and Yalwas, in front of the desk. She looked around the room from there: probing, curious, appraising. She glanced back at Yalwas.

"I . . . I did not tell them to do that, if that's what you think," said Yalwas. He was wide-eyed and seemed unsteady.

"I don't," replied Kalyna. With a wry smile, she turned to look back at Žydrė.

"Thank you, Kalyna," said Žydrė. "Clearly, *some* of us need to be reminded what a community is."

There was, at least, a little of the bite that Žydrė was capable of. I wondered if Vidmantas had convinced her to take a drink or two beforehand.

Kalyna nodded, then muttered something to Žydrė, who shook her head.

"Ah," said Kalyna, turning back to the rest of the room. "I thought we must've already had a way to vote here, but I suppose not." She sighed. "All right then! We'll go by carnival rules."

No one seemed to know what this meant, until Kalyna, once more, hopped up onto the desk. If she was weary from the day, or from the altercation she had just been involved in, none of it showed. She was graceful and gracious, seeming to enjoy the pomp and circumstance of the moment, while acknowledging its silliness as well.

"Let's just get to it!" She clapped her hands. "Unless anyone disagrees?"

Murmurs, but nothing else. It seemed the people of the Guild had made their decisions. The tension was thick, and I wondered how many other people were secretly armed like Ifeanyas.

"Lovely," said Kalyna. "All we need you to do, everyone, is use your best judgment for who you think should lead the Lanreas River Guild." Then she stopped and smiled apologetically. "That is, all of the *adults*. If you're still in one of the Trash Companies, you can't vote just yet."

There was an outcry of disappointment from a group of children, whom Kalyna then favored with a salute.

"So, *adults*, if you think it should be Yalwas"—she leaned toward him and held a hand over her head—"raise your hands." She grinned, inviting scattered laughter at how incongruous it was to treat the future of the Guild like a singing contest.

I looked around and saw hands in the air, but it was hard for me to count from where I was crammed into a group near the front.

Kalyna squinted and seemed to be counting, as did Yalwas, Žydrė, and everyone else with them.

"Don't worry if it's imprecise," she said to those on the dais. "If it's close, we can always try with ballots. But this is faster in case, well, you know . . . in case it *isn't* close." She smirked mischievously at that.

"Now," she continued, pivoting over toward Žydrė and raising a hand over the woman's head, "who thinks that—"

She was interrupted by a chorus of cheers accompanying the raised hands (which included mine). It seemed quite overwhelming in that moment, but soon angry voices were raised in opposition as well. I looked about the room and saw Guild members yelling in each others' faces, even pushing one another. Ifeanyas, who I noticed had not raised his hand for either person, seemed to be considering his knife.

Kalyna made a face of consternation and worked to quiet everyone down, urging patience.

"Well," she finally said, "that seems to be a win for Žydrė." Kalyna crossed her arms and looked out at the crowd. "But quite a few hands never went up, did they?"

"When do we vote for you?" called a voice from the crowd I didn't recognize.

There was a roar of agreement, joined a moment later by most of the Loashti when they heard someone say Kalyna's name. It was certainly *louder* than the cheers for Žydrė, but that didn't necessarily mean it was more people.

Yalwas had the same expression of surprise and fear he'd worn the entire time, but Žydrė's mouth became a very thin and fixed line.

"Me?" Kalyna seemed genuinely surprised.

"You said who we think should lead!" someone said.

Kalyna blinked a few times, looked around, then shrugged, and held her hands above her own head, in a sort of flourish.

The room exploded with noise, and based on the expressions of Žydrė, Yalwas, and their companions, the number of hands in the air was over-whelming. I did not raise mine (it seemed dishonest, as I'd voted for Žydrė), but Ifeanyas certainly did, waving it about to make sure he was seen.

Kalyna laughed in a way somewhere between surprised and trium-phant. Then she bowed and said, "I accept."

She hopped back down to the dais and moved behind the desk, ac-companied by cheers. There were dissenting voices, but they seemed to realize they were outnumbered: it was more the sound of disappoint-ment than of anger.

Kalyna spoke to Žydrė and Yalwas, but I couldn't hear it over the noise. I believe she was asking them if they'd accept this—if they agreed that the numbers were clearly in her favor. Žydrė eventually nodded curtly, Yalwas mostly shrugged.

Kalyna raised her hands to draw everyone's attention, and the crowd slowly quieted, although a few hecklers still made their voices known. She was breathing heavily now, positively beaming from, I think, the adulation. Those perfect white teeth gleamed as she took in the people of the Lanreas River Guild.

"Thank you, everyone. Thank you," she said. "It's quite the respon-sibility, and I hope I will do it justice. Žydrė and Yalwas will, of course, continue to work with me for the betterment of everyone at the Guild, and I hope that those who would've preferred them in my place will as well. Remember"—she winked—"I am not a king, and you can decide you're sick of me whenever you like."

Some applause, some angry looks from the dais. Vidmantas, I noticed, was glaring at Ifeanyas, specifically.

"But," Kalyna continued, "first things first. Yalwas"—she turned to face him—"tomorrow, when you have a moment, please bring me *all* keys to the river passage."

Yalwas sighed deeply but nodded.

"And second," said Kalyna, any hint of a smile or exhilaration vanishing, "Obinnas is exiled."

There were murmurs, but they quieted under the look of frightening intensity that Kalyna trained on her audience.

"Does anyone disagree?" she asked. "Am I being a tyrant?"

More murmurs, but nothing more.

"Vidmantas," she said, still looking out at the crowd, "you have a lot of knowledge and experience surrounding trade guilds. How would most of them handle an attempted murder between members?"

Vidmantas looked irritated to be brought into this, and angry at Kalyna, but he did not hesitate either: "By ejecting the aggressor. Or worse."

She nodded, still looking outward. "We do not turn weapons against our own," Kalyna continued. "I don't care whether Obinnas was told by someone to take up arms, or whether he acted entirely without thinking and did not even realize he had done such a thing. He nearly murdered a Guild member and by doing so, has forfeited his own membership, yes?"

Silence.

"Just so," she said. Then she looked very directly somewhere toward the back, seemingly making eye contact with someone. "Obinnas, you have tonight to make your goodbyes and gather up your belongings. Tomorrow morning, we will give you a day's worth of food, and you will never return. Do you have any money?"

"No," came a meek voice from behind me. "I gave it all to the Guild when I joined."

Kalyna nodded. "That was good of you." She looked to Žydrė, lowered her voice, and asked, "We must have a record of how much each person brought in when they joined. In case they leave?"

Žydrė shook her head.

Kalyna pressed her fingers to her closed eyes for a moment. "Gods. I'll add it to the list." Then she once more addressed the crowd: "Obinnas, you may also take twenty kudais from the Guild's coffers. But"—she looked around at the rest of the room sternly—"don't anyone go thinking that exile always brings with it a reward. Obinnas committed his crime during an admittedly confusing day. He is an exception."

There was another silence, until Obinnas' voice muttered, very quietly, "Thank you."

Kalyna nodded and added, "Oh, and Obinnas, you're not to tell anyone in the outside world about the passageway, or the water, or the livable part of the Tail, is that clear?"

"Yes."

Kalyna glared silently at him for a few moments, probably to hide the fact that she was thinking very fast. "Radiant," she said, pointing to me, "will know, from afar, if you betray our trust. In such a case, he will knock you dead with a wizard's curse. Is that clear?"

Gasps all around me. I wanted to curl up and never be seen again. But I held my gaze on her, because I knew it was what she wanted me to do.

Obinnas must have muttered assent or nodded his head, because soon Kalyna seemed satisfied.

"Lovely," she said. "Tonight, I would like to give everyone the freedom to grieve Adomas in their own way. I know that today has allowed little space for it. Drink, dance, cry, reminisce, sit quietly, congregate, or seek solitude. But please, be gentle with one another."

Eventually, everyone filed out of the Lecture Hall.

Kalyna and I walked north to Adomas' old house, in the shadow of the Estate, which she decided was now hers. A few minutes prior, Žydrė had voiced concern that the little hut would become a seat of power, just as the Estate had once been.

Kalyna shook her head at that. "I just need a home, Žydrė. I've grown tired of the dormitory. We will build up the space between his old house and the village with our new members, and soon it won't be apart from everyone anymore."

Žydrė clicked her tongue, but let it go.

As we moved toward the house, many people offered congratulations, which Kalyna deflected with things like, "It's only because of you," and "I only hope I live up to your expectations." Some glared as well, or muttered to one another, but she smiled beatifically at them.

As I watched her gracefully react to her victory, I wondered what was going on in her head. If this had been her plan, then why the ruse of backing Žydrė up until the last minute? Why the feigned surprise? This turn of events also further irritated the feeling that gnawed at the back of my skull: that Kalyna had murdered Adomas.

What was she thinking of these people, whom she had so often called fools, I wondered, as she smiled and nodded and talked to them about the importance of the duty they had given her?

Kalyna slowed a bit behind me as we approached the house, I assumed, because she was tired. I walked up the stairs ahead of her and opened the door.

The inside of Adomas' house looked the same as it had the last time I'd seen it, as though its occupant would return at any time. The bed was sloppily made; there was a pile of clothing on the floor that needed to be washed; and a book was open on the desk, next to an earthenware jug that may have still held water Adomas meant to drink. I suddenly felt the loss of the man who had lived here, while also being filled with a kind of quiet serenity in the cozy little home he had made. Something small skittered across the roof as I walked inside. I heard Kalyna follow me in and slowly, almost limply, shut the door.

She took a few steps, and then there was a loud impact. I turned and saw Kalyna had fallen to her knees on the hard, wooden floor. She braced herself with one hand against the floor, and the other one was at her forehand, fingers beginning to twist into her hair.

"Are you all right?" I blurted out. "That must have hurt!"

"Fuck," she said in Skydašiavos.

"What?"

"Fuck," she repeated, before speaking oaths in a score of languages.

I leaned forward, and put my hands on her shoulders. "What's the matter? It was just a little fall, you should be—"

She looked up at me, and her eyes were wild with fear, her breathing heavy.

"I can't do this," she said, shaking her head. "It's too much."

"Too much what?"

"Responsibility, you halfwit!" She pushed weakly at my hands. "I don't want to *lead* these idiots! Or anybody! I've done *enough*, and now they're putting their stupid fucking lives into *my* hands?"

I stood up, crossing my arms. "Well," I said, with a bit too much scold in my voice, "you should have thought of that before you intrigued to become their leader."

She glared at me and pulled herself shakily to her feet. "Intrigued?" she almost shrieked. "Is that what you think that was? You absolute—" something in Masovskani. "I never wanted this job. I didn't 'intrigue,'" she sneered, mocking the very word. "I'm just more charming and decisive than anyone these absolute bumpkins have ever met!" This did not sound like a boast, just a fact—a fact that made her livid.

"But Vidmantas was right," she continued. "This little cult would crumble without a leader its people can actually like and . . . and . . . *identify* with." She began to pace quickly and loudly across the small room. "So, since Yalwas is a big bag filled with nothing, and Žydrė has no gods-damned *presence*, I realized it had to be me! Realized it the moment I beat that Obinnas idiot."

"Then why didn't you put yourself forward as a candidate officially?"

"Because people need to feel like they're making decisions themselves, even when they are *not*." She growled and shook her head, as though explaining any of this to me was impossible. "You don't understand. People are fickle. I have to lead them to what they want, while pretending I don't know that they want it, because *they* don't realize that they do! It's the only way to do my kind of work."

"I thought you had a *plan*!" I slammed my hand on the desk for emphasis. As I held my hand there, I realized it was shaking. I had never seen her like this: with truly no control over a situation, or even over herself. Something about that stirred a deep fear in me.

She threw up her hands, and I flinched, thinking she would hit me.

"Radiant," she seethed, "are you a fucking child?"

"I . . . I . . . don't know what you mean."

Her anger and dismay turned into a truly horrifying rictus grin, and she laughed.

"A naïve little child," she spat. "Radiant, I never have a *plan*. I just . . .

fumble forward with whatever the world throws at me!" She clapped her hands together and laughed louder, spinning away from me.

"'Oh! I have three exact plans I'm working on!'" Kalyna began, in an imitation of herself. "'But I can't tell you, because they depend on the position of the moon tonight, and whether there's an angry ghost nearby, and which god is worshipped here!' and on and on, and on." She shook her head. "That was only ever a way to get Dagmar off my fuck-ing back!" She looked at me again, grinning, her eyes wild and scared, and her hands in the air. "Radiant, I never know what I'm doing! Does that truly surprise you?!"

I nodded my head slowly.

"And *you* were supposed to be smart," she laughed. "I'm trying to get these people to help you, after you pissed away all my work on Adomas. And then they go and offer me power over them. I would be *stupid* not to accept it. Even *you* must see that."

I was doomed. The Zobiski were doomed. Kalyna was not some preternaturally intuitive master manipulator. She was just a sad little woman who enjoyed holding sway over others too much to think about the consequences. Had she decided she was the best person for the job, or had she just wanted the crowd's adulation?

Kalyna turned away from me again, grabbed Adomas' desk, and overturned it violently. Everything he had carefully placed there fell to the floor: books, pens, a vase of flowers, the earthenware jug. The jug shattered, and there had still been water in it. I froze. I felt sure she would beat me next—burst my head open like that jug.

"Balls," she said. "I should run. It's that simple: I should run tonight, let the rest sort itself out. I've done what I can."

I felt an even greater feeling of doom at that: a low I hadn't thought possible. Kalyna was a fraud, but she was *here* and had some kind of power, after all. My despair became great enough that I decided I'd let her beat me, if she so chose.

I grabbed her wrist. "You absolutely have not done what you can!" I cried. "You can't run out now, while you—!"

She wrenched her wrist from me. "Don't you think I know that?" She sighed, although it turned into a sort of strangled sob. "Of course I'm not going to run *now*." She shook her head. "Grandmother always said I was a shirker," she muttered. "I can't let the old demon—"

She stopped, looked up at me again, and moved very close. Uncomfortably close.

"Radiant," she said through gritted teeth, "I will stay here, at least through tomorrow."

"That's good. Thank you. I—"

Her upper lip twitched. "Now get out."

"Sleep well!" When the second word left my lips, I was already at least a yard from the house.

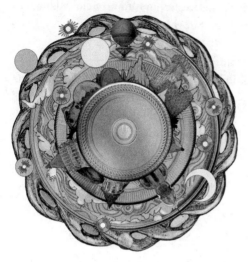

Chapter Twenty-Three

When the Lanreas River Guild Became the Site of a Miracle

At breakfast the following day, no one had seen Kalyna. But then, no one had seen much of anybody: the hall was largely empty, and breakfast—rice baked with eggs and spiced until it was a deep red—went largely untouched. Ifeanyas and I sat with a large table all to ourselves.

"This is ominous," I said.

"Maybe everyone is just tired of crowds," offered Ifeanyas, although he looked very worried.

Obinnas, the man Kalyna had banished, was at the back of the Meal Hall, near the kitchen, where he was quietly and solemnly scooping rice into canvas sacks. Sometimes, a friend or acquaintance would talk quietly to him for a few moments upon entering or leaving the hall. During one conversation, Obinnas noticed I was glancing at him and immediately cut off whatever he was saying to focus on his sad task.

I looked at Ifeanyas instead.

"What?" he asked, sounding almost worried.

"I'm just admiring you. Is that all right?"

"I suppose I'm not used to it."

"That's too bad." I leaned forward, elbows on the table, chin in my hands. "I'm not saying I expect you to sleep with me again. We can, or we can decide we had a lot of fun but that was that. Either way, I like looking at you."

He cleared his throat uncomfortably.

"Sorry," I offered. "Zobiski mores are very different from Skydašian."

"Well, I'm not really Skydašian anymore. But I'm still getting used to it."

I smiled. "Well, now that I've flattered you a little, will you accompany me to see Kalyna? I don't much fancy going alone."

"Of course!"

I didn't tell him that I wanted him as protection, in case Kalyna was still angry.

I knocked gingerly on the door to her new house, and it opened just a moment later. Kalyna was dressed, smiling, with her hair oiled but pulled loosely up to stay out of her way, and holding a mug of coffee. Behind her, Adomas' desk was right side up again, with everything placed neatly on it, including a neat little pile of shards that used to be a jug.

"Good morning!" she sang out. "I'm sorry I missed the communal meal, but I decided to take my breakfast in here and go over some plans."

Were those real plans for the Guild? Or the sort of fake "plans" she had apparently been making promises about for years? Kalyna was so chipper I began to wonder if I'd dreamed the previous night.

"Well, good morning," replied Ifeanyas. "You didn't miss much. Hardly anyone else was there either."

"I was afraid of that," said Kalyna, finishing her coffee.

She turned to put down the mug, then stopped, snapped her fingers, and turned back.

"Why, do you know that—?" She laughed musically and patted her forehead with her free hand. "No, of course you don't. You see, I was born thirty years ago today. Isn't that strange timing?" She shook her head at the impossibility of it all.

I reflexively replied with, "Many happy returns," in Zobiski.

"I will assume that was well wishes," replied Kalyna. "Loashti track that sort of thing more carefully than most of us from the Tetrarchia, don't they?"

"They do," I replied. "For bureaucracy."

"Nonetheless," she continued, "please don't go telling people or making a fuss. I think it would sound . . . unbelievable—like a cry for attention at a time when I should be focusing on everyone else."

We agreed, and I felt a little dazed. We began walking to the village, and soon enough, Ifeanyas left us to talk to some others he knew.

"Really? Your birthday?" I muttered in Loashti Bureaucratic.

She joined me and nodded, shrugging. "Really," she replied, almost dreamily. "It *is* just strange timing."

"Well, congratulations on your anniversary and your ascent to power."

Something between a wince and a snarl traveled across her face, and in that moment, I knew I had not dreamed the previous night.

Moving south, through the village and toward the farmland, Kalyna received a wide variety of greetings: smiles, scowls, pats on the back, mad dashes out of her way. We passed a Loashti whom I recognized but didn't know by name: she was broadly built, with delicate features, so I think I would have placed her as being from the southeast, not far from Quruscan. Upon seeing Kalyna, her eyes went wide, and she began to bow.

Kalyna put a hand delicately on the woman's shoulder and said to me in Skydašiavos, "Please tell her not to do that. I'm no prince or margrave or bey; I only have the power you all choose to give me." Even in this quick moment, she chose her words carefully, to ensure their impact when translated into Loashti Bureaucratic.

The Loashti woman stood up but looked unsure. Kalyna patted her shoulder again, harder this time.

"We can be friends," Kalyna said, "or comrades, or neighbors, but I'm no one's lord."

I translated this as well.

The Loashti woman trained a skeptical look at me. "Really?" she asked.

I shrugged. "Far as I can tell."

"Is she busted up in the head?" the woman added.

"Perhaps a little."

Kalyna definitely had to swallow her reaction to that last exchange. I took some kind of Loashti pride in that.

"And," Kalyna continued, "please tell her that you, Radiant, are going to start teaching me to speak Loashti, so I can better communicate with *all* of our Guild members." She said this part loudly, to make sure everyone nearby heard it.

I translated, of course, and wondered how quickly Kalyna would decide to "learn" Loashti Bureaucratic.

Near the northern edge of the farmlands, Žydrė stood in the bright sun, pointing to things and seeming to give orders—or, perhaps, suggestions. With her was a cadre of her allies, including Vidmantas.

"Where have you been all morning?" grunted Žydrė when Kalyna approached her. "Getting your beauty sleep? Oiling your luxuriant curls and rubbing cocoa butter on your soft hands?"

Kalyna laughed in a way that seemed to entirely disregard Žydrė's venom—that seemed to assume they were only friends ribbing each other.

"And your braids are immaculate as always," she replied.

Žydrė stared at Kalyna for a long time. Then she finally replied, "*Braids like these* take a community, Kalyna Aljosanovna. Like the success of our farms, they require a group. The 'immaculate' complexity you see here is because I have people here who care about me enough to help me look good. Do you?"

Kalyna laughed again. If she felt threatened at all by Žydrė's presence, she didn't show it.

"Not yet," she said. "I'm still new here, after all."

"And yet," said Žydrė, "you are apparently in charge."

Kalyna sighed and crossed her arms, moving into the shade of a nearby tree and shifting her weight to one side.

"Believe it or not, Žydrė," she said, "I was as surprised by that as you."

Žydrė seemed to chew something in her mouth, then sighed. "That is hard to believe. But, if you insist, I'll take you at your word."

Vidmantas stepped closer. "Do you honestly expect us to believe—"

"Vidmantas," snapped Žydrė. "Stop. You're worse than her when it comes to being pampered and vain, anyway." She spoke in the same tone she had used with Kalyna, with no sign of her usual friendly antagonism with Vidmantas.

"Well," he said, "I would argue that a desire to look *and feel* nice has no bearing on a person's—"

"I told you to stop," Žydrė interrupted. I'm sure I was not the only one who noticed she was still wearing only undyed linen dresses.

This uncomfortable scene was, thankfully, disturbed when Yalwas lumbered loudly up to us from somewhere vaguely northeastward. He seemed, for the first time, to feel the weight of himself, as though it was simply too much to carry. As though his muscles had lost all usefulness and were now only a burden; his fat no longer pleasant, but odious. He looked haggard, and he was entirely alone.

He approached Kalyna, eyes red, and slammed his large fist into the tree against which she was leaning. Žydrė flinched at the impact. Kalyna, of course, did not. Leaning against the tree, he lifted his other hand, and dropped a pair of keys into Kalyna's.

"There," he grunted. "One of those was mine, one was my son's. There was a third key, but it was buried with Adomas."

"Well, that was silly," replied Kalyna. "He won't be using it." She shrugged. "Thank you, Yalwas. I'm sure that wasn't easy to do."

Yalwas cleared his throat loudly.

"Or maybe," said Vidmantas, "Yalwas still has the third key."

Kalyna acted surprised, but I am quite sure this was another example of her leaving someone more tactless to say what she didn't want to.

"If that's the case, Vidmantas," she said, "it hardly matters." She pushed herself off the tree. "Because I am going to go unlock that door and leave it that way. Everything on the other side belongs to all of us."

She said this last part loudly enough for people nearby to hear, and as she began to march north toward the Estate, more and more members of the Guild joined her.

I remembered some of the things she had said in the previous night's outburst and now saw, so clearly, that she savored her power over these people.

By the time Kalyna arrived at the door to Adomas' secret passage, there were something like fifty people crowded about us, mostly of Tetrarchic extraction. I expected Kalyna to make some big speech or proclamation, to linger on the way she was keeping no secrets from the Guild, but she did no such thing. She simply allowed everyone to imagine what she would have said and, in doing so, appeared much more gracious as she unlocked and opened the door.

We filed through the passageway two at a time, Kalyna and I ahead of a long trail of curious people. I began to feel uncomfortable in that tight space, packed with human bodies, but at least I was in front.

It seems Kalyna did have a speech of some kind that she was planning to make when we emerged out into that small section of The Thrashing, Bone-White Tail of Galiag, with the Lanreas River running past us, but she had not accounted for just how loud those howling winds were. As everyone moved, blinking, into the light, she tried to speak, but even I, right next to her, couldn't make most of it out. Instead, all fiftyish of us stood in silent awe. Myself included, as I had not been there in the daytime before.

On my last visit, I hadn't reckoned with quite how *lush* the grass and underbrush were. We beheld an all-encompassing greenness the likes of which I hadn't seen since arriving at the Guild. The water of the river, dark though its depths were, still glimmered and showed some green at its edges.

And, of course, it was all brilliantly lit up by the searing winds pounding by above us, thick with the white refuse of the city of Galiag. So brilliant, in fact, that a few people looked up directly up at the sky and were temporarily blinded by the sun reflecting off of all that sand or dirt or whatever it was.

We all walked back through the passageway, which began to fill up with murmurs of surprise, wonder, irritation, and confusion. A few had to be led by their hands, but it wasn't long before their vision began to return.

"Fascinating stuff!" Kalyna declared once we were all back in the old, crumbling Estate. "Yalwas, perhaps tomorrow you can tell me what you and your son *do* out there. Cleaning, upkeep, and so forth. And, for that matter, what time of day you do it without going blind."

"Usually late afternoon or early evening," mumbled Yalwas.

"I see. It's like snowblindness!" said Kalyna. "They have other ways around that in Masovska: a blindfold with slits in it and the like."

Yalwas nodded numbly.

"As I said," Kalyna continued, louder, turning to the rest of the crowd, "this door will no longer be locked."

"What if someone sabotages the machinery?" asked Yalwas, grabbing onto a chance to defend why he had kept Adomas' secret.

Kalyna shrugged. "What if someone poisons our crops? What if someone kills Lini for food? What if someone burns our grain stores?

Our whole world is built on *trust*, Yalwas." She put her hand on his much larger one and looked into his eyes, seeming to genuinely sympathize with him. "That trust is fragile, which is why it's worth having."

"Now," muttered Kalyna, once she and I were alone, "how *do* we stop someone from sabotaging the machinery?"

This was some twenty minutes later, and I was sitting at the great desk in Adomas' library while Kalyna paced.

"Trust?" I replied.

She looked at me with derision and then realized I was being sarcastic. She smiled.

"Yes, exactly," she snorted. "I said I'd leave it unlocked, and that it belongs to everyone, so I need to think of *another* way to keep people out of there. Particularly strangers who may show up with the intention of ruining us."

"You went very quickly from arriving here to being suspicious of newcomers," I sighed.

"I'm suspicious of everybody." She waved her hand in the air, as though the motion concluded a line of reasoning. "Besides, I don't want to discourage new members, but this Guild is going to start attracting a lot of negative attention."

"Then why did you say you'd leave it unlocked?"

She walked up to the desk and slammed her hands down on it, and a sliver of who she'd been the night before crept into her face.

"Because it was what they *needed* to hear to keep *liking me*, Radiant. And no, I didn't plan it beforehand—that was simply what came out of my mouth in the moment. All right?"

"Did telling Obinnas that I'd curse him just come out of your mouth as well?"

"Obviously! I needed something to say in the moment that would discourage him from telling anybody."

"I wish you hadn't."

"Well, Radiant, *so do I*! But what's done is done. Besides, I rather hoped to get your people here and then make my exit before any consequences of my actions came calling. Leave you to deal with them. You're smart."

"That's not what you said last night," I replied.

I did my best to keep my voice even, but the memory of how much she'd scared me rippled through my body. I had realized, in the time since then, that the heady mixture of fear, anger, and unpredictability in Kalyna the night before had reminded me of my childhood: not of the times my father had hit me, but of the times when I did not yet know whether or not he would.

Kalyna, of course, picked up on this immediately.

"I'm sorry about that," she said, standing still again to look at me, but staying where she was rather than coming closer. "Not for my reaction, mind you, because I think *that* was entirely fair and justified. But I'm sorry my outburst twisted an old knife within you and made you fear for your safety. I hate to know that I made you feel threatened."

She sounded like she meant it, but I suppose Kalyna always did. She had told me once before that the difference between *meaning* and *not meaning* an apology meant nothing to her, so I decided to take it as genuine.

"Thank you," I said.

She smiled, clasped her hands behind her back, and began to pace again.

I wondered whether, now that we had access to the secret part of the river, it really would be possible for the Zobiski to take a boat down from Yekunde. I began inspecting a book of maps, and some ten minutes of silence passed between us.

"Speaking of threats," said Kalyna (I'd forgotten we were speaking of such things), "when were you going to ask Dagmar to help extract your people from Loasht?"

I nearly jumped, and the book of maps flew into the air. I almost caught it, but instead it spun around, out of my hands, and landed very loudly on the desk.

"What . . . what do you mean?" I squeaked.

"Well, I was planning to hire some sellswords with the Guild's money. She likes you, so she'd come cheap."

"What?"

"Look, she must've told you something, somehow, about how to reach her. Once she's actually invested herself in a task or person—which she does rarely—she dislikes quitting halfway."

I let out a very long sigh as I tried to think of what I would say.

"When you say 'a person,' do you mean me? Or you?"

"I'm not sure."

I sighed again and put my head face-first on the desk. I moaned loudly, which was as good as a confession, really.

"She did leave me a note," I muttered into the table.

"Which you burned your first day up here."

I moaned again.

"They were clearly recent ashes," she explained as I heard her walk closer to me.

"I didn't ask," I replied.

"What did she say?"

I dragged my head up to look at her. "That she's in Kalvadoti if I need her. And not to tell you."

"Going through so much trouble just to avoid me." Kalyna clicked her tongue loudly. "But also not going very far. She must miss me. Knows that if she sees me, her resolve will crumble."

"Could be," I said. "What of it? Is that what you want? For her resolve to crumble?"

She actually took a moment to think it over. "No, I suppose not. Probably best if you go to Kalvadoti without me. And don't tell her I know."

"Yes, Kalyna, I too would prefer she not think I *betrayed her trust*."

"Take Simurgh's balloon and whoever else you want, but tell them all that you're doing this without my knowledge. I won't have Simurgh spoiling everything."

"Fine."

"I suppose you can tell Ifeanyas the truth," she added.

"And how will we pay her? Along with a troupe of sellswords?"

"I'll worry about that—I've got an idea where to get the money. Just go get her help and offer whatever she asks. She'll probably give you a discount."

I shrugged. Kalyna began pacing again thoughtfully, and I watched her for some time.

Eventually, I said, "If we manage to save everyone, I'll understand if then you want to leave the Guild. I've asked a lot of you already, so I can try handling the consequences."

"That's kind of you," she said, with some irony, but not *so* much. Kalyna took a deep breath and rested her chin on her hand, with a look of what appeared to be resignation. "No, no. I'm not going anywhere. I've decided that."

I was absolutely exhausted and spent the rest of that day in my bed at the dormitory, not exactly asleep but in a state of, I suppose, half wakefulness. Dreams, realities, and fits of fancy all intermingled as I lay atop the covers and felt a breeze come in through the window now and then. My body wasn't really tired, but my mind was absolutely depleted. How in the world did Kalyna keep up her pace? Apparently, during that same day, she spoke to the three Guild members with clerical backgrounds, alongside meeting up with Yalwas and some others who had been close to Adomas to ensure that farming and trade with the outside world would continue as they had.

"I feel no great need to upend everything just because I can," she apparently said (or something to that effect).

Kalyna then went on to say she had some pressing issues to handle and wanted to give the day-to-day running of the Guild the attention it deserved later. I suspect she said this in a way that sounded less like she was avoiding work, because apparently no one was too angry about it.

I heard this from Ifeanyas, who was quickly becoming Kalyna's chief hanger-on. His earlier joy in working hard enough to not have to *think* about politics or philosophy seemed to be gone, replaced by an interest and eagerness beyond the wariness he'd shown when I first met him.

I began to feel as though everyone, Kalyna included, could find themselves here at the Lanreas River Guild, while I remained who I'd already been: an insecure little man who studied taboo topics and yet was desperate to please. Worse than I'd been, because while I still ached to be friendly and surround myself with people, I was becoming scared to. Worried, as I'd already put it to Kalyna, that I'd missed too much and been locked up too long—that this place was changing before I'd even gotten used to it. With my mind in such a state, it was easy to withdraw—to lie in bed or bury myself in studying—in order to avoid feeling out of step with everyone else.

Furthering my desire to hide from everyone, I was beginning to have a certain reputation throughout the Guild. Quite a few of the beds in the dormitory, which had recently been full of Loashti aliens, were now empty. At first, I took this as meaning that various newcomers had made friends and been invited into the homes of other members, which may very well have been true. There was also, now, a temporary encampment just north of the village, where many Loashti were now living, with houses planned to be built quite soon. But more than once, I saw people come into the dormitory and grab their things while giving me a look of . . . fear, perhaps. Disgust?

I must have looked asleep when one of Binturong's teenage children came in, looked at me, narrowed his eyes, and made an old Zobiski hand-flick motion of warding against evil. I should have continued to pretend I was asleep, but of course I did not.

"You know," I said in Zobiski, opening my eyes wider, "that warding spell is just as ancient and Zobiski and supposedly 'evil' as whatever you think I am."

"It's not a spell," he replied, angry and surprised all at once. "It's just a thing to do."

"It's the same thing, just watered down."

"Well, if it woke you up like that, it must have done *something* to you."

Then he ran out, leaving the small bag of his parent's that I assume he'd come there to retrieve.

I sighed and turned over, facing the wall so I wouldn't see whoever else came into the room.

"Hey. Hey."

I was being poked in the shoulder, so I turned over to see Vidmantas. I smiled dreamily, even though he looked serious. But he was dressed so colorfully, and he had fully regained control of his hair, which was glorious, so I kept smiling. He was sitting on a stool he'd pulled over, leaning toward me. No one else was in the building. I didn't know what time it was, nor did I care.

"What was that about a curse?" he asked. "I thought you were a 'wizard' in the sense of . . . well, an old hermit in the forest who can make some concoctions, and whose plants grow better than anyone else's."

"Except for the forest, that's not inaccurate."

"So the *curse* was a lie?"

I sighed. "Yes, but also sort of no."

"You're telling me you can really do that?" He did not sound like he believed it.

"Theoretically, I *could*. I've attempted minor curses, with help, but it's hard to say whether they worked."

"So she *was* lying then?"

I moaned in frustration as I forced myself to sit up, leaning back against the wall and looking at him.

"Vidmantas, what do you want me to say here? Are you looking for proof that I'm a dangerous sorcerer? Or proof that Kalyna is nothing but a liar? Or do you want the truth, which is more complicated than either of those?"

Vidmantas chewed his lip for a moment. "The truth, as you see it."

"I was, until recently, a scholar at the Loashti Academy, which paid me to research and write about anthropology. I chose to specialize in curses."

"That sounds like a good job."

"*It really was.*" I sighed. "Kalyna used my background—in what may well have been a moment of panic—to discourage Obinnas from telling our secrets to the world."

Vidmantas nodded slowly. "Radiant," he said, "I respect you, you know that."

"Is it just because I often blurt out whatever I'm thinking, the same way you do?"

He finally smiled, a little. "Perhaps. It's a shame we've ended up on different sides of—"

"There are no sides," I interrupted. "We're all here in the Guild together. I didn't choose Kalyna to lead—in fact, *I* voted for Žydrė—but the vast majority of our neighbors did." I threw up my hands. "And she may well be the best chance for my people."

The previous night had shaken my confidence in her, but unfortunately, this was still true. I certainly didn't know how else to help my community. I would simply need to barrel forward in the way that Kalyna, I now realized, always did.

"But Žydrė—"

"Vidmantas, *you* were the one who told Žydrė this place would fall apart when the 'charismatic leader' was gone, weren't you?"

"Yes," he said slowly. He clearly knew where I was steering him.

"Who else here approaches Adomas' charisma?"

"I know. But Žydrė has worked so long for this place, and—"

"And you used to make fun of her for it."

"But we grew up together! That's how we've always been." He sighed and let his head fall back, looking up at the ceiling. "Honestly, I still don't really believe in this place, but it's where I *am* now, and I think Žydrė can help it the most."

"And she still can. Kalyna is not the tyrant who will run everything, but her personality can hold these people together for a time."

"Like a figurehead?"

"Not quite. But she isn't Adomas."

"Radiant, do you remember that morning in the dormitory when she just kept slapping you?"

"I do," I replied. "I don't recall saying that she's a nice person."

I studied his face for a few moments and then realized how jealous I was of his beauty, so I had to say something to distract myself.

"What did Žydrė bring you here to do?" I asked. "In the first place, I mean. It seems she didn't plan for you to spend all your time dyeing clothes."

He shook his head. "I'm honestly not sure. Something . . . *intellectual.*" He strangled a laugh down in his throat. "Despite all the years of arguing, of telling me that I had no rigor to my ideas. Perhaps she thought I could help her lead."

"And is that what you want to do?"

"Not particularly. I enjoyed all those theories and back-and-forths when they were an escape from the drudgeries of the rest of my life. But now, given the chance to do whatever I want, I've gone right back to textiles." He laughed ironically, shaking his head. "My master would be so proud . . . at least until he saw what I was actually putting together for people."

"*Too* colorful?"

"The wrong kind of colorful. I'm mixing up markers of class, guild, location, and so forth, based on whatever appeals to me or what our people want."

"Why, Vidmantas, I had no idea your work here was so revolutionary!" I smiled broadly and patted his shoulder, hoping to put him at ease a bit. "Žydrė should be happy about that."

He smiled back for a moment, then dropped it. "Well, she isn't happy about *much* right now, Radiant. She feels that Kalyna usurped her, and I tend to agree."

"I'm sorry to hear that."

Vidmantas stood, making ready to leave.

"I don't know what Kalyna's planning," he said, "but she shouldn't expect any help from us."

"I'm sorry to hear that," I replied, "because she's planning to save people I love."

Perhaps it had been stupid to say, but I often default to honesty. Vidmantas looked awkwardly away, and I hoped he wouldn't ask how many people we planned to save, or in what way.

"And are those people more important than who is already here?" he asked instead.

"Of course not. After all, the people who are here—"

"Mostly voted for Kalyna, yes, I know." He sighed and looked back at me. "I would recommend distancing yourself from her, for your own sake. Look what one moment of uncertainty made her do to you. People are talking about your 'curses' and 'sorcery,' and they remember how much time you've spent locked away in Adomas' library."

"The library is free and open to whoever wants it."

"That isn't the point, and you know it."

"You're right, and thank you for the warning. Vidmantas, forget Kalyna for a moment. Are we friends?"

"I would like to think so."

"So would I."

I sat up straight. Despite my request to "forget" Kalyna, I tried to draw not just on her confidence, but the confidence she seemed to show in me. Did she just make things up as she went? Yes, obviously. But clearly some part of her thought I could play the role she'd assigned to me in her little drama.

"If you are my friend," I said, "then the next time you hear people whispering about me, please remind them that I am a *wizard*, not a sorcerer."

He furrowed his brow and stared at me. Then he nodded and took his leave.

I knew it was exactly the wrong thing to do, but I couldn't bring myself to have dinner with everyone in the Meal Hall that night. Knowing that rumors were spreading around me—apparently among both Loashti and Tetrarchic people—really got the Zobiski memory riled up in the back of my mind and throughout all my shaking limbs.

I stumbled my way up to the library. I knew I couldn't actually lock myself up in there, but the place usually provided solitude. Perhaps I'd just wait until the morning to eat. Could I sleep in the library, I wondered? If I bunched up my clothes on the desk, then . . .

The library was *not* empty when I got there. In fact, I heard excitable conversation as I came up the stairs. I slowed, wondering if, perhaps, someone was waiting to accost me, but soon determined that one of the voices was Kalyna's. I had many reasons not to trust her, but I sincerely doubted she'd have me strung up for a "sorcerer."

In the library, I saw a small table covered in grapes, crisped chickpeas and nuts, a large plate of greens dotted with red pepper, a smaller one of potatoes colored a brilliant yellow by their seasoning, and a tall pile of flatbreads. Around the table sat Kalyna and the Guild's three most priestly members: the smiling Skydašian man who followed the Tetrarchic goddess of the sea, the willowy Rot woman who had been a priest of the god who dwells in darkness, and the recently arrived woman from the order of the Loashti river god.

"Ah, Radiant!" called Kalyna. "Come, sit. You may find this interesting. I'm discussing the local miracle with our priests."

I smiled and then frowned. "I'm sorry, the local *what*?"

"The *purported* miracle," said the former priest of the god who dwells in darkness.

"This from the purported priest," grumbled the river god's priest in surprisingly passable Skydašiavos.

"I was nearly head of my order!" exclaimed the former priest, threatening to come out of her chair. "I only left because, on one *portentous* night, as I slept on the *cold rock floor* of my cave—"

The Loashti priest rolled her eyes. The Skydašian one smiled at me and shrugged.

"—my *god* came to me, and he *told me* that—"

"Ridiculous," sneered the Loashti river god's priest.

"Eminences, please," entreated Kalyna, "let's get back on topic. Surely this spot where the river and the Bone-White Tail meet, where the burning winds of Galiag twist out of the way, allowing life to flourish, *is* a miracle. The question is simply *whose* miracle and to whom a sanctuary should be built."

Now I understood what Kalyna was doing. If our secret little piece of The Thrashing, Bone-White Tail of Galiag was considered the site of a miracle, complete with a temple and a sanctuary, then our priests

348 | ELIJAH KINCH SPECTOR

would decide who could enter, even who was made aware of it. This would be her way of keeping newcomers to the Guild from knowing all of our secrets.

I began to think that even *blasphemy* was not a step too far for Kalyna. But I was also tired, and hungry, and very curious as to how she'd manage it. So I slid into a chair and began to scoop up potatoes with flatbread. Had I even had lunch? I don't think I had.

"Well," said the Skydašian priest, smiling broadly, "if it is a miracle, the sanctuary could be to my sea goddess."

"What power does a sea goddess have here?" asked the river god's priest.

"She also watches the rivers, of course," replied the sea goddess' priest, cheerily.

"Which flow into the sea. Not out of it," growled the river god's priest.

"And there is a separate Tetrarchic river god," the ex-priest of the god who dwells in darkness added.

"Quite a few, actually," chimed in Kalyna.

"You Tetrarchic fools seem to have more gods than people," grunted the river god's priest. "It's madness."

"Now, your eminence," began Kalyna, "no one here is Loashti or Tetrarchic, we're all members of—"

"Whereas," the Rot ex-priest interrupted, moving out of her chair and staring wild-eyed at the Loashti, "deciding that we, *mere humans*"—her voice rose and warbled—"know the *exact power structure of the gods* is entirely sensible!"

The Loashti and the Rot stared at each other for some seconds, until the ex-priest of the god who dwells in darkness turned away and raised her nose in the air.

"Do what you like!" she said, turning to leave. "I left my order and am but a *simple farmer* now!"

"Please stay," begged Kalyna. "I don't need fully practicing priests, I need wisdom. Those Galiag winds don't just sail harmless overhead, they power the works that bring so much water to our land. If your combined wisdom really says that this doesn't count as a miracle, tell me so, and I'll abide by it."

"It's not a—"

"Maybe if—"

"It's a moot point."

"Yes?!" Kalyna snapped her fingers and pointed at the river god's priest, who'd spoken last. "Why is it a moot point?"

"Because you people have too many wind gods, and none of them are represented here," said the Loashti. "You can't simply turn a wind miracle into a water one based on who you have around!"

"I don't know," replied Kalyna. "Whatever you may think of us down here, having so many gods means we have the space to be creative sometimes."

Was she being blasphemous? Or was this wheeling and dealing, this creativity, how her belief worked? Was it the way of the Tetrarchia? Or, at least, *one* way, given how fractured they were. And besides, that nice old river god's priest in my childhood had let me bend the rules too.

Kalyna did not give the Loashti time to finish, but instead turned to the Skydašian. "And why do you say maybe?"

"Well, to become a *sanctuary*, the miracle would need to have lasted for some time."

"Hasn't the wind been twisting around that spot at least since Adomas founded the Guild?" asked Kalyna.

"But no priest has seen it until now," replied the sea goddess' priest.

The river god's priest nodded in agreement.

"Is *that* necessary for you people?" laughed the ex-priest shrilly. "You and your fickle water gods. Any natural cave or tunnel is the work of the god who dwells in darkness, and we didn't have to sit and . . . *stare at it* for years to make our case."

"Adomas said," I began quietly, "that the tunnel from the Estate was already there. He just had it paneled."

The ex-priest slapped the table loudly and held her hand out toward me, smiling triumphantly. "Now *that*," she said, "sounds like a *miracle*."

"I know you left your order," offered Kalyna, "but perhaps we can form a new one here that's more to your liking?"

"Perhaps," replied the ex-priest, her voice even and noncommittal.

My mind immediately jumped to an unsettling conclusion: would this turn the Lanreas River Guild into exactly the sort of cult that Vidmantas, and Kalyna herself, had suspected it of being from the start?

The First Time I Attempted a Full Curse

My research was always meant to be theoretical and anthropological, rather than functional. This was for many reasons, including that:

1. I did not want to justify the beliefs of those who thought Zobiski were naïvely superstitious by letting on that I believed a curse might work.
2. If a curse *could* indeed work, I did not want to be seen as dangerous.
3. All traditions agree that a curse harms the one performing it in one way or another.
4. I *like* doing theoretical and anthropological research.
5. A curse large enough, and effective enough, to be confirmed as actually working would require a lot of help.

But of course I was curious. Who wouldn't be?

In fact, one of the lecturers who had sponsored my bid to become a researcher at the Academy turned out to be similarly curious. I tried to beg off attempting a curse, explaining that (theoretically, of course) the power to actually *change* the fabric of the world, even a bit, would require the assistance and belief of many people.

"Well," he replied, "isn't that what the senior students are for?"

I didn't want to explain my other reasons, and I was young and prone to risk anyway, so it was decided I would blight a small, predetermined square of sweet potato crop in the Academy's gardens. The anthropology department would, of course, reimburse the agricultural department for its crop, whether or not the curse worked. I was allowed to think the faculties of both departments had agreed on this, which was not in fact the case.

I was then given a group of ten senior anthropology assistants and spent a week, essentially, riling them up. All they knew was that we were attempting to ruin the agricultural students' crop, and that for the curse to work, they had to *want* the crops blighted, had to *need* the hybrids being created to fail. My students knew it was an experiment, but they were young, curious, and ambitious, and so easily allowed me to encourage their ire for the agricultural students.

Halfway through the week, I was told that no one in the agricultural department knew of our experiment. I was asked to keep this quiet, and did so, about which I still feel guilty.

I will not outline every piece of our attempted curse, but half of my students played the ritualized roles of blight itself, while the other half acted as the crops they would destroy, and I—under the influence of many substances—rent my garments and cried loudly over "my" destroyed crops. The anthropology scholars watching us apparently found it all very silly, until the intense emotions mixed up in all our symbolic playacting became too unsettling for them.

Did it work? No, but maybe. There was no blight, certainly, but there were happenings that may, or may not, have been results of my curse:

1. The sweet potatoes from that crop were extremely bland. But it was never clear if this was due to magic, because the hybrid hadn't worked correctly, or the result of simple bad luck.
2. The senior agricultural student guiding the hybrid sweet potato project fell into a deep depression for a year.
3. For at least the following five years that I continued to know her, one of my students could never bring herself to eat sweet potatoes.
4. Three of my students (not including the one just mentioned) continued to nurse a sort of angry disdain for the agricultural department. I could not shake them of this, and it caused me many sleepless nights.
5. When I drank my drugged concoction for the ceremony, I burned my tongue, which in and of itself is not so strange. However, the pain, numbness, and muted sense of taste

didn't last the normal day or two, but persisted for four and a half months. Long enough for me to despair that I would never have my full sense of taste again.

This last one I kept to myself and did not include in any of my official writing on the experiment. When it finally wore off, I was so thankful that I spent a week eating the most decadent and flavorful things possible—from the spiciest sauces to the most freshly picked mangoes—regardless of price.

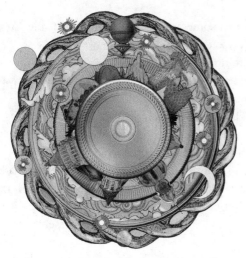

Chapter Twenty-Four

My Trip to Kalvadoti in Search of Dagmar Sorga

The next day, I told Ifeanyas about my intention to bring *all* of Yekunde's Zobiski to the Lanreas River Guild. I need the opinion of someone other than Kalyna or myself.

"Wow," he said, eyes wide. "I . . . wow. I can't wait to meet them, I suppose. Can I help?"

"You absolutely can," I sighed with great relief. "Fancy a trip to Kalvadoti?"

I wanted to bring Ifeanyas partly as protection for my trip. He was no Dagmar, certainly, but he was as tenacious as anyone I'd ever met. I had not forgotten that, on the day we met, he hazarded a jump from one barge to another while his hands were tied behind his back.

I also wanted his company because I trusted him as a comrade and a friend. Whether or not we chose to sleep together again.

So, the two of us approached Simurgh at her workshop, and I asked if she could fly us to Kalvadoti.

"Kalvadoti? Why?" she replied in Loashti Bureaucratic. She was sitting in a roughly hewn reclined chair, smoking something with a smell I didn't recognize.

"Because we want to visit someone there," I said in the same. "You took Žydrė to Žalikwen often enough."

"Yes. But I have a lot to do here."

Echoes harrumphed in a skeptical manner. The shaman-alchemist-whatever was straining a dark liquid through a sieve.

"What's that supposed to mean?" Simurgh snapped.

"Just, 'harrumph,'" replied Echoes. Her face was now painted in starbursts of bone white with centers of kohl black.

"These people," Simurgh said to me, "have only come here and made everything more difficult for me. When it was just me at the Guild, I was a nice little novelty, but now there are too many of us to be easily tolerated and too few of us to effectively advocate for ourselves. It's a difficult position."

I looked down at the Central Loashti from a good family, who had come here only because her ideas were too wild for her to succeed in our home. How abrasive and strange must she have been to fail in her own lands when she came into life with so much? And now, of course, she was reclining and smoking while the Kubatri "shaman" did the work.

Something must have shown in my eyes, because Simurgh immediately removed the pipe from her mouth and sat forward.

"Now, I know what you're thinking Radiant, but I'm just taking a break. Echoes takes breaks too, you know. It isn't as though I—"

"I know. I know," I replied.

"Simurgh does . . ." Echoes began, as though every word was being painfully dragged out of her, ". . . work very hard."

"Of course," I said. "But Simurgh, it must be so difficult for you to be treated like a *Zobiski*."

"Well, yes!" Simurgh cried, slapping her thigh for emphasis. "I don't know why you're acting as though you've *caught* me in something, Radiant. If being treated the way your people are was *fun*, you'd be going home with Aloe, wouldn't you? Which I assume you are not."

"No. No, I'm not."

"Precisely. You can hardly blame me for not liking being put in this position—I haven't had a lifetime of growing accustomed to such treatment."

I took a deep breath and tried to think of what in the world to say. I didn't know whether Simurgh was recognizing her own limitations of vision, or so oblivious as to think I would now pity her.

Thankfully, Echoes spoke up: "Oh, just take them, Simurgh."

"Where?" Simurgh frowned, then snapped her fingers and extinguished her pipe. "Right! Kalvadoti. It is a route I haven't tried before; would be interesting to see what the winds do along the way . . ."

"If it helps," I said, "we're going to meet someone who, we hope, will help us rescue *more* Zobiski from Loasht. Then perhaps you won't feel that our presence here is quite so . . . small." This felt, to me, like a very Kalyna-esque gamble, and I hoped it would entice Simurgh. Or at least rouse her curiosity.

Simurgh actually stopped and thought before she spoke, so I must've hit some sort of nerve. She looked into the middle distance for a moment, blinking, and even tried to take a puff of her pipe, before realizing she'd already put it out.

"What do you think?" she finally asked Echoes.

"That you should take them. And that I'll go too."

"You would say that," replied Simurgh. She thought for another moment and then added to Echoes, "Wait, do you mean just that you'll come with me to Kalvadoti? Or do you mean you'll be going back to Loasht for this . . . rescue?"

"Whoever's going to rescue these Zobiski will need a guide," said Echoes, as matter-of-factly as if she were giving directions. "I'm familiar with the land, I've already led one group of Loashti to the border, and my calling is to help my community. You know that."

"But what will *I* do without you?"

"Be proud that someone so brave and heroic has allowed you to order her around," Echoes replied.

"What if I say no? What if I won't take you?"

By way of answer, Echoes simply put down the sieve she had been using and folded her hands in her lap.

"Fine. Fine!"

Echoes returned to her sluicing and said, "We'll leave in two days. I need to prepare some surprises."

Though annoyed, Simurgh fixed us with a look that suggested we had something to look forward to. Poor Ifeanyas, of course, hadn't understood a word of it.

In the following days, aside from her normal glad-handing, Kalyna threw herself into three projects: expanding the reach and use of our Guild Farms; establishing a sanctuary on the hidden piece of the Lanreas River; and plotting while she pretended to be studying Loashti Bureaucratic. She also wrote a few letters, although I did not yet know to whom.

One of her earliest acts as leader of the Guild was to bring to her house all of the books and papers from Adomas' once-hidden study on the hidden banks of the Lanreas River. This way she could study them while also being easily available to anyone in the Guild. She was only interested in his naturalist works insofar as they could be passed on to me for possible use in our Guild Farms, but she remained convinced he had something scandalous in there that she could use.

She brought something else up from Adomas' study to her new home: the haunting sliver of eye, jaw, and tooth that had once been part of a creature bigger than I wanted to consider. Now it sat upright in a corner of her little house, watching her as she worked and slept. Sometimes when I came to see her, she would have papers spread out in front of her, but would only be staring at that dead thing. As though the two of them were seeing who would blink first.

Once it was time for our trip to Kalvadoti, Kalyna was decided: a boat from Yekunde was the only way. She would simply have to figure out how to make our secret piece of the Lanreas River accessible. (And also figure out where to get the money to pay mercenaries.)

On the morning we were set to leave, I found Echoes muttering over a mortar and pestle behind Simurgh's shack.

"So," I began, in Loashti Bureaucratic, "how are you feeling about—?"

She held up a hand for silence, so I waited as she very deliberately twisted the pestle, whispering to herself. A warm breeze passed us, and I heard a bird chirp somewhere in the trees. How much time was even left in the summer? I'd entirely lost track. What was autumn in North Shore Skydašiai? Surely nothing like Quruscan, or what I'd heard of Masovska.

"All right," said Echoes finally. Her face was adorned with orange boxes today. "I needed to count very carefully for that one. Five hundred and eighty-three grinds exactly."

"Or?"

"Or it may be a dud batch. Although no one would know until it was used."

"Have you ever tried a few more, or less, just to see what would happen?"

"No," she said, with great finality. "Do you know how hard it is to find dolphin blubber around here? It's difficult anywhere, really. To do it wrong on purpose 'just to see' would be a waste of money, time, effort, and the dolphin's unwitting sacrifice." She sucked her teeth. "Best to stick with what we know works. It certainly isn't my job to test new concoctions if I don't have to."

"That makes sense, I suppose. So is the 'eighty-three' part not—?"

"Yes, it's for the gods. And yes, we're no longer in the lands of the Eighty-Three. Forsaken, you could say, although I'd disagree."

"So would I."

"Some of our fellow Loashti outcasts think differently. Anyway, it certainly may have started as a useless flourish, or a way to ensure that the pestle made something in the neighborhood of six hundred revolutions. But it's good enough for me."

I nodded. "Maybe you should do one for every Tetrarchic god. Then you'll never finish."

This got a wry smile out of her, which was gratifying. And all I had to do for it was mock the people who'd taken us in. But I meant it with affection: I was coming to appreciate the Tetrarchia's messy, indecisive nature. I don't know whether the same was true of Echoes. She spent most of her time with Simurgh, but she also spoke more Skydašiavos than most Loashti at the Guild.

"What in the world are you making from . . . dolphin blubber, you said?"

She nodded.

"Something for the trip? To throw at someone, like you almost did to Obinnas?"

Echoes shook her head. "I'd never waste such a precious ingredient on a weapon. There are so many easier things to throw at someone." She held up the mortar. I saw a pinkish, reddish, viscous goop. "Once I add some other things—poison of a gecko, verdigris, and cinnabar among them—this, when burned at altitude, will turn a bit of sky red."

"That's for your return to Loasht?"

"Yes. Best to be prepared. And I'll leave some here as well, in case it will come in handy if"—she spat—"Aloe returns." She inspected the mortar, even gave it a sniff, from which she recoiled, before smiling with satisfaction.

"Handy how?"

"That will be up to Kalyna, won't it?"

I hope I haven't given the impression that all of North Shore Skydašiai was as provincial and isolated as the Lanreas River Guild. As a corrective, know that Kalvadoti was, in fact, the largest city I had ever seen in my life. I was impressed by its size when I first saw it from Simurgh's balloon, and then further amazed as we descended, and the city just grew and grew beneath me. When we landed in a clearing to the north, and its great, unpainted towers of sand-yellow and stone-gray rose up above me, I felt an immediate urge to lose myself in the city. I wanted to find every nook and cranny, every tavern, every fascinating person, and I wanted to know that there were places to hide if the city rose up around me. (Which, it turned out, was not so far from what was happening.)

Kalvadoti didn't have the color of other Skydašian towns and cities I had seen, but that does not mean it wasn't beautiful. The primary color of North Shore Skydašian plant life was gold punctuated by green and bits of reddish flowers, and the buildings of Kalvadoti reflected that. They were yellow and gold themselves, often with rows of wooden poles protruding here and there, along which there sometimes grew vines and flowers. It also seemed that every building had been constructed with the same sorts of carefully placed openings as the old Estate back at the Guild, redirecting breezes and keeping the interiors cool.

And there were just so many *people*: walking fast despite the heat, chatting, yelling, hugging, gesticulating. They appeared to be from all over: North Shore Skydašiai, certainly, but also Quru, Rots, Masovskans, and even a few Loashti. They wore robes of loose linen, not unlike some that were worn at Lanreas—less colorful than what

Vidmantas had been making and *more* colorful than what had been there before he arrived. I saw light colors, like dusty blues and pinks; faded colors; and plain linen with delicately sketched designs creeping about their edges. Almost to a person, the residents of Kalvadoti wore intricately woven sandals that seemed to cover their entire feet in strings of multicolored leather.

Before we entered the city, Echoes grumpily licked her fingers and rubbed off her makeup, smearing what came off onto the balloon itself, much to Simurgh's chagrin. Without her makeup, Echoes suddenly looked so very *plain*.

"Does anyone around here have tattoos?" I asked Ifeanyas, warily.

"Probably," he replied. "But not like you do."

I sadly covered my head in a linen hood and in we went, three Loashti led by Ifeanyas.

Most of the parts of Kalvadoti that I saw up close only had low buildings of a few stories, much like Yekunde, but its sprawl, density, and activity exceeded that of my home immensely. Perhaps the difference was due to the lack of humidity in some way; or perhaps the Central Loashti government purposefully kept all of its many, many, many (many, many, many, many, many, *many*) satellites at "manageable" sizes. In the distance, still as part of Kalvadoti, there loomed taller buildings of golden brown sunbaked mud bricks.

The bustle of the city, at least, helped us avoid much notice. But then, even if we were noticed, whom would they have reported us to? For at least ten minutes of wandering, we saw the Yams only sparsely: one or two at a time, lingering at corners with their orange uniforms, their swords, and their wheellock guns. They were often murmuring to one another and seemed worried, but that worry didn't seem to translate to Kalvadoti's citizens. What's more, despite our closeness to the border, not a single one of the city's guards gave *us* a second look.

"Dagmar said she'd be at the Hyrax Nest," I murmured as we moved through the streets. "Where's that?"

"How would I know?" replied Ifeanyas. "I've never been here before."

"A better question," said Simurgh, "is *what* is the Hyrax Nest."

"Or what's a hyrax," added Echoes.

Bad start. I began to feel that Kalyna would have been able to answer all our questions. But she wouldn't have been content to hide from Dagmar, I think.

"Well," I explained, "a hyrax is a sort of . . . well, a . . . let's say a *critter*. Squat furry things with fangs."

"Maybe it's the name of a tavern?" offered Ifeanyas.

Then we rounded a corner and realized why we had barely seen any Yams: they were all here.

There was a large square at the intersection of five or six streets, where Kalvadoti's twisting geography was suddenly beaten into solid, rectangular spaces. Beyond this square, many buildings seemed to rise up much higher, to perhaps seven or even eight stories—higher than any home I'd seen that wasn't a castle or an estate. But we could not see the neighborhood from which they sprung, because there were city guards everywhere and no visible citizens. Beyond the guards, there were barricades. I began to have a sinking feeling about where the Hyrax Nest, whatever it was, might be.

"Well?" hissed Echoes in Ifeanyas' ear. "Go on. Ask the big strong guards what's going on!"

Ifeanyas hung in place for a moment, flexing his fingers and seeming to drum up his courage. Then he approached a nearby group of Yams.

We three Loashti hung back and took solace in the fact that no one seemed to care about us. I watched Ifeanyas smile guilelessly, put his callused hand on the back of his neck and play the naïve bumpkin to a group of Yams who seemed vaguely amused.

Then, well, Dagmar appeared. She was standing atop one of the barricades, which seemed to be made of broken wooden furniture, rusted oven sides, and scattered pieces of statuary. In her right hand was the thin, Rotfelsenisch blade I'd seen her use in the past, while in her left was one of the wider and shorter ones that the Yams carried. She seemed as tall and immoveable as the large buildings behind her, and she bellowed out something that sounded quite forceful.

I couldn't make it out. Neither, it seemed, could anyone else. She was roaring drunk: I'm not sure she was using words at all. The Yams began to hoist their long guns, aiming at her, and then many things happened at once, or close enough to it, for my eyes.

The Yams fired their guns; Dagmar spun violently backward, out of sight; there was a great wrenching noise; and the barricade where Dagmar had been standing began to fall apart. I felt sure that we had come here just to watch Dagmar die, which would be both a great disappointment, and if I was being honest, not the *most* surprising turn of events.

The Yams cried out, as surprised by the collapse of the barricade as I was. Pieces of wooden furniture and stone masonry tumbled down in front and on top of them, as though the supposedly sturdy barricade had been ready to crumble spectacularly at any time. There were some sickening thuds and cracks, and mangled and confused yells, as the soldiers in front were crushed, and those behind them managed to move back. Then the cries of the Yams resolved into a cheer as many sections of the barricade now lay open, allowing them access to whatever was on the other side. They began to pick their way through the debris, and their unfortunately flattened comrades, toward these new openings.

"That was your friend, wasn't it?" Echoes said to me. "The big idiot?"

I nodded.

"Well, if they didn't already kill her, they're about to, and we can get through over there." She pointed to the farthest right opening in the barricade. "Let's go help her."

"We could die!" hissed Simurgh.

"And?" replied Echoes. Then she disappeared through the opening.

"Dagmar saved me once," said Ifeanyas. He screwed his mouth to the side. "I think. That day is kind of a blur." He followed Echoes.

I wasn't sure what *we* could possibly do to save Dagmar Sorga, of all people.

"We can just turn around," said Simurgh, under her breath. "We count this as a loss, and I fly us back."

I sighed and shook my head, before following the other two.

"Well, *I'll* be at the balloon!" yelled Simurgh. "And I'll leave without you the moment I'm in *any* danger!"

I ran through a maze of chair legs, stone blocks of statues, crates of rotted food, metal pipes, and who knows what else. I heard noise, yelling, impacts, and oaths, but for a few moments, I saw no one else and felt strangely alone.

I emerged into a battle. Yams, in their orange uniforms, were engaged in close combat with fast-retreating people who had no clear allegiances I could see. No uniforms—just an assortment of normal clothes, often with colorful accents. I flattened against a wall of debris and looked around for anyone I recognized.

What was *happening* here? While I'd been concerning myself with the petty politics of the Lanreas River Guild, had Skydašiai been falling apart? Were Loashti aliens fighting back against mistreatment, perhaps? Or were the North and South Shores getting ready to split? Or a thousand other possibilities?

"Smart Boy!"

I looked toward the voice and saw Dagmar, stumbling drunk and bleeding from her left shoulder. Her old sword was in her right hand, her new sword was sheathed, and she was moving awkwardly toward me, through the fighting. Behind her, there seemed to be more barricades: in fact, I saw barricades everywhere I looked. We were boxed in by makeshift walls.

Dagmar, impaired as she was, didn't see a soldier rear up behind her. I'm not sure where, exactly, Echoes had been, but she threw something at the Yam. He fell to his knees screaming and clawing at his face.

Dagmar grabbed my wrist and literally dragged me through the fighting, cutting up passing Yams while she seemed, at most, a bit irritated. We passed the man Echoes had stopped, and I saw that his eye sockets were bleeding—and empty.

I feel guilty about it, but for a moment, I wondered if Aloe and his followers had exiled Echoes *for a reason*. I was scared, and my mind was going everywhere at once, but that's no excuse. It was only shards of established Loashti thought that I had been unable to exorcise from my brain.

Dagmar dragged me toward an opening in the barricades, and I simply trusted her. We snaked our way through another labyrinth of garbage and emerged into a section of the square cordoned off by yet more barricades. This part of Kalvadoti was not only at war, but repeating itself endlessly.

We found Ifeanyas and Echoes alongside a number of armed people, many of whom greeted Dagmar with cheers. Then she and another woman with a sword were standing by the same passageway through which we'd emerged.

"Come on! Come on! Go!" Dagmar yelled, motioning along more and more non-uniformed, but armed, people, who kept appearing through the entrance, escaping the battle we'd just passed through.

"Not *you*," Dagmar growled, as a Yam pushed through, swinging his sword wildly.

Dagmar punched him with her empty left hand, even as her left shoulder bled, and he stumbled back into the barricade, fell over, and was stomped on by the next few of her allies to come through.

"That's everyone," grunted the other woman. "I think."

"That's everyone!" Dagmar repeated at the top of her lungs to someone I did not see.

There was much movement away from the passageway and its barricades, and then another wrenching noise as pieces of stone rained down, closing off the entry entirely. The Yam Dagmar had punched was buried entirely, and surely dead.

"Enough for today, I think," said a man with dark, curled beard, who seemed to have appeared from nowhere. He was unusually tall, round, and robustly built for one of North Shore extraction.

"Oh yes!" laughed Dagmar. "They'll run back and say they 'did their best'!" she sneered, imitating, I suppose, how she thought the Yams would talk.

The large man and Dagmar then did some silly thing where they acted like they'd punch each other, ducked and weaved, and then embraced.

It's only my own fault that I was surprised. I had simply assumed Dagmar Sorga had no life outside of Kalyna Aljosanovna.

There was more running and many more barricades, and I wondered how we would ever find Simurgh again. I even looked up for evidence of her flying away and leaving us. I saw many birds in the sky, and from down among Kalvadoti's towers, I couldn't tell if they were of normal or abnormal size.

After some time, we ended up in yet another square, beneath a stern-looking statue of an old Skydašian king, holding aloft his own infant child, who also wore a crown, more brilliant and intricate than his own. At the foot of the statue, where one of the father's legs was missing, was a pile of swords beside a pile of guns. Right next to that was a rounded, uneven *something* the size of two small houses and covered in a burlap sheet.

The square was full of battle-hardened people who were laughing and drinking, but they all stopped when they saw us and cheered, I assume, for Dagmar. A few stood guard near the mysterious thing under the sheet, waving away children who wanted to see it. Neither the children, nor their parents a little farther away, seemed particularly bothered by what was happening around them. In fact, as we approached, an old lady came to us and began peppering Dagmar's large friend with a long list of small complaints, as though he was a public servant.

The area surrounding the square looked much like the rest of Kalvadoti, except with barricades at its edges. Near those barricades were scattered pieces of refuse and masonry, but farther inward, the city seemed to be running quite normally. If the people we saw were scared of what was going on around them, they were not showing it. Some way north of us were Kalvadoti's towers, at least a few which were also within the barricades.

Dagmar and her friend, whose name was Žydrūnas (which is actually the male variant of Žydrė), took us across the square to a large tavern that was on the first floor of one of Kalvadoti's immense towers. Written above the door in Skydašiavos, and adorned with drawings of round and furry creatures, was: "THE HYRAX NEST."

The warriors drinking out in the square were positively sober compared to those inside, who all seemed to be either engaged in the most lively discussions or halfway to sleep. It was a very large place, with an upper level from which at least one man seemed to be dangling, and no windows, making any time of day feel like the middle of the night. Quite a roar went up at the arrival of Dagmar and Žydrūnas, which they accepted gracefully.

Then the group parted, revealing two great wooden thrones with a small man standing in front. He smiled, motioning to the thrones. Žydrūnas glided into one, and Dagmar flopped into the other, as the small man began to sing their praises to all present. And I do mean literally: he *sang* a rousing number about how valiant and fair they were. He continued to do this as he began dressing Dagmar's wounded shoulder.

Ifeanyas, Echoes, and I were brought chairs, although they were much smaller. We were also brought wine, although I turned it down. Ifeanyas sipped his slowly, and Echoes held hers, but I never saw her drink. Dagmar and Žydrūnas, of course, began to drink deeply, after they assured the crowd that they could go back to what they had been doing.

Dagmar Sorga looked different than she had when last I saw her. She partly wore the clothing of Kalvadoti: one of their elegantly faded robes cut into a shirt and the characteristic sandals of her new city, paired with the same old leather trousers and feathered, broad-brimmed cap. She had at least one new scar, for a start, which wound down the side of her face from forehead to chin. I must say that she appeared very happy, in a way I had only seen once or twice in the time I'd known her: she was laughing as though involved in nothing more mischievous than stealing melons from a neighbor.

"Smart Boy!" she cried, holding out her arms and frustrating her singing field doctor.

"Is that," Echoes muttered, in Loashti Bureaucratic, "Cöllüknit for Radiant Basket of Rainbow Shells?"

"Sort of," I replied.

Echoes nodded in vague understanding. Somewhere along our way through the barricades, she had reapplied makeup from a small tin she kept in her pocket. I began to realize that her need to control others' perceptions of her was nearly as strong as Kalyna's. (Or as mine, for that matter.)

"Welcome to my domain!" Dagmar continued. As with the last time I'd seen her, she spoke in Skydašiavos but continued saying *Smart Boy* in Cöllüknit.

"Your domain?" I asked. "You're revolutionaries?"

Dagmar threw back her head with a flourish of her stiff, straw-like hair and laughed uproariously. Žydrūnas, in the next throne, laughed softly with her, and she grabbed his arm for stability.

"No, no, no," she replied through tears. "Oh my, no. Smart Boy, we're bandits!"

Chapter Twenty-Five

Regarding the Devastator

"It's so *good* to see you again, Smart Boy!" cried Dagmar, crossing one leg over another on her makeshift throne. Almost languid, as if there weren't scores of soldiers just outside her little domain.

But within her little domain, everyone seemed to be jolly—and very drunk. Now that her arm was bandaged, her bard or griot or whatever he was walked among the revelers, singing of Dagmar's sturdy arm and Žydrūnas' wise counsel.

Žydrūnas, in the chair next to hers, was armed to the teeth. He had a shorter and heavier sword, like what the Yams carried, but with a hilt covered in curlicued gold leaf. He also had daggers strapped to each thigh and something tucked into his belt I'd never seen before: a gun small enough to fit in one hand. (I suppose the others had to be called "long guns" for a reason.)

"Oh, this?" he chuckled, when he saw me looking at it. "A little present from a Loashti lover.

Dagmar winked and punched him in the shoulder.

"Charming as it is," he continued, "it can't use the same ammunition as the Yams' long guns. So, now that I've run through the four or five bullets I was given, it's only for show."

Žydrūnas spoke with quiet force, as though every word was well considered. He and Dagmar appeared to be the greatest of friends and nothing more. But then, what would "more" even mean in this case? His companionship clearly made her far happier than Kalyna's had. Dagmar and Žydrūnas laughed, it seemed, at one another's every word, constantly clasping each other's hands in a strong, soldierly grip.

"Yes, yes, great to see you," Dagmar repeated. Then she looked at Ifeanyas. "And you as well, ah . . . ah . . . that is . . ." She snapped her fingers at him.

"Ifeanyas," he said.

"Right, yes, of course. That's it. And . . ." She looked at Echoes. "Um . . . something beginning with a 'V' . . . ?"

"We haven't met," said Echoes, in halting Skydašiavos.

"Of course!" laughed Dagmar, spilling some wine onto her thigh. "So! Smart Boy! What can I do for you?"

I was at a loss. Everything I'd just experienced had entirely knocked our purpose from my head.

"We need to get Radiant's people out of Loasht," said Ifeanyas, stepping forward.

"*Out?*" burped Dagmar, clearly surprised. "I must say, I assumed you'd returned home by now. That's why I was so surprised to see you here!"

"And almost got yourself killed," added Žydrūnas.

"*That* wasn't why I almost got myself killed," replied Dagmar. "I just thought they'd come a little closer before they fired, so we could hit more of them with debris."

"Why would they come *closer*, Dagmar?" asked Žydrūnas. "That's what guns are for." He patted her hand in joking condescension.

Dagmar shrugged, listing slightly as she sat back on her throne.

"So your barricades were falling apart on *purpose*?" I asked.

"Absolutely, Master Loashti," said Žydrūnas, leaning forward in his chair. "It's a trick I learned when I was a mercenary down in the Bandit States, which are heaped up on top of one another to such a degree that their wars are often won house by house and street by street." He leaned back again and waved a gloved hand toward our surroundings.

"Spend enough time staring at your own barricades under a siege, and you begin to have ideas."

"*You* begin to have ideas," said Dagmar. "I can't be bothered."

"You sell yourself short!"

"The catapults were also your idea, Žydrūnas."

"Oh, those are just boards and fulcrums—like a child's seesaw, but bigger, and throwing masonry about." He laughed. "None of us are in any condition to build *catapults*!" He leaned forward and pointed at me. "But if you want real genius, the *Devastator* was her idea."

"Devastator?" murmured Ifeanyas.

"An ultimate weapon, sir," said Žydrūnas, playfully lowering his voice further. "But don't you tell anyone."

Dagmar laughed and slapped Žydrūnas' shoulder. "It wasn't really my idea. I overheard it at your . . ." She waved at Ifeanyas. "Your talking thing."

"The . . . salon?"

"Yes! Yes! The ultimate weapon, so terrible that its very presence is meant to end the threat of war forever. Or such was the hope of the man who dreamed it up. *I* just thought a great metal shell with all sorts of guns and blades coming out of it sounded like a great thing to have." She shrugged. "And Žydrūnas drew up the plans."

"While you described them to me!"

"You're too drunk to build catapults," I marveled, "but not the Devastator?"

Žydrūnas shrugged and waved this off.

Dizzying. It was all positively dizzying. Why was any of this happening? And how could we possibly entice Dagmar to leave her friend and her comrades in the middle of their . . . war?

"So, Smart Boy," said Dagmar, "why do you want your family *out* of Loasht now?"

I began to explain, as concisely as I could, the shifting politics of Loasht, Aloe and his rise, and the historically precarious situation of my people. Dagmar's eyes, predictably, glazed over almost immediately, but Žydrūnas seemed quite rapt, even nodding now and again, his gaze fixed on mine.

Once I was done (I swear it was only a few minutes), Dagmar looked at Žydrūnas with a questioning expression.

"His people are in trouble there," he said to her.

"His family?"

"His whole community. Three hundred souls, give or take."

Dagmar nodded, and then she became contemplative, looking down at the dusty ground beneath her throne for a few moments.

"That sounds tough," she muttered. Then she looked up at me, all of her merriness apparently gone. "Do you have a plan?"

"We're working on that," I replied.

Dagmar narrowed her eyes. "Who is '*we*'?"

"Kalyna and I." I quickly sputtered out more words before Dagmar could object. "She doesn't know I'm here! Doesn't know where you are! This trip is secret from her—she only knows that we're looking for mercenaries who can see my people safely over the border."

Dagmar looked much more skeptical about this than she had over the idea of going into Loasht and saving a few hundred aliens.

"Really?" She leaned forward, hands on her knees. There was no trace of drunken gaiety or bloodlust in her expression now; she seemed coldly appraising. "Kalyna really doesn't know?"

"Really! I kept your secret. After all this time with her, I've learned to be a better liar." I suppose this was true.

Dagmar sat back and scratched her chin slowly. She looked contemplative and even came across as regal. What sort of "ruler" was she in this den of bandits, I wondered.

Žydrūnas silently watched Dagmar with a clear look of worry on his face. More worried than he'd seemed to be about her being shot no more than half an hour ago.

"What other . . . ?" Dagmar finally continued. "Oh, you know, what else . . . ?" She mumbled a few words of Rotfelsenisch.

"Resources," offered Žydrūnas.

"Yes! What other resources have you got? Yourself, Kalyna, scrappy Ifeanyas, and your witch friend there?" She gestured at Echoes. The word "witch" seemed to have been used with no judgment or ill intent—just the best she could think of in the moment.

Echoes, for her part, said nothing and didn't seem to be listening. She'd spent the entire conversation regarding her surroundings with a discerning eye.

"If you mean people," I said, "we'll be hiring more sellswords than just you."

"And," added Ifeanyas, "we have the efforts of the whole Guild to back us!"

"The what?" asked Dagmar.

"You know," I muttered. "The, ah, utopian farm where we were heading when you . . . you know . . ."

"Abandoned you?" said Dagmar.

"Sure. Well, the leader of the place died, and—"

"Kalyna is in charge now, isn't she?" sighed Dagmar. "Maybe officially, maybe not, but she's running the show."

I nodded. Dagmar closed her eyes and seemed very disappointed. Žydrūnas' lips tightened whenever Dagmar said Kalyna's name.

"How did the old leader die?" sighed Dagmar, her eyes still closed, head pressed to the back of her chair.

"Well—" began Ifeanyas.

"That's beside the point!" I interrupted. "We need—"

"Smart Boy." Dagmar's eyes snapped open and seemed to be looking right into my soul. "Did I not tell you to keep her from getting too full of herself? That she was heading somewhere dangerous?" She leaned slightly forward, elbow on her knee and index finger lightly tapping her lips. "But now, you come here, and you tell me she's conned her way into a leading a whole . . . *town*?"

"It's not fair to say that she conned her way in," said Ifeanyas. "The people wanted her!"

"Of course they did," replied Dagmar.

"Well, Dagmar Sorga," I grumbled, "what was I *supposed* to do? Stop her? How in all the world could *I* do that?"

Dagmar clicked her tongue slowly, nodded once, and sat back again. "I suppose that's fair."

"What about *you*?" I continued, perhaps ill-advisedly. "You said *she* was heading somewhere dangerous, but now you're a bandit? Cordoned off in a lawless part of the city? Ruling a . . . a criminal empire?"

"Hey!" Žydrūnas suddenly cut in. "You had better take that back, Master Loashti." His hand began to move toward his sword handle.

Suddenly, the tavern quieted around us. It seemed Žydrūnas could go from friendly to murderous as quickly as Dagmar. But I was too angry and desperate to care as much as I should have, even with everyone in the tavern staring.

"Sir! I have a name!" I stood up and threw my arms wide. "And if you wish to cut down an unarmed man for simply repeating what Dagmar has said, then—"

"Lawless!" he shouted, one hand still on his sword. With the other, he threw down the wineskin, which flattened to the ground and bled a little.

"What?!" I shouted back.

"Take back the word 'lawless'!" he bellowed, slamming his wine-stained free hand against the arm of his chair. "Our turf is more orderly than the rest of the blasted city!"

I stepped forward. Close enough that he could have leapt onto me from his chair.

"Well!" I yelled. "I didn't know that! You haven't given us the Grand Tour of your *bandit bureaucrats* and your *bandit parliament*, have you?!"

Žydrūnas stared at me silently, his face hard. Slowly, he removed his hand from his sword and sat back, keeping his eyes on me as though I was somehow dangerous.

"I like him," he then said to Dagmar.

The tavern resumed its normal noise and activity (and singing).

"Where were you going with this?" Dagmar asked me.

"You are acting," I began, heart still pounding, "as though Kalyna has done some terrible thing, while you are here lording it over an"—I looked at Žydrūnas—"impeccably regulated, I'm sure, den of thieves."

Dagmar cocked her head to the side, seeming confused.

"But, Smart Boy, I never said I was a good person. Look at who I am and how I enjoy spending my life!" She shook her head. "Kalyna, on the other hand, could be a good person if she tried. That's different."

"Well, she *is* trying to save my people. But, even if she doesn't realize it, she needs your help. That is," I added, "if you can leave all of . . . *whatever* this is." I sat back down in my chair.

"Smart Boy, believe it or not, we didn't mean for any of this to happen. I came here to get drunk, make a little money guarding merchants, fight some duels, that sort of thing." She sat back and looked wistful. "As a matter of fact, that's how Žydrūnas and I met. I was drunk in this very tavern, and I stepped on his foot."

"And that was enough to lead to a duel?" I asked.

"It hurt!" said Žydrūnas. "She was still wearing boots then, and I . . ." He motioned to his feet, which were in the characteristic sandals of Kalvadoti.

Dagmar nodded. "We fought, and wouldn't you know it, this horse-fucker *beat me!*"

Žydrūnas shrugged.

"Gave me this too." Dagmar pointed to the new scar on her face.

"You got me back at our next go-around," said Žydrūnas. "But I'd have to disrobe to show where."

"Maybe next time," I replied without thinking.

Žydrūnas, thankfully, grinned and said, "Maybe!"

Dagmar cackled. "I certainly did get you back. Three duels, and can you believe he won the first *and* the third?"

"But you've given out the most scars."

"*I* didn't touch your pretty face!" Dagmar motioned to her own but seemed quite aware that the new scar only enhanced her looks. "And now we haven't the time for me to get even."

Dagmar and Žydrūnas' friendly discussion of having injured each other was utterly baffling to me. I wondered if it was a Tetrarchic sensibility, but Ifeanyas looked similarly mystified. I suppose these two mercenaries belonged to a class that did things very differently than the rest of us. There may well have been people like them in Loasht too.

The singer returned, carrying a plate piled high with light-colored flatbreads rolled up into little bundles. They were quite different from those I'd eaten at Lanreas: the bread was spongy, with a tang that suggested fermentation. Inside was delicately spiced beef.

As we partook, the man with the plate sang, "The Yams had better beware, *beware*, beware! Beware of the Devastator!"

"Gods!" moaned Ifeanyas, through a bite. "I haven't had beef in so long . . ."

Even Echoes took one, but she did not betray her thoughts on the flavor. Žydrūnas placed a large pile of kudais on the plate and then settled back into his throne to continue the story.

"First," he said, "the Yams started saying that duels were no longer allowed in Kalvadoti. Which is, of course, ridiculous." He scoffed. "So we, and some other adventurers, mercenaries, and so forth, had a few light scuffles with the city guard."

"All in good fun," added Dagmar. "I don't even think we killed any, then."

"Who cares if we did?" chuckled Žydrūnas. "But then—"

"Then," Dagmar interrupted, "shopkeepers started offering to *pay* us not to fight in front of their stores and stands."

"Who were we to turn them down?" asked Žydrūnas.

"Quite so," agreed Dagmar. "Next thing we knew, it seemed we'd, well, rather *backed into* a protection racket. Entirely without meaning to, you understand."

"There was nothing for it but to stay the course," said Žydrūnas.

Dagmar nodded. "And I'll tell you, we don't take any more than the Yams did, and we never arrest or kill the locals."

"I think they even like us," Žydrūnas added.

"After a few days," Dagmar continued, "the Yams became rather cross with us, because they were no longer getting *their* cut. And, well, I was in a bit of a mood that day . . ."

"'I'll give you a cut!' she said!" laughed Žydrūnas.

"Not my finest moment," Dagmar sighed. "But you know how it is: things escalate. That's just the nature of *things*."

I was about to ask whether that was the nature of "things," or just the nature of "things" when a Dagmar Sorga was around. Ifeanyas seemed to read my mind, and he trained me with such a *look* that I held it in.

"And now you're at war with the guards in their own city?" I asked instead.

"Somewhat," said Žydrūnas. "They leave us be for a few days, then make a big push, then leave us be. I think most of the Yams would rather forget us, but their officers are embarrassed that we're here."

"I can't imagine this state of affairs will last," I noted.

"Oh, certainly not!" Žydrūnas agreed. "I wouldn't be surprised if today was a test before a bigger push."

"Then, Dagmar, are you too busy to help us?" I asked.

Dagmar scratched her head. "Well. I'd like to." She looked to Žydrūnas. "You really think we're getting near the end?"

"Dagmar," said Žydrūnas, "I've been telling you for the past two days that it's about time for us to disband and melt away into the countryside."

The blonde woman looked at me. "Kalyna hire anyone else yet?"

"I don't think so." I assumed she was still figuring out how to justify using the Guild's coffers to pay for mercenaries.

Dagmar grinned at Žydrūnas. "Well then, what if some of us melted into the *northern* countryside? That'd confuse the hell out of the Yams, wouldn't it?"

"That it would," murmured Žydrūnas. He shook his head. "Not all of us, of course."

"I think thirty of ours could do it. And would," said Dagmar.

I nodded excitedly. I knew Dagmar was only human, but she still *felt* invincible to me. With her, and with a plan from Kalyna, this might actually work.

"Depends on how many join up," she continued, "but I think two thousand kudais total would do it. Seeing as I trust you, and that we're already fat off this place, I don't need anything up front. Just have that waiting for us when we get your people to you."

Kalyna had told me to let her worry about how to pay for my community's extraction, so that's what I did. I nodded again as though we absolutely had two thousand kudais to hand over.

"And," Dagmar added, "I assume your witch will be guiding us?"

"How did you know?"

"Had a feeling."

"My name is Echoes in the Gingko-Wreathed Valley Sound like Grandfather's Voice," Echoes spoke up in her halting Skydašiavos. "And I'm not a witch—just an alchemist."

"What did you put in that Yams' eyes, old woman?" asked Dagmar.

"A little something," replied Echoes, holding unblinking eye contact with her interlocutor. "And don't call me old. I'm only fifty."

"I don't know that a Sorga ever made it much past that age," laughed Dagmar.

"How depressing," said Echoes. Her voice was so even that I'm not sure how she meant it. She then turned to me and said in Loashti Bureaucratic, "She is a drunken oaf. A stupid child playing at adult games, like so many in this place. But if she's the best we have, I'll try."

"She is. And thank you."

I saw Žydrūnas watching us and began to wonder if he spoke our language.

"I think," I said in Skydašiavos, "that you two will get along famously."

"Wonderful!" cried Dagmar. "Žydrūnas! What do you say we break out the Devastator tonight and say goodbye to Kalvadoti!"

Žydrūnas nodded vigorously and then led the whole tavern in crying out: "The Devastator!"

I began to feel guilty for aiding Dagmar and Žydrūnas in their plan to unleash a terrible weapon in Kalvadoti. I simply had to hope Dagmar knew what she was doing. Somehow.

The next few hours were busy ones for Dagmar and Žydrūnas, as they planned their final battle and rounded up bandits to go into Loasht. They drank heavily during all of this, and I kept picturing everyone waking up tomorrow, sober for the first time in perhaps a month, with the mother of all hangovers, looking at the state of Kalvadoti, and moaning: "We did *what*?"

After some time, Dagmar called Echoes, Ifeanyas, and me over to the table where she and Žydrūnas were concocting their schemes, and we began to plan the trip to Yekunde. Echoes claimed to know the way, and I knew Yekunde's big river boats were generally left unguarded.

"They're meant for the public good," I explained. "Besides, not a lot of stealing goes on in Yekunde."

"Sounds boring," replied Žydrūnas.

Sometimes our discussion would stop so we could listen to a breathless bandit's news. The Yams were panicking but beginning to regroup; they had heard about the Devastator and wanted to destroy it before it was used; the locals were all huddling inside until it was over. Yet no one in the tavern seemed particularly worried or in a rush, save the messengers themselves. Whether this was because of confidence in their Devastator, or sheer drunken ignorance, I did not know. I still don't.

"Smart Boy," asked Dagmar, "are you coming to Loasht? Lay eyes on the old home one last time?"

I shook my head. "I think I'd only slow you two down. Besides, I'm . . . terrified of what I'd find."

"Seems a shame that after all that work to get you home, you'd never see the place," she sighed.

"Plans change," I replied, thinking of how malleable Kalyna's plans always turned out to be.

"I suppose they do." Dagmar, leaning forward over the table, took a long gulp of whatever it was she was drinking, while studying me above the mug. Then she shrugged and looked at Žydrūnas. "And you, want to come along?"

Žydrūnas shook his head. "I think our little adventure here is enough for me, for a bit. I'm tired, Dagmar. I don't know where you find the energy."

"Neither do I," replied Dagmar, almost wistfully. "Maybe someday I'll figure that out."

"And then you can rest?" he chuckled.

"I rest all the time!" she cried. "It's one of my favorite things in the world, to lounge!"

"And yet . . ." I said.

"And yet," she replied, "here we are." She drained her mug, made a face, and slammed it down loudly on the tabletop, upside down. I assume this signified something in the Hyrax Nest.

"Besides, Žydrūnas," she added, "they couldn't afford you anyway, could they?"

Žydrūnas shook his head. "After what we're taking from this place? I don't rightly know who can."

"That's true," said Dagmar, as if she'd only just realized that being a bandit meant she might be rich now. The tall Rot stood up, loping one leg and then the other over the bench to disentangle herself.

"Well," said Žydrūnas, also standing. "Are you off?"

Dagmar nodded.

"Then I think it's time for the rest of us to disperse and give the Yams back their city."

"Let them suck it dry now," said another of their number.

"They certainly will," said Dagmar. "More than we ever would have." She yawned. "Or so I like to think. Who knows? I only ever met two—no, wait, *three*—people who could tell the future, and they were each differently unreliable."

Dagmar Sorga stood still, seeming lost in thought—contemplative, in her way. Even with the mess she'd caused here in Kalvadoti, I felt she was entirely capable of saving Silver and the rest. Certainly, they were in good hands, weren't they?

Then she stumbled, and I began to have my doubts. This was a Dagmar less aware of her surroundings than I had ever seen before—a drunker one, certainly. But she also appeared to be reflecting on something, which was also uncommon, in my experience. Perhaps time away from Kalyna was doing her good. Or, perhaps, Dagmar Sorga only allowed herself to reflect when she was deeply inebriated.

Whatever the case, Žydrūnas left her to it and so, therefore, did the rest of us.

"Smart Boy," she finally said. "Do you think I'm doing this for you? Or for her? Or to spite her somehow? Or out of hope that she notices or misses me?"

I wasn't sure what to say. Žydrūnas frowned, making a disapproving noise in the back of his throat. But he said nothing.

"You could do it because it's right," offered Echoes, as though it was the simplest thing in the world.

Dagmar grunted out a laugh. "I suppose I could."

Echoes stood and walked over to Žydrūnas, handing him a small bag. "Burn this to cover your escape."

"What is it?"

"A . . . big show that won't hurt anyone." Then she added, in Loashti Bureaucratic, "The wrath of the gods wrapped up in a nice little package."

Žydrūnas either spoke Loashti Bureaucratic or got the idea, because his eyes lit up and he thanked her profusely. Then he looked to Dagmar. "Just about time," he said.

Dagmar nodded. "See you again."

Dagmar and Žydrūnas embraced.

"You'll know where to find me if we both make it," he said.

Dagmar nodded and hugged him tighter. I admit I felt guilty for pulling her away from real friendship and back into Kalyna's orbit. But not guilty enough to do anything differently.

Once they'd disengaged, Dagmar began calling names as she wound nimbly toward the door of the tavern. Soon, she was standing at the door with Echoes and around thirty others. She looked back at everyone in the tavern and seemed very much like she wanted to say something, but didn't know what.

From across the tavern, Žydrūnas called: "Dagmar's leaving us! Do her proud tonight!"

The cheers became deafening. Everyone staying behind cheered, everyone about to leave (except Dagmar and Echoes) cheered. Dagmar stood in the doorway looking touched and also relieved that it was too loud for her to have to make a speech. She grinned and then slipped out the door, accompanied by Echoes and thirty bandits.

Žydrūnas turned to Ifeanyas and me. "The Yams are mostly coming from the south, and we plan to hold them a bit longer while we get things ready. I'll take you two out of here."

"It's almost a pity," said Ifeanyas, "that Dagmar won't get to see the Devastator in action."

Žydrūnas smiled and led us outside. It was already nighttime, and the moon reflected eerily off the now-uncovered Devastator. It looked rather like a great, metal turtle with carriage wheels. From its lumpy and misshapen shell protruded many, many, *many* blades and tips of long guns, pointing in all directions.

"We're arming it now," explained Žydrūnas, pointing to a number of his people going inside the thing and sliding spears, scythes, longswords, and even knives tied to broom handles through slits in the great beast's metal hide.

"How in the world will you make it move?" I asked. "I haven't seen any horses, and you'd need at least, I don't know, ten or twenty?"

"Oh, it won't move," said Žydrūnas.

"It won't?"

"Of course not. Look at it! It's just a big hunk of metal. The man who imagined the Devastator didn't have a means of propulsion—it was a rhetorical exercise!"

"Then why did you *build it*?" I asked.

"At first? Because we were drunk," said Žydrūnas. "But then rumors started getting around, and the Yams became scared of our secret weapon."

"That explains why you weren't very secretive," said Ifeanyas. He then began to hum a bit of "Beware the Devastator."

"So . . . what's your plan?" I asked.

"Well, when we realized the thing wouldn't move, we put in a trapdoor and blasted a little tunnel down to Kalvadoti's sewers. The Yams will think it's our final stand, and that our great weapon can't move. A group of us will lock ourselves in: shoot, yell, wiggle the blades around, and slip out one by one into the sewers. I'll be last of course."

"Of course," I said. "And with what Echoes gave you . . ."

"We can probably make the Yams think the thing's about to explode!" He grinned.

"Well," I had to admit, "that's a better plan than I expected. Dagmar's ideas have usually involved me falling a very long way."

Žydrūnas nodded thoughtfully. Then his eyes lit up, and he snapped his fingers, pointing at me. "Wait! Were *you* the one inside Farbex the Good Donkey?"

"I . . . Yes."

"Comrades!" he shouted. "Come meet Farbex the Good Donkey!"

Once I'd accepted the admiration of a number of bandits and answered their questions about Dagmar's story, Žydrūnas led Ifeanyas and me north through the barriers. I tried not to think about whether Simurgh had just gotten bored, or scared, and left us.

The sounds of fighting could be heard everywhere as we got to the edges of Žydrūnas' kingdom, but he assured us they mostly came from farther south. Sure enough, when we came out the other side of his barriers, it was onto quiet streets. Although it seemed every window was full of spectators.

"Just go north from here," said Žydrūnas. "You clearly aren't ours and aren't armed, so no one should bother you."

I thanked him and turned to go but was stopped by his large hand on my shoulder. I turned back.

"And Radiant," he said under his breath in clumsily passable Loashti Bureaucratic. "Dagmar is very hurt by this Kalyna person." He spoke her name like he was invoking a demon.

I nodded.

"Promise me Kalyna won't know Dagmar is in this now. I picture her miles away, laughing that she's got my friend under her thumb." He growled. "She still *grips* Dagmar's emotions."

"I promise."

He let me go, but I don't know if he believed me.

I worried Kalyna was turning me into someone as callous as she was. I told myself this wasn't true, because I was desperate, and because I still felt guilty lying to people I cared about.

Did Kalyna ever feel guilty? I began to consider the possibility that she did—perhaps constantly.

And desperation? Her life was easy now, but I wondered if she'd ever fully unlearned desperation.

"I waited so long!" yelled Simurgh as we approached her balloon, north of the city. "I almost left one time when I saw an *army* barreling toward me. But it turned out Echoes was leading it!"

She began coaxing up her flame as we got in.

"Did she say anything to you?" asked Ifeanyas.

"No! No matter how much I called to her! Ungrateful woman."

As we flew south over Kalvadoti, smoke began to billow up from somewhere in the center of the city. At first it seemed black, like the product of a small explosion, but then it became bronze, then crimson. There was a great whooshing from below, and the smoke began to spread out over the center of the city, engulfing it, hiding it from our view. In mere minutes, it became blood red, and through it writhed and pulsed what seemed to be tendrils, or fingers, of shiny blackness, often lined with even brighter reds—all of these colors were so stark that even at night they were clearly visible.

Imagining this red smoke spewing out of the Devastator's rounded shell brought to mind something very specific. In vicious magics from a few different parts of the world, invocations are made to the great "flame tortoise" goddess who supposedly resides in a volcano (which volcano exactly is disputed). Echoes had said this smoke wouldn't hurt anyone, but it was hard to look down there and not wonder what she had unleashed.

"She called it the 'wrath of the gods,'" I muttered.

"Who? Echoes?" asked Simurgh.

I nodded, eyes wide as I stared down at the smoke.

"I'll miss her," sighed Simurgh. "But if I think for a moment either of you will tell her I said that, I'll crash us on purpose and haunt your ghosts."

Chapter Twenty-Six

When I Learned What Kalyna Aljosanovna Really (Really?) Was

All the way back to the Lanreas River Guild, I thought about Dagmar's quickness to ask how Adomas had died. The sellsword certainly knew Kalyna better than I did, so this being her first thought made me suspicious all over again. On the other hand, Dagmar was quicker to kill than anyone I'd ever met.

But then, if Kalyna *had* murdered Adomas, what exactly did that change? Only, I suppose, my estimation of her persuasive talents, or of Adomas' stubbornness. If killing the old man would save hundreds more people—people he planned to expel or turn away—was the choice wrong? But was there any way for me to *know* that killing him had been the only way? Finally, if she had killed him, was it not entirely my fault for not keeping my fool mouth shut?

In the end, I hoped he had not been murdered, but my plans were the same either way.

When we landed, it was already the next morning. Simurgh went to sleep, or possibly sulk, while Ifeanyas and I went to find Kalyna.

"Thank you for coming with me," I said as we walked south.

"I don't know that I was much help. I was . . . *deeply* overwhelmed."

"But you were there, and I felt safer with you."

"I'm glad to hear that." He beamed up at me. "Maybe this is the exhaustion and bewilderment talking, but whether or not we try to fuck again"—he looked mischievous at using the word—"you can still kiss me. If you like."

"What if it's just to distract myself from the terrible things on my mind?"

He shrugged. "What if it is for me too?"

I took him up on it, and then we continued to Kalyna's house in the shadow of the old, crumbling Estate.

Her door was open, allowing in the breeze on what was another hot, dry day. The interior already looked less beholden to Adomas' sparse design sensibility (or at least, to the one he'd used in this house, less so in his hideout). Kalyna had hung up a few bits of colored cloth, and the sun trickled through them pleasingly. Through one of these, a ray of magenta crossed the room, landing on that sliver of the face of a long-dead creature, watching her from its corner.

She was hunched over the desk, which was covered in papers, with her back to the door, until I knocked lightly on the doorframe.

"Ah! I was starting to worry. Come in, come in." She turned and smiled brightly, waving us inside. "Close the door, if you don't mind."

We did so and sat down in two more chairs she'd had brought into the small house.

"You know," I began in Skydašiavos, "Dagmar would chastise you for sitting here with your back to an open door. You do have enemies here."

"What?" Kalyna snorted. "You think *Žydrė* would come stab me in the back?"

"Of course she wouldn't!" said Ifeanyas.

"I would like to see her *try*," Kalyna laughed. "I could be asleep, and drunk, and I'd still ruin her whole day."

"Awfully sure of yourself," I said.

Kalyna arched an eyebrow and smirked at me. "You certainly found Dagmar, didn't you?"

"We did."

I told her all about our trip to Kalvadoti. I rather hoped she'd betray some kind of emotion at hearing about what a good friend Dagmar had in Žydrūnas, but of course she didn't.

In fact, what she said when I finished was: "Oh, lovely! That saves me the trouble of finding other mercenaries."

Had Ifeanyas not been there, I would have asked her if she had really started looking for other mercenaries at all, or simply hoped that Dagmar would end up in that sort of company.

Instead, I asked, "And how will we find two thousand kudais to pay Dagmar and her bandits when they get my people here?" I asked, refusing to include the *if* that had intruded in my mind. "Push Yalwas aside and open up what's left of Adomas' coffers?"

"Oh, Radiant, we haven't got two thousand kudais in our coffers. I'm sad to say that, until you and I began our Guild Farms, this place was losing money."

"Well," said Ifeanyas, "making a *profit* was never the point of the Lanreas River Guild."

"No, it's not. But we'll need more money if we want to save the Zobiski and keep the Guild from being overwhelmed by a few hundred new members."

"Then where will that come from?" I asked.

"I have some ideas." She thumped a fist on a pile of papers on her desk. "These are all from Adomas' little secret study by the river. A lot of interesting things in here. How long do you think it will take Dagmar and Echoes to get there and back?"

"That's . . . very hard to say. Who knows what trouble they could run into on the way. A month, perhaps? But even that would only be *if* they can take a boat down here without crashing into the mountains where The Thrashing, Bone-White Tail of Galiag crosses the river."

"Couldn't they just disembark earlier?" asked Ifeanyas.

"That would mean a long walk for some very old people," I replied. "And a lot of chances to run into Yams on the way. Skydašiai still doesn't seem to want exiled Loashti running around."

"Don't worry about that," said Kalyna. "If they can get the boats, they'll be able to come straight here. Ifeanyas, do you mind leaving me alone with my wizard for a bit?"

Ifeanyas was more than happy to go eat and then sleep. My legs were terribly sore from so long in Simurgh's balloon, and Kalyna offered me her bed to lie on, so long as I didn't fall asleep while she was talking to me. I made no promises as I looked up at the gauzy, colored sheets that allowed the sun to paint the room in different colors as it moved across the sky.

"I'm on my way to handling the money," she said, "and a passageway from the river as well. You did good in Kalvadoti, and we simply must move forward trusting that Dagmar and Echoes can do what we need. Don't fall asleep."

"I'm not."

"I'm working through how best to break the news to the Guild that they're about to be outnumbered by Loashti aliens."

"Oh. I hadn't thought about that. Perhaps I didn't let myself." I sighed deeply. "That seems like a very good way to give Yalwas or Žydrė leverage."

"Truly. I wish one of them *would* just come at me with a knife. It would make everything simpler."

"Maybe," I suggested, "and follow me, if you will, on this flight of fancy."

She made an unamused grunt, but I continued looking at the colors on the ceiling. I was too delirious to think about anything before I said it—partially from lack of sleep, yes, but more so, I think, from how bizarre my Kalvadoti adventure had felt.

"I *say*," I continued, "maybe neither Žydrė nor Yalwas has tried to kill, beat, or greatly undermine you because what they both want most is to hold the Guild together."

"If that's so," said Kalyna, "it's no wonder they both lost."

"Kalyna, your outlook sometimes makes me very sad."

"But not so sad that you can't use me."

"Sad but useful," I agreed.

She let out a high-pitched, snorting, coughing laugh, and I heard her stomp on the ground from her chair

"'Sad but useful'!" she cried. "Gods. 'Sad but useful.' They should put that on my tomb, if I ever merit one. No names, no dates, just those words in every language of the Tetrarchia."

"You're welcome."

"Would a phrase like that work as a curse? You know, if someone was repeating it enough, believing it about someone?"

"No, no. They're much more complicated than that."

"In what way?"

Suddenly, I stopped letting my words wander and turned my head to look at Kalyna. She was sitting nonchalantly, but her eyes were fixed on me.

"Why do you want to know?"

"I was thinking that perhaps our plan could be further strengthened by a touch of retribution."

"Please just tell me what you're trying to get me to do."

"I'm not sure yet!" She threw up her hands. "You see, I'm being honest with you about how much I have planned and how much I don't. I just thought that, well, we've *got* a wizard—"

"That was something you said to make me sound impressive."

"Are you telling me you aren't impressive? Our crops grow better now, and everyone has less work in the fields. And you *could theoretically* strike Aloe down from miles away, couldn't you?"

I looked back at the ceiling. "How would that help us? He's already done his damage."

"I just want to understand all of the tools and weapons at our disposal."

"That is hardly at our 'disposal.' Take my word for it. I have never successfully cursed anyone before, I don't think."

She nodded but seemed unswayed.

"And," I continued, "a curse is neither easy to orchestrate, nor guaranteed to work. So much must be put carefully in place, the results are unpredictable, and—"

"I'm just curious—"

"—it would take a great toll on the caster. Which would be *me*."

"I just wanted to know our options, Radiant, so thank you."

I nodded curtly.

"I'll keep that in mind, so long as I am in charge." She winked.

"I certainly can't imagine Žydrė asking that of me."

"More fool her."

"And I'm not a—"

"Explain to me exactly *why* you aren't a wizard."

I turned over, putting my back to her and facing her wall. "I am going to go to sleep on your bed."

"Radiant, I've spent most of my life masquerading as a different sort of mystic."

"That doesn't surprise me."

I heard her chair squeak closer to me.

"No, no. This isn't like pretending to be a Bari captain, or an acolyte of Adomas', or any other small con I've done. This was my life. It still is, although now I'm able to take breaks now and then." She laughed bitterly. "Believe it or not, this whole time with you is essentially a lark, a vacation."

"You're welcome."

"I'm trying to be honest with you."

"And I'm trying to sleep."

She sighed and leaned in close. I felt the weight of one of her hands on the bed, propping her up.

"I've spent my whole life not just wishing I had access to an other-worldly power but *cursing* myself for the lack of it. Feeling empty and worthless and broken, because I did not have it. Being forced, every day, to act as though I am the person I was meant to be—was raised to be—and therefore being constantly reminded that I'm not. And never will be."

My back was still to her, even as I felt myself open up to what she was saying. "This is why you hated your grandmother so much, isn't it?"

"Oh yes."

"I'm sorry, but—"

"I envy you."

I did not know how to respond to that.

"You're a normal person who worked very hard and is now some-thing more," she said. "I worked very hard and *knew* I would never be what I wanted. I envy you. I envy that you've immersed yourself so deep in your field that you don't even realize what how extraordinary you are."

I took a deep breath. "Thank you for your honesty, but I've still never cursed anyone."

"And I," Kalyna replied, "have a lifetime of experience in *dragging* results out of recalcitrant mystics."

I think that I fell asleep while puzzling over what that could possi-bly mean.

The rest of that day was a haze, but the following morning, I learned how Kalyna meant to make our Guild accessible from the river: through the transformation of Adomas' once-secret refuge. The work was mostly done in the early morning, when the sun was not directly hitting the gleaming sand that flew through the air above our heads, so that no one risked being blinded.

A crew of workers, which Yalwas insisted on being a part of, had begun by building a scaffolding using wood from the Estate and the secret tunnel, as well as a bit from the hidden little house by the river—which Kalyna called "Adomas' summer home," much to Yalwas' chagrin. The scaffolding reached out over the river, so that workers could begin chipping away at the opening in the northern mountain wall, where the Lanreas River entered our (secret) domain. As it was now, water could pass through, but even someone on a raft, let alone a large boat, would likely hit the mountain.

Very quickly, the work of building the scaffolding, and then of dropping huge chunks of rock and dirt into the river, began to stir up things that lived, or traveled, in the waters. It became normal to see the outlines of irritated creatures twist beneath the scaffolding.

"Let's try to keep the refuse out of the water!" Kalyna yelled over the howling Galiag winds above. She actually had to yell it in the ear of someone standing near her, who then conveyed it to another, and then another, all up close.

"Bad things can happen if we disturb their home," she explained to me in what passed for a murmured aside out there (another yell).

That evening, at dinner, Kalyna was surrounded by people trying to understand *why* this work at the river was being done.

"You told us it would bring in money for the Guild," said Yalwas. "But I fail to see how."

He was at the same table, sitting across from her, and it would have looked like an interrogation if he hadn't also been eating scallion pancakes. Ifeanyas and I sat near her, and the rest of the seats were filled as well. More people crowded around the table, while Žydrė, Vidmantas, and some others sat at the next one over and looked skeptical.

"We can't very well start charging ships to go through," piped up Vidmantas from the next table. "I worry that our ownership of this land is tenuous enough, but we definitely don't have legal dominion over the river."

"Our ownership of this land is secure!" Yalwas yelled. "The paperwork says—"

"A lot of things without precedent," interrupted Kalyna. "It *says* we own the land collectively, but Vidmantas is right: Skydašiai could easily decide it doesn't recognize such a strange arrangement." She sighed with some theatricality. "Not to mention Adomas' original, noble family. They exist, and they know he's dead."

"How?" asked Yalwas.

"Were we keeping it secret?" Kalyna retorted. "If so, I wish someone had told me."

"Well, no, but . . . Hm."

She smiled at Yalwas, a touch condescendingly, yes, but nothing like how she'd relished making him uncomfortable before she came to power.

"The work by the river," she explained, "may help us keep a surer grip on our land and will definitely bring in more money, which is, unfortunately, something we need."

"Now wait a moment," said Yalwas. "Just because I control the coffers doesn't mean—"

"This isn't about blame." Kalyna shook her head. "After all, making a *profit* was never the point of the Lanreas River Guild. But kudais are necessary for some things, and we are quite low. We could, perhaps, get by on what we have, now that the Guild Farms save us more money, but we would be wiped out if there was, say, a flood or drought."

"You've convinced us we need money," groaned Vidmantas. "How are we going to get it?"

Kalyna folded her hands in her lap and began to look very serious. "There's a group of Loashti desperate to escape the country that's turning on them—a predicament we're all quite familiar with by now. As you all know, Skydašiai isn't terribly interested in giving them a place to live, but we can. We already have, for some, and they're now part of us."

Yalwas looked unconvinced. He had always been close with Adomas, so it was likely the old naturalist would have told him he didn't want more Loashti coming here.

"How many?" he asked.

"That," replied Kalyna, "will depend, frankly, on how many survive their treatment in Loasht and the trip here. In fact, making the river accessible will help them to survive. But it would be no more than three hundred."

The room erupted into noise. They were not all out-and-out refusals, but there was much hand-wringing over what this influx would mean.

Kalyna, naturally, stayed entirely calm and patient. Waiting for them all to finish.

Yalwas eventually quieted the group down enough to voice their concerns directly: "That many Loashti will inalterably change the culture of our home!" he said.

"Every new arrival changes our culture a bit," she replied. "Once they're here, they won't be Loashti. They'll be members of the Guild."

"But they'll outnumber us!"

"Who is *us*, Yalwas?"

"Well . . ."

"Are we the Lanreas River Guild," asked Kalyna, "or are we nationalistic separatists? If our goal is for the Guild to remain chiefly Skydašian no matter the cost, then I want no part of it. Shall I leave?"

Murmurs, grumblings, but no one took her up on it.

"I'm all for helping people if we can," said Žydrė eventually. "But how does this bring in money?"

"Thank you, Žydrė," said Kalyna. "There is a rich Loashti benefactor who is embarrassed by her country's recent turn and doesn't want an entire community slaughtered on her doorstep." She smiled ironically and rolled her eyes. "That said, she is still a classic noble Loashti and doesn't really want them on her doorstep *at all*. Either would be embarrassing for her in the current climate. The Yams won't take them, and she understands that we can't feed and house so many people as we are now, so she proposed a resettlement scheme."

"Really," muttered Yalwas.

Kalyna smiled and nodded.

"And how much will she pay us to take these . . . people?" someone asked.

"We're still negotiating," said Kalyna. "But at least ten thousand kudais."

The room exploded into noise of a very different tenor: amazement, trepidation, excitement, and imagination.

It only took a few days of suggesting ways the Guild could be improved with a fraction of that money before enough people were on board. There were also many appeals made along the lines of, "Well, look how well this or that Loashti has become part of the community!" which I did not love. But I took it as a very good sign when Yalwas started asking around for a dragoman to translate his welcome lecture.

About two weeks after my trip to Kalvadoti, I was becoming quite anxious. We had heard nothing of Dagmar's Loashti expedition—which wasn't terribly surprising but was still maddening—and I still didn't know how Kalyna intended to pay her either. I both wanted to know more and was scared of what would happen when thirty bandits appeared at the Guild expecting money we did not have. So I went to Kalyna, hoping for more information.

Outside of her house, I ran into a few Guild members who had the quality to their manners that can only be described as Lingering and Gossiping. One of them told me, excitedly, that a strange someone had come in a carriage and was currently having an audience with our leader.

Curious and hopeful, I quickened my pace though the little garden that had once been Adomas', which was now overgrown and unruly. In that garden, I saw a strange chair outside with casters on its legs. The door to Kalyna's house was open, as usual, but through it I heard a stream of excitable conversation, in constantly shifting languages, from a voice I didn't know.

"You mean to tell me you're in *charge* of all these people? That's not right, Kalynishka, not right for us at all. I'm *proud* of you, of course. Of course. That is, *of course*, if people are allowed to pick their own leader, they'll pick you! Who else? But we aren't supposed to have that sort of power! To tell people what to . . . what to . . . what to . . . what to *eat* and to wear and to say, Kalynishka, that isn't at all . . . I mean, that is . . . it isn't . . ."

"I promise I don't tell them any of that," was the soft reply from Kalyna.

As I walked into the house, a man was still talking. In the far corner of the room, almost obscuring the strange slivers of the dead creature that she kept there, was a disorderly pile of cases and parcels. Kalyna sat on her bed, with a look of serene patience I don't think I'd ever before seen on her face. Her back was to the wall, with her arm around a man perhaps in his fifties, who gesticulated wildly as he spoke. At first I thought he was very small, swallowed up in a great silk caftan, but then I realized he looked that way because he didn't have legs.

"—because I love you so much, Kalynishka, so much, and everyone else should too. All the *world* should love you, each until their final moments whether by famine or sickness or violence or being enveloped in a great fire. *The* great fire, I think it will be."

"Is that so, Papa?" Kalyna nodded as though he had just told her a neighbor's dog had finally had puppies.

"Oh yes, yes. Awful. Awful. But we'll be long dead." He wiggled his hand to show there was nothing to worry about. "And anyway, I shouldn't be bothering you when you're so busy and important with leading your community and talking to that pretty wizard and— Oh." He turned his head and finally saw me. "He's right here, Kalynishka, right here. Well"—he pointed—"right there."

Kalyna smiled at me and then patted his back. "Do you want to . . . ?"

"What, Kalynishka, what? 'Welcome to the tent of so and so and such and such'? No, no. No longer." He winked at me.

She laughed quietly and introduced me to her father, Aljosa Vüsalavich.

"After I won the election," she explained to me, "I realized I would be here for some time, so I sent for him." She smiled at me. "You see, Radiant? I wasn't going to run out on you."

I looked at her father's wide-eyed, adoring expression as he beheld his daughter, and then looked to me for confirmation of his regard for her.

"I never for a second thought that you would," I lied.

Aljosa then went on to chatter about a great many confusing things. He was charming, in his way: even when saying absolute nonsense, he maintained a tone and rhythm that made it sound almost like a rehearsed patter. That he was Kalyna's father would have been clear even if they did not share the same aquiline nose, deep-set eyes, and broadly enveloping smile.

I had stopped paying attention to his exact words when I realized he was looking directly at me and asking, "So how's Dagmar?"

"Dagmar? Well, I . . ."

"Because I certainly hope she isn't dead. Was it Kalvadoti you said, Kalynishka? Why, I haven't been there in years, I think. Have I ever been there? I hope Dagmar's all right. I often assume she's already dead, but of course, I can't know that, and I do like—"

"Papa, we don't know," said Kalyna, patting his hand. "And I don't think you've been to Kalvadoti." She stood up and moved back to her desk, looking for something in her papers.

"Ah, well that's too bad. Say, wizard, are you here to talk my daughter into taking that ghastly thing out of our home?" He pointed to the piece of a long-dead creature, which seemed now to be spying on us from a hiding place.

"I can try. Who told you I was pretty?"

"Oh. Oh? No one, no one. I have eyes, you know."

"But you hadn't seen me yet."

"Eyes of the brain, wizard, eyes of the brain. You understand."

I wasn't sure whether to nod as though I understood, or to ask what he meant.

"Smiling Zhuldyzem, from Desgol, was more than happy to see that Papa, and our things, got here," explained Kalyna. "I paid him well, of course."

"Such a generous daughter. I hope Zhuldyzem is careful on the way back. I'd hate to see him die again."

I could not begin to parse Aljosa, so I turned to the parcels and cases in the corner. "So in there is your pipe and your wooden chicken, and so forth?"

"Mother's pipe," Aljosa corrected.

"That's right," said Kalyna. "Everything we own in the world."

"And the chicken is named Dietlinde!"

"Including our remaining money."

"I don't suppose that's ten thousand kudais?" I asked.

"Absolutely not!" said Kalyna. Then she and her father laughed in near unison. "But it's a bit, and it will allow us to hire an advocate, and to buy some nice, new clothes that weren't designed by Vidmantas to be iconoclastic."

I looked to Aljosa, who was smiling. I don't know if he understood what she was talking about, or if he simply enjoyed hearing his daughter speak, but he nodded at me excitedly, as if to say, *Go on. Ask her. Go on!*

"Why do we need nice clothes?" I asked.

"So we'll look presentable when we sell the Lanreas River Guild."

Excerpt from *The Notes of Echoes in the Gingko-Wreathed Valley Sound like Grandfather's Voice* (translated from Kubatri)

Getting out of Skydaš city harder than getting into Loasht.

Loashti border just takes Wrath of the Gods, then we slip through easily. No one stabbed.

Big Rot suggests cutting the lines to Skydašian balloons; send occupant off into the sky. I like the idea but tell her no.

Run for hours, back the way I came with the other aliens. Rot and her bandits all hearty despite drunkenness. Difficult to keep up with.

Finally stop for the night. I'm more tired than rest. Rot disappears. Bandits all fall asleep.

Rot reappears hour later with two horses. Says tomorrow she and I will scout ahead.

I don't know how to ride and tell her so. Stares at me dead-eyed for a minute, ties both horses to a tree and leaves.

Try to sleep in grass, surrounded by passed-out bandits. No one on watch. I stay very still. Both sides of border crocodile country.

Can't sleep. Jot down memory notes instead.

Next morning, Rot returns with third horse, much bigger than first two. We are to ride together.

Bandits hungover.

Rot tells them to use other two horses as pack animals and begin northward.

Ride north on big horse, clutching big woman. Uncomfortable, very fast.

I ask why she isn't hungover like the rest.

Grins, tells me she's still drunk. Pilfered wine bottle in saddlebag.

Chapter Twenty-Seven

Our Time Aboard the
Ikennakas Family Leisure Ship

On the day that we went to sell the Lanreas River Guild, someone looking out into the endless ocean from the west coast of North Shore Skydašiai, might have beheld an odd sight. Specifically if they were right around where the inland Skydaš Sea emptied out into that ocean—where the domain of the Bari in their barges ended, giving way to the Skydašian navy, which patrolled the coast in great warships—they would behold what appeared to be a gigantic stork mounting a ludicrously humongous swan.

This swan-shaped vessel was not even the biggest nor most extravagant leisure ship to (I'm sorry) swan about the coast, but it was large enough that Simurgh could land her marabou balloon on its deck and easily avoiding being skewered by its masts.

"This . . . oh gods . . ." Kalyna was sitting on the floor of the marabou's basket, looking sick and making gulping noises as she spoke. "This is a very delicate operation, Simurgh . . . so . . . ugh."

"Yes, yes, I remember."

Kalyna nodded and began to take deep breaths.

The purpose of Skydašian leisure ships, I was told, was for the wealthy nobles of the kingdom to move between North and South shores easily—to always be part of both in a noticeable and meaningful way. It wasn't actually convenient, as they only had easy access to the coasts, but it let them feel cosmopolitan and withdrawn at once, and allowed them to move from shore to shore without relying on the Bari (who were, of course, "beneath" them).

"Once upon a time," Kalyna had told me, "the nobles had barges on the Skydaš Sea, but they ran into the same problem as the Yams: their rowers kept defecting to the Bari."

This ship, like all of its type, did not have a traditional title. Instead, the surname "Ikennakas" was emblazoned across its side, as though someone had taken a branding iron to the poor swan. This false bird had been endowed with a visage that towered above the rest of the ship and could easily have fit two or three adult humans in its beak, but the collections of gemstones that made up its eyes actually served to make it look vacantly surprised.

The founder of the Lanreas River Guild's full, legal name had been Adomas Albinakas Rutorie Marijonkwo Ikennakas, and this swan that could have housed every member of his guild belonged to his sister, Rozalija. (I do not remember her full name.)

Kalyna and I stepped out onto the ship's vast deck, and she took a series of deep breaths meant to calm her stomach before anyone reached us. I was quite used to the suspension of the marabou but had never been on the ocean before, so it was the rocking of the ship's deck that made me feel a touch sick.

Kalyna was dressed in lightly woven, and closely cut, wool. She carried an unused red cloak over one arm and wore trousers that matched it, over which was a black doublet trimmed with silver, which glimmered perhaps too brilliantly in the sun. Also glimmering were a number of rings and a gold necklace worn over the doublet. Kalyna had admitted that even she could never pass as a noble, and so was dressed as a merchant—the sort that made Skydašian nobles hate the trade guilds for "elevating" commoners just a bit.

I wore a silk robe not unlike what Vidmantas had on when I first met him. It was turquoise with yellow flowers, and I looked forward to wearing it again when the seasons turned cooler. Most wonderfully, there was no need to cover my tattoos for this trip.

An attendant, who was attended by sub-attendants, greeted us, said some nice things about the marabou, took Kalyna's cloak, and offered us chilled lemon liqueur in little glasses. We drank it beneath a parasol carried by a sub-attendant.

"Oh, none for her," said Kalyna, nodding back toward Simurgh. "She must keep the thing flying or else the flame dies out. She'll be back for us in an hour or two."

As we were led across the deck, with the marabou rising behind us, the attendant pointed out other ships that could be seen nearby. The pleasure ship in the shape of an enormous blue frog belonged, we were told, to a Skydašian prince. Even further out was a battleship that seemed just as huge as its decadent neighbors.

"Now *that* is the Goddess of the Summer Sun. Pride of the navy, patrolling our waters." The attendant's eyes flashed with excitement, and he whispered, "And below? Our biggest prison: the Goddess' Guts!"

Kalyna smiled wide, enchanted to see such a famous craft. I leaned on the fact that I was acting as her foreign manservant (really her charity case, or her pet), and kept my expression neutral. Were the others from the Žalikwen Salon still there? Still alive deep in the Goddess' Guts? Are they there even now?

We were led belowdecks into a hallway that appeared to be made from the smoothest brass, showing our warped reflections in deep orange as we walked along it. Confused as to why a ship with brass innards wasn't *sinking*, I touched the wall to find that it was actually wood. Whatever they'd done to paint it so convincingly amazed me as much as a ship of brass would have, or possibly more.

We turned a corner and found ourselves facing a well-dressed man in his thirties who looked, well, rather like a young Adomas must have. He was of a lighter complexion, his ears stuck out a bit, and his eyes didn't have the same endlessly searching quality, but he was certainly sporting the same warm smile that Adomas had been able to bring out when he needed to.

"You must be Kalyna Aljosanovna!" he said, bowing in the most fluid fashion. "We have been in correspondence. Enyivdas, I was Adomas'—"

"Favorite nephew, yes, I remember!" Kalyna bowed back. Hers was much stiffer, and I didn't know if this was lack of practice or pretending to have a lack of practice. "Absolutely charmed!"

I wondered how many little truths and lies they were communicating to each other with their tones, their clothes, their movements. Loasht is absolutely a place that can stand on complex ceremony, but less so in the south, and far less for Zobiski. (This is, perhaps, another reason people didn't like us.)

What's more, I had never seen anything so decadent as this ship we were on. The Loashti Academy came with its own prestige—Aloe was a noble with a longer pedigree than anyone in the Tetrarchia—but its bones had been built before anyone could do the kind of trickery that just this hallway demonstrated.

Enyivdas began walking alongside us and chatting with Kalyna.

"My aunt Rozalija hasn't any children," he said. "I wonder if this ship will come to me when I'm gone?" He laughed airily. "Or perhaps she'll want it sunk with her—a burial at sea!"

"Perhaps," Kalyna replied. "And if you're to inherit from her, why do you need to buy the Lanreas Estate?"

"Well, because I don't know, do I? And I certainly wouldn't like my darling aunt to leave us so soon."

Kalyna bobbed her head from side to side, as though she was weighing her options. Even though we were on our way to an appointment, she walked slowly, both to give the young man his time, and also to make him anxious at her seeming disinterest.

"You must understand," Enyivdas continued, "Rozalija never leaves this boat. She wouldn't be a good ruler of that land—not if you still want to guarantee that your workers can stay there."

"I do," said Kalyna. "That's an important point, my lord. My workers and I will run the farm as they see fit, and send their crops and other products to . . ." She acted as though she was about to say a name and then stopped, smiling coyly. "Well, to whomever ends up owning the land. Wouldn't an absent landlord be more useful for my purposes?"

"But she won't understand, you see. She'll be off in her boat, or *perhaps* attending balls in the south, and so she'll simply lay down quotas with no thought to what is actually feasible. What if you have a drought and can't produce this or that amount of sorghum, but that's what she insists upon?"

Kalyna pursed her lips thoughtfully and bowed her head toward him. "And you . . ."

"Well, I love to travel, you see. A regular vagabond. I would greatly enjoy coming to the farm and seeing how things are done, what you all need, and what you can spare. And then . . ." He snapped his fingers and waved his hand. "I'd be off to some other corner. You see?"

"I do. I do." She rubbed her chin, and we stopped walking right outside a door that was bigger than all the ones we'd passed.

Our attendant flourished toward it and opened his mouth, but Enyivdas stepped on whatever he was about to say.

"Rozalija's in here, my good Kalyna. If you wish to say anything to me before we're in her presence, now is the time."

He bowed low and took her hand, not quite kissing it. From the look on the attendant's face, Enyivdas was not supposed to treat a commoner this way, not even a rich one.

"You make a good case," said Kalyna. "But I can't know who will be the better owner of the land." She took her hand from his in order to snap at me. "Loashti? How much is the Countess—?"

I shuffled some papers, smiled simperingly, and replied, "Her most recent offer was six thousand, ma'am."

Kalyna did another little bow of her own. "Numbers are something I can know right now, my lord. So consider that."

"How very bourgeois," sighed Enyivdas.

The attendant opened the door, and we were ushered in to meet Countess Rozalija Something Something Something Something (Something?) Ikennakas. The chamber was stunning, although I'm not sure if it was stunningly beautiful or stunningly ugly. It was beyond my senses and experience, I think.

If the ship itself was a swan, then the room was like being nestled to a swan's bosom, beneath its wing, or perhaps like being inside of its body, if that body were the abstract concept of a swan, rather than guts and sinews. The walls were covered in what appeared to be white feathers, each as long as my forearm and patterned so tightly that nothing beneath was visible. The far wall sported a series of portholes—all shaped like eggs—which were open so that the ocean breeze could gently sway the feathers. (When I came closer, I realized the feathers were not real, but painstakingly handmade.)

I was disappointed to see that all the furniture in the room—desks and chairs and couches and lamps—was sumptuous but did not particularly match the theme. The floor, on the other hand, made me gasp audibly: it looked so much like the quiet, serene surface of an impossibly blue pond that I almost worried I would fall in. There was a pattern of ripples throughout that made it look as though something light, like a leaf, had landed gently in the very center of the room—a trick of the light made it sometimes seem that the ripples were moving.

"Rozalija! You've impressed the Loashti!" laughed Enyivdas.

"Well of course," said the Countess, who was standing perfectly in the center of the room—that is, in the center of the floor's ripples. "Please. Please. Come in and sit down. I'm so *glad* my nephew has been keeping you company."

Rozalija looked much less like Adomas than her nephew. She was small and delicate, with thin wavy hair and a pinched face. The Countess struck me as someone who would have been very awkward had we not been on her ship, where she wielded all the power.

We made our introductions and were brought to a set of large armchairs near the portholes. An attendant brought us wine and pastries so precious they looked like they'd fall apart if one breathed on them.

"I saw your approach through the windows, you know," said Rozalija, with none of the chumminess of her nephew. "I've never seen anything like it."

"Such was the freedom your good brother granted us while he was alive," I said. "The freedom to dream. And create!" Part of my job in this little play was to be the sycophant of poor, departed Adomas, so that everyone else could tear him down.

"And in so doing, left us with no money and a . . . complicated ownership situation," added Kalyna.

"That does sound like Adomas," said Rozalija. "But when my brother—to everyone's surprise—found himself *un*-outlawed, the family gave him your plot of land, because it would have been embarrassing for the oldest of my generation to not own any estates. We considered it to be worthless, so why is it now worth six thousand kudais?"

I began to fidget nervously with my papers. After all this, was the Ikennakas family suddenly uninterested? But Kalyna feigned surprise—which is to say, she purposefully looked as though she was feigning surprise to play along with their game (I think).

"Well, I know that you know it has been verdant and bountiful for ten years now," said Kalyna, pointing playfully, but I assume rudely, at the Countess. "I also know you've had your people scurrying around the nearby towns, asking for information, for at least the last five."

"And mine too!" laughed Enyivdas. "I don't want to feel left out!"

Kalyna smiled graciously at him.

"It's true that things started growing better there, somehow," said the Countess. "But there were also a lot of strange rumors."

"None of us," said Kalyna, "are here to argue that your brother *wasn't* a strange man. My point is only that what he did worked for the land."

"But not for your coffers," Enyivdas chimed in. "Else you wouldn't be selling."

Kalyna nodded, smiling. "Yes, but I'm not just selling you the land; I'm selling you *potential*."

"For?" was the Countess' brusque reply.

"I don't know how up-to-date your news of our farm is, but we've recently improved it much more and are on the cusp of being able to do something truly wondrous with that land. And our secret weapon"— Kalyna waggled her eyebrows—"is the second reason you should want that land."

"I assume you mean the proximity to Loasht," replied Enyivdas.

"You're welcome to that, nephew," said Rozalija. "I am old enough to know better than to trust this Blossoming."

"But there's never been anything like it before! Not in hundreds of years!" I chirped.

"You don't have to trust something to make money off of it," said Kalyna. "The fact is, what was once a contentious border is now a trade route. But even more importantly for the Lanreas River Estate, Loasht is currently, ah, cleaning house, if you catch my meaning."

Both nobles nodded understandingly. I looked at my feet on the marvelous floor.

"And that," said Kalyna, "means an evergreen source of fresh, cheap labor coming to our little farm. *That* has been the secret to our recent success." She held her hands out, indicating me—my entirety—as though I were an object. "Why, my Loashti here was a respected advocate in his own land. But he has the misfortune of being the wrong kind of Loashti, so he now keeps my papers for a pittance!"

I nodded.

I should point out here that while this aspect of my role was Kalyna's idea, she did not push it on me at all, and promised we could go another route if I preferred. But I insisted, because I thought it might be fun to try playing a part the way Kalyna so often did, and because I thought of it as a good way to learn just how abhorrent Adomas' family were.

The answer was: quite.

"But to bring in more workers," continued Kalyna, "we need the money to build homes, buy equipment, and feed everyone before the farm is up to its full *potential*. There's that word again." She grinned her great, big Kalyna grin.

Rozalija tried to look uninterested, but if I didn't believe her, Kalyna certainly did not.

Enyivdas shrugged and said, "Well, now, that seems decent. I suppose I'd pay as much as . . . oh, four thousand."

Rozalija harrumphed out a laugh before she could help herself.

"Does that mean your offer's still on the table, Countess?" asked Kalyna.

I dug out the letter in which she had offered six thousand.

Rozalija looked at her nephew for some time and then said, "Yes." It was hard to know how much was greed and how much was a desire to show up her nephew.

"Well, I . . . I . . . I could probably go higher than that," said Enyivdas. "But how do I know this scheme of yours will work?" He smirked. "Besides what *my people* have told me, of course."

"Of course," Kalyna repeated. "Speculation is always a gamble, but the core of it is letting us run the place our own way, which is baked into the contract my Loashti here has drawn up."

I nodded with great seriousness.

"Less work for me sounds lovely," said Enyivdas. "Seven thousand."

"Eight," said Rozalija.

Enyivdas opened his mouth, stopped himself, closed it, and then shrugged. "I must leave my final offer at seven. I couldn't do more in good conscience."

"Seven and eight," said Kalyna, pointing from one to the other. "Well, naturally eight wins."

"*If* I like this contract," replied Rozalija.

"And if she doesn't, and I do . . . then seven!" laughed Enyivdas.

"Of course, of course." Kalyna snapped her fingers at me and held out her hand.

I reached into my satchel and pulled out a crinkled, old paper, sliding it into her hand delicately. Kalyna made a big show of holding it up, moving it farther, then closer, wetting her lips, and then squinting.

"'I'm surprised at how fast I've gotten used to the idea,'" she read and then looked at me, irritated. "This isn't the contract! What is it?"

"I . . . I don't know, ma'am." I began rooting through my satchel, looking mortified. "But it must be related to the Lanreas Estate. I haven't brought anything that isn't, I swear!"

"Why," said Kalyna, "it's dated to ten years ago. How odd. And does this look like Adomas' handwriting to you?"

I looked over her shoulder and agreed that it did.

She furrowed her brow in mock curiosity and continued to read: "'What was unthinkable is now my only way forward. I've spent my whole life running, and I'm tired of it. If I poison King Piliranas and then save him with my own concoction, no one else will ever have to know'?!" Kalyna looked up, aghast.

"What is this nonsense forgery?" growled Enyivdas.

"But we found this in Adomas' own study after he died!" I insisted.

"Why would he write that down?" demanded Rozalija.

Kalyna shrugged. "Narcissism, perhaps? So that someday people would know how clever he was? Does that . . . does that sound at all like him to you?"

Silence.

"Still, it must be a forgery," said Enyivdas. "This isn't enough proof."

Kalyna then began to let on by smiling slightly. "Wait, wait. There's more. From the next day." A throat clearing. "'I pondered for some time about how best to get poison to the King, considering I'm outlawed, but now I've hit upon it. That wastrel Enyivdas—' Oh no. I'm so *sorry*, Enyivdas. You must understand I'm just reading what it says here. 'That *wastrel* Enyivdas is so desperate to fill the void my brother left in his life that he's been trying to cozy up to the King as a new father, when he isn't bothering me for the same.'"

Enyivdas' mouth was hanging open.

Kalyna shrugged apologetically, then grinned with relish and continued: "'He was just telling me that his next overture—'"

"You were speaking to Adomas when he was *outlawed*?" growled Rozalija. "That's treason already!"

"We both know you were too!" her nephew yelled back. "And besides, this is all falsehood. There's no proof!"

Kalyna smiled and waited patiently for them to be quiet. Once they were, all pretense was gone. She was possessed of a vicious glee far beyond her enjoyment when toying with Yalwas or a commander of the Yams.

"'He was just telling me that his next overture,'" she repeated, slowly, "'will include a gift of the Leopold volume *A History of North and South Shore Monarchs in the Years Before Skydašiai.* I learned a trick in—'Well, let's not give away all his secrets." Kalyna winked. "The trick is 'to contaminate the binding of a book with arsenic such that repeated usage will poison the reader. Enyivdas isn't much for books, so I'm sure the boy will be fine.'"

Enyivdas had his head in his hands. If I hadn't seen his eagerness to exploit my people, I would have felt sorry for him.

"'In this form, it will be slow acting,'" continued Kalyna, "'so once the King gets sick, I'll just need to swoop in and . . .' Well. You get the idea." She shrugged.

"Give me that!" Enyivdas came out of his chair, reaching for the paper.

Kalyna easily avoided his grasp without getting up. "This isn't the only page, my lord. Your uncle was quite detailed. For posterity, I suppose. Or maybe as leverage—this is a level of treason that would bring down your whole family even if you weren't directly involved."

Enyivdas stood above her, fuming.

"You still can't prove it," said Rozalija. "Even if my fool nephew has confirmed it here, you have a piece of paper. And if we kill you here, then who will ever know?"

Kalyna opened her mouth.

"Have you mailed more pages to an accomplice?" Rozalija interrupted. "I can't see how it would matter. It looks like his handwriting, but how could they prove the story is true?"

"Adomas didn't poison a bottle of wine, Countess, he poisoned a book, which is probably still sitting in the royal library."

"And?" laughed Rozalija. "Do you think we haven't friends at court? Do you honestly believe you left your other pages with someone who can get to the royal family before—" She stopped and knitted her brow. "What? What are you pointing at?"

Out the portholes, over Rozalija's shoulder, was the frog-shaped pleasure ship of a Skydašian prince. A great and terrible stork was hovering above it.

"Our balloon," said Kalyna, "will land on the Prince's ship any minute, agiving him everything he needs to learn of the plot against his grandfather."

Enyivdas collapsed back into his chair.

"Unless, of course," she added, "your semaphore men send a signal that I will tell them."

Enyivdas moaned.

"Didn't King Piliranas die just a few years later?" mused Kalyna. "I wonder if he kept reading that book . . ."

"But . . . but . . ." spluttered Rozalija.

"Oh, give it up!" Enyivdas chided. "I inscribed the damn thing!"

Rozalija blew a loud breath out of her nose. "How much do you want?"

"No more than you each offered." Kalyna smiled at me. "The contract, if you please."

I handed it to her.

This contract, written up by an advocate Kalyna paid quite a lot for, was much more exacting than Adomas' original will, which had simply promised the land to "the members of the Lanreas River Guild." Now the Guild would be granted all the legal protections of being owned by nobles, but those nobles (undersigned here) could act only as "sponsors," with names on the deed but no rights to change, take, or do *anything* to the land. There were, the advocate told us, precedents for organizing "village law," wherein a group of elders were in charge. For our contract, he simply added a clause that defined elders as "anyone over sixteen."

"You're welcome, of course," the advocate had said to us. "But who in the world would sign such a thing?"

Kalyna had just grinned and paid him.

And thus, the Lanreas River Guild laid claim to fifteen thousand kudais, to be delivered by the end of the week.

Kalyna was still much too skysick to enjoy her victory on the way back, but once we were wandering the Guild, she looked elated.

"I don't mind telling you, I was worried for a moment there." She stretched her arms above her head as we walked. "If Simurgh had actually needed to land on the Prince's ship, I think we would've been out of luck. Imagine her parlaying with royalty!"

"You sound like you enjoyed how close it was."

"Well, yes! And I'd almost forgotten how much fun it is to stomp all over powerful and awful people. Didn't you enjoy it?" She turned to look at me. "After all, you were— Oh, no. No, you didn't at all."

"The very beginning was fun, as was the end, when we knew we'd gotten away with it. But the middle was all . . ."

"Demeaning, shameful, abject."

"Yes."

"I warned you."

"You did! I'm not upset with you at all. I'm . . . I'm in awe. How do you do it? And enjoy it?"

"I don't always. But . . ." She stopped walking and tapped her foot in the dirt for a moment, watching Ifeanyas slowly coming toward us, pushing Aljosa in his chair. "I don't know. You can waste a lot of time trying to convince people like them that you aren't the scum they expect. It usually gets you nowhere." She looked at her hands, still covered in rings, and pressed her fingertips together. "Conversely, it can be . . . *freeing* to just act like what they think you are."

"Maybe."

"Well, for *me* anyway, and the ways in which I am broken."

"Kalynishka!" Aljosa cried as Ifeanyas brought him closer. "*Never* say that about yourself! You'll make me cry! And then I'll see crying people. All sorts of crying strangers, from all over and all when!"

Ifeanyas looked at me and shrugged.

"I'm sorry, Papa." Kalyna took his hand.

"You sound like Mother when you say things like that about yourself," he said, looking into the middle distance.

"Don't you miss her? Isn't it nice to be reminded of her?"

He brought up his other hand to pat hers absentmindedly. "Yes I do, but no it isn't, you know that. Mother is gone, and if we just stand here talking until the sky bleeds, these boys won't get to go kiss, and I *know* you don't want to be responsible for that."

"No, no. Of course I don't," said Kalyna. "Never in a million years."

Excerpt from *The Notes of Echoes in the Gingko-Wreathed Valley Sound like Grandfather's Voice* (translated from Kubatri)

Yekunde not far, but trip is slow. (Way back faster by boat?) Rot and bandits must pilfer to eat and accumulate horses.

Also wine: if they go immediately from heavy drinking to none, will be useless for a day or two.

Rot expects me to "mix up something" to help ease transition, but I don't. Limited ingredients. Brigands will have to manage.

Light scuffles on the road, but no great trouble. Soldiers not everywhere, citizens still trusting. On the surface, southern Loasht unchanged. I hate that.

Faster when we have more horses. Lose track of time. Exhausting way to travel.

At a week (more?) we make Yekunde. Rot and I go into city at night. No guards, no gates.

Never been to Yekunde before. Seems normal, subdued.

Follow Radiant's instructions to Zobiski quarter. Very quiet. No Zobiski.

Houses still stand, interiors untouched, possessions in place—clothes, books, toys, dishes, chairs—but no people.

Yekunde people stole nothing from neighbors. Still happily watched their removal. I begin to feel sick.

Dagmar swears many Rot oaths. I think she is crying.

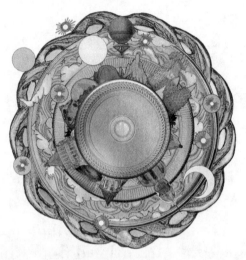

Chapter Twenty-Eight

Regarding the Final Piece of Kalyna Aljosanovna's Plan

Fifteen thousand kudais from the Ikennakas family did in fact come at the end of the week, as promised. By that time, we were nearing a month since Dagmar and Echoes had taken off into Loasht with a small army of bandits. Should we have been expecting them soon? And if something had happened to them, was there anything we could do about it? Or any way we could even know?

Kalyna saw about finishing the work being done inside our hidden piece of The Thrashing, Bone-White Tail of Galiag, which would (if the Eighty-Three were merciful) allow for the swift arrival of Dagmar, Echoes, thirty bandits, and some three hundred Zobiski, including Silver. There was still some grumbling about the effort going into the project, but it cooled considerably when she brought in the contract ensuring the Guild's future, the ten thousand kudais she promised, and another five thousand besides. (Two thousand of which would be held to pay Dagmar and her bandits when, or if, they returned with the Zobiski.) Even Žydrė had to admit she was impressed.

At the hidden riverbank, Ifeanyas, who was not tall enough to be much use in chipping away the rock, had taken with relish the job of messenger. He ran to and fro, conveying words between Kalyna, different groups of workers, and the Guild architects (such as they were) who tried to ensure the widened opening would not simply collapse. Some messages were simple enough for hand gestures, but for everything more complex, there was Ifeanyas. The burning, whooshing, howling winds of Galiag still rushed by above, of course, drowning out most noise.

In order to get it done before Dagmar crashed a boat into the mountain, they were now working through midday, when the sunlight made the winds glitter a blinding, rushing white above us.

On the day they were set to finish, I went to go see their work. Everyone there wore some sort of blindfolds with slits in them—just as Kalyna had said were used to avoid "snowblindness"—made of light, thinly cut wood, and carved vaguely into the curves of a face. When I was issued mine by a small Masovskan woman sitting at the end of the tunnel, on the lowest stair, I was still told to avoid looking straight up if I could help it.

"If curiosity can't be shaken," she said, in slightly awkward Skydašiavos, "look at the river's reflection."

I immediately did look at the bright, shimmering reflection in the river. Then, *of course*, I looked up at the sky for a moment, to see just how these wooden goggles worked. It was very bright, but I had my vision back in just a few moments. Quick enough to see, but of course not hear, Kalyna laughing at me.

She was standing with one leg up on a little hill, a way back from the water. I actually think the hill may have been some meerkat's home: I'm sure her treatment of it would have horrified Adomas. But so would most of what was happening here. She was watching a group of workers—many of the Guild's tallest—on their scaffold over the water, some thrusting upward with picks and shovels to loosen stone, while others built yet more scaffolding to, I suppose, hold the rocks in place.

Just at the banks of the river, there were a number of people whose job was to stand there with sticks or farm implements, discouraging curious crocodiles that tried to come ashore. Every now and then, one of the beasts would peek out and perhaps waddle slightly from the water, but they never took much convincing to go back: there were a *lot* of humans out here, and the creatures may not have liked the noise any more than we did. The only ones I saw were of the common four-legged kind. None of my unsettling, and strangely beloved, upright Yekunde variety.

Inside Adomas' "summer home," or what was left of it, were the architects: three Guild members who'd been around since the start and had worked on building the simple houses that dotted our lands (but not the one in which they now sat), and a Loashti alien who'd arrived in the same group as Echoes and Binturong. The Loashti had, I learned, been the chief planner for a number of large government buildings in the western reaches of Loasht, before she was accused of laying out their corners and halls to correspond with older, and less savory, symbology than the Eighty-Three. ("Ridiculous," she told me. "When I sat before their supposed 'tribunal' of three dirty and small-minded idiots, I told them the absolute truth: that I just prefer to have nice, symmetrical, even numbers of things.")

I had caught a glimpse of these architects through the open door as Ifeanyas ran out from the "summer home" to carry some complaint or worry of theirs to Kalyna. The door was closed quickly, so that they could continue talking in the quiet hut.

"Remind them," Kalyna screamed hoarsely to Ifeanyas, "that this opening does not need to stand forever! Just long enough! It may even do us well to close it up afterward!"

Ifeanyas nodded and was off. He was winded, but frightfully energetic. I got tired just looking at him.

"This will be ready for Dagmar and the rest, if they can get to the boats!" Kalyna said (yelled) to me. "And if the boats can hold them all!"

"They should! The river boats are used to carry many passengers up and down the Lanreas!"

She nodded and looked out to watch the work. Talking for too long out there got exhausting. I took a few moments to watch a man I didn't know use a pitchfork to shoo a small crocodile back into the water. It regarded him coldly with its glassy, unthinking eyes, but backed up awkwardly and swam away. Then I saw Ifeanyas, running toward the workers out on the scaffold, take a short detour to pass the man with the pitchfork and kiss him on the cheek, before veering back toward his original destination. The man I didn't know smiled and stretched a hand out for Ifeanyas, who was already out of reach.

This made me feel . . . *something*. But I wasn't sure what. Was it jealousy? Ifeanyas owed me nothing, and I'd never been jealous over someone who owed me nothing. Had I even ever been jealous of anyone but Silver? It was hard to remember, and that made me feel old.

Perhaps I was jealous because Ifeanyas and I, though we were friends who sometimes kissed, had not fucked since the night of the dance. We had tried, but I'd simply been too tired, too frayed, too nervous. This was understandable, due to everything that was happening, but it made me feel unattractive nonetheless. He had already gravitated toward someone else and, for maybe the first time in my life, that made me feel as though there was somehow *less* attention and warmth for me. Or perhaps I was simply jealous that *anyone* was having fun and companionship, while I felt more and more that I was becoming the wild-looking, old hermetic wizard from a story.

Besides, Ifeanyas was the first person I'd fucked in . . . Eighty-Three, in *two years*. That was bound to cause some uncomfortable feelings.

I didn't hear the splash, or the screams of alarm, or whatever Kalyna said in response. All I knew was that Kalyna was standing there next to me, and then suddenly she wasn't.

I looked up and saw her running to the river, throwing down her goggles behind her. Ifeanyas, and a few people on the scaffold, were shouting and pointing downstream to something moving in the water. Everyone else simply stared at what looked, to me, like a person being swept away.

I began to run south along the river, parallel to Kalyna, although she was much closer than I cared to be. She was soon right at the water, yelling frantically. From her lips, she seemed to be saying, *Swim, idiot!*

I saw a hand reach up out of the water, followed by the emergence of half a gasping face, and realized the person in the water was Yalwas. But why he wasn't swimming to shore was beyond me. The way he was being pulled downstream, he would soon hit where the surface of the Lanreas River met the Galiag winds, and . . . well, *something* bad would happen. I still didn't fully understand that strange phenomenon.

Then Yalwas was under again, and we all saw why he wasn't swimming to land. A tail thrashed, long and ridged. I'd know a crocodile tail in a heartbeat, but I had never seen one this large. It twisted and dragged Yalwas about, holding part of his midsection in its jaws, which were as big as he was. The thing thrashed such that its exact size was hard to tell, but it was easily bigger than two normal crocodiles; bigger than Lini the cow.

Kalyna saw all this too. She also saw that she was, by far, the closest to Yalwas. She ran along the water, staring down at it with eyes wide—seeming more afraid of the river itself and whatever else might lurk within than she was of the creature attempting to devour Yalwas.

I believe I saw her utter a quick prayer, although, based on her expression (and depending on the god), it may have been closer to an accusation, or a frustrated, *Why me?*

She threw off what clothes she could, kicked her boots away, and dove into the waters. I had no idea she was such a fast and forceful swimmer. The woman never ceased to reveal new talents.

What, exactly, she intended to do about a crocodile almost as large as the Devastator when she got to it, however, I did not know.

She got her arms as far around its thick neck as she could, fruitlessly attempting to wrestle the thing. She also tried yelling something to Yalwas whenever both of their heads were above water. I mostly saw turning bodies and thrashing limbs, until Kalyna began to *punch* the beast in its great, globular eye. It did not let go, but twisted out of Kalyna's grip until it was moving downstream tail first, putting Yalwas' limp body between itself and this new annoyance.

Moments later, the beast was gone. Not into thin air, exactly, but into the winds of Galiag where they arced down to meet the river. I saw the very flesh stripped from the beast's bones as its eyes, which had already looked blank and dead, stared back at Kalyna. First green flesh, then white, dissolved into tatters and were swept up in the wind, or carried away by the rushing water. The bones would take longer, but I could see them beginning to be pockmarked as well, before they dropped out of sight into the water.

Then the same thing happened to Yalwas' left leg, with which he had been trying to kick away from the crocodile. His brown flesh gave way to pink, as Kalyna tried desperately to swim upstream, lugging his body. She screamed something in his ear, and eventually Yalwas began to weakly swim forward with his free hand, while the other was over her shoulder.

Somehow, the two of them made it to shore. When Kalyna heaved Yalwas up onto land, his left leg was entirely missing below the knee. The bone of his thigh was still intact, but there was no flesh attached to it any longer. There was also a great, bloody rent in the left side of his chest and stomach, and it was hard to tell how much of his midsection was missing.

Kalyna began to frantically wrap his wounds while yelling. Finally, Ifeanyas recognized that she was calling to him, and moments later, he was off down the tunnel to the Estate to get help.

Yalwas screamed the entire way to the village, and no one could blame him. By the time we got him to the gaunt Loashti alchemist-doctor who had arrived with Echoes, Yalwas was unconscious, which was likely a blessing.

In the following hours, his extraneous thigh bones were sawed away, and he was bandaged up as much as possible, but he hadn't regained consciousness.

"His heart is untouched, thanks, I suppose, to the great thickness of his chest," said the alchemist-doctor, "but I'm afraid the beast damaged, or took, other important innards. He'll survive the day, but I don't know beyond that."

Despite Yalwas' grim chances, many Guild members made a point of heaping praise upon Kalyna for risking her life to save him.

"I was simply the closest," she kept saying. "Any of you would have done the same in my place."

"No one would have done the same in my place," she seethed that evening, in her hut. "I shouldn't have either. It was daft. I punched the thing."

"But you did, and it worked."

Added to the brightly colored cloths hung in her home were now a small clay incense holder (shaped like a smiling, floppy-eared pig), and a faded, old tapestry depicting a sea beast capturing and dragging down a ship. The tapestry was old but not particularly artful: no visionary had strung it together, although I did appreciate the beast's angry, human-like eyes. It sat above those ancient, watchful remains of eye, jaw, and tooth, as though she'd made that corner a shrine to creatures too big to comprehend. The more stressed she was, the more often her eyes shot over toward them.

Most parcels of her possessions that Aljosa had brought still sat unopened. But his own had been unpacked, and their contents were with him inside the tent, which sat just outside her hut, crushing more of Adomas' garden. He seemed to greatly enjoy sleeping in a tent.

Kalyna had pulled the desk away from the wall, so that we could both eat our dinners there: cooked greens and beans with sorghum flatbreads. Today, though, the flatbreads were also coated with oil and garlic. It was delicious, but I wasn't very hungry.

"*Maybe* it worked." Kalyna's appetite seemed unaffected, and she took big bites, even as she looked peevish. "He still may not survive."

"But you did your best."

"Why are you being so nice to me?"

I shrugged. "I suppose because you did a good thing, which no one else was brave enough to do."

"Well," she said, wrapping up greens in a flatbread, "it wasn't just bravery."

"What else?"

"Radiant, he wouldn't have been in the water to be half-eaten in the first place if it wasn't for me."

"That's not—"

"And for you," she added. "It's your fault too."

"Fine." I threw up my hands.

She took a large bite and then stared down at the remaining rolled-up bread, with green innards visible inside, for a long time.

"He often worked by the river before we even knew about that place," I finally offered.

"But not on a scaffolding over the deepest part." She closed her eyes, and repeated to herself, very quietly, "The deepest part."

"Is this conscience?" I asked. "Or something else?"

Her eyes snapped open and regarded me with irritation. "A bit of both, Radiant Basket of Rainbow Shells. Just . . . just know that the beast I *could* see was the least terrifying thing about diving into those waters to me."

"Why?"

"I do not feel like discussing it."

"All right. And the work at the river . . . ?"

"Will finish tomorrow, of course. You've been good enough to tell us the sizes of your Yekunde river boats, and we're almost there."

I nodded.

"I admit," I sighed, "that I hadn't thought of myself as partly responsible for what happened to Yalwas until you said it."

"You're welcome."

"He was against violating Adomas' little secret haven by the river, but he still did his part there once we got started."

She nodded.

"If our doctors can save him," I asked, "what will happen to him?"

"He'll be fed, clothed, and housed the rest of his life, of course. If he wants to work, there's plenty he can learn to do without his leg. But if he'd rather relax and do nothing for the rest of his days?" She shrugged. "Who would tell him no? That's the way of this place, isn't it?"

"You almost sound fond of it."

"I'm fond of a lot of stupid and hopeless things. You, Dagmar, the Tetrarchia, and so forth."

My next thought was interrupted by the sound of someone *screaming* just outside Kalyna's home.

"Really! Now?!" she growled to herself.

Then she bolted up and ran out of the house. I followed her outside and around to Aljosa's tent. She yelled, "Don't come in!" a moment too late, and I was already inside.

Kalyna was shaking her father as he wailed and moaned a stream of nonsense in at least five different languages. At first I thought he was having a nightmare, but his eyes were wide open.

Kalyna glared at me as she held him and rocked him slowly, muttering to him in a similar mélange of tongues. Then she rolled her eyes and, in as frustrated a manner as possible, motioned that I sit down. She continued to comfort him for a few minutes, while I looked around at how artfully cluttered his tent was: skins and rugs and little tapestries, a shrine. I hope Kalyna appreciated how hard it was for me to not consistently ask, "What's happening to him?" and, "Is he all right?"

Eventually, he began to calm, and his breathing slowed. Whatever he was saying, too, slowed and quieted, although it did not stop until he suddenly broke from his gibberish to say, in Skydašiavos, "Kalynishka. Kalynishka. Does your friend the pretty wizard have a friend with a big"—he raised his hands and wiggled his fingers, perhaps to mean glittery—"cape?"

"Yes, Papa."

"He's not my friend," I said.

Aljosa seemed shocked by my presence. Then he stared at me, while Kalyna stared at him, as though waiting to see whether my presence would hurt him, calm him, or something else entirely. I remembered, then, back in Desgol when she hadn't wanted me to come near him.

"Who's not?" he asked.

"The man with the glittery cape. Aloe."

"Aloe? Aloe's not what?"

"My friend."

"What?"

"Radiant," Kalyna said through her teeth, "trying to make sense of it won't help him. He's *always* trying to make sense of it, and to have someone else's perspective is confusing."

"Make sense of what?"

"Papa, did you see a man with a cape?"

"Just now? Isn't that what I've been telling you?!" He growled and gripped the bridge of his nose as though we were the most irritating people to exist. "The man! The pretty wizard's friend! With the"—he wiggled his fingers again, but angrily—"cape! He will come . . . Do you hear me? I say, he will *come here*!" He was shouting now, which was very uncomfortable in such a small space. "And then! His soldiers! At the border! Will take him! Up the river!" He pointed north.

Having gotten out what he needed to say, Aljosa sagged against Kalyna and looked relieved.

"Thank you, Papa. That must have been hard."

He nodded with great intensity.

The three of us sat quietly for what may have been thirty minutes, until Aljosa fell entirely asleep on Kalyna's shoulder. She sighed, slipped him carefully onto his bedroll, looked at me, and pointed imperiously out the door of the tent.

The sky was now orange and purple with the sunset, and there was a slight chill in the air, but only just. Downhill from us was the temporary encampment for Loashti Guild members who didn't yet have sturdy homes. I could hear snatches of many languages from home drifting toward us, and saw spouses, friends, comrades, and neighbors working to live some kind of a life in this new place. A place *so very new* to a Loashti, in the larger procession of history. At the southern end of the encampment, the frame of what would soon be a new dormitory had already been nailed together.

"Do you think they heard him screaming?" she asked, nodding toward the encampment.

"Probably."

"Great. That's the first time that's happened to him in months; you should be flattered."

"Kalyna, I'm *flattered* by his insistence on calling me the 'pretty wizard.' *That* was just confusing."

She sighed and steered me away from the encampment, toward the forest, where we'd have more privacy. Kalyna walked with her thumbs hooked in her belt, focused on the trees bathed in the moonlight, barely looking at me.

"Radiant," she said, "my father can see the future."

"Ah. I was afraid that was it." A few things began to click into place, and I tried not to sound excited. "Your grandmother, as well? But not you?"

"Yes, yes, and that's why she hated me." She turned toward me, half bowing, and held out her hands. "You solved my *rrrriddle*. You must be so proud."

"If it's so painful, you may be lucky not to have it."

"It was always painful for my family, but Papa's different." She kicked a small stone, and it flashed through the moonlight as it bounced. "In the last few years, though, it got better for him. Partly, I think, because we've had great comfort and safety, and, yes, partly because Grandmother is gone. But, even now, it's very difficult for him to pick out a given detail, a given throughline, from any of his visions. It causes him a lot of pain."

"So you're saying he understood that Aloe coming here would be important to me, and he forced himself to . . . to . . . retrieve it all?"

She nodded. Somewhere nearby, Lini was making soft lowing sounds in her sleep.

"Well then. I'm flattered. And also very worried."

"Yes. Assuming that—my gods willing—Dagmar and Echoes have been successful, they may bring all of Yekunde's Zobiski down the river right into Aloe's hands."

"The timing could work out. They may miss each other."

"Maybe. But even if Papa didn't know *why* this was important to tell us, he knew it was. I think we should move forward with the assumption that they will encounter each other on the Lanreas River. North of the Loashti border."

"All right, so I have that assumption. Now what? I'm even more scared, but I don't know what we can possibly do."

"He's coming back here first, isn't he?"

I stopped walking and looked at her, incredulous. "You're much too smart to be considering killing him while he's here. Our little contract wouldn't protect us then."

"No, it wouldn't. Aloe will be untouchable while he's here." She gazed off into the evening.

I moved in front of her view, forcing her to look at me.

"You want me to curse him."

"I want to save your people however we can."

"It would be very difficult and possibly deadly for me."

"But isn't—?"

"Of course it would be worth it," I said quickly. "If we could guarantee it would work."

"And how do we do that?"

"Oh, Kalyna, we don't. But we can be more sure depending on the curse, and on what we have to aid me. What and *whom*. To even come close to making it effective, the combined wills of a large group of people would be absolutely necessary. After all, Aloe doesn't think he's doing anything so base as 'sorcery,' but the lines between magic and simple willpower are porous, and he's rallied a great many people to his cause to support him, whose beliefs are in tune with his."

"If only," she said, with a snicker, "we had a community of people who were, I don't know, under the influence of a charismatic leader." She sounded very proud of herself.

"But do you really control them? Or are you just their mouthpiece?"

"Guess we'll see, won't we?"

"Perhaps," I suggested, "you shouldn't approach it as though they are in thrall to you."

"I'll consider it. What else do we need?"

"Not sure yet. Whatever it is, the curse will need to be terrifying enough to scatter Aloe's soldiers. And, well . . ."

"Kill Aloe, yes," she said, completing my thought. "Which is still unlikely to stop what he's begun in your homeland, but may at least give us breathing room."

"So, in essence . . ." I paused, took a deep breath, and failed to calm my blood. "So," I tried again, voice cracking, "you want me to carry out a political assassination. Put him out of the way when he doesn't see it coming."

Kalyna took a deep, satisfied breath and started walking again.

"Is that," she asked, "any more ethically dubious than, say, if you shot him from an unseen rooftop while he held a knife to Silver's throat?"

"Of course it isn't," I replied immediately. "You misunderstand me, Kalyna." I couldn't help smiling, just a little, and added, "For once."

She smiled back weakly.

"I only wanted to be honest," I said. "Honest with you, with myself, with the gods, about what we are planning. I'm worried about how I'll manage it and how I might survive it, but those are my only qualms."

Kalyna's face brightened. "Ah! Yes, good. An assassination, then!" She reached out and grabbed my hand, gripping it tightly.

I nodded absentmindedly. My thoughts began to swim with possibilities. I—who had never undertaken a real, full, truly harmful curse—would now try, at a distance, to kill a man. A powerful man, no less. I saw no way out of it that did not, at best, leave me a wreck of a person.

"He'll never know what hit him," added Kalyna, happily.

Something about that sentiment made me sad. But I didn't yet understand what.

"Did Adomas?" I asked. "Know what hit him, I mean."

"I certainly don't know," said Kalyna. "I clearly don't mind telling you when I think assassination is appropriate, so believe me when I tell you I did nothing of the kind to the old man."

"And if you couldn't have convinced him, would you have?"

"Perhaps."

"And you didn't even know yet that he'd poisoned a king."

"If I had," she replied, "I might've liked him more."

Excerpt from *The Notes of Echoes in the Gingko-Wreathed Valley Sound like Grandfather's Voice* (translated from Kubatri)

Woman in a Zobiski house. Not Zobiski. Looks Central. Going
  through a chest of clothes. Neighbors stealing after all.
Dagmar wishes to kill her. I agree but want information. Radiant
  deserves to know. Some things said are worth remembering exactly:
"My large, savage friend wishes to know exactly what happened to the
  dead people you're robbing."
Sword to throat, tears in eyes. Woman commendably brave.
"They aren't dead, and I'm not robbing them. I'm keeping their things
  in order for when they return."
I laugh, then translate. Dagmar also laughs.
Woman—named Casaba Melon Water Soothes at Noontime—shows
  us where Yekunde Zobiski are being held outside the city. At the
  edge of the swamp: smells terrible.
Fifty soldiers, with guns, camp around stone ruin. Four walls and iron
  door rising out of brown and green land, grown over with vines, no
  ceiling. Was once dungeon, but rest of fort is gone. Inside, cell walls
  still stand. Casaba played there as a child.
Three hundred Zobiski prisoners are locked in those cells. Sweltering
  and open to the rain.
"The Zobiski will be taken to Central Loasht," says Casaba, "where

they'll be put through some kind of education. And brought back
here, to their homes."
Even hidden in the swamp, so close to our goal, Dagmar and I laugh
at her more. Bitterly. Sadly.
I tell her the only way she'll see them again is to help save them,
which will make her as much alien as I. Even if "educated," those
who survive will no longer be themselves.
Casaba agrees immediately. We're impressed. Take her back to camp.

Chapter Twenty-Nine

When Aloe Pricks a Mare upon the Mountain Bluff Returned to the Lanreas River Guild

Yalwas survived the next few days, because our Loashti alchemist-doctor worked with Simurgh on a novel way to keep him alive, at least for now. By his bed there now sat a pair of glass globes, each as tall as a toddler, filled with blue and red liquids, and from these were extended tubes of Simurgh's poppy rubber that went right into Yalwas' left side. It was certainly beyond my understanding, but it seemed to be working. The globes had to be refilled and moved around every other hour, but he wasn't going anywhere. That a couple of Loashti were preserving Yalwas' life was not lost on anyone

I, meanwhile, spent those days doing just about the opposite: ruminating on deadly curses.

After so much time thinking about plots, and politics, and farming, it was comfortable, a *relief*, to think once more on my subject of choice. Chances for success seemed low, but, as Kalyna liked to say, it was a fascinating problem.

I did not do this thinking in the library, because I didn't need to do any research yet; I had all the basics in my head. So I further enhanced my wizardly reputation by wandering around the Guild for hours at a time, deep in thought, sometimes mouthing words no one could hear, with my hair wildly unkempt.

Then we heard from Simurgh that Aloe was almost upon us. She had been going up in her marabou balloon regularly to look northward for signs of Dagmar and Echoes, of which she had found none. This meant it was extremely likely Aloe would encounter them upon the Lanreas River.

If that happened, there was little chance Aloe would simply allow Silver and the others to leave. Of course, they weren't *wanted* in Loasht, but neither had they been officially exiled, so far as I could tell. What he might want with them, I couldn't say. Perhaps an example to reeducate, or a tool for my good behavior, which would certainly be a problem once I refused to go back with him. He would recognize the great river boats of Yekunde immediately, and his soldiers had Loashti guns that were more than capable of slaughtering everyone onboard. That darkest possibility loomed large in my mind, because Aloe got to decide who was no longer Loashti, and nobody is easier to kill than the stateless.

Of course, all this planning would be moot if Dagmar and Echoes had failed, and were dead. I tried to stop thinking about this possibility and to instead focus on what I was capable of doing.

After some late nights, I finally hit upon what seemed the best way to strike at Aloe from afar, with the least likelihood of implicating myself or any "occult" elements unfortunate enough to still be in Loasht. I also hoped that this method would not turn him into too much of a martyr, but that is hardly ever predictable—particularly without knowing exactly what he'd been telling his followers all this time.

Kalyna got started on her piece of willing such a horrendous curse into being right away. She made circuits of the Guild, speaking to absolutely everyone she could, more tirelessly than she ever had before. She was gauging different members' capacities for concentration, imagination, and acting. Among the Skydašians and other Tetrarchic peoples, she exulted in spreading stories of how nefarious Aloe was. Speaking to the Loashti aliens (having fully "learned" their language), she gently looked for who was best able to revisit—or even inhabit—their oppressors, and who was possessed of a deep-seated need for revenge.

When people wondered why she was doing all this, she told them cheerily, "Our wizard is preparing a powerful spell, and he needs your help."

"This is utterly mad," said Vidmantas.

He had finally found the time and will to return to his clothes-dyeing station and continued concentrating on his work as he spoke.

"Oh, I know!" I replied, laughing. "Extremely!"

"When I first called out to you in the Žalikwen Salon," he began, elbow deep in dye, "if anyone had suggested you could do something like this, I would've castigated them for their narrow view of the Loashti."

"And correctly! I've never really done it before, and have little reason to think I'll succeed. Besides, very little of the spell will actually be Loashti."

He sighed. "I don't know how I feel about all this."

"You know what Žydrė would say if she were arguing for me."

"That I'm so caught up in being an idealist that I won't accept an imperfect answer now." He lifted his hands out of the dye and stood up to wash them. "But that doesn't change the fact that I'm going to help you *curse* someone. Ugh." He shook his head and then looked at me. "What do you need from me, then?"

I took a moment to, I hope, show in my face that I respected his frustrations. Then I couldn't help smiling, despite everything. Impish, it might even have been.

"Have you got anything that can . . . glitter? Shimmer? Like silk brocade?" I asked.

"I absolutely do not."

"Could you approximate it? Just enough to evoke the real thing from afar, even. Or, say, the *abstract suggestion* of silk brocade."

"No, I—wait, yes. Maybe with delicate work."

I explained what I would need from him, but no more. Even Kalyna did not know the full details of what I'd planned. It was best that there be genuine surprise and horror and wonder on our end. I had not even written down all the details for myself, only scrawled nonsensical notes in my Commonplace Book as I refined my curse. And it was *mine*, synthesized from countless traditions from all over the known world, but entirely, and damningly, belonging to me in the end. I never did put every step of it in my Commonplace Book, and neither will I include such here, as that would allow people to attempt replicating it.

And then, Aloe Pricks a Mare upon the Mountain Bluff arrived.

There was much commotion in the Guild, but here was another reason it was best not to let everyone in on the full plan. In no world could Aloe have walked through an entire town of people planning to kill him and not learned what was coming. A select few knew, while the rest were simply preparing for a sort of performance (not untrue). They would learn more when the curse was imminent, but today was all preparatory.

Nonetheless, Aloe did not walk alone into the Lanreas River Guild this time: he marched in with some twenty Loashti soldiers, each with sleek long guns far beyond the Yams' piddling wheellocks. I'm no expert, but I was told these were much more accurate, with a longer range, and could fire twice before reloading. The larger number of Yams who were escorting him still waited outside the Guild, obeying old King Piliranas' agreement with Adomas.

This time, Aloe wasn't smiling either. He strode right into the center of the Guild, ignoring anyone he saw and fuming with the anger of one unused to ever being denied or inconvenienced. (What a short memory he had.)

"What, by the Eighty-Three, is going on here?" he growled in Loashti Bureaucratic as he moved purposefully toward the square in front of the Meal Hall. "Where's the old man?"

Aloe stopped in front of a group of Loashti and threw back his colorful brocade cape, placing his hands on his hips like someone's cross uncle. "Well, why don't you answer? You must understand me!"

Binturong, and a number of other Loashti Guild members, looked very much like they wanted to tear Aloe limb from limb, and like a few bullets and deaths would be a small price to pay for getting close. I could relate, and I felt for them, since they didn't know we had a (mad, impossible, evil, dangerous) plan. All I could do was restrain myself and hope the rest followed suit.

426 | ELIJAH KINCH SPECTOR

The Tetrarchic Guild members had a healthier fear of those long guns—it's quite likely they assumed the weapons to be more powerful than they were—and largely regarded him with expressions ranging from suspicion to curiosity.

"Ah! Radiant!" Aloe called, his eyes lighting up when he saw me. "There you are." He smiled broadly and crossed the square toward me, reaching for my hand as his language became less formal.

I took his hand, and I let him embrace me. I could not think of how to avoid it.

Aloe still thought of me as his friend, and this gave me pause regarding our plans for him. I didn't feel guilty or wrong—it was something else I couldn't identify. I reminded myself that my job right now was not to agonize but to catalog his every tic and movement, expression and mannerism.

"What in the name of the Suzerain happened here, Radiant? Where's Adomas got to?"

Over Aloe's shoulder, in a shadowed spot between two buildings, I saw Vidmantas furiously sketching on large sheaves of paper.

"I . . ." I gulped. "Well, that is . . . you see . . . I . . . I . . ."

"I'm afraid Adomas died," said Kalyna in Loashti Bureaucratic, as she walked out from somewhere behind me. "Sad, but he was quite old. I'm in charge at the moment." She gave him a very stiff and sharp bow. "Kalyna Aljosanovna. How can I help you, Aloe Pricks a Mare upon the Mountain Bluff?"

Aloe stepped back from me and studied Kalyna for a moment, hands still on his hips. "So, do you take responsibility for what's been going on here?"

"I don't know to what you refer, but I am responsible for the Guild now, yes."

"I see," said Aloe, wandering back toward his soldiers, with a clearly and purposefully feigned casualness. "Why are so many of my people here on your lands? Radiant, I understand. He was stranded out here, but the rest . . ."

"Were kicked out and had nowhere to go. Were we to leave them to die?"

"They weren't going to *die*," replied Aloe, laughing at her simplicity. "There was just a misunderstanding at the border."

"Ah! A misunderstanding!" cried Kalyna. "Which seems to have led them here. Now what, exactly, is the problem, Aloe Pricks a Mare upon the Mountain Bluff?"

"The problem, Kalyna Aljosanovna," he began, "is that you've kidnapped my people and are keeping them from their home."

"This is their home."

"Eighty-Three," he grumbled. "What have you done to them? You must have some sort of hold on them to keep them from leaving, to keep them from"—he turned and snapped his fingers in Binturong's general direction—"responding to me. I don't know if this blackmail—"

"Your excellency—"

"Minister Investigator!" one of his soldiers yelled.

"Minister Investigator—" Kalyna corrected.

"—or hypnotism, or—" Aloe continued.

"—they don't like you," Kalyna finished.

"What?" growled Aloe. Hands back to his hips.

She smiled in friendly condescension and batted her eyelids at him. "Oh, Minister Investigator, try to understand: they hate you."

Aloe furrowed his brow and looked again at the faces of the various Loashti. He didn't look at me, though—I suppose he felt secure in my friendship. It wouldn't have mattered anyway, as he didn't seem capable of seeing the hatred in any of them.

"Look," Aloe finally said. "Just give me back my people."

"Which ones are your people?"

"Anyone Loashti!"

"Well," said Kalyna, "I have some Loashti blood in me. Am I included?"

"Being Loashti isn't about blood, barbarian. It's about culture."

Kalyna was actually quiet for a moment, thoughtful.

"Interesting," she said. "I admit that sounds a bit better. In theory."

"You have no idea," said Aloe. "And you never will."

Kalyna shrugged, still smiling. "I suppose I'm just a barbarian."

"Give me back my people."

"I'm sorry," said Kalyna, "I'm still not clear on who those are."

"But—"

"If it's not about who has Loashti blood, then you haven't got any people here. None of them want to go back with you."

Aloe's whole being filled with irritation. This was, I suppose, Kalyna's real power, far more so than the "planning" she seldom actually did, or the roles she took on.

"Of course they don't *think* they want to go back! They're confused!"

"Confused by what?"

Aloe shook his head in disbelief. "Are you actually so dense?" he asked. "Or are you being willfully ignorant?" His look became imploring. "They are but misguided. Don't you see that I want to *help* them?"

By the Eighty-Three, he really meant it. I suppose I already knew that, but seeing such naked sadness on his face—such pity for those Kalyna was cruelly keeping from his tender care—was arresting. Kalyna was taken aback as well, because she finally lost her smugness for a moment and had no response. Then I realized I was, perhaps, paying too much attention to Kalyna, when I needed to be watching Aloe.

"Please," he said. "Allow me to help my people." His face strained with sadness. "Do you want me to kneel? I will get right down on my knees in your barbarous dirt. I will debase myself and plead in front of my people, whom you hold hostage, and my soldiers, who will lose their respect for me. I will do it, if you tell me to, in order to help them."

Kalyna stood silently for what felt like a long time before she said: "No need, Aloe. I believe you would do it, and I believe you think you would be helping them. But they will only go with you if they wish to. Which"—she looked around, at the Loashti-derived Guild members—"it seems none of them wish to do."

Aloe turned to address the crowd. "Please," he entreated.

A moment or so of silence passed. Then one of Binturong's children called him a pig-fucker.

Soon it became a deluge. Binturong next, then someone else, and soon there were insults in at least eight Loashti languages being hurled at Aloe until it became one great amorphous bellowing. The incoherent anger of the mob: likely a perfect encapsulation, to Aloe, of exactly the ignorance he wanted to save them from. I'm sure this exact point occurred to most of them as well, but they didn't care. For at least this one moment, they didn't have to worry, or even consider, what a man like Aloe thought of them.

I say "them," because I did not join in. Satisfying as it would have been, I was too busy studying his movements, the sincerity in his face, as well as watching Vidmantas attempt to sketch as Aloe spun about, his cape glittering and undulating, as he looked for a friendly face and found none.

It was wonderful Ifeanyas who was the first of Tetrarchic origin to begin yelling insults at our guest from the north. I was surprised and heartened when Žydrė joined him, followed soon by many more.

Kalyna stood still and silent, smiling at Aloe.

"Radiant!"

I was watching Aloe's face but had become entirely removed from what was happening, or so I felt. It was almost like being up in the clouds on bhang; reality was a thing that was happening around me, but in which I had no part.

"Radiant!" Aloe shouted louder, putting his hand on my shoulder. "Let's get you away from these fanatics and back to your family. Come on."

I was so unmoored that I actually took two steps after Aloe before I realized what I was doing and stopped. I looked down and realized he had taken my hand, like he was my older cousin leading me out of a dangerous cave, or corner of a swamp. When I stopped, he pulled my arm taut and was then yanked backward in surprise. We were both about the same in size and strength.

"Radiant . . . ?"

I shook my head. "I'm not going,"

The boos and insults continued around us. But Aloe, who had only so far seemed confused and surprised, now looked utterly crushed.

"What? Why?"

"Because I don't want to join the Ministry."

"Eighty-Three, Radiant! Then you won't have to! You can go right back to your spot at the Academy!"

"No."

"No? Why 'no'? What in the world is the problem, Radiant? You told me—"

"I changed my mind," I lied.

"But I'm your friend!"

"And I'm your friend, Aloe," I lied. "But I have to stay here and . . ."

"And *what*, Radiant?"

It was a good question. For the sake of my plans, I didn't want him to suspect how I felt about him, how laughable I would have found his life's work if it wasn't hurting so many. If Aloe even began to suspect, then no matter his opinions on "magic" or "the occult," he would begin defending against me. Even if he did not know it, he would be aware of me as a malign presence and would bring his followers' willpower to bear upon me.

"And help these people," I said.

Aloe looked at me as though I was speaking nonsense.

"Help them by coming back! By working at the Ministry! Eighty-Three, Radiant, I threw myself to the Grand Suzerain for you! I risked *everything* for you!"

"I'm sorry."

Aloe let go of my hand. "You're not making sense, Radiant. I don't know what she's done to your mind, which was once so acute and . . . wonderful. I can't force you, but I won't give up on you!"

It was not exactly a Kalyna Aljosanovna master class in lying, but he was confused by me more than he was angry at me, and that was better for my purposes.

Aloe stomped away with his guards, and Kalyna finally joined in on the jeering. She cupped her hands to her mouth, and, of course, her voice soared above all others: "May a crocodile eat your pecker and spit out its remains at your sister's feet!" This was an old southern Loashti saying, which only took four words in Loashti Bureaucratic.

Aloe heard that one and looked back, once, with anger, as he yelled something that none of us could hear.

I gave Kalyna a look.

"What?" She shrugged. "It's a perfectly normal thing to say. He won't think anything of it, I promise you."

"Incredible," Binturong said to me. "You're an amazing teacher. Kalyna's gotten so good at Loashti Bureaucratic."

"I take no credit. She has a gift."

Binturong nodded. In the distance, I saw Vidmantas making a hand gesture at me that I didn't understand. But based on his expression, I assumed it meant "all is well."

Excerpt from *The Notes of Echoes in the Gingko-Wreathed Valley Sound like Grandfather's Voice* (translated from Kubatri)

At camp, Casaba says Zobiski will be held in the old dungeon for another week. Then another fifty soldiers should return with paperwork.

"Authorizing their education," she says. "At least, that's what everyone in Yekunde is saying."

"Likely authorizing their murder," says Dagmar.

"Or," I say, "education for those they think can make the trip. Murder for the rest."

Casaba starts to cry. It is decided to not kill her.

I ask Dagmar if I should treat blades with fast-acting poison. She gets angry: I've insulted her honor.

"Echoes!" she yells. "Of course you should! Why even ask?!"

Treat all blades in camp. They must dry for a day and a night. Then we attack.

First, I will use Mist, rather than Wrath of the Gods, to keep soldiers from seeing and shooting us. Its greenness makes sense near the swamp; its fresh scent will clash with swamp's heavy one.

Once obscured, we will cough loudly, make soldiers think Mist is noxious. Then the butchery will begin, if we're lucky.

Can't let them know we're there for Zobiski—even obscured by Mist, easy for soldiers to shoot in general direction of three hundred prisoners.

If we lose, remaining Skydaš bandits will flee to save themselves. Don't blame them.

Dagmar, Casaba, and I will either save the Zobiski, or we will die.

Always been my purpose, but those two surprise me, and I tell them so. Meant with admiration; Dagmar takes as sarcasm. Or pretends to.

I pray for two hours beforehand. Some bandits join me, as though I am a priest; some watch and seem unsettled.

Notes must end here. Too much to do next.

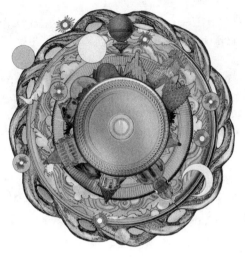

Chapter Thirty

The Culmination of Years of Study

Three days after Aloe left us, Simurgh came down from her balloon and told us that, this evening, he'd be back in Loasht. She also did not yet see any large boats heading down the Lanreas yet, meaning if Aloe did indeed travel by water, he would absolutely pass Dagmar, Echoes, and Silver, and do so in Loasht. Unless they had already failed.

"If they've been stopped," said Kalyna, standing outside Simurgh's home beneath the slowly deflating marabou balloon, "then at least we may get some kind of revenge on Aloe, yes?"

"I don't know that this would be worth it for revenge," I said.

"You may be surprised," said Simurgh.

I hadn't quite expected that from her.

"Besides," said Kalyna, "killing him could help some of those still remaining in Loasht."

"Or hurt them more," said Simurgh, before I could. "By putting in his place someone who does not even consider themselves to be doing a kindness."

"Well, obviously," agreed Kalyna. "It can always be worse. Those of us able to bend the world around us in *any* way must simply accept that. We can only do what we can."

"Forgive me," I said, "if that doesn't—"

"Comfort you? It wasn't intended to."

"Of course," I sighed.

There was silence. Birds chirped, and a light breeze fluttered its way through the summer morning. I wondered whether the days were beginning to cool at all in Yekunde yet, such as they ever did.

Simurgh kicked at the dirt. "Well," she said, "I'm off to the north if I'm going to do my daft part. And see if I can pick out Echoes and the rest."

"Do you want to take anyone with you?" asked Kalyna. "To help?"

Simurgh shook her head. "No, no. I fly faster alone—due to both weight, and, well, reckless abandon." She smiled. "On my own, I will do things that would scare a passenger."

"And if you crash and die?" I asked.

"Radiant, I've always expected to go that way. I'd be disappointed if I didn't. What sort of simurgh would I be, otherwise?"

"Well then," said Kalyna, putting a hand on her shoulder, "please be as careful as you wish to be." She favored the Loashti inventor with a smile that was much more reserved than I was used to seeing.

I nodded. "I'll look for your signal. But, if it takes too long, I'll have to assume you crashed and move forward anyway."

"Naturally," said Simurgh.

Within ten minutes, she was aloft.

I spent about an hour alone in the library with a mirror, practicing moving like Aloe. I did not have to perfectly imitate his expressions: this was broader than that, more concerned with using him as a totem—a symbol. Unfortunately, that meant I had to engage, intellectually, with Aloe's ideas, which I did not particularly want to do. He had quite purposefully made himself into just such a symbol, so that people would feel correct in following him. Why else was he so attached to, and conscious of, the eye-catching cape that conveyed his power? But to do what was required, I would have to fully look at, and absorb, the awful thing he had become. And the awful person he had clearly always been. No one else, not even Kalyna, with her years of deception, was capable of doing this.

Once I felt I would make no more progress with practicing (though I certainly did not feel ready), I put on a simple robe of deep-blue-dyed linen and went down to the Games Hall, which was empty except for Kalyna.

She smiled weakly at me, and I did my best to respond in kind.

"How are you feeling?" she asked as she handed me a cup of coffee.

"Terrible. Hopeless."

"Well, know that I have faith in you." She rubbed my back and led me to a chair in front of a large mirror of hers.

My hair, by then, had grown into what I felt was a quite agreeable halo, but that wasn't how Aloe wore his hair, and so Kalyna took up a pair of scissors.

"Don't worry," she said. "I used to always cut my hair, and Papa's, and even Grandmother's when she was alive. They were all of differing textures."

"Texture hardly matters," I sighed. "Just as short as possible." I sipped my coffee. It tasted wonderful.

"I know. I saw him. And the texture does still matter."

Large black and gray clouds of hair fell to the floor of the library, and the face in the mirror became more . . . *spare*. It was as though the hair had given it definition, or character, and now I had no way to hide or distract—there was only my aging face with its fading beauty. Ifeanyas wore his hair similarly, but his face was almost cherubic and full of energy. Yalwas was bald, but he radiated a hearty power—or at least he had before they began leeching him with rubber tubes. I sat and stared at this unadorned version of *myself*.

Until, of course, Kalyna adorned me. In a way.

Aloe and I were of similar skin tone, and Kalyna had combined some of the makeup Echoes left behind to match my hue, which she used to cover the tattoos on my face. Then she took black kohl and used it to make my face into a sort of grotesque of our target. First with arched eyebrows that would read to the cheap seats as an angry man; and then shadows just under my face, to approximate the jawline I did not have anymore, but Aloe still did (for some *unfair* reason). Finally, she added his tattoos: three slim, squiggly lines beneath each eye, and then muddled them a bit with the dark brown that covered my own, so that they would look faded. This also served to hide my high cheekbones, a feature I was proud of that he did *not* share.

"That's very good, for having seen him twice," I murmured.

"I'm observant. Now drink that coffee carefully. I don't want you to muss it."

"Of course. But I'll need much more coffee, and—"

"It's got everything mixed in, yes."

"Good."

"Your heart may simply burst out of your chest during this," she said, not unkindly. She ran a hand over my short hair to inspect her work; it was a nice feeling.

"That is one of many dangers I'm facing today, yes." Another sip. "I told you I'd be risking my life."

"I suppose I'm just now seeing how that may happen." She clasped my shoulder, looking me over in the mirror, her head above mine. "And I suppose I'm worried about you."

I shrugged and carefully finished my coffee. She took the mug and disappeared into the back.

I spent at least an hour simply staring at myself, as Kalyna brought me more and more coffee. A few times, she did have to redo parts of the makeup, as my hands had begun to shake quite intensely, but she didn't chastise me for it. At this point, I needed silence. When the shaking began to slow, Kalyna silently put a hand on my back and left. She needed to make sure all of our collaborators—my assistants—were ready.

I sat alone in the Games Hall, staring in that mirror, allowing myself to feel my pulse rise, my mouth become numb, my hands turn leaden, my body heat up immensely.

In that coffee there had been many, many other substances, which were all now bouncing through my veins. I won't list every one here, because, again, I don't wish for what I did that day to be reproduced, but there was: some bhang, for an expansive mind; a few ground roots that added dirt-like smells beyond even that of coffee, to bring me back down from wherever I would be lifted; a sprinkling of purely ceremonial substances, as far as the Academy was concerned.

Of these last, I will say that many were from growths, or animals, associated with very specific gods—both from within and without Loasht's Eighty-Three. There were also tree onion and elderberries, just in case my Fortresses might really protect me as they did our plants. I don't know whether any of these ceremonial substances affected my body, or if only the knowledge that they were swirling within me did. (And "swirling" *is* the right word—I felt very sick to my stomach, to a degree easily beyond the mixture of fear, excitement, and coffee.)

Once my breathing and my extremities had slowed to, well, almost normal, and the speed of my heartbeat began to *seem* as though it, too, was normal, I felt a rarer sensation: I felt as though what coffee, tea, khat, and so forth do to one's body, blood, and mind was happening *only* in my mind, but a thousand times over. Behind my eyes, you could say.

I had some truly excruciating moments, in which I became convinced that, in such a state, I would forget all the steps of what I had to do. But then, in an eternity or in another moment, I would realize that I didn't know how to do anything else.

Eventually, some sad, backward little representation of the barbarous Tetrarchia came into the hall and spoke to me in her doggerel language. She was like all the worst things about our childish neighbors rolled into one. Then the pitiable thing repeated herself, in a laughable approximation of our own tongue.

"Radiant!" snapped Kalyna. "Are you ready?"

I looked up at her with the utmost disdain. Then I understood what my mind—with its many substances—was doing. I softened my expression.

"I'm sorry," I said in Loashti Bureaucratic. Even knowing full well what was happening, and who I really was, I could not bring myself to speak *Skydašiavos*. The very thought gave me a new wave of nausea.

"Sorry for what?"

"For thinking unkindly of you."

She snorted. "Silly thing to start apologizing for now. Your thoughts don't hurt me."

"Well, they hurt me."

Understanding, at least to the extent that she was capable, came into her face.

"Ah, I see. He's really in you now, isn't he?"

"Very much so."

"*Good.* That's the idea." She beckoned me with a broad motion. "Come on. Simurgh must have made it partway at least, because she's done it. Even from here, through a telescope, it's awful to behold." Kalyna was not being glib. She looked quite genuinely disturbed by what she'd seen.

I nodded, stood, fell back into my chair, and stood again.

"Can you walk on your own?" she asked, offering her arm.

"I'll have to. I certainly can't show any weakness now."

"If you say so. But I can ask them to go easy—"

"Don't you dare," I growled. Was this someone else's tone, or my *idea* of someone else's tone? Or was this who I really was?

I decided it didn't matter. I had something to do and, on top of that, something quite oppositional to myself to do. I focused on the dirt flavor that still clung to the edges of my mouth, letting it cut through the fog and remind me where I was.

"Let's go before I lose my nerve," I said, even though I don't think I had ever had more nerve in my life.

She nodded. "I know you can do this, Radiant," she said, with what I took to be quiet awe.

She swept my cape onto my shoulders and then gave me one last pat on the back. (Why did she dare touch me?)

"Your thralls await you," she said.

At first glance, the Lanreas River Guild looked normal enough, if empty. As I strode through it, uphill toward the Estate, that emptiness became more acute. Sometimes people looked at me from their windows, but when I turned to them, they disappeared. Quite a few of the buildings were empty, as I well knew.

I remembered when, early in our time here, Kalyna had wondered if these strangely cheery people got up to human sacrifice. This, now, felt like how the place would have been if such were the case. And, in a way, we were doing exactly that.

Kalyna and I passed the crumbling old Estate and continued north. She fell easily into step behind me, like my inferior, and this felt natural. My cape was pleasantly heavy on my shoulders, even in the summer heat. Comforting. Sometimes, I looked down at my sides and saw brocade catch the light of the setting sun with gold, green, red, and blue. I radiated power.

The clearing where Simurgh's marabou balloon normally sat looked like an entirely different place—another country, perhaps. There were some fifty people waiting for me, standing in carefully regimented rows and wearing undyed linen cut to resemble Loashti army uniforms. They held sticks and farm implements like they were long guns. I'm sure, to an outsider, it would have looked like a pale imitation, but what mattered was how real it felt to us. Mostly, to me.

The crowd greeted me by saying my name in Loashti Bureaucratic: Aloe Pricks a Mare upon the Mountain Bluff. Some of them pronounced it clumsily, as though they hadn't been speaking the language their whole lives, but I forgave them. (Or rather, Radiant Basket of Rainbow Shells did.)

The Tetrarchic amalgamate woman behind me said something, and my soldiers—my people, my siblings-in-arms—parted for me. In the center of the clearing was a fire pit. My soldiers must have dug it for our upcoming evening camping here, right over the border, back in our home at last. Here they would light an alchemical fire meant to keep away pests, and perhaps much worse things.

I moved to the pit and looked up into the northern sky. I gasped, and my soldiers all looked too, beginning to cry out in fear. The sky to the north was red and black: it was on fire.

Moments later, the same was true of the sky above us. It was mystifying and portentous. That this should happen *now*, when we had just returned home, was ominous. Our home was meant to welcome us back; the world was meant to bend around us. My loyal followers began to cry out in fear. In great, big (perhaps exaggerated) fear. Some cried out about the wrath of the gods, others simply moaned wordlessly.

A flame went up in the fire pit, but it would not dispel the clogged and bleeding sky, nor the terrible, unseen things that seemed to twist their way effortlessly through those red clouds. I called for calm, but my followers only grew more senseless in their fear.

Something was thrown into the fire, and it flared up higher for a moment. Soon enough it, too, was leaking red and black smoke, through which my panicking followers ebbed, reappeared, ran, and fell.

Then something else was in the smoke, a sharp smell, and for the moment, I was Radiant. Radiant Basket of Rainbow Shells.

In the north, I knew, Simurgh in her balloon had filled the sky with red smoke, for both its terrifying and its obscuring properties. We could only hope that Echoes, wherever she was, if she was alive, had seen this and answered in kind, but there was no way for us to know.

I also knew that once I had been greeted by my followers, Ifeanyas and Vidmantas had lit yet more of the dolphin blubber mixture up in the Estate's library, fanning it through the broken opening at the top of the tower. This red sky now covered much of the Guild's lands, especially here at the northern end. Now I saw the world quite similarly to how I hoped the other *I* was seeing it.

But for a short time, I was Radiant again, and Radiant had things to do.

"Keep screaming! Keep capering!" came Kalyna's voice from somewhere in the darkness, first in Skydašiavos, then in Loashti Bureaucratic. "There will be time to rest later. Scream! Run! Fall!"

First, I circled the fire, spitting on the ground as a sort of ward to, perhaps, protect me from some of the danger I was going to bring on myself. This piece of the ritual I'd concocted was Masovskan, and Kalyna had spent a good hour making sure I pronounced the invocation perfectly, with all four syllables crammed into one in the split second between each spit. "Find a rhythm to it," she'd said. "That's how Masovskans do it."

Next, I did a sort of capering dance, kicking up dirt and mixing the places where I'd spat into mud. This bit was Zobiski, but had never been part of a curse. It was a plea for good fortune and a show of thanks for the privilege of still being alive at this point in time. By using it toward such a harmful purpose, I was perverting it, but it nonetheless came easily.

I shut my eyes and pronounced a string of chants in twelve different languages: four Loashti, the four official Tetrarchic, two suppressed Tetrarchic, and even two from the Bandit States. More than a few of those languages were barely spoken anymore, yet Kalyna still walked me through some of the pronunciation. No, I will not tell you which languages they were, nor what exactly I was saying. Besides, by then, despite knowing who I was, my mind was traveling so far, buzzing and shaking and babbling with such force, that I did not even know what I was doing. I only knew that I was enacting what I had practiced.

The scale on which we were enacting our imitation was, itself, Skydašian. Long ago—as had been depicted in *The Miraculous Adventure of Aigerim*—there had been sorcerers who owned fiefdoms and fortresses, forcing their people into carrying out massive spells. It had begun in the South Shore, moved to the North Shore, and eventually came to be falsely attributed to Loasht.

There were other pieces of scattered magics from throughout the known world that I synthesized to create this amalgamation of a curse, but I will tell you only two more.

One was a very old Quru ritual meant to protect mountain towns and encampments from striped bears. It had only ever been used defensively, and required people wearing bear skins to act as the bears themselves, running away from the place that was being protected. More on that in a moment.

When everything was in place—the herbs burned, the pleas muttered, and Kalyna doing her part to keep the Guild members on task—I began the last piece.

This was Rotfelsenisch, but *old* Rotfelsenisch that I had found at the Academy more than a decade ago, preserved as proof of our neighbors' barbarity. I didn't have the Commonplace Book volume where I'd written it down, but it had remained in my head with no effort.

"I've never heard of that," Kalyna had told me.

I had to, essentially, strangle myself as far as was possible.

"But," she had continued, "it sounds like them."

I took a deep breath. I stared at the fire. I heard the screams around me grow in frenzied intensity, arcing in and out of the blood red fog. I picked up a silk scarf, which was tied in a loop to a thick piece of wood. I put the loop around my neck. I waited.

Eighty-Three, I couldn't do it. I thought of Silver, of their family, my people, my hatred for Aloe, but I couldn't bring myself to begin twisting the stick, tightening the silk. It was cool and smooth against me. It reminded me of life, of why one should remain on the ground as long as possible, rather than rushing toward—

"Kalyna!" I wailed. "Kalyna, I can't—!"

"I worried this would happen." She was already behind me. She had been ready.

Knowing the importance of this part of the ritual, Kalyna immediately began tightening the silk garrote.

"How long?" she gasped. Even she sounded panicked now.

"Until I fall."

Remembering pain is a tricky business, or at least it is for me. I don't really recall what I felt or thought or did as Kalyna Aljosanovna strangled me, other than that I almost fell on purpose many times, just to make it stop.

But when I was truly unable to stand, she immediately untwisted the silk and let me drop. I don't know if she helped me to the ground, said anything to me, spared me a look, or simply left. How could I? I wasn't there.

I was up on a bluff in southern Loasht, in view of the border—or such would have been my view, if not for the smoke surrounding me and my soldiers. Now those red-blooded and strapping Loashti fighters were panicking and shooting at nothing. Certainly it was frightening, but I didn't understand what had possessed them to entirely lose their composure this way. Or, for that matter, why I had so suddenly collapsed, unable to breathe. But now, on the ground, I was able to regain my breath.

(Was I hallucinating what I wanted to happen, or had I traveled in some way to embody Aloe? Whatever the case, I felt removed from all I saw and heard, while also absolutely in the center of it.)

I cried out to my people to contain themselves, but to no avail.

("Now! Now! Go!" cried a voice that sounded like it was beneath an ocean of swamp: miles and miles of mud choking it out.)

Screams of terror turned into something else, but I did not understand why. Then Hail, one of my soldiers, ran past me, with a great gash in her head. There was something out there worse than smoke. Something solid was moving through those red clouds now.

The face of Elderflower, one of my first followers, whom I had known for years, emerged. He screamed for me to run.

I made it to my feet and moved toward him, but he motioned that I go the other way. Something appeared over him. Scales, glinting red in that morass. Teeth. Dark, dead eyes.

Then Elderflower's face was gone. His body, still pointing in the direction he wanted me to run, flopped to the ground.

When the crocodile emerged more fully into view, I became sick with sorrow and shock. The great thing walked on two legs, in a mockery of humanity. Such upright monsters weren't supposed to be so near the border; they all lived farther north, around Yekunde. This one must have traveled south for days, and by mistake, just to appear now as a phantom of my home. It made no sense.

What's more, it didn't stop to devour its kill—my poor Elder-flower—but instead continued toward me.

I had never seen one so close before. Its stooped gait, its arms, used for balance but with claws—I was struck with the *wrongness* of it. Standing upright, sort of. Lumbering. A piece of Elderflower's cheek dangling from its jaw. Not going back for its meal but coming for me.

It almost made me believe the old stories that my ancestors had told, about the Zobiski somehow *being* these things, or descended from them. As though the very embodiment of their atavistic nature was coming for me, to punish me for trying to cleanse them of it. But this wasn't possible.

I pissed myself as I began to run from the thing. It was only a freak occurrence that it was here. Happenstance.

"Crocodile!" cried someone to my left, as the thing loped after me.

"Crocodile!" someone else screamed from my right, as I kept running.

Directly in front of me was the sound of rending flesh and screams. But the beast was behind me, and I couldn't stop. I ran forward, until I hit something and fell back. Something hard. Not just another croco-dile, but another *upright* one.

"Impossible," I murmured to no one.

(I exulted when I found myself saying this.)

More came out of the red fog. More and more. More upright croco-diles than I had ever heard of being seen in one place, all killing at once. At least twenty, but it was so hard to count.

Some of my followers were still alive out there. I could hear them screaming as they ran away, moaning for help as they bled out. Why these predators had not finished them off and begun to dine, I could not understand.

Even stranger, these two-legged crocodiles—these unnatural, an-cient, human-like, provincial mistakes—all just . . . stopped. They stood over me, around me, regarding me with their glassy eyes, housed in great big heads that would have made more sense upon their four-legged siblings. Were their teeth red from the reflection, or my people's blood? Why didn't they feed? What were they looking at? What in the world could they have been waiting for?

("Go! Do it!" shouted a familiar voice. "It's Aloe! Don't hold back!")

I didn't see the first one; it was behind me. I felt only incredible pain: tearing or beating. Then there were great, scaly bodies slamming themselves upon me, and they began tearing off pieces. But not my head—nothing so quick. It was almost as though these dumb creatures, that only knew hunting and eating, wanted to hurt me as much as possible.

The pain was excruciating. The fear was absolute. But the most overpowering thing in that moment was my utter confusion.

(And then, as I felt all of Aloe's pain—or felt the pain I imagined he was feeling, in my own hindered and expanded state—I, Radiant Basket of Rainbow Shells, realized something. For days, an element of this plan had bothered me. Not the morality of killing Aloe, which was justified. Not the very real pain and possible death that I would suffer, which I had resigned myself to. But something I wasn't sure of.)

(As I watched, felt, and experienced Aloe's possibly dreamed dismemberment, I wondered if my reservation had been the painful nature of the death I'd planned for him. The cruelty of it.)

(But no. No, it wasn't that. It was something uglier, something that may have always been in me, or that may have come from Kalyna's influence. What bothered me was Aloe's *confusion*. The fact that he didn't understand why this was happening.)

One of the beasts, instead of biting me, was using its claws to gouge out one of my eyes. I screamed. Why? Why was this happening? I had achieved greatness, but had so much more left to do! And now I was here, bleeding from where my limbs had been, beset by senseless creatures. Crocodiles more interested in causing pain than in eating. Why were the gods doing this to me?

As I began to mercifully fade from life, my mouth started moving of its own accord. Not to scream—I had been doing plenty of that already—but forming around words. Words that were not in my head.

"Not the gods," I said hoarsely to myself. "Radiant is doing this to you."

Impossible. Radiant was my—

"I was never your friend."

I didn't understand how it had happened, or why, but the last thing I thought, as the crocodiles *finally* moved to rend my body down the middle, was a deep sadness. Betrayal. Realization. Helplessness.

("That's enough! Enough! Stop!")

Epilogue

I, Radiant Basket of Rainbow Shells, did not regain full consciousness for almost a week. Apparently, I spoke a lot in my sleep, often seemed "awake" (after a fashion), ate and drank, and even sort of held conversations. But it would quickly become clear that I was not actually present and that my "conversations" made no sense.

Much of this had to do with the many substances I'd imbibed in order to enact my curse, with the fact that Kalyna had strangled me nearly to unconsciousness, and with whatever it was I experienced when I saw-felt Aloe's supposed death. But it was also because I had a great deal of physical healing to do.

As I've said before, magic is imitative, and this was certainly true of the Quru bear-ward that I had repurposed as part of my curse. Instead of people in bear skins acting as though they were giving Quru towns a wide berth, we had put Guild members in crocodile masks so they could "kill" me. But weakly miming as though they were biting at me would simply not have been enough: they had to actually beat, kick, gouge with their fingernails, and even bite and tear with their (thankfully, human) teeth. It had to be that way: the more real the pain, the more intended the harm, the more uncontrollable the violence, the more likely our desired outcome. Besides, if the beating had been carefully planned, I might have tried to avoid it.

I am sure that to an outside observer, those people in masks beating me while I screamed would have looked silly, and certainly nothing like what I was seeing at the time. But this sort of magic is not concerned with observers.

In the days before the curse, I had met with my stand-in crocodiles many times, told them it was what they needed to do, what I *wanted* them to do, assured them I would not be angry, and would indeed be thankful, even if I died. Swore up and down that I would not haunt them. Even so, it had taken much coaxing and encouragement from Kalyna to get them to do their part.

At least it appeared that I had not died.

When I finally awoke, the first thing I saw was the face of Silver Petals Alight on Sand. I shouted in joy and reached for them. Somehow, my hand missed.

Their large, round, perfect face hovered over me, showing relief and worry. They reached out and took my arms, placing them around that thick neck I'd so missed. I started to cry, and that was when I felt the bandage over my right eye. A moment later, I realized the eye was gone entirely. Our crocodiles had truly done their work.

"Radiant," they said, "what exactly did you *do*?"

"I saved you," I gulped.

"You frustrate me."

"I love you too."

Behind them, I saw Casaba Melon Water Soothes at Noontime, and farther back, in the doorway of the room, stood a worried Ifeanyas. Silver held me and kissed me for some time. I began to realize that I was sore all over, and Silver knew this, but they held back only slightly, because they also knew me.

"Please help me up," I finally said.

Silver put their arms around my waist and began to pull me out of the bed.

"Maybe," said Casaba, "you should rest a little longer."

I felt Silver's head shake as I fixed my hands weakly around the back of their neck.

"Bring him a stick," they said. Then Silver smiled sadly at me. "Your left foot is broken, love."

That was when I realized the foot in question was wrapped tightly and held in a splint. Soon I was sitting up on the bed, my legs dangling over the side. Silver put their hands on my shoulders, kissed me on the forehead, and moved aside, so I could see myself in a full-length mirror hung on the wall across from me.

The space where my right eye had been was covered by a bandage, as though the eye itself was still there and just needed time to heal. But I knew it was gone. Perhaps I could feel its absence, or perhaps a part of me remembered when it was gouged out.

I expected my face to be covered in bruises—and it was—but I found myself surprised by the rents and tears. Deep lines left by fingernails and Eighty-Three knew what else spiderwebbed their way across my face, complicating the tattoos and lines of age that had already been there. Some were scabbing over; some were still red.

I was struck, suddenly, by how beautiful I had still been just before this happened. How lovely my face had been, even with its flaws and age, which I had been unable to see until now, when even that version of me was gone.

I began to cry again. Silver held me but, knowing me well, did not block my view of the mirror.

I was brought a walking stick and helped to my feet. I began to slowly make my way outside, stepping lightly on my splinted foot, with Silver next to me in case I needed a hand. Casaba and Ifeanyas walked close by, each looking a slightly different combination of worried and relieved.

"It is . . . It's nice to have all of you with me," I managed to say.

I realized then that we had been speaking Zobiski the whole time, of which Casaba had a decent grasp, but certainly not Ifeanyas. I turned to him and smiled.

"Have you been introduced?" I asked him in Skydašiavos.

"Yes!" he replied. "We've all been doing our best without you to translate. Kalyna can, and Simurgh; Echoes, a bit; some others too."

Silver nodded and muttered in Zobiski, "I'm glad to see your tastes broadening." They would have elbowed me in the ribs, had I not been bruised and unsteady.

I limped into the next room and finally realized where I was: the mid-sized building that had become our infirmary of sorts. Lying there, still hooked up to a pair of glass globes, was Yalwas. And much to my surprise, he smiled at me.

"Glad to see you're . . ." He wheezed and took a moment to regain his breath from the effort of speaking. ". . . up and about, Radiant. Afraid I'm . . ." Another breath. ". . . not quite there yet."

"But you're awake! That's wonderful!" I hobbled toward him excitedly.

Was I happy for Yalwas, or was I happy that Kalyna and my plans had not killed him? (At least not yet.)

He nodded. I was struck again by how small he looked now.

"Talk more . . . later," he grunted. But he continued to smile, which I hoped meant he did not resent me or the Zobiski for doing this to him.

The sun was brilliant when we got outside, and I felt myself trying to squint through my empty eye socket wrapped in a bandage. It was warm out, but when I would pass beneath the shade of a tree or a house, I would become almost, slightly, cold. Autumn was beginning to trickle in a little.

Looking around me, the Lanreas River Guild was buzzing with activity, with noise, and with people. I heard the beautiful sounds of Zobiski around me, mixed in with Skydašiavos. Houses were being built, roads were being made flatter and even, food was being prepared, and the ranks of the children's trash-collecting companies had swelled. Uzochi looked up from roasting chickpeas and smiled at me, waving.

Ifeanyas giggled and leaned in close to me. "Just before everyone arrived the other day," he said, "Kalyna told Uzochi, 'You start roasting and being friendly, and you don't stop until I tell you!' Then she made sure he knew some basic Loashti phrases."

"Of course she did. Where is Kalyna, anyway?"

"Probably south, by the farms."

I asked to be taken to her. Silver understood enough to make a disapproving noise in the back of their throat.

As we walked south, I looked around the newly crowded Guild in bewilderment.

"Did . . ." I began in Loashti Bureaucratic. Then I stopped. I didn't want to ask the question. I wanted to live forever in the moment where nothing, besides my injuries, had gone wrong.

I took a deep breath and tried again: "Did everyone make it here?"

"Most," said Casaba. "Some Zobiski were killed by soldiers when they were rounded up in Yekunde. Some died of unattended illness while interned. In all, I think we lost some fifteen to twenty—there are exact numbers, but I did not want to dwell on it."

"She blames herself," said Silver.

I opened my mouth to reassure Casaba but then thought better of it. I doubt I had anything to tell her that she had not already heard. Or, if I did, it was because I was still woefully uninformed about how the Loashti extraction had even gone.

Instead I asked, "Is Dagmar here?" As soon as it was out of my mouth, I realized how badly I wished to see Dagmar. To thank her.

Casaba shook her head.

"Is she dead?"

"I don't think so," replied Casaba, with a laugh.

It felt strange to furrow my brow, half of which was beneath a bandage.

"She fought like a demon and got us all onto one of Yekunde's river boats," explained Casaba. "The trip south was easy enough, especially once Echoes explained that the red smoke we saw was 'part of the plan.'" Casaba smirked. "Although when asked what the plan was, Echoes admitted she wasn't sure."

"She left us some of her Wrath of the Gods to use as we willed," I said.

"And you certainly used it," added Silver, patting my midsection lightly.

"We floated easily into the Tetrarchia," explained Casaba. "When we were nearly here, Dagmar had a conversation with Echoes about this . . . Kalyna person." She gestured southward. "They were speaking Skydašiavos, so all I understood was that name, which they'd discussed before. Then Dagmar shrugged, gave her bandits some sort of farewell, and dove into the crocodile-infested waters of the Lanreas River. That was the last I saw of her." She shrugged and smiled. "Echoes seems to think she made it to shore. Says Dagmar asked that the full two thousand kudai payment be split among the remaining bandits."

"Although," added Silver, "a few have chosen to stay here."

"As to *why* Dagmar would do such a thing," Casaba continued, "Echoes only said, 'She'd rather risk the crocodiles than see that woman right now.'"

"You can imagine," said Silver, "that some of us began to worry about whose hands it was we were being delivered into." Their tone told me they were still unsure about Kalyna.

"Well," I grunted, "Dagmar did say 'right now,' didn't she?"

I received skeptical looks from both Casaba and Silver. Poor Ifeanyas continued alongside us with no idea what we were saying.

"They used to be lovers," I added.

"I figured that out myself, sweet."

We found Kalyna sitting in the grass beneath a tree with her father. Nearby, Guild workers were harvesting sundry crops from where they had been planted right up against one another, according to my system: carrots, squash, artichokes, and whatever else was deemed ready. Kalyna seemed, somehow, to be simultaneously giving all of her attention to Aljosa and to the harvest work.

It took some assistance for me to sit with them without putting too much weight on my foot in the process. Kalyna stood up and made as if to help but was not given the chance. I was well protected and enveloped by Silver, Casaba, and Ifeanyas. The latter two also sat. Silver remained standing, leaning against the tree and watching Kalyna intently.

"Well, hello there!" cried the old man in Loashti Bureaucratic, smiling at me. "If it isn't the pretty wizard."

"Hello, Aljosa," I replied. "Afraid I'm not quite so pretty anymore."

"Well! You're certainly a wizard! And, I don't know. This? All this?" He waved his hands vaguely at my face. "This will heal somewhat! And scars give a face character."

Kalyna pointed to the mark on her upper lip. "He's been saying that since I got this as a child."

"Well, it's true. Just don't get tattoos to cover them, pretty wizard."

I had already been planning to do exactly this.

"Get tattoos to *complement* them," continued Aljosa, with great seriousness. "That's what the veterans of the revolution will do."

"Revolution?" asked Casaba.

"Oh yes! The one that will split Loasht into a thousand, thousand pieces! But I'm sorry to say, my lady, none of us will live to see its awful carnage." He sucked his teeth and blinked a few times. "I think? Not sure."

"Papa," said Kalyna, switching to Skydašiavos, "I think poor Ifeanyas must feel quite left out of this conversation. Why don't you let him help you test the new road?"

"Oh, you should see it, young man!" Aljosa told me. "If only you could see now how it will be in a month: truly grand. Nice and even for my chair, and for anyone else." He motioned toward my walking stick, while Ifeanyas and Silver helped him into his chair. "Not just for me, oh no. After all, we'll be leaving soon."

"Leaving?" asked Ifeanyas. "Why?"

"Well, Kalynishka has saved everyone, hasn't she?"

Kalyna shook her head, but her father didn't notice. Ifeanyas moved to wheel him away.

"Wait!" I rasped, gripping Ifeanyas' sleeve. "Please kiss me first."

He hesitated. My first thought was that he no longer found my face pleasing, torn up as it was. My second was that he felt shy doing so in front of Silver. My third was that he worried he would hurt me.

Whatever his reasoning, I felt I saw a genuine consideration of whether or not he wanted to do so, making it very gratifying when he did. Gently.

Kalyna watched Ifeanyas wheel her father away with a sad smile and then turned it upon me. It was not the dazzling one she put on to draw people in, but a look of acceptance, of regret, of sympathy, and of gladness that I, and she, and her father, and all of us were, well, *here*. Alive, if not well.

"I'm sorry about your eye, Radiant," she said in Loashti Bureaucratic.

"Yes, I'd like to know more about that," murmured Silver, with a tinge of anger in their voice.

"Later, later." I shook my head. "Did it *work*?"

"Well," said Kalyna, "we know Aloe died that night. That much news has reached us from across the border." She shrugged and looked up at Silver towering over her, and then to Casaba, who was sitting primly, her legs folded beneath her. "We don't know how he died. 'Natural causes,' they said, and I can't imagine Loasht will ever let anyone learn more."

"Crocodiles are natural," I muttered.

Kalyna's mouth quirked into a more ironic—more *Kalyna*—smile. "That's true."

"I saw it happening," I said, staring at nothing. "Felt it happening. I spoke to him, even, as myself, from his own mouth." I felt it again, just then—in my bones, in the rents in my flesh, in my soul. I closed my eyes and shook my head. "But that may have all been a dream."

"Maybe," said Kalyna. "But we wished him to die, and he died. So, to me—" She stopped herself and leaned toward me, putting out a hand. "You must be sore. May I touch you?"

I nodded.

She put a hand lightly on my shoulder. "To me, that means your curse worked, Radiant. I know no other way to measure it."

I nodded slowly.

I will tell you now that, in the years since, I have vacillated on whether the curse worked and, if so, to what extent. Did Aloe die because of me? If he did, was it actually by the jaws of crocodiles, or did the curse end him in a less extravagant way? Did he know it was me? Did I truly *speak* to him? All I can do is hope, and accept that I'll never know. That's normally how magic works, if it does at all.

"Thank you," I said to Kalyna. "It helps to know you have faith in me."

"Of course I do."

"You told me so," I added, feeling myself start to tear up at the memory, "right before cutting my hair."

"Oh, Radiant." She squeezed my shoulder and looked into my eye. "*That* was a lie. I just needed you to be confident. But *now* I do."

I laughed, and she let go of me. Silver did not find it quite so funny.

"So," they said, "you didn't believe his curse would work, but you still let those . . ." They let whatever word they had been about to say die in their mouth. "You let those people beat him, break him, and take his eye?"

"Silver—" I began.

"No, no," interrupted Kalyna. "They deserve to have their anger." She looked up at Silver, taking in the large, powerful person standing above her. Kalyna made no move to stand, or otherwise change the difference in power and intensity between them.

"But," I tried, "I chose to—"

"They know that, Radiant," said Casaba. "That isn't the point."

"I was the one who suggested he curse Aloe," said Kalyna. Then she shook her head and corrected herself. "I was the one who *pushed him* to do so. And when he carried out the curse, it was my job to make them stop when I judged the timing to be right. Too soon, and Aloe would have survived; too late, and Radiant would not have." She held unwavering eye contact with Silver, her hands folded neatly in her lap. "I could only do my best, Silver Petals Alight on Sand. It was a disorienting situation and one that changed rapidly. Every moment I fancied I was watching my friend die—for, indeed, he was acting the part of a dying man—and every moment I had to decide whether *now* was the time to put a stop to it. Knowing that if I did so too early, it would mean your life, and your community's, for which my friend would never forgive me."

Was Kalyna playing Silver or being honest? I'm inclined toward the latter, because she didn't theatrically stifle any tears, nor let her voice quaver. I'm sure she was being calculated with her honesty—because that was second nature to her—but I chose to trust that it *was* honesty.

Silver's nostrils flared as they let out a long breath. Then they looked at me. I shrugged and nodded slightly.

"All right then," they said.

Silver grunted and sat in the grass beside me. I lay my head on their shoulder and smiled, and they began to stroke what little hair I had left, after I'd been shorn to look like Aloe.

Kalyna blew out a sigh of relief and braced her arms against her knees, looking jokingly relieved.

"Oh, thank the gods," she gulped. "I was expecting you to hit me a few times." She put up her hands. "Which would be only fair! But I'm not sure I'd have survived." She winked at me. "Radiant likes them strong and protective, doesn't he?"

I nodded against Silver's shoulder and smiled. They patted my cheek.

"He's our little weakling," they said.

"Well, I don't know about that," argued Kalyna. "How many people have *you* killed from miles away?"

I spent much of the day slowly traversing the Guild, with assistance. I was reunited with Silver's parents—Crane's Gift on a Summer Morning, Cedar Cones Pelt the Naughty Mangabey, and Sharp Rocks

Split the Amber Waves—who were greatly impressed with all I'd accomplished here.

I also saw my own parents, who seemed to be greatly, truly, disturbed by how badly beaten up I was. I held back the unkind responses that occurred to me, and instead said it was good to see them, and that I was glad *I* had been able to save *their* lives. This seemed to confuse them. I also allowed myself to be hugged. Gently.

Echoes was already back in the northern part of the Guild, doing chores around Simurgh's home. It was as though nothing had happened, as though she had not risked her life to save my community. Echoes staunchly refused to be thanked for it.

"*You're welcome*," Simurgh said to me, pointedly. "I helped too, didn't I?"

I thanked Simurgh profusely until Echoes got embarrassed enough to leave.

And before I knew it, the time had almost come for dinner. What would have been a three-minute walk now took at least ten, with a break. I hobbled into the Meal Hall and saw Žydrė and Vidmantas sitting alone at a table. I asked if I could join them, and Vidmantas said yes before Žydrė could answer, so I did, flanked by Silver and Casaba, neither of whom yet spoke Skydašiavos.

"Go on," said Vidmantas, elbowing Žydrė. "Just repeat what you said to me earlier today."

Žydrė shot him a look, then sighed. "Radiant, I am glad to see you're up and recovering."

"Was that so hard?" asked Vidmantas.

Žydrė clearly had more to say, though, and let her silence linger.

"But?" I asked her.

"But," she repeated, "I must say, I'm rather . . . disturbed by the whole thing. By your magic and . . . and what it required."

"So am I." I smiled widely at her, and I felt the scabbing on my face pull with the movement. "I think being disturbed is the correct response to the forces we—the forces *I*—took hold of."

She leaned forward, clasping her hands on the table. "But it wasn't *forces* that tore your face apart, Radiant. It was our neighbors."

"Those forces and our neighbors became one and the same, Žydrė. That's . . . just how it works."

"Well, you understand I'm just worried about the, you know,

cohesion of our community after such a thing." She began to avoid eye contact, drumming her fingers.

"And with Zobiski now outnumbering everyone else?" I asked.

"It's . . . it's certainly a shift. And, well, Adomas—"

"But Adomas," Vidmantas cut in, "isn't here anymore. And when he was, the old man was fine to change his ideas to suit a new context, wasn't he?"

"Of course he was!" said Kalyna, coming up and sitting down at the table before anyone could tell her no. "Adaptability and all that, yes?"

Žydrė's eye twitched.

"Would you have preferred," Kalyna continued, "that all these people"—she motioned to Silver, Casaba, and a number of other Zobiski filling the hall—"died or were imprisoned, than be here?"

"Of course not," said Žydrė. She closed her eyes, as though she did not want to see anyone's reaction to what she said next. "And," she grumbled, "I must admit we have enough of a surplus, now, to support them for a time."

"Not a 'surplus' anymore," needled Vidmantas, "now that our numbers have grown."

"That's fine," said Kalyna. "A real surplus is an invitation to begin hoarding and acquiring, which I don't think is what we want. Is it, Žydrė?"

The other woman opened her eyes to see that, as far as anyone could tell, Kalyna was not being ironic or cutting, but seemed to mean what she said.

"No," Žydrė agreed. "No, it isn't."

"And besides," added Kalyna, "you wanted to spread Adomas' beliefs to the world. Now you have three hundred more adherents."

Žydrė shrugged.

"What are they saying?" asked Casaba. "Is it about us?"

"Sort of," I replied. "But not really."

Later that night, Silver and I huddled together in the tent they'd been using, and I once more leaned my head on their shoulder. They pointed to a pile of leather satchels just a foot away and told me to open them. I shook my head.

"I'm too tired to move," I said.

"Trust me."

I exaggerated my pained groan and lurched forward to open the top satchel. Inside was volume 1 of my Commonplace Book.

"They're all there," they said.

I began to bawl, to sob, to wail as I opened the satchels and gazed at my books, held them, smelled them.

"Now, why didn't you cry like that when you saw *me*?" asked Silver, although they could not pretend they weren't happy at my reaction.

"Because . . ." I gulped. "Because I could never imagine living without you and so had refused to face the possibility. But I had resigned myself to never seeing these again."

I cried much, much, *much* more that night. Probably for many reasons.

I eventually healed, but beyond even my eye, I would never be the same again. My face did end up scarred, and though my broken foot has mended, it continues to give me pain, now and then.

But worse than the physical transformation was the social one. It soon became clear that many people at the Lanreas River Guild would never view me as a normal person. (That this included some of those that beat me to enact my curse makes me particularly sad.) Some avoid me, pretend not to hear me when I speak, and whisper about me when I'm not around. I'm told that it's mostly in a tone of awestruck fear, which is, I suppose, better than disgusted and hateful fear.

Neither did all the Zobiski come to like me, given how much fear of "the occult," and of their own history and traditions, had been drummed into them over the years. Even in exile, it is not so simple to leave those judgments behind.

But I still have many friends, and lovers, and family, as well as people who respect me, like me, and even—Eighty-Three!—wish to learn magic from me. I have *admirers*. I'm the Lanreas River Guild's own wizard now, no matter how silly that seems to me.

And sometimes I lean into my new role. One of my beloved Zobiski tattoo artists had indeed made her way to the Guild with Echoes, and I came up with an idea for how she could *complement* my missing eye. She put a truly terrifying crocodile skull, with no skin and flesh, around it, as though delicately holding my eye socket in its jaws.

Kalyna threw herself into getting the new arrivals acclimated, and having more dormitories, houses, and halls built as soon as possible. She also began involving others more and more in the running of the Lanreas River Guild, ostensibly because she wanted to be a better leader, but probably because she wanted less responsibility.

Žydrė was the first, of course. She was cooperative and happy to help but could never bring herself to *like* Kalyna, exactly.

Yalwas began to take a greater role in leadership as well, being unable to work in the fields as he'd used to. He turned out to be uninterested in making decisions but had an inexhaustible knowledge of the Guild's past and Adomas' whimsies, which often came in handy. He never publicly blamed Kalyna, or me, or the Zobiski for his condition, and I always appreciated that. (Some others did, but not too many.) Simurgh worked with our Loashti alchemist-doctor to continue improving the system they'd made to keep Yalwas alive. It was an astounding success that the man lived a full three more years, and seemed to enjoy much in that time.

Whatever happened next in Loasht remained mostly a mystery to us, and I began to understand a bit of why my home country had always been so frightening to the Tetrarchia. Any information or insight into events there disappeared entirely from view. Snatched away, as though it had never been. As though the country to our north was not a place full of bustling masses, but a fortress.

Sometimes, new Loashti aliens would arrive at the Guild, but only in small numbers. They would tell our large expatriate community about what was transpiring "back home," but often only within a small orbit. I am sad to say that Aloe's death did not, of course, miraculously end what he had set in motion, but his movement did splinter, which we all hoped would turn out well for everyone else.

Speaking of division, the Lanreas River Guild was now more Zobiski than not, which was not without its complications. A full history of the time between then and now is beyond the scope of this document, but know that, as I write this, nearly a decade has passed since the events I've described, and for now, we exist.

I put these words down in Skydašiavos because it is what nearly everyone here speaks. Zobiski is still heard quite often, but it is seldom taught to children, which both makes me sad and strikes me as entirely understandable.

Almost a year to the day from when Aljosa Vüsalavich was brought to the Lanreas River Guild, we woke up one morning to find that both he and Kalyna Aljosanovna were gone.

I don't think anyone saw it coming, as Kalyna seemed to have truly settled down, to be happy and content here. Aljosa had often spoken as though they were soon to leave—as though Lanreas was one leg of a longer journey—but I'd taken that as more of his pleasant nonsense.

They took some of their personal effects but left many more—paintings and shrines and textiles and incense—for whoever wanted them. But Kalyna did take that great sliver of an eye, a jaw, and a tooth of some long-dead thing that Adomas had once kept hidden in his secret study.

And, of course, not to be outdone by Dagmar Sorga, Kalyna left a note for me in the latest volume of my Commonplace Book.

Letter from Kalyna Aljosanovna to Radiant Basket of Rainbow Shells

I think I would have liked to stay, if for no other reason than to see what this daft place will become, but Papa is growing restless.

Well, that's not quite fair of me. Yes, Papa is growing restless, but he also likes it here, and I could probably convince him to stay. The truth—and I will tell you this, Radiant, because you're my friend—is that I'm scared of what I will become if I stay at the Lanreas River Guild.

That sounds very dire, but I don't mean it in the way that I'm sure you, and perhaps Dagmar, despaired for my future: that I'd become a cult leader or a despot. I mean that this place is too damned nice and too blasted provincial. And, Radiant, a sick little part of me *likes that*.

If I were to stay, how long until I began to really, truly, derive satisfaction from well-executed leadership? From conciliation and compromise? To be satisfied with, for the most part, only knowing Skydašian and Zobiski folk? To only knowing the ins and outs of one little patch of land in this wretchedly big country? Gods, just the thought of it makes me long for freezing winters—for a change of pace!

I can't become that person, Radiant. I already knew that, but it became even clearer to me when we were aboard the pleasure ship of Adomas' stupid, worthless family. That gaudy thing, with the feathers everywhere? I loved it. And I loved running circles around them.

I tell you all this for your own records, because I know you'll write it down someday, and I won't have a version of these events that doesn't give me the final word on why it is I'm leaving. Or, by the time you read it, why I left.

Besides, looking through Adomas' papers has made me realize something important: the world deserves to know how exceptional I am. Of course that's arrogant, but if Adomas gets to have a legacy, why not me? (Perhaps having one will someday excise Grandmother's voice from my head.)

Anyway, speaking of Adomas' hidden papers, I know it's not in keeping with the Guild's principles for me to take selections of them for my own use, but I've done so nonetheless. I think I will have more use for decades of blackmail material and poison recipes than you all will.

> Sorry about your eye,
> Kalyna

Selected Sources

Paradise Now: The Story of American Utopianism, Chris Jennings (2016)

    On the one hand, you should read this book because it's both fascinating and entertaining. On the other hand, if you do, you'll realize just how much I stole from it. (Even if it also contained about a hundred bonkers things I didn't have space for.)

To the Finland Station: A Study in the Writing and Acting of History, Edmund Wilson (1940)

    A useful and well-written—if at times outdated—overview of certain strains of revolutionary thought. The chapters on Fourier and Owen are what really got the gears turning for me on *Kalyna the Cutthroat*.

Mutual Aid: A Factor of Evolution, Peter Kropotkin (1902)

    A huge help in molding Adomas' philosophy into something cohesive, in part because Kropotkin was also an ex-noble with a background as a naturalist. (That's where the similarities end, though.)

The Faggots & Their Friends Between Revolutions, Larry Mitchell, illustrated by Ned Asta (1977)

    Artforum once called it (pun clearly intended) a "fairytale-cum-manifesto," and that's better than anything I'll come up with.

The Terms of Order: Political Science and the Myth of Leadership, Cedric J. Robinson (1980)

    I wish I could say I read this whole book as research, but I honestly only had time for the bits about charismatic leadership, and why it doesn't have to be inherently despotic. Someday!

Paths in Utopia, Martin Buber (1949)

    An interesting survey of utopianism on the left . . . until you realize Buber's thesis is that the one *successful* attempt at utopian socialism is the Zionist experiment in Palestine. From the depths of my Jewish soul: fuck that.

The Book of Charlatans, Jamāl al-Dīn ʿAbd al-Raḥīm al-Jawbarī, edited by Manuela Dengler, translated by Humphrey Davies (thirteenth century, translation in 2020)
  A treatise on scams and con artistry by a man who definitely had a shady past of his own. There's a bounty of wild shit in here that I can't wait to mine for more.

The Necessity of Art: A Marxist Approach, Ernst Fischer (1959)
  A major part of Fischer's study is the idea that (emphasis his) "art in its origins was *magic*." Fischer even includes a passage about a curse being done through imitation, which provided the foundation for how magic works in *Cutthroat*.

"The Rebbe of Apte and Tsar Nicholas I," S. Ansky, from *Radiant Days, Haunted Nights: Great Tales from the Treasury of Yiddish Literature*, translated and edited by Joachim Neugroschel (story in 1923, anthology in 2005)
  This story of a curse being put on the Tsar fully solidified my decision to write about magic as imitation, and for Radiant to study harmful magic specifically.

Frederik Ruysch and His Thesaurus Anatomicus: A Morbid Guide, edited by Joanna Ebenstein (2022)
  Most of the inspiration for Adomas' collection. I always love seeing how science was approached before a lot of our ideas around it had been formed.

TikTok: Mike Hoag, @transformativeadventures
  Yes, I learned about permaculture—the method of agriculture Kalyna and Radiant bring to the Guild—from a TikTok account. It's also where I snagged some of the plants that are used as Fortresses, Enticers, etc.

Acknowledgments

As always, I can't thank my agent, Hannah Bowman, enough. She helped me figure out what a sequel to *Kalyna the Soothsayer* could even look like, and when the rough draft was done, she also provided its first feedback in an email with the delightful subject line "OMG THOSE CROCODILES."

In no way would anything like *Kalyna the Cutthroat* exist without everyone at Erewhon and Kensington. Sarah Guan, my editor, didn't just *allow* me to make Kalyna more arrogant and frightening this time around, she actively encouraged it—egged me on, even. I'm hugely grateful to Viengsamai Fetters, who stepped in for part of the edits, providing a vital perspective on a story that I worried was impossible to tell. Also Cassandra Farrin and Leah Marsh, who've now gotten both books out into the world, and with stunning design.

Martin Cahill sold the absolute *fuck* out of *Kalyna the Soothsayer*—introducing me to wonderful authors and booksellers as a side effect—and I can't wait to see what he does with this one. And yet again, Lakshna Mehta and Rayne Stone heroically put up with all of my weird, dumb, or archaic stylistic tics, turning them into something cohesive.

The cover, by Bose Collins and Samira Iravani, looks perfect next to the first book and caused me to tear up with joy when I first saw it. I had the exact same reaction to Virginia Allyn's beautiful map, which made the Tetrarchia feel *real* to me in a way it hadn't before.

And now, I must thank my whole family, and everyone who loves me, for putting up with how distant and useless I got at many points in this process.

None more so than my spouse, Brittany Marie Spector. Not only did she keep me going just by continuing to be an impossibly smart, funny, stylish, and loving presence in my everyday life, she was also indispensable for talking through where I got stuck in the story. There are so many pieces of *Cutthroat* that wouldn't exist without her, but I'll just mention one: it was her vivid imagination, not mine, that drew us into a mutually reinforced obsession with crocodiles while I was writing this book.

It's thanks to Peter Rowland, a dear friend since high school, that a story about a stranded refugee turned into one about utopian communism. He had the idea for us to start a two-person leftist book club in 2020, which began with *To the Finland Station*, leading to my fascination with bizarre pre-Marxist socialists.

Then I learned even more about the history of separatists, anarchists, and communes from another close friend since high school, Martine Neider. While helping her father downsize his library, she sent me all sorts of fascinating and relevant books, including his old copy of *Mutual Aid*.

I also have to mention my close friend Mattie Lubchansky, because the two of us keep simultaneously, but inadvertently, reading and getting inspired by the same things. This time, it was *Paradise Now*, which is why, on a beautiful day at Jacob Riis Beach, Mattie talked me into putting the goddamn Devastator into this book.

Finally, I'd like to thank extended-release Adderall. Learning I have ADHD made a lot of things (including *Soothsayer*) suddenly make sense in retrospect. I'd rather not imagine how long *Cutthroat* would've taken to write without proper medication.

Thank you for reading this title from Erewhon Books, publishing books that embrace the liminal and unclassifiable and championing the unusual, the uncanny, and the hard-to-define.

We are proud of the team behind *Kalyna the Cutthroat*:

Sarah Guan, Publisher
Diana Pho, Executive Editor
Viengsamai Fetters, Assistant Editor

Martin Cahill, Marketing and Publicity Manager
Kasie Griffitts, Sales Associate

Cassandra Farrin, Director
Leah Marsh, Production Editor
Kelsy Thompson, Production Editor
Lakshna Mehta, Copyeditor
Rayne Stone, Proofreader

Samira Iravani, Art Director
Alice Moye-Honeyman, Junior Designer
Virginia Allyn, Map Artist

. . . and the whole Kensington Books team!

Learn more about Erewhon Books and our authors at erewhonbooks.com.

Find Erewhon Books on most social media at @erewhonbooks.